P9-AFW-579

The Little Giant of Aberdeen County

The Little Giant of Aberdeen County

A NOVEL

Tiffany Baker

Doubleday Large Print Home Library Edition

GRAND CENTRAL PUBLISHING

NEW YORK ~ BOSTON

This Large Print Edition, prepared especially for Doubleday Large Print Home Library, contains the complete, unabridged text of the original Publisher's Edition.

Grand Central Publishing
Hachette Book Group USA
237 Park Avenue
New York, NY 10017

Printed in the United States of America

Grand Central Publishing is a division of Hachette Book Group USA, Inc.
The Grand Central Publishing name and logo is a trademark of Hachette Book Group USA, Inc.

ISBN-13: 978-1-60751-512-8

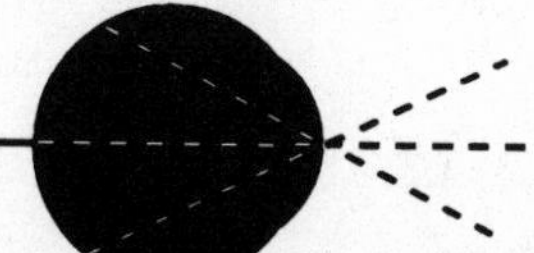

This Large Print Book carries the Seal of Approval of N.A.V.H.

For Edward

Acknowledgments

Thank you first and foremost to Dan Lazar, my champion agent at Writers House, who always believed in this novel. And then to my sterling editor, Caryn Karmatz Rudy at Grand Central Publishing, for making my vision come true. Words aren't enough.

Thanks to everyone in the Drever clan, especially Jan, Papo, and Lala for taking the pictures and amusing the kiddies. Thanks to my own tribe: Ned, Willow, Raine, and Auden. You all are the reason for everything.

And a special remembrance for some souls who have traveled on ahead: Joe, Tommy, Mimi, Wyby, and Wendy. Peace.

Part One

Prologue

The day I laid Robert Morgan to rest was remarkable for two reasons. First, even though it was August, the sky overhead was as rough and cold as a January lake; and second, it was the day I started to shrink.

I remember standing by the open grave, the muddy earth clotted like wet dung, waiting for Robert Morgan's body to be lowered into the hole. The other, scattered mourners had begun to take chill and leave, but I wasn't cold. There were layers and layers of me folded together like an accordion. So many that I would be warm in a blizzard. I could stand naked at the North Pole and be just fine.

I watched the coffin drop slowly into the ground, the supporting velvet ropes sliding under its belly like devious snakes. Before his death, the doctor had chosen a mahogany casket trimmed with brass and lined with a somber maroon satin. He brought a picture of it home to show me, and I examined it with suspicion. It looked phony somehow, like something you would find at Disneyland or a waxworks museum. All of it was too perfect. Now, however, as it settled with a lonely thump at what seemed like the bottom of the world, I saw that it would rot as soon as anything else down there, brass scrolls or no. I pictured Robert Morgan laid out in the elaborate box, his hair slicked down over his scalp like an otter's, his spindly fingers gnarled together in a knot over his heart, awaiting judgment.

I had chosen the doctor's favorite black suit for his burial, had brushed the cloth carefully before delivering it to the undertaker's with a striped tie curled in one of the pockets, socks and underwear stuffed in another. I didn't know why a dead man needed underpants, but there you had it. If Robert Morgan had been giving the directives, he would have insisted on aftershave, a belt, and cuff links, but since he wasn't calling the shots anymore, I left these items home. Now that the doctor was shut up in his box and I would never see him again, I wondered what the undertaker had done to close the cuffs on his shirt. Did he keep a spare pair for such an occasion? Had he used wire or thread? The plastic twist ties from a garbage bag?

I threw a fistful of earth onto the coffin and held my breath for the accompanying thud. I thought of all the patients Robert Morgan had buried and wondered if any of them were down there, waiting to meet him. If so, were they a polite ensemble with decorously folded hands or a nasty throng, eager to anoint him with the press of rotten flesh? I thought of all the other Dr. Robert Morgans scattered around the cemetery—four of them in total—and imagined one subsuming the other like those cannibalistic Russian nesting dolls, the parts of them mixed together into a Frankenstein monster of local history.

I shifted my bulk, kicking more dirt and

pebbles down on the casket. Along the sides of the grave, the exposed roots of weeds and trees dangled their anemic arms, as if pleading for clemency. I was reminded of Robert Morgan's dying patients who would come to the house and beg the doctor to do something—anything—to end their pain. They used metaphors of burning, of hot steel, or of blades carving a mysterious alphabet into their bones, rewriting the familiar language of the senses until they were desperate and confused. That's how Dr. Morgan saw them, at least. "Pay them no mind, Truly," he'd say, shaking his head as a son would lead a mother down the sagging porch steps or a hunched woman would teeter down them on her last strength, her fiery hands wrung in despair. "They are no longer themselves."

But I thought differently. Robert Morgan might have rolled the naked flesh of his patients under his palms, probed their organs with his skeleton fingers, but he never paid a whit of attention to their souls. If one ever did emerge, slit free of the body by an incandescent blade of pain, Robert

Morgan simply would have had no reference point for it. He prescribed morphine, suggested supplements, provided balms and creams, but he had no answer for the naked yearning to get it all over and done with. In his mind, the body was a self-regulating clock. It would wind down on its own volition and in its own time, and the soul would just have to accept it.

Of course, toward the end of his own life, the doctor had really not been himself at all. Swaddled in the famous Morgan family quilt in his bedroom, he'd howled, and thrashed, and finally just whimpered, his whole body coated in a fine sheen of sweat that lent him a radiance I didn't think he deserved. I brought him chicken broth on a tray and ice cubes to suck, cold compresses for his head. And when Robert Morgan grew delirious, crying out for his estranged wife and the son who'd left him, I took the doctor's own advice to heart and paid him no mind. "Robert Morgan, you're not yourself," I'd say, gently dabbing the new crevasses in his lips with petroleum jelly.

Now all that was over, shut up forever in

Robert Morgan's brass-studded box. For the first time in a hundred and fifty years, Aberdeen was left with neither a Robert Morgan in it nor a doctor, but rather than feeling as raw as the open grave in front of me, I was surprised to find myself completely numb. I thought about returning to the house I'd lived in with Robert Morgan for the past decade, a dinner of roast beef and green beans covered and waiting for me on the stove, a table setting for one laid out in the kitchen, television later. But for the first time in my life, I wasn't hungry.

I didn't normally leave the doctor's white-gabled house unless I could help it. My childhood companion, Amelia Dyerson, came to clean the doctor's premises once a week, bringing groceries, and in the spring, summer, and early fall, Marcus Thompson, another childhood friend, clipped the garden to kingdom come. These visits—Marcus slurping lemonade on the back porch, a sodden bandanna slung around his neck; Amelia muttering over her feather duster—constituted enough society for me. There had also been Robert Morgan's patients, of course, but they weren't always in the mood to chat. They entered a different part of the house, anyway, and departed with their heads bowed, locked into themselves, chastened by the disobedience of their own bodies.

If anyone ever asked, I could have told them all about that feeling. How it felt, for instance, to watch as my limbs stretched and spread of their own volition, as if I were some sort of mutating lizard. What it was like to sit on the Morgan family furniture and hear it creak and complain, threatening to split for good if I eased back any farther. How, when I stepped on the scale in Robert Morgan's examining room, the weights never wanted to balance but slid all the way to the ends of their metal strips, as if giving up in the monumental task of measuring me.

"Any bigger and you could get work in a sideshow, Truly," Robert Morgan chuckled during the last exam he gave me, and noted my weight on one of the endless charts he kept. Somewhere in his filing cabinet, a growing library of papers told a thousand and one versions of the strange story of my body. The doctor exhaled on his stethoscope to warm it, then slipped the metal disk in between the complicated folds of my breasts. "You're like the fat lady who died in the circus, and who was so big, she could only be moved by the hippo cart." I sighed. I knew the story. He told it to me every time he examined me—as a kind of parable, I suppose, a fable about the laughable indignities of excess.

He moved the metal circle to the other side of my chest and arched his eyebrows. "It's true. I promise you that. One hundred percent. Good thing you're not in the circus, eh, Truly? By the way, how's the heart? Any pangs or pains you want to share?" I shook my head and said nothing about the melancholic roots that were spreading through my body like willow reeds. Robert Morgan didn't need to know anything about those, I thought, especially since he'd caused most of them.

Some people in this world are born bigger than life, and some grow to be that way, but I know it's not a matter you can pick and choose. If it were, then I would opt to be doll-sized. Maybe even a dwarf. Then I'd have to be carried everywhere I went, ceremonially, in a sedan chair borne on the oiled shoulders of nubile young men. I would pick out a seat of gold with scrollwork of its own, maybe even a dragon or two, and hire children with clashing cymbals to accompany me, singing out my name. My life would be like a parade. As it happens, however, my feet are bigger than most men's, along with my hands, my hips, my neck, and the vast expanse of my shoulders and back. And the only parade I've ever attended is the defunct May Day festival, where the mayor used to drive a gaggle of the town's prettiest girls down Main Street in his convertible. Every year, it was the same. Dick Crane, senile in the end but still able to perform this one civic task, beeped the horn of his classic Caddy, and the girls all screamed and waved, hysterical with their own beauty.

Even before I gained all the weight, my body pressing outward like a balloon getting ready to take flight, I was always huge. *Solid as granite,* my father used to say, *and twice as thick. Not like your sister, that's for sure. Serena Jane takes after your mama. A real living doll.* Which was, after all, the whole reason Robert Morgan wanted my sister in the first place, even if he had to stalk her and steal her away like the wolf in a fairy tale. I sometimes wonder what would have happened if it had been the other way around—if Serena Jane had been the one pursuing Robert Morgan. Most likely he would have turned tail and run, his long, lupine teeth chattering in fear. Robert Morgan never liked a thing in his life unless he got to take the first bite out of it, and he never let a thing go, either, until it was chewed all the way down to skin and bone. Even his narrow, prowling walk told you he was a man of limitless appetite—hungry all the time and yet never filled all the way up. Not like Serena Jane, who was about as dense as spun sugar, who picked and pushed at her food and grew so light that she eventually flew away, and certainly not like me, who always ate what was given to me but who, anyone could see, always ended up paying double for it.

After the burial, I veered from the main path of the cemetery, headed deeper into the graveyard to pay my respects to other souls. If I'd turned around and looked, I would have noticed that the trail of my footsteps through the grass was growing lighter and less emphatic, but I just trudged with my nose pointing to the bulging wilderness of my abdomen, my chins tucked up tight against my neck, my thoughts lost in the familiar ocean of my own labored breathing. The other mourners gathered themselves, shaking the sound of dirt thudding on the doctor's coffin from their ears, drifting back toward town and the wake.

The jagged iron gates of the cemetery glittered in the distance, the black spikes sticking up into the darkening afternoon like a row of rotten teeth. They reminded me how Robert Morgan's breath had stunk right before he died, as if his body were cleaning house, sweeping out all its rank corners and dubious crannies before it gave up its ghost once and for all.

A bitter gust of wind skidded up behind me and lashed at the backs of my legs. I was wearing a black rayon dress I'd sewn myself—a sacklike, drooping shroud of a garment that did little to disguise my bumps and bulges—and no stockings because there just weren't any that would fit. On my feet, I had the black workman's boots I wore from October to April, and over everything I'd draped a moth-eaten greatcoat from the doctor's attic, which still only barely gripped the plinths of my shoulders.

At the burial, I'd stood with Amelia. I knew that people were whispering and nudging one another, darting significant looks when I heaved myself right up to the grave's edge, panting like a dying elephant. *At least we don't need to worry about her falling in,* Vi Vickers had muttered to Sal Dunfry.

Sal had giggled behind her imported calfskin glove. *She'd get stuck halfway down.* I blushed, but Amelia, who'd cleaned the doctor's office for the past ten years and probably had enough dirt on him to bury him herself, pointed out that I was an angel to have put up with Robert Morgan for so long and that no one, least of all decent people with good sense, should be mocking me. Sal shut up then but cast another dubious glance at my lank hair and fleshy limbs and concluded that Amelia Dyerson was blind as well as dumb. She gave a backward glance over her shoulder as she left the graveyard, watching as I lumbered away from her. *Truly's no angel*, I heard Sal snicker to Vi, rearranging the buttery folds of her cashmere scarf closer against the unusual weather. *Why, for one thing, she'd take up half of heaven, and for another, she's too big to get off the ground.*

An irate crow flapped out of the nearby trees, squawking its displeasure, leaving its bare branch vibrating in the unseasonable cold. The noise made me look around at the world, the ground cosseted with a freak blanket of frost, the headstones stark as ancient relics. I peered up at the sky, the light dwindling to an echo of azure, and watched the crow flap its way to the horizon. And at that moment, the hard stone I'd been carrying around in my chest—the one that weighed as much as all of Aberdeen's tombstones piled together, the one that kept me pinned inside Robert Morgan's house, even on days when the town roses made the air into a honeyed liqueur—that stone began to melt, sending oily tears slicking down my cheeks. I wiped them away, ashamed to be blubbering over something as silly as a crow bobbing in a great big sky, but relieved, nonetheless, to be standing under something huge enough to contain me. You see, for the first time in longer than I could remember, I'd found something larger than me.

Chapter One

Technically speaking, I guess you could say I killed Robert Morgan, but I did it only because he insisted on it, and because death had clearly already gotten its mealy hands on him, and because I knew the very act of asking must have made him madder than hell.

"Look at me," he'd cackle from the foul nest of covers on his bed, "and then take a look at you. It just doesn't seem right." I knew what he meant. Let's just say I had more than my fair share of resources shoring up my bones. "You could live through two winters back to back, Truly," he rasped.

"You could swallow the whole damn world, and no one would notice."

He was lying under his great-grandmother's famous quilt, the one embroidered all over with flowers and vines, some of them nice and neat inside a diamond-edged border and the rest running riot around the edges. It was a peculiar piece of work all right. In fact, if you looked at it hard enough, you might get to thinking it was almost two quilts—the tidy, inner square worked up all careful and the crazy border that looked like a floral explosion. That's what I'd concluded, at least, after ten years of staring at the thing.

Soon enough, the doctor quit talking altogether. At first, I welcomed this development, banging into his room with trays of food I knew he couldn't eat but tormented him with anyway. "That story about the dead lady in the hippo cage?" I asked, waving a spoonful of tapioca under his nose. "It's the dumbest thing I ever heard. So what if it's true?" I watched him shake his head, then popped the pudding into my own mouth and rolled the beads across my tongue, satisfied with their slick sweetness. "For one thing, what'd they do with the hippo? And for another, you don't even know any of the details that would make the story really good. For instance, what kind of coffin did they put her in? Or did they just throw her body in the cage and pull her along to a giant hole in the ground?"

I leaned down so close, I knew he could see the tiny hairs that limned my upper lip. "Do you want to know the difference between a good story and the truth?" When he didn't respond, I went ahead and gave him the answer. "The little bits, Robert Morgan. That's all. If you get those right, you can get away with murder." I smiled and patted his arm. Then I finished off the tapioca.

After a few days, however, I found myself unsettled by the silence between us. For twenty years, I'd endured his barbs and insults, but now I could feel his stony stare roving over my flesh, as if he wanted to devour me raw. I'd watch out of the corner of my eye as he cricked his jaw open and shut like a ventriloquist's dummy, trying to make a noise and failing, and then

I'd collect his untouched tray, half wishing he'd snarl at me like the old days and half hoping he wouldn't.

In spite of their best intentions, death has always had a way of stalking the Morgan men, as far back as any of them could remember, at least as far back as the history of Aberdeen. The first Robert Morgan arrived in Aberdeen from the South, just as the Civil War was winding down. In the war, he'd served as a surgeon, up until the very end when Sherman's hot swath of vengeance proved too much. Death, the first Robert Morgan decided as he followed lines of ghost-eyed soldiers through the fetid air of the South, was a perpetual motion machine—a spiked instrument of butchery that would roll on as long as there were men willing to feed it. He was not one of them.

He deserted just outside of Savannah, stowing himself in the wrecked husks of plantations and barns, making his way north via the coast, and then, when he hit Delaware, he turned inland and worked his way through the Tuscarora Mountains, all the way up to New York State. Everywhere he went, he inquired the same thing:

Did anyone know a way to ward off death? He was shown crucifixes, amulets of twine and grass, rosary beads, and an eagle's feather. He would examine each object politely, then hand it back to its owner and shoulder his pack, his mind already racing ahead of him.

By the time he got to New York State, the answer to his question started to change. "I don't know 'bout scarin' death away for good," one gap-toothed farmer told him, his skin as wrinkled as linen, "but you might try askin' the folks in Aberdeen. They're all older than a bunch of mummies. If anyone's gonna know, it's them."

Intrigued, Robert Morgan accepted the man's offer of his barn for the evening, and that night, Robert Morgan slept peacefully and deep, awakening well before dawn to hoist his dwindling pack before heading the opposite direction of the sunset. He didn't have the foggiest notion where he was, but it didn't matter. For the first time since he'd deserted, Robert Morgan had a destination to get to.

❧

When he arrived in Aberdeen at the onset of winter, he found the population of the village in the middle of an influenza epidemic, with just one woman treating them all. Her name was Tabitha Dyerson, and she was the relative of a famous witch.

"Judith Dyerson. Burned at the stake," Ebert Pickerton, the proprietor of Aberdeen's alehouse, told Robert with a wink. "A heretic. The whole family upped and left Massachusetts after that. But some say"—and here the innkeeper leaned conspiratorially close to Robert Morgan—"they brought her shadow book with 'em. That's where Tabitha gets the healing touch from."

Robert Morgan tilted back and took a blessed breath of neutral air. "Is that why everyone here lives so long? Because of old Judith's secrets?"

Ebert Pickerton's belly danced with laughter. "Hell no, son," he brayed, smacking his palm down on the counter. "That's on account of our bad tempers. The good Lord won't have us." His face fell, a balloon caving in on itself. "Lately, though, seems people in this town are dropping off like anyone else. You can go out and see for yourself." So Robert Morgan went to Mass on Sunday, toting the medical instruments he'd stolen from the army, to offer his services as a physician.

The first patient he attended was a child, a girl about nine years old. She screamed when he approached her. To the delirious child, Robert Morgan, gaunt from seven months of walking, his beard too wild for any scissors to tame, was an evil Father Christmas.

"You'd best go," the girl's father told Robert Morgan, his hand clamped firmly on the doctor's elbow. "We'll call for Tabitha."

Robert Morgan raised his eyebrows. "Your daughter needs proper medical supervision."

The man just shrugged, opened the door, and ushered Robert Morgan into the miserable November cold. "Tabby has herbs," he said. "They've worked before."

Robert Morgan acquired his second patient after a thorough session with Aberdeen's barber. This time it was an ailing grandmother, down with the flu. Seventy-three and prune-faced, she lay stoutly in a brass bedstead—the bed she'd been born in and the bed she was prepared to die in—watching as Robert Morgan unwrapped his instruments. Her beady eyes roved over him like a chicken guarding an egg. "Please," she whimpered. "I want Tabitha." Robert Morgan sighed deeply—a great defeated wind sinking to his boot tips—and wrapped his instruments back in their chamois. Her hulking son gave an apologetic half-smile. Tabitha, at least, wouldn't charge anything expect maybe a pumpkin or two or a loaf of his wife's molasses bread.

Robert Morgan retreated to the shadow-shrouded back room he had taken at Widow Dunfry's house with a small bottle of whiskey wrapped neatly in plain brown paper. So far, Aberdeen had stonewalled his search for longevity, refused his good-intentioned attempts to cure, and even its weather was foul.

Robert Morgan took another, bitter swill of Ebert's homemade whiskey and sank farther into the widow's mildewed armchair, reviewing the afternoon's case. *Tabby has herbs,* he recalled the little girl's father saying. Robert Morgan snorted, expelling a small plug of snot. Skullduggery, that's what it was. He tipped the bottle back to his lips, upending it. The liquid ignited in his throat like a firecracker. He pursed his lips, the sear ghost of rye singeing the insides of his cheeks, his nose, and the secret canals of his ears.

When he woke, he found himself in bed. He hitched himself onto his elbows, feeling his eyes swim in his head, losing his balance. Then he realized he wasn't alone.

The diminutive woman sitting in the corner sighed, put down her knitting, and walked over to him. She reached under his wrist to test his pulse with lily-stalk fingers. "You're over the worst," she told him, sweeping back to her place in the corner, her skirts whispering like contrary angels. "When you can, you should bathe." She began to leave.

"Wait," Robert Morgan cried, his voice muted by phlegm. "How ill have I been?"

The woman cocked her head. "You're over the worst," she said again. "You'll soon be better."

Robert Morgan hitched himself onto his elbows again, wavering. "You're the witch."

Tabitha Dyerson drew herself straight, narrowing her eyes like a snake getting ready to strike. "I'm as Christian as you are, sir," she snapped. "Possibly even more so. You owe me your life."

It wasn't until hours later that Robert Morgan realized she'd taken the last of Ebert Pickerton's whiskey with her.

She lived on a farm on the outskirts of town, Robert Morgan learned, with her father and brother, the father swimming in the mad sea of old age, the brother a recluse since he'd returned from the war. Robert Morgan trudged over the rough track of mud that served as a road, announcing his presence at her door with three harsh knocks, the only kind he knew how to give anymore. His bare knuckles stung from the cold.

She spied him from the window and answered the door warily, her hands clutching the wood. From around the sides of her seeped the scent of lemons, of gingerbread and camphor. Feminine odors that Robert Morgan had forgotten existed in the world.

"You've recovered." Her voice rang as flat as his raps on the door. Robert Morgan produced from his pocket an apple—a gnarled piece of fruit, but an offering all the same.

Tabitha received it warily, tucking it in

the depths of her apron. "Do you have a specific reason for calling?"

Robert Morgan could feel the heat radiating out of the house and sensed that she was impatient to be rid of him. He listed on his cracked boot heels like a ship about to sink, then brought an arm forward to steady himself. Slowly, the world settled back into some semblance of order, the porch boards still warped, the chimney still aslant, but all the pieces more or less fitted together. It was probably, Robert Morgan decided, as close as he would ever again come to being arranged. Tabitha folded her arms and waited. "I have come," he stammered, "with a proposal."

They were married on Michaelmas, the ceremony witnessed by Widow Dunfry and Ebert Pickerton. They celebrated Christmas with a goose and chestnut stuffing. The brother drank too much cider and wheeled about on the wooden leg he would never get used to. The father slumbered over his dish, and Robert retired early to the corner of the parlor he had transformed into a makeshift laboratory. No one sang.

Three things amazed Robert Morgan

about his new life. The first was that no one asked him about his past. The people of Aberdeen just seemed to regard him as Tabitha Dyerson's new husband, and a prior existence neither occurred nor mattered to them. The second thing that needled him was that even though he was a doctor, he had yet to heal one single patient in the town. His remedies either failed, or the people dumped his powders in their chicken feed. They unwound his bandages and replaced them with Tabitha's poultices made from crushed wolfsbane and pig's urine.

The final source of wonder, of course, was his wife. Impervious to the wild whip of a New England winter, moon-skinned under the covers when he took her at night, circumspect in all matters relating to herself. With her father, she was patient, forgiving; with her brother, resolved; and with Robert Morgan, she was serene.

"Tell me what your earliest memory is," he demanded one night after lovemaking. The air outside was so cold, the stars appeared to be shivering.

Tabitha loosed one of her arms from the sheets and brushed a piece of hair away from her eyes. When she spoke, her breath escaped in a visible wisp. "Gathering herbs," she said. "An iron pot bubbling on the fire. The odor of wet leaves." She half closed her eyes and smiled but offered no elaboration.

"What is your favorite food?" Robert Morgan asked. They'd been married only a short time, but she already knew that he liked venison stew with nutmeg and juniper berries, that he preferred whiskey to ale, soda bread to brown, while he could only guess at her tastes. It bothered him a little, this advantage she had over him.

Tabitha stretched one of her long arms toward him, and he grew excited at the thought of her touch, but she merely rearranged the blankets closer around her chin. "I eat the same as you, husband," she whispered. "We are one flesh now. Please, let's sleep."

On his better days, Robert Morgan indulged her behavior, told himself he was lucky to have wed an obedient and untroublesome woman. On his bad days, he skulked in the parlor, cursing her witch blood.

By June, Tabitha's belly was drum-tight

under her altered skirts, the baby riding so high that Robert Morgan was certain it must be a girl. Tabitha merely murmured over his predictions. She dreamed whole afternoons away, wrapped in the floral quilt her grandmother had begun. Sometimes, Robert Morgan found her replacing the batting, mending the quilt's weak seams, shoring them up for the generations.

He moved them into town, and when people called at the new house, it was Robert who greeted them, ushering them into the parlor's laboratory, asking them to breathe against the discerning disk of his stethoscope. On the shelf above his head, he had jars of tablets ordered from Boston, powders from New York. He had a canister of ether and a paper cone to administer it. When Tabitha's father died, Robert Morgan turned his room into an examining office and then built a whole separate cottage in the back for his practice. He quit accepting eggs and skeins of yarn for payment, demanding a deposit of silver up front. It took only the turning away and subsequent death of one young mother, spotted with fever, for the town to learn that death is an impatient master.

Even the poorer households acquired clocks and began putting pennies in the bank for the hours the doctor charged.

By the time his son, Bertie, was five, Robert Morgan had hired a young man to keep his books and appointments. He had finished the cottage in back of the house and turned it into an office and an examining room. The recalcitrant brother moved back to the defunct farm. Tabitha had two more children after Bertie. With each successive pregnancy, she grew quieter and quieter, until she finally ceased to speak at all. The bouquets of herbs she was accustomed to fix to the rafters lost their shape, then their color, and finally relinquished their earthy scents, crumbling into twigs and dust. She stayed in her room, working at her quilt, adding pieces, making it bigger so that its ends draped off the bed and swept the dusty floor. Tabitha lay in the covers, wishing her arms had no bones.

Occasionally, Robert Morgan savaged the house looking for old Judith's shadow book, the one Ebert Pickerton told him about on his first day in town. He ripped apart the larder, biting indiscriminately into pork pies and wedges of cheese. He knocked down the woodpile, upended Tabitha's linen cupboard. He pried apart floorboards, thumbed page by page through the family Bible, then burned the whole thing. He ordered a new Bible from Boston, and when it arrived, it was bound in supple calfskin, its pages gilded, the cover embossed with his initials and his alone, in real gold. He penned the names of his children inside, flourishing the dips and curls of the letters, lining them up perfectly on the page, but he left Tabitha Dyerson the witch, the crone he'd tried to make a Morgan, off the family register.

At church, Robert Morgan's lips moved, but it wasn't the words of God he was uttering. Instead, he was silently cataloging his stores to himself: *carbolic powder, laudanum, aspirin, alcohol, ether*. In his experience, salvation came droplet-sized, issued from the pinched nose of a beaker, from tiny grains of granules measured and slid into an envelope. The prospect of heaven had been bottled and stoppered by him and his brethren. It was easily dispensed.

One morning, while shaving, he ran the razor over himself by feel, averting his gaze from the aging stranger in the glass, and when he turned back to his image, he found he'd nicked himself. A trickle of blood wormed its way down a crease on his face and cavorted along his jaw. He turned to Tabitha, but she was marooned in a melancholic swamp in the middle of their bed, her brow as smooth as an egg. She ignored him. Her hands were twisting and turning, knotting and looping. Under them, as if by magic, the outlines of nightshade, belladonna, and hemlock bloomed in silken leaves across the quilt. A mortal garden stitched for the immortal soul.

Robert Morgan thrust his jaw out toward his wife. "Help," he demanded crossly, and received the press of Tabby's little fingers, wrapped in a square of cast-off linen. As if by magic, the blood stopped, and Robert Morgan scowled. He wondered briefly how Tabitha did it, but the clock downstairs chimed, and he rushed to put on his hat. For him, knowledge was a plain thing, like a neatly labeled bottle, transparent and tucked on a shelf. It was not in his character to pick and follow the threads of an idea like a woman unraveling a skein of yarn. Besides, he was running late.

"Thank you," he growled, and loped out of the room, his thoughts already on salvation, his belief that he was in charge of dying in the town of Aberdeen fully intact—an idea that would persist for the next hundred and fifty years until I came along and overturned the apple cart of history.

Chapter Two

Even before I emerged from my mother's womb in 1953, people began warning my mother that the infant she carried was going to be huge. "It's bound to be a boy!" Reverend Pickerton boomed at her after church when she was only four months pregnant, laying his stout fingers on her stomach. The world, it seemed to her, had been transformed into pairs of groping hands.

"He's already rough-and-tumble!" Reverend Pickerton chortled, patting my mother's belly. As if in reply, I tilted and spun in her uterus. My mother was so enormous that Robert Morgan IV had checked her twice to make sure she wasn't carrying twins.

"I just can't believe it," he said again and again, shaking his head. "A baby this big. It's bound to be some kind of record." When his own wife gave birth to a hefty boy a year and a half before (another Robert, called Bob Bob), her abdomen had been only the size of a melon. Nevertheless, Dr. Morgan heard only one heartbeat, one fetus growing in Lily. Unless, of course, he thought, the baby had somehow devoured its twin, winding itself into its sibling, a possibility the doctor didn't present to my mother.

By midsummer, her wrists and ankles sloshed with fluids. Her knees were so puffy, it was painful to bend them. Her breasts were two cones. She was ravenous all the time, eating the strangest things in spite of herself—jelly and raisins on rye bread, anchovy and mustard sandwiches, lime-flavored gelatin with bits of ham and sweet potato floating in it. Her thighs expanded, turning gummy and pale. Her fingers plumped into sausages. My sister,

Serena Jane, was two years old and no longer liked to sit on her lap. Her tiny fists prodded my mother's legs, searching for the old, slender ones. "Bad bump." It was Serena Jane's opinion that I was consuming my mother and would eventually fill her all the way up.

My mother sighed and slid Serena Jane back onto the floor. Of all the trials of motherhood, she'd been the most unprepared for the critical scrutiny of a toddler. Serena Jane screamed when my mother read her the wrong story at night. She combed her fingers over my mother's face, outlining every crease and fold. She inspected the cheese sandwiches my mother made her at lunch with the offended air of a restaurant critic, whining if the crusts were still on. My mother could only imagine her daughter's reaction to a bald, squalling infant. She ran her palm over Serena Jane's butterfly hair and tried not to care when my sister yanked her head away. My mother sighed again.

"Don't be silly," she said. "I had a bump with you, too. I was round before you came out." But they both knew she was lying.

This time was different. Something really was eating her from the inside out.

Dr. Morgan found the lump in my mother's breast in the eighth month of her pregnancy, four weeks before she was due to deliver. It rolled under his palm like a hard-boiled quail's egg. My mother cried out from the pressure.

"How long?" he asked, pushing his glasses up on his nose, as if they would make the elements of the situation clearer.

My mother bowed her head. Her neck wattled. "About three months."

"This size the whole time?"

My mother shook her head. "It's gotten bigger." Bob Morgan sighed, and that single exhalation told my mother everything she needed to know. She splayed her knees on the examining table and contemplated the reproduction going on inside her body—copies of copies of copies, a garbled message being passed around her organs. An unbreakable code.

She refused offers of a ride home. She wobbled down Bob Morgan's porch steps, her knees as flexible as rubber bands, and waved to Maureen and little Bob Bob, who were cavorting in the sprinklers by the side of the house. Bees weighted with nectar hung in the hedges. Bob Bob, his buttocks swaddled in a diaper, scooted over to my mother and hugged her around her calves, throwing her off balance.

"No, darling," Maureen scolded him gently, detaching his fingers from my mother's puffy legs and flashing a weary smile at her full-mooned face. "I'm sorry," she said, her eyes roving the mountainous curves of my mother's body. "He's completely uncontrollable. He just wants what he wants. I can't keep up."

My mother looked down toward her feet, toward Bob Bob, but her monstrous belly, her mutinous breasts, blocked her view. She felt the child's wormy fingers trying to creep in between her own, and she opened her hand wider.

"It's okay," she told Maureen, moving her palm up to her belly. "You don't have to explain." After all, she'd just learned that even something microscopic could have an unstoppable will.

❧

When her labor began, my mother was brushing Serena Jane's baby-floss hair.

Serena Jane was beautiful, my mother knew, a miracle of physical arrangement—perfect eyes, perfect pearls of teeth framed with a cupid mouth. *The girl should be in pictures*, my father used to chortle, hoisting Serena Jane up as if to display her to an adoring crowd. It pleased him no end to have produced a commodity like my sister. He took almost as much delight in the starched baby ruffles, the rose-patterned, crocheted toddler clothing, as my mother did. He was an ordinary citizen, a small-town barber, but he had produced a princess, a queen. And soon, to go with the little monarch, there would be a prince.

"Put her down," my mother scolded. "I'm not done." In her hands, a limp length of pink ribbon drooped like a tired tongue. My father deposited Serena Jane back on the bureau top, where she stood with eyes fixed, limbs poised, as if waiting to receive a benediction. My mother anointed Serena Jane's hair with a double-looped bow. Her fingers looked as if they were wrapping a present they couldn't wait to give away. "There!" she said, sunbeams in her voice. She turned Serena Jane to the mirror, angling her small body from side to side. "Who looks pretty?"

Serena Jane merely blinked. She knew she was pretty. She accepted it as her due. In the summer heat, at birthday parties or picnics, when other little girls' clothes were sticky and smeared with cake, hers remained buttoned and pristine, crisp as sails on an arctic lake.

The mothers of Aberdeen sighed and envied my mother. They didn't know that every night she stayed up late—sometimes till two in the morning—devising ever more elaborate costumes to set off her daughter's remarkable beauty. While my father slumbered beside her, she squinted in her weak pool of bedside light and smocked the fronts of dresses. She embarked on a marathon of embroidery, embellishing Serena Jane's new winter coat with rosebuds and silk ladybugs. She crimped extra ruffles onto cuffs, edged collars with ribbon, replaced plain bone buttons with mother-of-pearl. When she finished stitching, when her hands ached, she would climb out of bed and iron the layers of Serena Jane's clothing for the coming day.

Only when the little shoes were spit shined, the socks rolled together just so, did she haul her huge self back into bed and allow sleep to claim her. Although she hadn’t said so to my father, or to anyone, for that matter, she was looking forward to the birth of a boy, to a creature she would not have to decorate every day like a cake. Then she drifted into the mire of pregnant sleep, her dreams muddied with bats, and baseballs, and vibrating with the hopeful color blue.

Take her,” my mother said to my father, handing over a stiff-legged Serena Jane when she felt the first pain claw at her back like an impatient animal. It was a Sunday in July, the air sticky, unpleasant, and inclined to fight its way down into people’s lungs instead of sliding. The pain was two weeks early. My mother grabbed the nicked edge of the bureau and tried to hold on while another jolt jigged through her with molten feet, then she staggered her way into the bedroom, where her water broke. Saucer-eyed, my father and Serena Jane stared at her. “Don’t just stand there like twin monkeys," she barked. "Go get me Bob Morgan."

By the time my father returned, my mother had smashed the Union Oil alarm clock, her bedside lamp, a vase of flowers, and gone on to shred the sheets. Bob Morgan found her in a knot on the floor, gnawing at the cotton, her hair a conflagration around her face and neck. A lodestone of calm and reason, he set down his black bag and turned to my father and my sister.

"I'll take it from here," he told them. "You'd best take that child into the kitchen and get her something to eat." Dumbfounded, my father obeyed.

Everything about my mother's labor was sized to scale. The puddle of her water on the bedroom floor invited comparisons to a small sea. Wrenching jabs shook her body, then the bed, then rocked the house so that all anyone in town had to do to know how the birth was progressing was saunter down Maple Street and stand outside number seven. Over the next several hours, a curious knot of spectators developed on our front lawn, growing from a few concerned neighbors to the better half of the town. Soon, picnic baskets appeared, along with frosted bottles of ginger beer and lemonade. Estelle Crane, the brand-new mayor's wife, arrived with a cherry pie she was saving for supper that evening and began passing pieces of it around.

"Ten pounds, seven ounces," said John Hinkleman, who owned the general store, slapping five dollars into Ebert Vickers's outstretched palm, and the Reverend Pickerton countered him with a guess of eleven pounds even.

"I'll go even higher than that," Roger Thompson blustered. "Put me down for eleven-five. Doc Morgan says this kid's going to be some kind of record. He still can't believe Lily's not having twins." His remarks led to a new whirlwind of furious betting, men revising and upping their stakes.

"With a boy like this on the team, Aberdeen's bound to win every time." Dick Crane, the youngest mayor Aberdeen had ever seen, took a long swallow of beer.

"Got a few years yet there, Dick," John reminded him, but Dick shrugged.

"Still."

The men thronged tighter, resuming speculation, until—from far away, it seemed, the voice was so quiet—a question was offered.

"What if it's a girl?" The group of men, and several of the nearby women, fell silent. Heads swiveled to regard August Dyerson, the town oddball, resident collector of junk, unsuccessful horse breeder, and general outcast.

"What if—what if—*what* did you say?" Ebert Vickers stuttered, his chubby fist full of humid dollar bills, a pencil clamped between his steadfast teeth.

August repeated his query slowly and carefully, as if enunciating for a particularly stupid, non-native speaker. "I said. What. If. It's. A. Girl?"

Roger Thompson spat and gurgled like an incontinent whale. "August, what the hell are you talking about? Lily's in there about to give birth to a tank. No female infant is that robust. Besides, look at Serena Jane. She's not exactly gargantuan."

August ignored Roger's reasoning, squared his shoulders, then handed Ebert Vickers a wad of notes. "I'd like you to put me down for Girl."

Ebert thrust the money back at August. “We’re not betting on the sex, Gus. We’re betting on the weight. Either put your number in or step aside.” August’s arm flagged a moment, as if independent of his body, then took the money and shoved it into his sweaty pocket. The men roared with laughter as he sidled toward the white hot strip of summer pavement.

“There’s no accounting for women and fools,” Dick Crane said, wiping his eyes.

“There’s no accounting for the likes of Gus,” John Hinkleman replied.

The shoving began again.

“Twelve-seven!”

“Twelve-nine!”

The digits went up and up, rising like bread in the moist July air.

Inside the cool cave of the house, my mother and Robert Morgan IV were floating in their own detached universe, one that ticked along at the slow rate of bones expanding. On the slumping mattress, my mother lay with her legs bent back like a pair of exhausted wings. The insides of her pale thighs glistened, as if snails had danced down the length of her. When a contraction gripped her, rattling her teeth, Bob placed his hands on her cheeks and riveted her stare with his own. "Not yet," he instructed her. "Don't push yet."

But I wanted air and light. I was brutalizing her with my impatient head. "I can't," my mother whispered, her voice crushed. She pictured all the cells of her body neatly ironed and creased, ready to be folded up and put back on a shelf. All the cells, that is, except for the stubborn ones in her breast. Nothing, she knew, would stamp them out. In the past four weeks, the lump had grown from a minuscule egg to a child's fist. She hid it from my father with the padding of her maternity bra, turning her back to him when she dressed in the morning.

"Yes, you can," Bob insisted, and by saying it, he made it so. My mother felt Bob Morgan's hands palpating the gap between her legs and winced as he inserted gloved fingers into the doughy depths of her. She knew he had delivered twelve babies in Aberdeen, including his own son and Serena Jane, but she still felt shy in front of him.

"Lily . . ." Bob anchored her with his

eyes again. "I'm going to prop you up with pillows and then you can push." He tucked pillows and a blanket behind her and pushed up the hem of her nightdress farther. A pain arrived that was so enormous, my mother ceased to care what Bob Morgan saw, was grateful, even, for his gaze, which was needle-sharp and capable of remembering who she was before the layers of pregnancy camouflaged her.

"I have blue eyes," she muttered to remind herself of herself, high-pitched, feverish words. "I like the color green," and then her tongue loosened and gave way to an unbroken wailing pouring from her throat, a noise like a cat bleeding in the rain.

She was still lost in the delirium of her mental catalog—a letter to her son she would write down when the pain was finished with her—when Bob Morgan pulled me out of her, using no small amount of muscle and marveling at my hefty shoulders, the Neanderthal sprawl of my cranium.

Corned beef, my mother thought, her favorite supper. *"Amazing Grace,"* her favorite hymn. *Dear Son,* she thought, her fingers stretching for a pencil, eager to begin composing the details of herself. She wanted her boy to know these things about her before she forgot or was no longer there. *Christmas*, her favorite holiday. *Dahlia*, the flower she loved best.

She missed Bob Morgan's squawk when he finally pulled me free from Lily and saw that I was a girl. His hands slipped under my slimy head. He almost dropped me.

"Lily," he whispered, moving up beside her. "Look, it's a girl, not a boy. You have another girl." Then he saw the indiscriminate puddle of red seeping into the bedclothes. "Lily?" he rasped again, just as I began to squall. He glanced from my mother's pallid cheeks to my pug-nosed face. He put me down on the soaked sheets, the umbilical cord still attached, and when he reached to my mother's neck to feel for a pulse, his fingers left a bright red smear on her throat. A faint throb beat under his fingers, but not, Bob Morgan knew, for much longer. He didn't bother with the afterbirth, merely cut the cord from my stomach and knotted it, ignoring my furious cries.

"Lily," he demanded again, shaking my mother's shoulder and leaving more red smudges on her chest so that she resembled a savage painted for war. He laid me on top of her. "Lily, you have to give your baby a name."

But my mother's head lolled, and her eyes stared back at him, jelly in their sockets. Inside the cage of her skull, her mind was still wheeling through its marvelous inventory of herself, the list she would present to her child—favorite pastries, films. *Little Women*, the book she loved more than any other. Not that a boy would want to read such a tale—the small dramas of burned dresses and chopped-off hair, the stuff of sisters. She tried to think of a book for boys, couldn't, and so decided to end her letter. *Yours truly*, she whispered into the swampy air of the room, but it was hard. There was an animal sitting on her chest, plucking at the lump in her breast. *Take it*, she thought. *I never wanted it in the first place.*

"Truly?" Bob Morgan puzzled, wiping his hands with a cloth, glistening finger by glistening finger. "Lily, what the heck kind of a name is that?" But he never received an answer. By the time he removed me from my mother's breast, cupping my enormous head with the spread palm of his hand, my mother's lips had gone as blue as the sky outside.

"Well," Bob Morgan said, looking into my eyes, "you may be ugly as sin and heavy as an ox, but I guess your mama loved you truly." Wide-eyed, I suckled my fist and took in the doctor's words with a look of gravity, as if I knew that for the next three decades, it would be the only direct reference I would have to the word *love*.

Chapter Three

Had August Dyerson insisted on sticking with his bet of Girl, he would have won a substantial sum of money off the men of Aberdeen, but as it was, no one profited from my birth because I outweighed even the highest estimate. There was mirth and much laughter when Dr. Morgan announced the official figure and then silence when he explained how all of that was irrelevant owing to my mother's death. Chastened, people shut up their picnic hampers and clustered empty bottles to their chests in clumsy bouquets. The next morning, Ebert Vickers returned limp dollar bills to their rightful owners, making a door-to-door town circuit on foot, his hat held over his heart in sympathy for my poor, dead mother and her monstrous newborn babe. No one in Aberdeen said so, but it was clear they all believed I had killed my mother. A baby as big as me was just not natural.

Bob Morgan took careful pains to explain to my father that the birth had been messy, yes, but that my mother didn't have much time left anyway. He described the lump riddling her breast, lurking in her body like a spy, ready to send out emissaries. "It would have been a losing battle in the end, Earl," Bob said, "a fight she never would have won. You wouldn't have wanted her to go through that now, would you?"

My father, muted by grief and stuck with two motherless daughters, stared at the lank body of his wife stretched out on their bed and felt as though the walls of his throat were about to gum closed. It was unacceptable, he decided—the brown clots of blood seeping into the mattress, the metallic sour smells in the air, all of it. Like a meal left half-finished on the table, the candles still burning, someone's fork poised at the edge of a plate. He looked at my mother's body—a scrap, a leftover from life—and then at Robert Morgan IV, and he intuited that the man was asking to be let off the hook. His black medical bag gaped in his hands like a dumbfounded mouth trying to explain.

My father didn't want to hear it. He almost pushed Bob out the door, away from his house and girls, right down his porch steps. "You go on," he said. "Get. I'll take it from here."

Still shamed from the ruinous carnival of my birth, nobody in town wanted to attend my mother's funeral, so it was just my father, my sister, and I who clustered at the lip of her grave to watch her disappear into Aberdeen dirt. Reverend Pickerton read a few hasty Bible verses, then beat a quick retreat, dabbing his forehead with the immaculate and reassuring corner of his handkerchief.

"My condolences, Earl," he muttered, squeezing my father's biceps with crablike fingers and studiously avoiding the moonscape of my newborn face. My father, stunned by the weight of his grief, blinked. Reverend Pickerton hesitated, then squeezed my father's arm again and jutted his chin in my direction. "I'm sorry the baby was a girl," he said, and squeezed once more before fleeing.

The afternoon thickened around my father. In front of him, my mother's grave leered like a jester's laughing mouth. Next to him, my sister snuffled, her head bowed like a bluebell, the bow of her upper lip only enhanced by all the snot. And then there was me—more of a boulder than a baby, rough-skinned and bug-eyed, impervious to the significance of the chasm yawning in front of me. My father tilted me toward it. "That's your mother in there. Tell her good-bye."

My father watched in horror as I gummed my pacifier, broke the teat in half, and spat the remaining plastic down on top of my mother's crude pine coffin, where it clattered and spun like a lost top. Later, much as he wished to chalk it up to the stupidity of infancy or to a soul trapped in the primitive and clumsy cage of the body, it still seemed to my father that I knew exactly what I was doing. And in a way, he was right. Even back then, I guess, I suspected that sometimes the only available choice in life is to spit on death and run.

❧

My life as a girl came to an abrupt halt at the age of one and a half, when I suddenly outgrew all of my sister's old clothes. Trying to shove my head into one of the frilly bonnets my mother had sewn, my father quickly concluded, was like attempting to stuff a watermelon through a keyhole. No matter which way he tugged, how much he heaved and pulled, the bonnet strings would not tie. The bonnet would not even cover half of my red scalp.

My father stepped back and examined me. Whereas Serena Jane possessed the limbs and features of a vain little pixie, my physiognomy brought to mind the heaviest and roundest of objects—a cannonball, perhaps. Something impervious to smashes and collisions. Since I began walking at the unprecedented age of seven months, I had fallen down the stairs twice, plunged unharmed into the flower beds from the front porch, and survived being pushed into oncoming traffic by Serena Jane in our rusted red wagon.

After each disaster, my father patiently checked me for signs of concussion, broken bones, or ravaged flesh but observed nothing. I never had any welts or bruises—I never even cried. In fact, the only way he ever even knew about any of my early calamities was the unholy noise I made when I fell. It was, he told his customers in the barbershop, like an asteroid colliding with the Earth. Except for that, I could have been made of rubber.

He sighed now and reached for one of the lace-trimmed chemises my mother had made before she died and which I could still fit into until a few months ago. But he was again unsuccessful. He held the shirt up to my robust chest. Next to me, the shirt looked comical, like a doll's. It came to a halt a full inch above my hips. My father rummaged in one of Serena Jane's bureau drawers and pulled out a smocked dress—brand spanking new, a gift from the reverend's wife. Still no luck. Finally, in desperation because he was late for his shift at the barbershop and because there didn't seem to be anything else to do, he put me in one of his own shirts, the sleeves rolled over and over on themselves, peeled back like banana skins, the hem scraggling at my feet.

Fatherhood had become a series of negotiations he suspected he was losing. Without my mother, my father simply had no precedent for raising two daughters, especially when they differed as much as Serena Jane and I did. The things that made Serena Jane happy—tea sets, and baby doll clothes, and the leftover bottles of my mother's nail varnish—made me howl in misery. My father learned quickly enough to give me plainer toys: empty cans to rattle and tower into pyramids; lengths of scratchy rope to coil and knot; a cardboard box with a hole cut in it for a window.

And then there was my appetite. My father couldn't keep up. He cracked open tin after tin of formula, heating it carefully on the stove the way he'd seen my mother do, then pouring it into a series of sterilized bottles I gulped down as if they were milk-filled thimbles. I cut teeth at three months, and soon after that, my father gave up on the bottles, spooning piles of tapioca pudding into me instead.

"You can't feed a child that young solid

food yet!" Amanda Pickerton scolded during one of her early mercy visits, and my father, his eyes glazed with exhaustion, hunched his shoulders and agreed with her.

"I can't do any of it," he admitted, and that's how Amanda Pickerton came to be briefly in charge of my existence.

Every weekday morning, before he went to cut hair in the barbershop, my father delivered my sister and me to the better judgment of Amanda. The arrangement suited my father (he didn't care who took us off his hands as long as he actually got to use them), and it suited Amanda, whose children were grown and gone. She was one of those women who needed to hold dominion over something smaller than her, and that was always the whole problem between us. I was never minute enough to squeeze through the cracks of her world.

The morning my father left me on her porch wearing his old shirt, Amanda knit her brows and pulled the corners of her mouth down like sickles. My father shoved us into the house without speaking, his jaw clamped tight, his eyes already focused on the reassuring world of male hair. Serena Jane, highly verbal, did his talking for him.

"Look, Mrs. Pickerton! Truly's busting at the seams!" she crowed, delighting in my clownish attire.

Amanda stared at Serena Jane and discovered nothing wrong with her, at least. As always, Serena Jane's hair held its braids perfectly, the ribbons at the ends of them a little crooked, maybe, her skirt not really pleated as stiffly as it could be, but that wasn't our poor father's fault. He was just a man, after all, doing his blessed best. It was me who was giving him a run for his money.

That morning, to add insult to the injury of the floppy shirt, I had crumbs clinging to my ample chin and, Amanda noted, a smear of butter glistening on one of my wobbly cheeks. My father put me down next to the placid Serena Jane, and Amanda noticed for the first time that I was getting to be bigger than my sister. Serena Jane's legs and arms were tender stalks, feminine in their every curve, but my limbs hung awkwardly from my torso as if I were wearing padding. Even my lips looked as though they were squeezed onto my face. Amanda sighed deeply and held an unenthusiastic hand out to me.

"Come on with me, darling," she cooed. "Let's see if we can get you fixed up." She made cow eyes at my father, who was shuffling his feet on the other side of the screen door, eager to get going. "Don't you worry about a thing," she simpered, smiling at Serena Jane and gripping my fist a little harder than she needed to. "I've got some old clothes of Gina's upstairs that should do the trick. Why, you won't even recognize her when you get back!" My father flashed a grin, relief making his jaw relax, and turned and lurched down the Pickertons' steps, blind to how white Amanda's knuckles were around my hand.

As soon as he turned the corner from the house, Amanda's smile disappeared. The transformation was remarkable, like a house reverting back to plainness once its holiday baubles were stripped. Without her church face, Amanda Pickerton looked almost like a fox. "Now, dear," she said to Serena Jane, tidying one of her pigtails' wilted ribbons, "why don't you go and play in the sunroom? I've set the dolls out for you, and there are some books as well."

Serena Jane cast an uncertain glance in my direction. "But my sister—"

Amanda cut her off. "Don't worry your pretty little head about Truly. I'll take care of her."

Serena Jane walked over to me and planted a dry kiss on my cheek. I made a grab for her waist, but she held me off. She didn't like my sticky fingers on her clothes. "Truly likes dolls, too," she noted to Mrs. Pickerton, and then wandered to the back of the house, where an absorbing array of molded plastic figurines with realistic eyelashes awaited.

Upstairs, in her grown daughter Gina's old room, Amanda roughly divested me of the offending shirt, then sat me nearly naked in a hard chair with wicker caning. The straw dug into the tender backs of my legs, and I tried to wriggle free, but Amanda caught me and pushed all her weight on my shoulders. "You stay there!" she commanded, her red, red nails digging into my skin. "You sit until you're told." Even though I couldn't form words yet, I was perfectly cognizant of the message. I stopped wriggling and stared at Amanda. On my shoulders, half-mooned welts bloomed.

I watched Amanda sift through several boxes stowed at the back of the closet. Whenever she pulled out another item of clothing, the scent of mothballs billowed through the air. I sneezed, and Amanda looked once sharply over her shoulder but then went back to her task of rooting through the closet. The mothballs didn't seem to bother her. Sentinel, Amanda's orange kitten, appeared out of nowhere and began batting at my calves with his claws. I tried to shoo him away, but he refused to go. Amanda turned around and smiled, then gave him a shove with her foot, and he disappeared under the bed. "Good kitty," she purred at the animal.

She dug up a number of child's dresses, some of them flowered, some of them smocked with Peter Pan collars, a few pinafores and white lace blouses to go underneath them, and a pair of black patent-leather shoes with straps that circled the ankle. To the top of the pile she added a pair of frilly pantaloons and some ruffled socks. I watched, breathing through my mouth, making unpleasant sucking noises in the stale air of the room. Amanda marched over to me and hooked two fingers under my chin.

"Stop that," she said, her eyes shining like mean jewels. She lifted me to standing with considerable effort. "You sound like a hog yard. Now, put this on." Her hands parted the frothy layers of a pink striped dress with embroidered ducks cavorting on its bib. She ballooned open the fabric and tried to shove it over my head. The neck was plenty wide enough—if anything, the dress might even have been too big—but no matter what Amanda Pickerton tried, there was no way to pull the garment over me.

"Sit still!" she barked, but I wriggled and lurched like a fish on a line. In one swift movement, Amanda lifted me onto her lap, taking my place on the chair and clamping her knees tightly around my waist, squeezing until my eyes goggled with surprise and my lips fell slack. Amanda dug one elbow into the back of my ribs, pinning me in place, and wrestled again with the dress.

"If I didn't know any better," she spat between clamped teeth, heaving the pink stripes backward over my hair, "I'd say, child, you have got the makings of Satan in you." As if in protest, I flapped my baby arms, but Amanda laid her own forearm down over my torso and pushed up into my windpipe with one of her knees, gagging me. She spun the dress around and sat me up, forcing my arms into the puffed sleeves, then finally deposited me on the floor.

"There!" Amanda chirped, trying to put her mussed hair back in place with one hand and do the buttons on the dress with the other. "You're still not pretty, but at least you're decent." I ogled her for a moment, and then, with what Amanda would always recall as uncanny adult resolve, I tore the candy-stripe dress from hemline all the way up to collar. Sentinel leapt from under the bed and began batting at the strips.

"Oh!" Amanda gasped, as if someone had punched her in the stomach, and placed a fist in her mouth, biting so hard that she tasted the sour tang of her own blood.

When my father returned at five o'clock, he was met by a glowering Amanda Pickerton. Amanda, he noticed, had a bandage tied around her right thumb, a single spot of blood decorating the gauze like a ruby. I was still wearing the same shirt he'd deposited me in that morning. Before he had even finished crossing halfway over the porch, Amanda lunged toward him and shoved me into his arms as if returning a particularly offensive gift. My father noticed tiny spider lines twitching around the corners of Amanda's mouth.

"Didn't she fit in the clothes?" he asked hopefully, casting an eye over the threadbare shirt shrouding me. His heart sank a little. He didn't earn much from his job cutting hair, and without my mother's gift with a needle and thread, he didn't know how he would manage two feminine wardrobes. Amanda growled, her voice as bitter as snake venom.

"Nothing about that child will ever fit *anything*, Earl. You mark my words. She's little better than a wild beast, and I, for one, am through."

My father blinked at her, confused. In his arms, my weight was as familiar and reassuring as an old stone. He looked me over but saw no bruises, no scabs or signs of tumbles or spills. Neither was there any evidence of the belt Amanda had taken to my bottom before she'd used it to buckle me to the chair for the rest of the day.

"She didn't fall out a window again, did she?" he inquired, squinting, and Amanda Pickerton snorted.

"She'll do worse than that before she's grown and gone, you mark my words. That girl's got the devil running right through her bones." She glanced down at Serena Jane, who was planted next to her on the porch. She ran a hand over Serena's glossy hair. "This one, however, is a piece of heaven. I'm always happy to look after her."

She gave Serena Jane a quick kiss on the cheek, then went inside and slammed the front door. In the semidarkness of the hall, surrounded by the respectable scents of furniture polish and a roast in the oven, she paused to examine the gauze on her thumb—a single darkening drop marring the white—before ripping off the bandage and sucking greedily, opening the wound deeper to get a good, long taste of herself.

As my father clumped down State Street back toward home that evening, me asleep over his shoulder and Serena Jane burbling on about tea sets and dolls, he was grateful that it was the weekend. It meant he would have at least two days to sort something out for me, though he couldn't think what. At home, he heated up a half-hearted can of soup for himself and Serena Jane and warmed a pan of tapioca for me. The shirttails rode up my thighs as he lowered me onto the sofa, but the skin there was rosy and plump—all signs of Amanda's sharp nails, her pinching fingers, absorbed.

After we were in bed—Serena Jane angelic, her winglike arms spread wide; myself bunched in a ball—my father poured an emergency measure of whiskey and set to thinking. He ran through the women my mother used to know, but sympathetic as they may have been, they all had children and worries of their own—too little time, too little money, too few hands. He sighed and knocked back the rest of the whiskey. That left just one option, even though he wasn't fond of it. Still, it was better than nothing: oddball August Dyerson. Everyone's last resort.

The next morning, my father dressed Serena Jane in one of her few remaining dresses and tied a pair of stained pink ribbons into her hair. Serena Jane frowned when she saw the oily marks but said nothing as our father looped the lengths of satin, his clumsy thumbs digging into her scalp. She knew Mrs. Pickerton would do them over right. She always did. My father dumped me into another one of his old shirts, a plaid one this time, and once again rolled up the sleeves over my wrists. I squealed and waved my arms with vigor. I looked like a miniature maestro conducting a crowd.

"That's good, Truly," my father told me. "You go on giving 'em hell."

"Daddy," Serena Jane asked when he buckled her into the front seat of the Ford and plunked me on her lap, "why are we taking the car?" Usually we walked to the Reverend and Mrs. Pickerton's.

"Because," my father told her, "I don't think Mrs. Pickerton wants your sister around. I got to take her somewhere else." He expected Serena Jane to be a little anxious, at the very least disappointed, but she exhibited no remorse that he could see. Instead, she shifted under my bulk and crossed her ankles neatly.

"Oh," she remarked. "That's okay, then. Mrs. Pickerton will give the clothes to *me*."

My father glanced down at his two daughters—me jam-smeared and epically proportioned and Serena Jane dainty as a tea cake—and had to concede that she had a point. A girl like me was probably better off in overalls and dirty sneakers than buckled shoes and a crimped dress, he thought, no matter what people said. He wondered what our mother would have done. He told himself it didn't matter, but then he remembered the miles of fabric she'd adorned during all their nights together and felt a pain in his heart so sharp, it was like being pierced with a silver-edged embroidery needle—the kind you might use to decorate a baby's pillow so that when it slept, it dreamed only of you.

Besides her impressive quilt, the other legacy of Tabitha Dyerson Morgan in Aberdeen was her family's farm, passed down through generations of hapless Dyerson men—a trait reflected in the farm's general appearance. Although the Dyerson farm was no more than two centuries old, it looked to be Jurassic. All of its structures lumbered and leaned. Scraggly weeds tufted up like witch's hair around the farmhouse's foundations, and the windows were rendered moot by fixed layers of sediment and grime. A little ways behind the main house, a defunct windmill hulked, its blades frozen like rusted wings.

"Bird!" I cried, stretching my arms up in the back of the car.

Dad switched off the engine and shook his head. "That's a windmill, Truly," he explained. "See, its blades go around and around." He squinted at the rusted planes of metal and corrected himself. "Sometimes."

A small child was squatting in the grass in front of the main house, poking at earthworms with a stick. She stood up when she saw my father approaching and pulled down the grubby hem of her dress, one of her legs winding around the other. When we got close, we could smell urine and see two pea-sized tears shimmering on the girl's cheeks. Her bottom lip wobbled as she fluttered her hands, but before she could burst into full song, a stringy woman strode across the yard to her and scooped her up close, urine or no. She smoothed the girl's ratty hair. Even though the woman's fingers looked as rough as tree twigs, they were also surprisingly limber.

"It's okay, Amelia," she soothed, one eye on us. "We'll clean you up. I have pound cake inside." Amelia laid her head on her mother's shoulder and tucked two fingers in her mouth. The woman turned slightly so she could see my father over Amelia's head. "Earl. What can I do for you?" Her words were pleasant enough, but years of ravenous creditors had honed a guarded edge in her voice.

My father dropped me at his feet and pursed his lips. "Morning, Brenda. Gus in?"

She jerked her head to the barn and set her jaw. "Messing with the horses. There's another race this week." August's horses had never once come in anything other than dead last in any race—a fact that had, of late, proved very lucrative. Certain well-connected gentlemen were making a mint off Gus Dyerson's predictable losers, and they weren't hoarding all the winnings, either.

"Thanks," my father said, and shuffled across the unruly grass, me stumbling at his heels. He heard the rickety screen door of the house slap, then Brenda humming inside. "*That's a good sign*," my father mumbled. According to him, only happy people hummed.

Dad found Gus sandwiched between a mottled mare and the splintery wall of her stall, brushing the beast's tired-looking flanks. When my father approached, both horse and man looked over at him with myopic eyes, but then Gus smiled, and it was as if the sun had just bloomed across his face. The sags and pouches of his skin reconvened into more amenable wrinkles, and his jaw tilted forward. "Earl Plaice!" he cried, and gave the woeful horse a smack on the haunch for emphasis. The animal snorted and shifted her weight.

I suppose it was a testament to Gus's character that he was able to greet visitors with any measure of decency, much less delight, for no one ever came to the Dyersons' farm unless it was to collect on a debt. Even the mail didn't travel that far. It stopped just after the Dunfrys' place, right before the road turned to dirt and all hell.

My father kept a sharp eye on me as I headed for a mangy cur curled up in a pile of hay, but then he saw that the dog was as weary and worn down as everything else in the place and not much of a threat. He folded his hands in front of his belly. "I need to ask you a favor," he rasped, expecting Gus's shoulders to hoist themselves straight or at the very least for his jaw to harden. But the man's features remained as open and loose as the barn's weathered doors.

"Shoot," he said, one distracted finger probing a sore patch in his mouth.

"I wonder if Brenda could keep an eye on Truly for me. Just during the week. I wouldn't ask, but things aren't working out too well with Amanda Pickerton."

Gus extracted his finger and examined something yellowish on the end of it. "What about Serena Jane? You want us to take her, too?"

My father shifted. "She's not the problem."

Gus's gaze drifted over to me, curled up now with the flea-bitten dog, and took in my attire for the first time. "Why's she dressed like that?" he asked.

My father sighed. "She won't fit into anything I've got for her, and she won't wear Amanda's girl's clothes."

At that, Gus chuckled and hocked a wad of phlegm into the muck beside him. "A real live wire, eh?" He grinned, and my father finally relaxed, seeing that maybe this was a good place for me after all. I couldn't possibly make more of a mess than already existed, for one thing, and even if I spent my days naked as the Lord God made me, no one would care. August walked over to me and smiled down like a shabby but benevolent god. "You'll be all right, little one," he said, and I stared right back at him, stupefied by the erroneous prediction.

When my father returned that evening, he found that Brenda's solution to my clothing dilemma had been to dress me in boys' clothes. Where they came from, my father had no idea, but there were so many odd pieces and bits around the place—the rusted bugle abandoned under the kitchen table, the frying pan lurking on the porch steps, stacks of newspapers and racing reports spread over a chair—that he didn't bother to ask. All he knew was that when he walked into Brenda's kitchen, I was alive, well, and buckled into a pair of black-and-white denim overalls like a train engineer, the sorrowful dog curled loyally by my side in a corner, Amelia crouched next to me, watching with savage interest as I wielded a pink plastic doll leg. My father glanced around, but there was no evidence of the rest of the figure. Side by side on the floor, Amelia and I seemed to be not so much companions as individual islands—Amelia silent and half-feral, me spilling over my edges. Amelia made a lunge for the doll leg, but I wasn't ready to give it over to her yet. She stuffed her mouth full with her fingers and waited, making odd, off-key noises, halfway between grunting and music. I looked up at my father and held out my arms, babbling a string of nonsense. Amelia quickly reached out and snatched the doll leg for herself with a snarl before retreating under the table.

"What's the matter with that one?" my father asked, jutting his chin toward Amelia. "Doesn't she talk right?"

Brenda shrugged over the biscuits she

was mixing. "She will when she's up and ready."

My father bent down and hoisted me onto his hip. "Has she been good?"

Brenda sighed. "Good enough." She whacked her wooden spoon on the side of the bowl, then passed it to Amelia, who abandoned the doll's appendage and began licking the buttermilk batter in long, enthusiastic slurps.

My father sidled to the door. The heat from the oven was making him sweat. "Well, okay, then. Thanks for everything. Especially the clothes."

Brenda didn't miss a beat in the punishment of her dough. "You'll have to buy her more," she said from behind a piece of fallen hair.

My father paused. "More clothes for a girl, or more clothes for a boy?"

Brenda stopped kneading for a moment, and it was long enough for my father to remember that she used to be pretty. "What do you want her to be?"

My father considered. "Well, she is a girl."

"So?"

My father thought back to those perfectly

round and expectant days just before my mother gave birth, a memory that shimmered for him now, frail as a soap bubble. He remembered the football he'd brought home and tossed gently to my mother, the new pigskin slapping in her hands as if it belonged in them. He remembered my mother finishing matching blue booties and cap, holding up the cobwebbed yarn for inspection on a knitting needle. My parents had liked names that began with the letter *C*. Caleb. Christopher. Clive. It must have seemed impossible to my father that there had once existed a period in his life so ripe with optimism and hope. But why shouldn't I be what suited me best? If he sped, my father bet, he could get to Hinkleman's department store before it closed. He reached for the screen door and saw that it was torn in several places.

"Thank you," he said again, but Brenda just shrugged and turned back to her baking, scooping round moons out of the dough with the rim of a glass and the heel of her hand, then pushing the leftover pieces back together. If there was one thing Brenda Dyerson was good at, she knew, it was cooking up the scraps destiny had laid out on its plate for her.

"Bring her back tomorrow if you want," she spat, sliding the tray of biscuits in the oven. "Amelia likes the company, and I ain't got nothing but time on my hands, anyway."

My father put a hand to his temple, tipping an imaginary hat. Time, he figured, was better than nothing. We would take it.

Chapter Four

If the purpose of education is to reshape the self, carving and digging like a whittler's blade, then my education surely began on a glimmering autumn morning in 1958 when I heard myself called "giant" for the first time.

As a special treat, Serena Jane woke me up early that morning and fixed me a proper breakfast—cereal, toast, and a glass of milk. "Be glad Dad remembered groceries," she said, sliding the food across the table to me. "Half the time I go to school with a rumbling belly, but I've learned to live with it."

I nodded and tried to chew my food slowly. I knew what she was talking about. The more I grew, the hungrier I got, and we never had much food in the house. The Dyersons didn't, either. They ate straight out of the ground from their wilted garden and off food vouchers the rest of the time.

Serena Jane brushed toast crumbs from her lips and stood up, holding out her hand. She was being so nice to me this morning, it was almost as if she were a different girl. "Come on, I'll brush your hair before we go, but we have to hurry." When it came to the issue of being on time, Serena Jane was as tightly wound as the steel hand of a stopwatch. She rushed me everywhere we went, but I tried not to mind. It was just her way of saying she was the boss of us in life.

She whipped a comb through my hair, rubbed my shoes with some spit and a tissue, and then I let her propel me out the front door, waiting while she dutifully turned the key and locked it. We trundled down the sidewalk past Sal Dunfry's house and then past the Pickertons', but when we passed the cemetery, I dug in my heels and stopped cold, as immovable as a mule.

I almost never came by my mother's grave, but now, in the early morning's golden sunlight, I could see the white square of her headstone winking at me, and before Serena Jane could say boo, I'd torn my hand from hers and dashed through the iron gates. "Truly, wait!" Serena Jane called, her voice a hollow reed in the distance, but I kept going to the corner plot where our mother was buried. I couldn't say why I needed to kneel on the grass, brushing my hands along the tops of weeds, but the action calmed me. If I closed my eyes, it was almost as though my mother were alive, stroking my hands and telling me things would be fine, that I would love school.

I felt a sharp yank on the back of my collar, and then Serena Jane was leaning over me like an impatient crow, asking me what on earth I thought I was doing. "You do realize that there's a whole living world waiting on us, don't you, Truly? I swear, sometimes I think that head of yours is really a pumpkin or something." Sadly, I patted the grass one last time, then got up and followed her.

Eventually, we arrived at the one-room

schoolhouse, and Serena Jane ushered me up the steps by the hand but dropped my wrist as soon as we were inside. Even though my sister was two years older than me, I was taller. Over the past year, I had shot up so fast, I was two inches bigger and pounds heavier. It seemed that the nearer I came to Serena Jane in size, the more distant and unlike me she grew. She hung her sweater on one of the coat pegs and smoothed her collar, her eyes scanning the yard through the open door for the friends I'd heard about but whom she never brought home. "Stay here," she said, turning her back. "I'll come back and tell you what to do soon."

"But I want to come with you." I wanted to follow my sister but knew I would be banished. I felt tears fill my eyes.

Serena Jane pursed her lips, considering. More than anything, I knew, she hated it when I cried, not because she felt pity, but because she hated the sensation of guilt. It was the one weapon I had over her, but I used it only in times of duress. Serena Jane sighed and held out her hand again. "Oh, for goodness' sake, all right, if you're going to be like that about it. Just don't say anything, and you have to do exactly what I tell you."

Just then, however, a bell rang, sending the raspy scent of chalk dust, glue, and freshly sharpened pencils deep into my cortex. A hawk-eyed woman in a sweater set marched to the front of the room. Serena Jane guided me to a row of desks. "Sit here," she whispered, and pointed to the desk next to her. It was nicked and so old that it still had an inkwell. I squeezed my thighs into the seat as best I could and folded my hands up like a tent. I looked over to my sister, but she was staring straight ahead, her ankles crossed, her fingers all lined up evenly, the model student.

All that morning, I learned how much I didn't know. The alphabet for starters—a string of crazy angles and curves with a lilting, singsong tune. How to write my name. The numbers from ten to twenty. How many sides a pentagon had. My head swelled with facts like a gutter after a rainstorm. The bell clanged again, and the children started filing outside for morning recess. Once again, I followed my sister. Through the open door I could spy the generous leaves of the chestnut tree fluttering, and I yearned to go and stand under it, listening to its chatter. Serena Jane and I were almost through the door when the teacher's voice snapped through the air like a crocodile tail sweeping for prey.

"Girls. A moment, if you please."

Serena Jane sighed and watched the other girls huddle into groups. She took me by the wrist again and returned to the front of the classroom. When my sister and I stood side by side like that, her chin was level with my shoulder. "Yes, ma'am," we said.

The teacher sniffed. Her lips bunched themselves up like bees. "Which one of you is Truly?"

Serena Jane pointed at me. "She is."

"And how old are you, child?"

I half raised my hand. The teacher flicked her eyes down to the roster in her hand, then back to me again. I held my palm up higher, all five of my fingers extended, eager as soldiers before a battle. The teacher squeezed her eyes open and shut. "But this can't be right. You're a little *giant*!"

I blushed. It was a word I'd heard before

in Brenda Dyerson's fairy stories, wherein magic stalks grew out of regular dried beans, ordinary geese laid jewel-encrusted eggs, and enchanted harps sung of their own accord. To me, it was a word that swirled with extraordinary promises of castle spires and treasure chests. That's not how the teacher said it, though. She spat the word through the front of her teeth, as if she were expelling used toothpaste. "Huge!" she elaborated. "Surely it's not normal."

Serena Jane and I blinked at her. It wasn't normal not to have a mother, either, or to have a father who drank beer at breakfast, but we did, and we put up with those things, just as we put up with hand-me-down clothes, and no birthday parties, and Christmas without a tree. The bell rang again, and the teacher put the roster back down on her desk. "Recess is over," she said, as if she were flicking a fly off her shoulder. "But this discussion is not. Please come and see me when the school day is over."

My sister and I shuffled back to our desks in the center of the room. Maybe Serena Jane managed to learn something that afternoon, but I didn't. My mind was stuck on a single phrase, like a shoe in gum, and I knew that no matter how hard I tried, I'd never be able to pull it loose. *Little giant*. The words rolled around and around in my empty head, my education stalled before it got started.

The teacher was named Miss Sparrow. Fresh-faced out of a ladies' seminary, she was new in town and thus unfamiliar with the peculiarities lurking among some of Aberdeen's children. Which was unfortunate because she was exposed to them all at once. Aberdeen's population was so small that its children were educated together in one classroom, with the older pupils helping the younger ones. Miss Sparrow, who hailed from the comparative metropolis of Albany, found the entire concept charming when Dick Crane, Aberdeen's youthful mayor, described it to her in a job interview in the seminary's chintz tearoom.

"How adorable!" she'd exclaimed, inhaling her Darjeeling and fluttering her long eyelashes at a man she guessed was at least eight years younger. "How very basic!"

And Dick Crane, charmed himself by the length of Miss Sparrow's delicate legs (whose allure belied her thirty-five years), sipped his tea and neglected to correct her vision of a rural Arcadia.

In 1958, Aberdeen was stuck somewhere between a village and a town. Its sidewalks had weedy cracks that gaped bigger every winter. The bells at the firehouse sometimes locked when the weather was damp, and the newspaper had quit printing its Saturday edition. There was still a recreational softball team, a ladies' gardening committee, and a brick library, but the team never won, the collective age of the gardening committee was four hundred and seven, and the print in half the books in the library was so faded and smeared, it was no longer legible.

Even the town trees were looking a little stunted. Starting in early autumn, their leaves merely mottled and dropped instead of igniting into the traditional yellows and reds. On the first day of school, the steps leading into the school hall were already so slimy with desiccated foliage that Miss Sparrow had to stop and scrape the smooth bottoms of her spectator pumps back and forth across the door lintel. When she looked up, she discovered Marcus Thompson, the smartest and smallest boy in school, skulking behind the globe on her desk.

"Oh—but—my goodness," she gasped, for Marcus had the general appearance of a garden gnome.

"Hello," he spat through a gap in his buckteeth. "I came to clap erasers."

Miss Sparrow smoothed a manicured hand over her abdomen and sucked herself a little taller. "Of course." She smiled, her Satin Primrose lips blooming into a harsh curve like a sickle. "How sweet. I'm Miss Sparrow, the new teacher." She stepped behind the desk to escape Marcus, but he was not to be thwarted. He enthusiastically began to bang the felt erasers, releasing a maelstrom of chalk and dust.

"It's like intergalactic dust," he crowed, screwing up his face to watch the white particles fly. "Maybe this is what Laika saw out the window of her capsule."

Miss Sparrow put a fist to her mouth and coughed. "Who?"

Marcus increased his pounding. "Laika.

You know. The Russian space dog. I read all about her in the paper."

Miss Sparrow put down her fist. "You can read?"

"Oh sure! Laika was on *Sputnik Two,* which orbited the earth two thousand five hundred and seventy times." His brow furrowed, and he momentarily halted the erasers. "All the scientists are always talking about sending a man into space, but I think Laika is the real hero. She died, though, you know."

Miss Sparrow frowned and brushed dust from her hair and camel skirt. "The Russians are not our friends, young man."

Marcus considered this. "Does that mean we should be glad when their space dogs die?"

Miss Sparrow did not get a chance to answer, for the rest of the children tumbled into the schoolroom in a noisy knot. Marcus's dust set off a towheaded boy's asthma. Immediately he began gasping and wheezing, his poor lungs squeezing themselves like faulty bellows, his aspirin-colored face blooming into a dusky pink.

"Marcus Thompson!" Vi Vickers scolded,

holding the gasping child by the elbow. "Stop it! You know you're supposed to do that outside!"

Miss Sparrow looked at Vi and saw a strawberry-sized birthmark ringing her left eye, giving her a surprised expression. But Vi Vickers was one of the older students in the class. Almost nothing surprised her anymore. She escorted the coughing boy outside, her left eye startled and amazed, her mouth caved into a bored sulk.

When Marcus's genie cloud of dust settled, Miss Sparrow got a good look at the rest of her class and was relieved to see that several of the girls were even very pretty. She noted with pleasure which of them had on smocked dresses for the first day of school and which of them had new ribbons braided into their hair, which of the boys' cowlicks had been pasted down with Brylcreem so their heads shone like angels. All in all, she surmised to herself, running her red-tipped fingers down the tiny shell buttons of her cardigan, they were workable. Hope began beating again in the birdcage of her breast. Then the door flew open, and the prettiest child Miss

Sparrow had ever seen descended upon her, holding the hand of the ugliest.

But surely your family must have seen a doctor," Miss Sparrow said to my sister as we continued our conversation after school, giving my bulk the same critical eye the judges used on the heifers at a county fair. I shifted, adding to Miss Sparrow's bovine assessment of me.

It didn't help that, for once, I was dressed as a girl. In a fit of compassion, Mrs. Pickerton had sewn me a school wardrobe of dull brown pinafores, army green skirts with suspenders, and tan blouses. As attire went, it was a prison sentence—a solitary confinement of the soul. On me, the pleated skirt and Peter Pan collar looked cartoonish, almost freakish, the product of a sewing pattern gone terribly wrong. In fact, Mrs. Pickerton had had to increase the measurements by four, resulting in circuslike proportions that did nothing to hide my lumps and bumps. I hung my head and let my sister do all the talking.

"We don't go to the doctor," Serena Jane told Miss Sparrow, her voice as sweet as a dulcimer, but flat, too, as if the notes hit were just slightly the wrong ones for the music.

Miss Sparrow shook her head, as if trying to dislodge water from her ears. "Why, what do you mean you don't go to the doctor? What happens if you get sick?"

Serena Jane shrugged. "We don't."

"You don't get sick?"

Serena Jane shrugged again. "Not real bad."

Miss Sparrow smoothed a nonexistent wrinkle out of her lap and took a deep breath. "But surely you must have noticed that something is, ah, *not right* with your younger sister. Surely your mother must have wanted to know what was wrong with her." Miss Sparrow's eyes flitted from the fairy child to the ugly duckling. I shuffled my feet and bowed my head farther.

"Our mother's dead." This time, Serena Jane's eyes went flat to match her voice.

"Oh, I see." Miss Sparrow squinted at me, as if by reducing the size of her gaze, she could also shrink me. I could tell she still found it hard to believe that Serena Jane was related to me. She reached into her desk for a piece of paper and her enamel fountain pen, which showed to very best advantage her prize-winning penmanship. She looped her hand across the page, making elaborate dips and swirls, then blew on the ink to dry it and folded the note into an envelope.

"Here," she said, giving it to Serena Jane. "Take this home to your father tonight. It says that you have to see the doctor if you want to come to school this year. You need your shots, and a hearing test, and a checkup. The board of education has its rules, and we can't just ignore things like that, can we?" She eyeballed my fantastic bulk again. Clearly, I was out of the bounds of normality. Why, I was an absolute giant, and although Miss Sparrow was more than expert at cutting people down to size, she was also certain that anything of my magnitude just wasn't in her job description.

What's this?" my father asked when Serena Jane handed him the note over supper that night. He unfolded the paper slowly, as if unwrapping an ancient map, and squinted to decipher Miss Sparrow's florid script.

In the years since my mother's death, my father had melted and spread around his edges like an ice-cream cone halfway through consumption. Everything about him seemed to be dripping, heading straight back to the ground—an impression only reinforced by his lamentable personal hygiene. His wrinkled trousers sagged over his backside and dipped beneath his buttery belly. His shirttails hung defeated. The cracked tongues of his shoes lolled. Even his shoelaces straggled on the ground in perpetual surrender. Customers in the barbershop were reluctant to let him near their hair, choosing instead one of the more youthful employees who had found their way into the shop. My father didn't mind. He had grown weary of pompadours, and ducktails, and handlebar mustaches. He was like a baker who never ate sweets, or a goldsmith who wore only silver. He spent most of the day hunched in the corner of the shop, reading the papers and checking the racing reports. He'd made a small bundle betting against August Dyerson's woeful horses, but he never told anyone his secret. He simply took the money home and shoved it in a shoebox under his bed.

He placed Miss Sparrow's note on the

table in front of him, where the corner came to rest in an ignoble drop of tomato sauce. Most nights, I made the dinner and ate it alone. I just opened whatever jars I found in the cupboards and poured the contents onto plates. Then I sat at the table by myself, sucking olives off my fingertips or swirling a pinkie around the rim of a tapioca pudding can, while my father lolled on the busted sofa across the room. On the nights he did come to the table, it always left me feeling a little uneasy, as if I were faced with a volatile, uninvited guest. He burped once, lightly, and leaned over closer to Serena Jane.

"Did you tell this teacher we don't see the doctor?" he asked, blinking at her in the room's squalid light, as if she were an angel descended in the wrong location—an assessment of herself that Serena Jane seemed to share. She nodded.

"And did you tell her why?" he persisted.

"I told her Mama was dead."

Small reserves of spittle gathered in the corners of my father's mouth. Two of his teeth were broken. The rest were as yellow as old socks. "Did you tell her it's because the doctor stood by while your mama was dying and didn't do a damn thing to help her?" He smoothed his fingers over the surface of the teacher's letter. Watching him, I had the urge to cover his hand with mine, trapping his battered knuckles in the cage of my palm and holding them tight until they smoothed again into the reasonable knobs I remembered. My father pounded his fist on the table.

"We don't need no witch doctor. We've been just fine without him." His gaze ricocheted back and forth between the miracle of physical arrangement that was Serena Jane and the mystery that was me.

"Not a lick of your mother in you," he said, then chuckled. "More like three licks. No wonder Lily died pushing you out. Hell, you'd block a barn door." He doubled over, coughing, then remained that way, his beer can balanced on his knee, halfway between upright and spilling over. I had an urge to kick it and watch the liquid go flying. After one of my father's harangues, I always felt like one of our sour-smelling, holey dishrags thrown in the corner of the sink. I thought about the X-ray glasses advertised on the back of the cereal box we'd bought last week. Right then, I wished my father could have put them on. Then maybe he would have seen that I was more like my mother than it appeared. Instead, he burped and wiped his lips with the back of his hand.

"Just fine," he repeated into the empty air, ignoring the tiny razor teeth that were nibbling at my soul and quietly eliminating it, making me small in spite of my heft. Making me less than half the girl I wanted to be.

Dr. Robert Morgan's office smelled of rubbing alcohol, and peppermint, and dispenser soap. It was the way I imagined the tops of mountains would smell—rarefied, antiseptic, frosted. Everything in the office was cold. The stainless-steel sink, where chilly beads of water clustered and shook like frightened fairies. The linoleum floor, which numbed my feet through my socks. The row of callipered instruments lined up on a metal tray according to shape and size. Even the leather examining table was cold. I shifted my weight on it, and the paper underneath my buttocks and thighs crinkled. I tried to pull my thin cotton gown together around my midsection, but the fabric resisted, gaping open like a laughing mouth all the way down the back of me. Embarrassed, I put my hands in my lap and waited. Across the room, the door flew open.

Above the thick black rims of his glasses, Dr. Robert Morgan had the complicated eyebrows of a fairy-tale huntsman. I stared at his eyes—watery, bloodshot around their edges, but gentle—and decided I didn't mind. That man in the stories was always kind. He saved Snow White from the evil Queen. He rescued Red Riding Hood from the moist jaws of the Wolf. If a huntsman brandished his ax, I knew, you should stay still and let him do his work. Dr. Morgan lifted the hinged metal cover of his clipboard and peered at the papers underneath it, as if peeking at a script to remind himself how to start a conversation. He paced over to the little counter and balanced the clipboard on its edge. I waited to see if it would fall, but it didn't.

"Hello, Truly." He stretched one of his long-fingered hands in my general direction. "We haven't met in a very long time. Since you were born, in fact. You've grown up quite a lot since then."

I ducked my head. "Mrs. Pickerton says I'm growing too much. She said I'm even too big to wear the devil's britches. She makes my school clothes." I could feel my cheeks flush scarlet, which made them mottle and blotch. When Serena Jane blushed, it just made her more beautiful.

Dr. Morgan wiggled his stethoscope into his ears and lifted the disk. "Mrs. Pickerton is an old nanny goat," he said, and pressed the circle to my chest. He listened as I took careful breaths, but after a few minutes, his smile turned into a slight frown. He moved the disk of the stethoscope down a few inches. "Interesting," he said, snapping the earpieces back down around his collarbone. "I'd like to weigh you." He led me over to the upright scale in the corner and showed me how the metal balance slid back and forth on its incremental metal bar, smallest to biggest. I pinched my gown together behind me and stepped on the scale. The balance stopped halfway.

"Very good," Dr. Morgan said again, scribbling something on the clipboard. "Just stay there, please. I'm going to measure you." He slid another steel bar along a vertical ruler until it rested flat against my head. "Uh-huh," he said, squinting and scribbling. "Interesting," he repeated. I liked the way he said it, chopping up the syllables—*in-te-rest-ing*—so that I felt like a puzzle he was slotting together in his mind.

I was used to plenty of people staring at me, but no one had ever paid such deliberate attention to me before. My father saw me only through the haze of his evening beers. Serena Jane mostly ignored me. Brenda Dyerson, busy with a hundred things in her falling-down house, kept me pinned firmly in her peripheral vision, along with Amelia, who was always so close to me that we could touch hands without blinking but who never said a word, just smiled from time to time, offering me her broken toys when she was done playing with them. And while it was true that Mrs. Pickerton focused on certain bits of me with the ferocity of an enraged wolverine, they only ever seemed to be the bad bits. Until then, no one had ever bothered to scrutinize the whole mass of me, connecting neckbone to backbone, shinbone to anklebone, in an entire picture. I felt as if I were a rare and beautiful insect being inspected through a magnifying glass. *Maybe*, I thought, *Dr. Morgan will give me a name for what makes me different*. Maybe if he could classify me, I would know what to make of myself and know what to say when people gawped at me as if I were the prize exhibit in the county fair. My heart beat a little faster with anticipation.

I climbed back on the table and let Dr. Morgan whack me in the knees and elbows with a small, rubber tomahawk, as if we were playing Indian chief—a game the taciturn Amelia and I sometimes played in the woods at the Dyerson farm. Amelia was always the princess, subdued and in mortal peril, and I was the Indian brave—barreling through shrubbery and trees, arriving in a huff of wobbling arms and legs. The husk of Amelia was so light, I could carry her with one arm, and I greatly enjoyed this. It made me feel competent and gave me the illusion of capability. *Don't worry,* I'd pant, dragging Amelia toward the barn, *I'll keep the both of us safe forever and ever.* Amelia would close her eyes and giggle, but when I looked at her face, she always still managed to look worried, as if all her life experience as a Dyerson had taught her better than to hope for even an ounce of salvation.

Dr. Robert Morgan wound a tape measure around my forehead, my chest, and my thighs. More numbers flew from his pencil into the clipboard. He shone a penlight and watched my pupils contract and expand—twin universes being born and dying right in the center of me. He peered into my nostrils and ears. He thumped, and prodded, and poked. He had me cover one eye and read nonsense letters off a chart. When I switched hands, the letters scattered and wheeled like magpies in a field.

"Do you ever feel dizzy or faint?" Dr. Morgan ran his thumbs down the sides of my neck. I shook my head. "Short of breath? Tired? Extremely thirsty?" I shook my head again. No, no, and no, although it wasn't true. My heart did sometimes heave and thump in my chest as if it had a mind of its own, but I didn't know how to explain that to the doctor. Also, I wanted him to write that everything was fine with me for Miss Sparrow. A wild animal heart and regular dizzy spells weren't going to get me the correct diagnosis.

Dr. Morgan slammed down the cover of the clipboard. "Okay, Truly." He patted my knee and gazed at me over the black rims of his glasses. "We're all done here." They were scientist's spectacles—square and thick and utterly reasonable. If I put them on, I wondered, would I see everything in angles and perfect straight lines? Would the world fall in order? Dr. Morgan handed me my limp pile of clothes. "You can get dressed. I'll just wait outside, and then I want to talk to your father."

I took my clothes. They were my weekend boy clothes: dungarees, a plaid shirt, wool hunting socks. They hung in my hand like a shed skin. I looked up at Dr. Morgan and took a deep breath. "Am I a giant?"

Dr. Morgan turned back to me, his hand on the doorknob. "A giant? Why, wherever did you hear that?"

"Miss Sparrow. She said there must be something wrong with me. She said I'm too big to believe."

Dr. Morgan crossed back over to me. He took off his glasses and wiped them carefully, swirling the corner of his white coat around and around each pane of glass, clearing it, making it shine. "Is that why she sent you here?" he finally asked. My bottom lip quivered. I nodded. Dr. Morgan patted my shoulder with the absentminded rhythm of a mother soothing a child.

"You shouldn't listen to people like Miss Sparrow, or Mrs. Pickerton, either. They don't have medical degrees. They have no idea what they're saying." He tipped my chin up and wiped my tears away with the pad of his thumb. His fingers were surprisingly warm. "Have you ever heard of the pituitary gland?" I shook my head. He moved his fingers to the base of my skull and tapped, marking the spot as if he were going on a treasure hunt.

"It's like a little clock in your brain. It sends out messages to your body about when to grow and how fast. Some people have a slow clock, so they don't grow very much. Those are the little people in the world. And some people, like you, are in a hurry to get as big as you can as fast as you can. It's like your body is in a race against everyone else's, and it's determined to win. The regular people in the world, all the ones in the middle who aren't special in any way, well, some of them don't like it, that's all. They're jealous, Truly. They don't know what to make of you."

I blinked at him. "Are you a witch doctor?"

He threw back his head and laughed, the rough sounds rolling out of him like bark off a log. "Who told you that?"

"My daddy. He said we don't need no witch doctor. But you don't look like a witch to me. Besides, I thought witches were girls."

Dr. Morgan smiled. "So they are, Truly. So they are. And one day, you, too, might grow up to be enchanting. You and that pretty sister of yours. Now get dressed and I'll take you home." He crossed the room and closed the door behind him, taking his clipboard and pencil away, along with whatever kind of conclusion he'd drawn about me.

Chapter Five

From the outside, our house looked almost like the other homes on Maple Street. It had a shallow front porch with a swing on it, a white picket fence, and lace curtains in all the windows. Daisies sprouted by the bottom stoop. In the winter, the stocky chimney belched puffs of smoke. But our house also had some features the other homes didn't have. Weeds grew in the mouth of the porch's loose drainpipe. Paint flakes riddled the clapboards. The mailbox teetered on its support like the head of an unruly drunk. The mailman had taken to leaving the few pieces of our correspondence tucked under the edge of the door, where Dad would find them and kick them into the corner of the front hall until the pile grew big enough for him to do something about. Waiting for my father to answer the doorbell, Dr. Morgan peered down between his black wingtips and noticed two envelopes wedged in between them. Behind the door, there was a crashing sound, then footsteps padded closer, and my father appeared, blinking in the afternoon light. In front of him, he saw me standing on the porch holding the hand of Dr. Robert Morgan IV.

"Get in the house," he barked. "Brenda Dyerson called over to the barbershop. She's been wondering where you are."

It was Saturday, the busiest day for my father at the barbershop. Serena Jane was at the Pickertons'. I was supposed to have waited for August to pick me up at my house that morning and take me to the farm, but I'd struck out for Dr. Morgan's instead, clutching Miss Sparrow's note, which babbled about giants, and medical records, and vaccinations, albeit in very beautiful script. I gave a quick squeeze to the reassuring hand of Dr. Robert Morgan and scampered upstairs to the room I shared with my sister. Downstairs, I could hear footsteps shuffling—the clumsy, half-hearted ones of my father mixed together with the precise sounds of Dr. Morgan's wingtips. His feet sounded the way a father's feet were supposed to, I thought. Solid, decisive. The kind of footsteps I wanted to hear climbing the stairs to tuck me into bed at night, instead of my father's stumbling ones.

I sat on my bed, elbows planted on knees, and faced the mirror that was glued to the back of the door. Already, I almost filled the whole narrow span of it, edge to edge, my body lumpier than any monster I could imagine. I tilted my head in the mirror, grimacing, then put my hand to the back of my skull, to the place where Dr. Morgan had told me there was a little clock. I moved my fingers around but didn't feel anything, then listened, holding my breath, but didn't hear ticking. I arched my neck and spread my arms, copying one of Serena Jane's ballerina poses, but I didn't transform into a swan princess the way Serena Jane did. I just stayed myself—goggle-eyed, pucker-lipped, chin upon chin upon chin. I returned my arms to my sides and slumped back on the bed. I wasn't a dancing bird-girl. Apparently, I wasn't anything as exotic as a giant, but neither was I ordinary-sized. I sighed and fished in my pocket for Miss Sparrow's note—tattered and sweat-stained now, but still lovely for all that.

I scooted off the edge of the bed and tottered to the room's single desk, the drawers of which I'd filled with crayons, and pens, and paper, the surface of which Serena Jane had cluttered with hair ribbons, lip glosses, magazines, and a jar of cold cream. I cleared a small space in the detritus and smoothed Miss Sparrow's note as best I could, then I took a blank sheet of paper from one of the drawers and uncapped a green felt-tip pen. After laying the blank sheet of paper over the top of Miss Sparrow's writing, I began to trace the whirlwind of her lettering, letting my wrist relax in order to better copy the eddies and flourishes of her words. I finished the first row of the note, then sat back and admired my handiwork. Not bad. I hunched over and set back to work again, determined to master the linear vocabulary of elegance, determined to make one thing about me as beautiful as possible.

Downstairs, Dr. Morgan took a seat on the lifeless sofa, his buttocks sinking deep in the cushions. A vaguely sour odor emanated from the kitchen. Dr. Morgan closed his throat up and breathed through his mouth, keeping his face carefully neutral, the way he'd learned to do in medical school. From my perch at the top of the stairs, I could just about peer into the room. I leaned forward for a better view.

"Well, Earl, it's been a long time," Dr. Morgan said, avoiding any mention of my mother. In the years since her death, he'd become more and more introspective, brooding over the small handful of patients he'd lost during his career while Cody, his Labrador, followed him mournfully, snuffling at his heels, swiping the pink rag of his tongue over his chops. Dr. Morgan planted his hands on the bony corners of his knees and cleared his throat. "I don't suppose it was you who sent Truly over to my office this morning."

My father snorted and opened another

can of beer. "There ain't nothing on the planet that could send me to you. Whatever I've got coming, I figure I'll deal with on my own. But the girls"—he shrugged—"well, they're getting big now. I guess they've got their own ideas."

Dr. Morgan placed a discreet fist over his mouth and coughed. "Actually, that's what I wanted to talk to you about. Surely you must have noticed that Truly is bigger than other girls her age. She's even bigger than Serena Jane, who's two years older."

My father swallowed. "Yeah, she ain't the prettiest."

I frowned. Even though I knew my sister was the beauty of the family, I secretly preferred my own pug features and familiar heft. They were so much more comfortable. Serena Jane was too porcelain, too painted up and satiny. I was always worried she would chip and break, like a temperamental china doll.

Dr. Morgan shooed a fly away from his ear. "Pretty is as pretty does," he said. "What I'm worried about is Truly's growth. It's way out of line for a normal five-year-old. She obviously has some kind of hormonal imbalance, probably stemming from her pituitary gland."

Across the room, my father continued to slouch. "Huh. How about that."

"If I could just run some more tests, do some bloodwork, I'm sure I could isolate the problem and—"

"No."

"But—"

My father stood up. In the half gloom, up this close, he was bigger than Dr. Morgan remembered, his chest still barreled, his cheeks sunken, but his shoulders still broad. "No tests," my father said, the words coming out remarkably clear for a man on his fifth beer of the afternoon. "No bloodwork, no needles, no showing off for your medical buddies. No one's making my daughter into a circus freak."

"Come on, Earl. It's not like that. I'm only trying to help."

My father narrowed his eyes. It was the same expression he used in the barbershop, on the rare occasion right before he cut into someone's hair. "I think you helped enough five years ago," he said through his front teeth.

Dr. Morgan hung his head. "She would have died anyway, Earl. There was really nothing I could do. She'd lost too much blood, but even so, the tumor would have had her sooner or later."

"You don't know that. No one knows for sure. Maybe it would have shrunk. Or she could have had radiation or something."

Dr. Morgan stood up. "No. I don't think so. You would have found that out sooner or later. In spite of what you wish to think, there are some things I do know for certain, and some things I can't do anything about, no matter how painful they are. And, Earl, I'm telling you now, something is wrong with Truly. But you can do something about it. You can save her from what's bound to be misery."

"The Lord helps those who help themselves," my father said. "I ain't too good at the saving aspect of things."

I am, Dr. Morgan wanted to say, but he realized it wasn't true. He hadn't saved my mother, after all. "What about Truly?" he finally asked.

My father shrugged. "I guess she'll get what the world has coming to her, like it or not, the way we all do." He clumped over and slapped Dr. Morgan on the back. His touch stung slightly, the way it was meant to. He stumped into the hall and opened the front door wide. "Thanks for coming," he said. "Now get the hell out of my house."

My father waited for Dr. Morgan's black suit jacket to disappear around the corner before he closed the door. He stood for a moment in the hall, then smoothed his greasy hair over his skull, tucked in his shirt, and climbed the rickety stairs to our room. I was sitting hunched at the little desk. My father squinted, but it was no use. No matter how hard he tried, he never found a scrap of my mother in me. If I hadn't been born right here in this house, he probably would have thought I was switched at birth.

Hearing my father's beery breathing, I looked up from my paper. The tips of my right forefinger and thumb were stained green, and I had emerald smudges dotting my nose and cheeks. My father leaned over me to see what I was doing. Underneath the span of my hand, a line of green ink cartwheeled across the paper.

"Let me see." He gathered up my script

and held it to the window, where the light shone through the page, making my writing into a vine. *Resembles a giant,* it read. *Clearly out of the bounds of normality.* He sighed and put down the paper. It was that new, stuck-up teacher's writing. Of course, I had no idea what any of it said. He put his hand on my head, wishing he were better at stories, wishing he could make up one now where the giant wasn't bad, just misunderstood, where the princess was huge—the bigger the better—where beauty on the outside always matched beauty on the inside, wicked queens looked like the hags they were, and uppity schoolteachers were locked in towers for perpetuity.

"Why don't you come on down for something to eat?" he asked. "I think we got some tuna. I'll make you a sandwich."

And I, always eager to fill the empty place squatting in the middle of me, followed him down, the green description of me fluttering between my fingers like the thorny stem of a fragrant, poisoned rose.

The Dyersons were the most genuine of upstaters. Weedlike, they had long, complicated roots that stretched back to Tabitha's drunken brother, James. A veteran of the Civil War, he hadn't weathered the fighting as well as the first Robert Morgan, having lost a leg in battle along with the livelier portions of his soul. He returned home to Aberdeen on crutches, a wooden leg strapped onto his thigh, his gait unsteady not just from the unfamiliar appendage, but also from the moonshine he'd learned to distill in the hollers of Appalachia. After his sister married Robert Morgan and moved into town, he kept company with the foxes and crows that haunted his farm, growing pale, ragged rows of corn with which to brew more hooch. When he died, the town was astonished to learn not only that James had been keeping a half Oneida woman he'd startled in the woods one afternoon as she was raiding his still, but that he'd also fathered her child.

"That was Amelia's great-great-grandfather Jeremy Blood Moon Dyerson," August drawled with pride out in the barn, patting one of his horses on its tragically bony flank, then reaching over to smooth the dark tangles of his daughter's hair. "He's the one we get our powers of intuition from. It's what makes us so popular around here." He tapped his forehead and winked, and I stifled a laugh behind my mitten. Whether it was because of their mixed blood or the tangy whiff of grain alcohol that always clung to their clothes, the Dyersons were anything but popular in Aberdeen, and the same went for their unlucky horses.

August loved the beasts regardless. "They're winners in their own way," he said. "The math's just a little different, is all," and Amelia nodded in rapt agreement. I stared at the withers of the nearest horse and then at the saggy flanks of August Dyerson and decided that if the world hated its losers, it must loathe its winners even more. What else would explain the rusted windmill decaying in the Dyersons' yard, I wondered, and the stubborn stones that bloomed in all the farm's fields, and most of all, the melancholy stare of Amelia, who, with her ink-pot eyes and ability to creep silently into a room, seemed to have inherited some of Jeremy Blood Moon's gifts of secrecy?

In my new life with the Dyersons, Amelia and I shared a room, all our meals, and even some clothing (Amelia wore what I outgrew), but I could never overlook the fact that she was the utter antithesis of my sister—dark where Serena Jane was golden, skinny where Serena Jane was plump, and, most important, mute when Serena Jane was busting with opinions about everything from the sorry state of my stick straight hair to the proper angle of the safety pin on her kilt.

It was Amelia's silence that was the hardest thing for me to adjust to. For the first time in my life, I was the one doing the bossing, and it was a lonely business, I was discovering, especially given a subject as sleepy-eyed and reticent as Amelia. "Do you want to go outside and play?" I would ask after Brenda had slid some eggs across the beat-up table to us. "Let's go into the woods behind the barn and look for arrowheads." But Amelia, absorbed in trailing her fork tines through the runny yolks, wouldn't answer. I would shovel down my food and stomp outdoors on my own, missing the brashness of Serena Jane, who was always telling me to hurry.

The woods, alive with the chattering of insects and the furtive rustling of thousands of leaves, were always a relief after the cavernous weight of Amelia's quietude.

One day, however, about six weeks after I'd arrived, she surprised me, slipping up on me so quietly that she reminded me of a deer trying to sneak past a bear. "Play now," she announced, and handed me a rooster feather.

My mouth fell slack. "You're talking." In all my time spent with the Dyersons, both before and after my father's death, I'd never heard her utter a solitary word. When she wanted something, she usually pointed or described the object with her hands, and Brenda and Gus obliged.

"Why doesn't Amelia ever say anything?" I'd asked Brenda.

She'd just smiled her slow smile, wiped her hands on her apron, and shrugged. "Does it make any difference?"

"I guess not."

"Well, then, there you go." And she'd turned back to her oven.

In the fresh air of the woods, Amelia's voice emerged rougher than I thought it would, like a curl of tree bark. "Play now," she repeated. She had a hard time pronouncing the “l” in *play*.

I twirled the feather in my hands, trying to hide my surprise. “What do you want to do?”

Amelia plopped herself down right there in the dirt and blinked at me. “Story,” she rasped, then closed her lips again, retreating back into her eerie calm. I ran the feather back and forth under my chin. It tickled like velvet. Amelia sat patiently at my feet, staring at me. I stared back. I marveled at the bravery it had taken Amelia to utter those few words and wondered how best to honor it. Amelia became impatient, however, and pounded her little fist in the dirt, so I opened my own mouth and just started saying whatever popped into my head.

“Once upon a time,” I began, “there was a beautiful princess with an ugly name—Bugaboo. All she ever wanted was for folks to like her, but as soon as she opened her mouth and introduced herself, they about busted their seams laughing. Not only did she have a real silly name, but her voice was about as croaky as an old bullfrog courting in a pond.

"No one believed Bugaboo was a princess until one day, she found a magic feather, kind of like this here rooster feather." I held it up. "She thought it was real pretty, and she tucked it in her hair, but it was cursed, and it took away her voice.

"At first, Bugaboo thought that was a bad thing, but then she realized that no one could laugh at her anymore. And so, she grew up to be the wisest, best, most beautiful princess in the whole world, and she never even needed to speak again, for people just naturally figured out what she wanted before she said it, and she lived happily ever after."

Amelia's mouth fell open. Her little hands were folded in front of her chest, as if she were a victim of frost. For a moment, I wondered if maybe she really did have something more wrong with her than problems talking, but then she burst into applause so enthusiastic, I worried that she'd rip her clothes.

The next day, she brought me a circlet of twigs she'd bound with rawhide and demanded another Bugaboo story, so I told her about the time Bugaboo made a raft out of wood and sailed a sea so wide, it took her a year to get across it. Soon, I had an entire collection of Amelia's found objects cluttering up the drawer in the chest between our beds, every day adding something new, until gradually I came to see that I wasn't entirely alone and that Aberdeen still held some gifts for people like Amelia and me, even if we did have to make them up for ourselves.

Now that we had bonded, Amelia began tagging after me like a sticky shadow, whether I wanted her to or not. I even started taking her with me when I ventured into town to meet Serena Jane at Hinkleman's soda fountain on Saturdays—the one day Mrs. Pickerton had decreed that we could visit. Mr. Hinkleman shook my sister's pearly hand as though she were a highborn lady and gave her extra cherries for her soda, but when it came time for him to push Amelia's and my drinks across the counter, he never said anything, and he always made sure never to touch our skin when he plucked the sticky quarters from our palms.

"Bad luck slips off easy as soot," I heard him telling the pimpled counter boy as he swept the shop in aimless circles. My stomach did a flip-flop, but I ignored it. Without moving my eyes, I lifted my soda and drained it in one greedy swallow, pushing all the sweetness into me at once, letting it fizz good and hard right in the center of my belly. Next to me, swinging slowly from side to side on her stool, Amelia sipped her drink more conservatively, savoring the burn of bubbles in her throat, mixing pleasure with pain until the one became the other. I turned away from her and faced my sister on the other side of me. In public, I never bothered to talk to Amelia. She wouldn't respond, I knew, just furrow her brow and suck harder at her straw.

"She talks," I'd insisted when Serena Jane had made fun of Amelia. "She just won't do it around strange people." But Serena Jane had just tossed her curls and sniffed that Amelia was the strange one.

"What would you rather have on a desert island?" I inquired of my sister now, hooking my feet on the stool's rungs. "Tools or food?" I was aware of Amelia picking at her cuticles. She seemed to be considering the question, even if she was going to answer it only in her head.

Serena Jane half shrugged and glanced

at the clock. Amanda Pickerton was going to take her to the movies at one. "Who cares?" She tired easily of my games. In her new life, apparently, Serena Jane never had to make choices of any kind. When I'd asked her what she got for breakfast after we'd been apart for the first week, she'd looked at me as if I were from Mars. "Whatever I want," she'd said. "Mrs. Pickerton just ties on her apron and whips it up. She produces marvelous cuisine."

"But what if you wanted both pancakes and eggs," I'd pressed, trying to imagine Brenda offering that choice and failing. Breakfast at the Dyersons' was whatever the hens decided to give you. "Which one would Mrs. Pickerton fix?"

Serena Jane had flipped her hair over her shoulder. "What a stupid question, Truly. Why would I ever eat that much at one sitting?" I'd looked at my sister's white knees nestled together like a pair of Brenda's eggs and had the urge, not for the first time, to crack her right open. I wanted to pick her ribs apart until I got to the messy center of her—surely somewhere inside my sister there must be some sort of mess, I thought—and dip my fingers in.

Instead, I tried to make her make choices. I stuck us on theoretical desert islands, stranded us in dark jungles, dropped us out of smoking planes into cities in which we were the only two people alive. Then I presented some options. Starvation or cannibalism? Escape or befriend the natives? Hunting or fishing? I was the one who ended up doing most of the answering.

"I'd pick tools," I said now, "because then you could catch fish and stuff, and make your own food." I stretched my hand out toward hers a little on the counter. "I'd catch some for you, too. If we were on a desert island, I'd share everything I had."

Serena Jane stifled a yawn, then squinted at my overalls. Now that I'd been liberated from the wardrobe clutches of Amanda Pickerton, they were all I ever wore anymore. "Really, Truly," Serena Jane said, flicking a piece of lint off her cardigan, bored with my fantasies, "you might at least acknowledge that you're female."

I gazed down at the bulging universe of my body. "Why?"

"Because you *are*."

I spun a quarter on the counter, watching it wobble harder and harder before it fell. I was a lot of things. Bigger than most boys. Stronger, too. But that didn't matter if you were a girl. All anyone ever saw about me, I thought, were the parts that were missing: lovely clothes, and proper manners, and tidy hair. No matter what Brenda did to it, my hair refused to curl or behave in any kind of reasonable way. Amelia had long hair that could have held promise, but she always wore it tied up in a single braid she wove herself, and that suited Brenda just fine. "Doesn't matter anyway," I mumbled, slurping the dregs from my soda. "I'll never be pretty."

Serena Jane sighed. "That's not the point."

"Then never mind." I smashed my straw down in my glass. But I knew what she was trying to say, even if I didn't like it. She was trying to make me make a real choice before the world up and did it for me.

All that winter after my father's death, Amelia and I learned to play five-card stud and rummy in the bittersweet air of the barn, the pungent odors of horses and hay wavering around us. By the end of January, August had taught us how to twist and throw a pair of dice so that one number, at least, would end up low and we wouldn't lose our shirts. "That's what you call evening up the odds," August said, squatting next to us, the better to assess our technique.

Amelia fixed him with her clear and steady stare. Only in the barn with her father did her words come clear and easy, maybe because given August's track record, it was impossible to believe you could disappoint him. "It's what you call cheating," she said, and August let loose a great bark of laughter.

"Who would have thought it?" he said. "A Dyerson on the straight and narrow!" And Amelia scowled.

"Come on now, girl," August soothed. "Let's see what the cards got in store for us today." In the weathered air of the barn, his breath billowed out in defeated clouds and mingled with the exhalations of the horses. It looked as though halfhearted angels were descending, as though something almost wonderful were about to happen. Amelia and I were at the age where wonderful things sometimes still did happen, but far less often than they used to.

August pulled a deck of cards from the sleeve of his coat, shuffled, cut, and then told us to take the one from the top. He took a card for himself, then asked us to pick again.

"Hold 'em close now. Don't let me see." I clutched the pair to my chest, the laminated cards slipping back and forth between my mittens. Amelia looked at hers once, then closed her fist around them and stared at the ceiling. August took another card for himself, then frowned.

"Now, it don't matter what color you got or what the shapes on the cards are, all that matters is how *many* things you got. Are you good at your numbers, Truly?" I shrugged. Miss Sparrow had tried with me, rapping her pointer on the blackboard so hard that she'd sometimes gouged the slate, but I couldn't seem to keep anything straight.

"Now, do either of you have a picture of a lady on any of your cards? Or a king?"

I checked and shook my head. Amelia didn't answer.

August paused, then continued his instruction. "Okay, that's good. So just go ahead and count up what you got."

I ran my eyes over the black-and-white shapes on the cards. "Six hearts on one card and eight black things on the other."

"What about you, Amelia?"

"A king and a queen."

August whistled. "Well, now, that's pretty damn good. I'd stick with that." He turned to me. "And you've got fourteen altogether?" He bent down, and I could see the yellow tobacco stains on his teeth, the crow's-feet lurking at the edges of his eyes. "The aim here is to make all your cards add up to twenty-one. Royals are ten. Aces can be one or eleven. You can ask for another card if you want, but it might put you over. You still got another seven to go, Truly, so I'd go for it, but it's up to you." He straightened up and stood over me like a judge while I tried to make up my mind. I'd never expected that one tiny thing would matter so much.

"Okay," I finally announced. "Give me another card."

August's face bloomed into a panoply of creases. "Good girl." He grinned. "Take that one right off the top." His thumb slid out another card. But when I took it, drew it to my chest, and peeked at it, I saw that

I had the king of hearts, his narrow eyes suspicious as a trout's, his helmet of curls cut severely along his jaw. My face fell.

"Now what's the matter?" August's scarecrow features filled up the space in front of me. "Are you bust?" His gnarled fingers, one of the tips shorn off, tilted my cards. "Aw, that's too bad. That gives you twenty-four. Too much. Let's see what Lady Luck delivers me." His fingers siphoned off a card. "Damn." The word drifted from his mouth, a disappointment reluctant to leave the warm nest of his body and become manifest.

"I got twenty-seven. That's even worse." He showed his cards to me. A nine of hearts, an eight of spades, and the pucker-lipped jack of diamonds. I spotted a family resemblance to the king of hearts in the scaly stare, the pompous curls, the shoulders that didn't look as if they were going to give in to Lady Luck anytime soon. The stamp of royalty, I figured, must make a person successful but cruel. I tucked that fact in the back of my mind to use in one of my Bugaboo stories.

"Don't worry," August said into the brittle air, laying a straw-boned arm across my shoulders. “That’s chance for you. The chips don’t always fall where you want ’em to.” His chin slackened with this admission, then tipped up, the stumps of teeth in his mouth little gravestones swimming in a yellow tide. His way of smiling. “Next time I’ll teach you girls grand hazard.”

His palm disappeared into his pocket and emerged with a trio of black-tipped, ivory dice. They gleamed in his hand, smooth and round, the way his teeth never had and probably never would.

At night, I took to sleeping with the deck of cards August gave me slipped under my pillow and hoped that when I woke, the bulbous eyes of the jacks, the haughty lips of the queens, and the ridiculous crowns on the kings would be squashed flat. Every morning, however, they were unaltered, and it was my own face—puffy and moon-sized in its proportions—that displayed all the damage. Week by week, my cheeks grew rounder, my head more elongated. My legs sprouted like vines. Soon, my ankles protruded a good three inches from under my pants hem, and my legs shivered in the raw air, but there were only so many sets of boys' clothes the Dyersons could afford to buy. More and more clothing piled up on Amelia's side of the room.

Serena Jane, on the other hand, was gathering more clothes than she knew what to do with at the Pickertons'. Mrs. Pickerton sewed them for her—dresses with butterfly collars and perfect white blouses with sheer sleeves puffed on them like dandelion fluff. Each week, Elsie, Mrs. Pickerton's maid, laundered and ironed the garments back into elaborate shapes, ready for their next promenade. They stood at attention in the wardrobe like little tin soldiers. When I went over to visit her, I liked to comb through her closet.

"How come you never wear this?" I asked, extracting a green plaid kilt. I liked the way it looked with its brutal safety pin—like something for a Celtic warrior. Serena Jane didn't even look up from her movie magazine.

"I don't know." It was raining, and we hadn't felt like going to Hinkleman's.

I reached into my hip pocket. "Want to see a card trick?" But the only sound was

Serena Jane turning a page. I hung the kilt back in the closet. "If it was me, I'd about wear this every day."

Amanda Pickerton knocked, then stuck her head around the door. Sentinel—stouter and slower, but no less obnoxious—mewed violently at her heels. Instinctively, I edged away from him. "Serena Jane? Chicken pot pie for dinner." My mouth began watering, but Amanda curdled her lips into a smile for me. "Don't worry, dear. August knows to come get you. He'll be here shortly." She noticed my hand on the kilt in the closet and shook her head. "Oh no," she said. "No, no, no. You would be a disaster in plaid. Absolutely." She shut the door behind her as if she were locking a reptile in a cage.

I went and flopped on the bed next to Serena Jane, causing the mattress to lurch. She didn't even know how lucky she was. She had chicken pot pie—hot and bubbling, straight from the oven—whenever she wanted it and a ruffled bedspread that was flecked with snooty primroses. She had pocket money every week, whether she deserved it or not. I nudged my sister with my shoulder, sending the mattress lurching again. "Do you ever miss me?" I kept my eyes pointed straight down, my gaze swimming among the bedspread's primroses. *If anything,* I thought, *she should be the lonely one.* After all, I had Amelia in the bed next to me at night, snoring her funny, snuffly snore. Serena Jane had no one here.

Serena Jane tossed her magazine on the floor and flipped over to her back. "Sometimes, when I go to sleep. It's weird without you." She blinked up at the ceiling, and I pictured her doing that in the middle of the night, her arms raised over her head like wings. I reminded myself that nothing came for free. My sister's piano lessons and new wardrobe had a price. Maybe it seemed steeper in the dark. Serena Jane rolled back over to her stomach and brushed the hair off her cheeks. "In the morning, everything is fine, though. I'm getting used to it."

I pictured her drinking coffee and milk out of Amanda Pickerton's basket-weave wedding china, spooning fresh fruit out of the crystal bowl, and tolerating the Reverend Pickerton's rapturous gaze. Whenever I came over, I noticed that he spent a lot of time hiding behind his paper if Serena Jane was in the room. When he was done with the front page, he busied himself with drafts of his sermon and budget forms until Serena Jane left, wafting behind her the unusual scent of tuberose. Once, I watched him sniff the air tentatively, like a dog investigating a new bone, allowing himself one sharp inhalation, one perfumed blast of sin—his rapture for the day.

If he had been a gambling man—and he wasn't, not by any means—I bet the Reverend Pickerton would have laid his entire fortune out in front of Serena Jane's fairy feet just for the pleasure of it, just to watch her lithe arms scoop it all up to her bosom. He was a man of the spirit, but he wasn't totally ignorant of the ways of the flesh. I bet he would have paid to put himself on Serena Jane's side of the stakes any day of the week. He wasn't a fool. He knew that in this world, beauty always comes out on top.

Chapter Seven

As the days after my father's death turned into months, and as January led into February's dreaded chill, I refused to return to school. Nothing Brenda said to me made any difference, either. "Don't you miss Serena Jane?" she asked. "Don't you want to spend more time with her?" I shook my head. At school, Serena Jane had always made it a point to sit as far away from me as possible, and she'd consistently ignored me in recess, flocking instead to the more pleasingly proportioned girls.

Brenda tried a different tack. "Don't you want to see your friends?" I snorted.

"Suit yourself." She shrugged. "Saves us on gas. You can stay out here with Amelia." Because of Amelia's mute spells, Brenda taught her at home. Amelia had never set foot in that schoolroom, and I intended to follow her lead. At the sound of her name, the muscles in my throat slackened as though they'd been given a balm. *Amelia*. My main companion now. Amelia, who bubbled like a soup kettle when she tried to speak to anyone but me, who glided unseen in the edges of shadows, whose skin was so pale, it seemed as if the daylight might break her in half.

Not everyone was pleased with my new arrangement, however. Miss Sparrow, for one, was starting to stew in her classroom. What was it about me? she wondered. Why couldn't I be fenced within the reasonable bounds of educational authority? According to her view of the universe, if ever a creature needed institutional shaping, it was I. And even though she found me absolutely grotesque and personally repugnant, she was still more than willing to have a whack at whittling down the bulk of me.

She waited until after Valentine's Day before she paid her first visit to the farm, sparing me the usual flurry of construction paper hearts passing in and out of everyone's hands but mine. Through the grime of a frosted upstairs window, Amelia and I watched her mince her way from her car toward the rickety front door, her rabbit-skin boots leaving a refined calligraphy in the snow. There was a series of machine-gun raps on the door, and then Brenda answered. Priscilla Sparrow's eyes raked over Brenda's thin shoulders and paisley head scarf, and Brenda's jaw tightened like a bow. Then Brenda's lips moved and released all the arrows she was hiding in her mouth, piercing Miss Sparrow's armor of nail lacquer, and hairspray, and Coral Gables lipstick. The nicked wooden door swung closed in Miss Sparrow's face. Upstairs, I dug a single fingernail into my palm, scratching a line into my flesh to keep score. Downstairs, I could hear Brenda banging pots and pans in the kitchen.

"Girls," she crowed, "come on down here and help me set this table." She clattered a handful of forks together like sabers. "That damn fool woman," she muttered, slamming bowls of Irish stew onto the table.

"Thinks she knows it all." She ran her eyes over the bumps of my body, then over Amelia's skinny cheeks, and paused. "She doesn't know the first thing about us."

The sentiment proved to be equally true on Brenda's part when it came to underestimating Miss Sparrow. For in spite of her carefully limned makeup, and clattery high heels, and fancy words, Priscilla Sparrow was a warrior at heart. In her opinion, she had right on her side, and she had no intention whatsoever of letting an illiterate like Brenda Dyerson call the shots. She tromped back to her car, the heels of her furry boots leaving a trail of cruel crescents, and drove home, where she brewed herself a strong cup of tea, spiked it with a splash of sherry, and regrouped.

The day of Miss Sparrow's second visit, the snow was up to her knees. She had to abandon her car on the main road and stumble down the dirt lane to the farm, but it didn't deter her from reaching the farmhouse door and pounding on it like a refugee. This time, I was in the kitchen, drinking cocoa at the scabbed table with Amelia, and I could see large wet flakes staining Miss Sparrow's painted cheeks. Once again, Brenda blocked the doorway with her meager body and cocked her jaw, resenting the heat that was curling around her ankles and out into the air. Priscilla Sparrow might have been good at math, but she wasn't even aware of the calculations we went through in deciding whether or not to put another log on the fire.

"What is it?" Brenda spat.

Miss Sparrow didn't waste precious words. She scrabbled in her pocket with her finely gloved fingers and produced an envelope.

"From the superintendent of the board of education. It states that, by law, you're required to send any children in your care to school, and that if you don't, you can be found negligent and have the children removed." She glanced over Brenda's broom-handle shoulder and took in my bulk and Amelia's greasy hair and sleepy eyes. Unattractive girls, both of us, she thought, but that wasn't her concern. She was merely here to see that the rules were followed, that justice was done, that no one fell through the cracks on her watch.

Brenda accepted the envelope, stuffing it into her apron pocket without looking at it. She was an expert in receiving unwelcome news. In her experience, bad correspondence always arrived dressed up—splashed with red ink, embossed with seals and a lot of stamps, as if written threats needed extra muscle the way loan sharks needed heavies. She knew all about them, and they knew about her.

Brenda shivered with a blast of icy air and scuttled her shoes on the floorboards. On the other side of the door, Priscilla Sparrow was still craning her neck, trying to get a good look us.

"Is that all?" Brenda closed the door a fraction of an inch.

In the cold, the tip of Miss Sparrow's nose was turning bulbous and red. Nevertheless, she managed a sickly smile. "Unless you have any special circumstances of which I'm unaware." Her teeth hung in her mouth like icicles.

Brenda produced a sickly smile of her own. "No special circumstances. Truly will be back at school in the morning."

Priscilla Sparrow's stained lips retreated even farther over the ridges of her teeth. "Oh, but this letter stands for *all* the children at this residence. I believe you and your husband have a child of your own? A girl? Whom you've never sent to school?"

"I teach Amelia here at home. She's shy. She has a hard time with her speech."

The corners of Priscilla Sparrow's eyes narrowed into poison-tipped darts. "And what makes you think you're qualified to meet that responsibility? Do you have any kind of formal training in pedagogy? Any familiarity with child development and psychology?"

At that moment, Amelia snuck up behind her mother and peeked around her apron. A life passed amid gangsters, horse thieves, smugglers, and gamblers had granted Amelia an unerring nose for greed, vanity, and other assorted venal characteristics, and in Miss Sparrow, she smelled rancid pride combined with the bitter char of unrequited love. She smelled the lemon tang of loneliness mingling with despair. Just under Priscilla Sparrow's skin, Amelia could tell, a rosemary blast of judiciousness rippled, followed by the musty decay of jealousy and a lingering note of envy—in short (and in spite of all of Miss Sparrow's better attempts with Dick Crane), the odors of a lifelong spinster.

I didn't think a person like Priscilla Sparrow was going to have any more luck getting Amelia to speak up than her mother did, and even if she succeeded, it wouldn't change anything. At the end of the day, Amelia would always still be a Dyerson—soft-spined, down at the heels, patchworked. She was what she was, and she didn't mind, either. Not like me, who would have given anything to shed my cumbersome skin and bones, stripping myself down to marrow, to nothing more than a gambler's heart, which beat fast and true and still believed that somewhere out there, a deck was stacked entirely in my favor.

I was correct about school. Miss Sparrow hated me, but she hated Amelia even more. It turned out Amelia was unable to make any progress whatsoever with elocution, dictation, repetition, or any form of memorization. For an entire month, Amelia was kept so late after class that the moon would begin to rise in the schoolroom's paneled window, but it did no good. No matter how many chalky columns of letters and words Miss Sparrow tallied up, no matter how much she banged on the blackboard, Amelia simply couldn't force out a sound. She did better with her numbers, having a firm grasp on the concept of zero. She knew, for instance, that nothing divided by nothing was still nothing. "Things are what they are," she muttered to me on the long cold walk home, her tongue loosened after the confines of school. "You can't change them."

Not that Miss Sparrow didn't try. First, she punished Amelia for being unwilling to speak, sticking her in the coat closet, then she tried coddling, intimidation, and, finally, wheedling. "Come on, darling," she'd say, hooking a finger under Amelia's chin and tipping it up to her for better eye contact. "The other children find recitation easy. You should, too." When Amelia merely blinked at her, silent as an owl, Miss Sparrow dug her finger harder into Amelia's skin. Her teeth seemed to grow a little longer in her mouth. "You know, don't you, that children who refuse to repeat their lessons don't get visits from Santa? You wouldn't like that, would you?" Amelia, for whom Santa was an abstract concept, merely blinked again.

In the end, Miss Sparrow gave up, ignoring

the listless presence of Amelia in the back row and contriving to have her miss school on the day the state assessment exams were held. Amelia didn't mind. She spent the afternoon at home, curled in a nest of blankets, reading the Sears catalog, and helping Brenda bake.

My reentry to school was hardly smoother than Amelia's. The day she skipped the test, I muddled through the pages of questions, my tongue trapped between my teeth, my ankles squeezed together under my desk, as if by tightening all the screws of my body, I would summon up the answers. I gave a glance over to the seat next to me, where Marcus Thompson scratched his pencil across his paper as fast as he could, his lips whispering the answers to himself as he scribbled, adding extra facts and explanations in the margins as he saw fit. I leaned forward, hoping to overhear an answer or two, but it was all mumbo-jumbo to me. "Smarty pants," I hissed, and he jerked his head up, startled. Then he grinned.

"Big bones," he snapped back, but his eyes twinkled as he said it.

Ever since my return to school, Marcus

had been the only pupil with any kind words for me. Even my sister was as distant as a ghost, gliding past me at recess like an unattainable spirit, and it was this canyon of strangeness between us that pained me even more than my troubles with numbers and letters or the rude comments I got from everyone else.

"Hey, Truly," the kids taunted, "come sit on this here rock. You'll crush it, and we'll have us some marbles." Or, "Truly, Truly, two-by-four, couldn't get through a barnyard door." Always, I searched for my sister, but she was usually too far away to do any good, as flickering and unreliable as a lightning bug.

During classroom hours, if I turned my eyes to the desks on the far left side of the room, I could pick out her waxy curls. Sometimes she wore a sweater set the color of orange sherbet or a skirt so fully pleated that she resembled a flamenco dancer. On her wrist dangled a charm bracelet Mr. Pickerton had given her for her birthday—a silver heart, a small key, and a little cross studded with seed pearls, just like the one he'd given his real daughter. When Serena Jane moved her arm, I could hear the charms jingling. I would close my eyes and pretend it was a secret code Serena Jane was sending just to me. During lunch and recess, Serena Jane was immediately swallowed by a phalanx of admirers—girls who cooed over the fringe of her new kilt and boys who wondered how her eyelashes had gotten so dark while her hair was still so blond. Even Miss Sparrow flickered around her, returning Serena Jane's essays tattooed with soldierly exclamation points and warm words of encouragement. Mine only ever had the letter *C* curling into itself on the last page, as if it were giving up.

Amelia and I ate together alone on the big rock shaped like a turtle, peeling the waxed paper off our sandwiches silently and eating glumly, hunkered into our own separate miseries. Soon, however, I noticed Marcus staring at us from his perch across the schoolyard, muttering nonsense to the air. I nudged Amelia. "What's his problem?" She just shrugged and bent back over her soggy bread and tuna fish. I glared at Marcus, making my eyes bulge until he turned scarlet and beat a retreat inside to pester Miss Sparrow some more with his endless facts about Russian space dogs, the chemical properties of curare poison arrow tips, the physics of the curveballs thrown by Yankee Mel Stottlemyre, and anything else that struck his fancy.

One afternoon, though, he either decided he'd had enough of my eyeballing him or he was full up to bust with information, but he abandoned his bench across the yard and sidled up to our rock with his rucksack, settling so closely to me that his leg touched mine. Amelia and I were just finishing the sandwiches that Brenda had packed for us, chewing the chalky slabs of government cheese as slowly as possible to make them last.

"What do you want?" I scowled, bracing for a comment about my butt being heavier than stone or some other such nonsense.

But Marcus merely reached into his rucksack and withdrew a bunch of comic books, fanning them out on the rock between Amelia and me. "Want to see these? Some of them are really good."

I shrugged and picked up a copy of *Spider-Man*. On the cover, Spidey was throwing a web out of his wrist big enough to swallow an entire apartment building.

Marcus tapped the page. "Really, it should be coming out of his abdomen because that's where spiders spin their silk. Did you know they make different kinds? Sticky for traps, and smoother, stronger pieces for moving around on. They weave both kinds into their webs so they can cross them without getting stuck." Marcus squinted. "What kind do you suppose Spidey's using here?"

I rolled my eyes. "The sticky kind, obviously. Because he's catching bad guys."

"But there aren't any bad guys in the picture."

Across the yard, I could see my sister telling an elaborate story, her head thrown back in laughter. I put the issue back down and pushed it toward Marcus. "Okay, so maybe the other kind. Who cares?" It was nice to have company, I thought, but I was like Spidey. I worked alone. I stuck my chin in the air. "Don't you know that no one ever talks to Amelia and me?"

Marcus flipped a comic page. He was small, but I could see he didn't scare easy. He shrugged. "No one ever talks to me, either. They don't want to know all the things I know, like about spiders. Did you know they can live underwater? One type even weaves a waterproof web." He ducked his head. "It's shaped like a bell." Next to me, her forearms resting on the boulder, Amelia leaned over the cover of a vintage *Superman* comic, enthralled by mousy Clark's transformation from spectacled milquetoast to man of steel. Marcus jutted his chin toward the magazine. "*Superman*'s okay, but I like *Spider-Man* better. I just collect *Superman* for the resale value. So far, my collection is worth ten dollars, but I only paid two."

I crossed my arms. "If you're so smart, maybe you can tell me how Superman manages to change his clothes so quick."

Marcus blushed and without asking began gathering up his comic books one by one, his pale fingers worrying the corners of the covers like light-drunk moths. A brace of clouds overhead buckled and began spitting out snow. "I don't know the answer to that," he said as if it were the saddest thing in the world. "Some things are just pretend." He leaned in close to me. His eyes were very, very blue. Just then, Miss Sparrow appeared on the steps with her bell, ringing it with grim precision. "But not everything," he whispered. I bent close to hear what he was saying, and as soon as I did he planted a quick kiss on my cheek. I looked over at Amelia, but she was absorbed by the falling snow and hadn't noticed a thing. I tugged her wrist, my face scarlet. Suddenly, going inside was the last thing I wanted to do.

"Come on," I said. "We better head in."

After school, Marcus was waiting silently for Amelia and me by the coatroom door, and he proceeded to trail us the whole length of town, waiting for some kind of signal to come closer. "What's he doing?" Amelia said, twisting her neck around, and I had to confess that he'd kissed me earlier.

The sun came out briefly from behind its frill of clouds, making Marcus's shadow coast along like a bat. I pointed it out to Amelia. "Look at that." She twisted her head and smiled one of her rare smiles. "Stop it," I hissed. "If you keep encouraging him, he'll just follow us forever."

Amelia kept smiling, though, as if she knew something I didn't. In front of us, our three shadows danced and jigged—Amelia's a happier version of herself, Marcus's elongated and elegant, and mine so big, it slid off the cement and into the street, where it morphed and stretched until I couldn't tell anymore where I stopped and the rest of the world began.

"He must be in love with you," Amelia whispered, kicking up a light dusting of snow. Even after all of Miss Sparrow's instruction, her tongue still stumbled over her consonants, so that it took me a minute to figure out what she was saying. When I did, I scowled.

"Don't be ridiculous. He wanted to show me his comic books, that's all."

Amelia shrugged, as if love were no big deal. "Sometimes," she said in her funny drone, "that's all it takes."

The only things I bothered to bring with me when I moved to the Dyerson farm were my mother's tortoiseshell mirror, a wedding photograph of my parents, and my half of my father's winnings from August's horses. They were only three items—not very many to keep count of—but over the course of my life, I would manage to lose them all. I started with my mother's mirror. Of all the things my mother had left behind her in this world, the tortoiseshell mirror was one of the few possessions Dad hadn't given away. Year by year, the silk slips, the dresses in my mother's closet, her round-toed shoes, had leeched into charity bins and the garbage.

"They've got moths," Dad would bark, coming down the stairs with an armful of sweaters. "It's frayed all along the seams," he explained when he gave away her coat. "No one wears this style anymore."

I never knew why he kept the mirror. It wasn't particularly valuable—in fact, there was a crack running down its back and handle, and the glass was speckled and hazy, giving anyone gazing into it the semblance of a pox victim. Still, the tortoiseshell was genuine, and even after years of neglect, it shone with a gentle luster that reminded me of well-oiled wood. Sometimes I used to sneak into my father's room and pull the mirror off the bureau, twisting it around and around in my hand or tilting the glass so it caught the light and made a little circle of luminescence on the ceiling. After each of my father's purges, I would creep to the chest of drawers and check that the mirror was still there, and it always was, facedown on a yellow linen runner.

One rainy afternoon when I was about six and Serena Jane was eight, we decided to play May Queen—just like the real May Queen that Aberdeen crowned every spring. I assumed that Serena Jane would make herself the queen—she always did—but that afternoon, she just smiled and said, "No, Truly, let's make it you this time." And so I let myself be swaddled in a toilet paper sash, crowned with a tinfoil tiara, and given the mop to hold for a bouquet. I'd felt silly until Serena Jane's breath tickled the back of my neck and she whispered, "Look, you're a princess." She held up the flecked oval mirror in front of my square jaw and bulbous nose, and for once, I believed her.

At night now, tucked up in my cot under the dormer window in Amelia's room, I listened to Amelia's ragged snores and thought about Serena Jane's rose-sprigged room at the Pickertons'. Amelia's bedroom had old horse blankets thrown on the mattresses and flour sacking for curtains. When darkness fell, we would light the stub of a candle to see by, the same one for days, until it was little more than a nub. Even in the dark, it wasn't a room that inspired fantasies of tiaras and ball gowns. Neither was it a room that required the glossy sheen of a tortoiseshell mirror. I could see plain enough what was around me without it. I wasn't like my father, however. I couldn't just get rid of things.

"Why don't you give the mirror to Serena Jane?" Amelia suggested one night after I'd told her a Bugaboo story. Earlier, she'd come in the room and caught me staring miserably at my reflection. "I bet Serena Jane would like to have something from your mother." She didn't say that she thought Serena Jane deserved to have the mirror more than I did, but she didn't have to. Between my sister and myself, Serena Jane was the pretty one, with the pretty life. She'd have a better time staring at herself than I ever would.

I rolled over and slid the mirror back under my bed. It was the last piece I possessed of my mother, but maybe Amelia was right, I thought. Maybe if I gave it to Serena Jane, the gift would tie us together again. I slept badly that night, tossing and turning but resolved. Before I set off for school, I wrapped the mirror in an old scarf and stashed it in the bottom of my satchel, carefully doing up the straps.

All morning, through a tedious math lesson, I squirmed, eager for recess when I could give Serena Jane my present. I watched my sister bend her head over her paper, then straighten up and stare out the window, bored. Beauty didn't need long division, I thought, a stump of pencil clenched between my fingers. Beauty had its own system of partitioning up the world.

The bell rang, and Miss Sparrow glanced up foggily at the class, as if surprised to find herself standing at a blackboard in front of twenty-odd children. Time was not being particularly kind to her. Tiny lines were starting to colonize the spare skin around her eyes, and her lips, once as plump as summer berries, were beginning to thin along their edges. She still bought herself a new pair of high-heeled spectator pumps every year, though, even though she always complained that her toes were killing her and that all the sidewalks in Aberdeen were cracked to kingdom come. She blinked now and clapped her chalk-tipped fingers together dryly. “Recess, children,” she called. She fisted one hand, held it to her mouth, and cleared her throat.

I waited until everyone filed out of the room, then reached into my satchel and withdrew the mirror. Slowly, I unwound the moth-eaten scarf I’d tied around it. Serena Jane was outside, laughing at something a boy was saying and showing off her new skirt. I planned to leave the mirror on her desk, where Serena Jane would see it and understand. She would wait for me after school, and walk with me to Hinkleman’s to slurp sodas, our heels hooked up on the stools. *Here,* she would say, and slip off the tinkling charm bracelet. *You can have this.* She would know how badly I needed something small and frivolous with which to decorate my life.

I had just laid the mirror facedown on Serena Jane’s desk and was turning the bulk of myself around when I heard Miss Sparrow chirp from behind her desk, “What have we here, my dear?” Her heels clicked in my direction and stopped at Serena Jane’s desk. She picked up the mirror, pinching the palm of her hand in the process.

"Oh!" she cried, and dropped the mirror at her feet. A spidery crack spread across the surface of the glass, and one jagged shard fell next to her shoe. "What's this?" She sucked the skin of her hand and nudged the broken glass with her foot. "Don't you know you're not allowed to bring things like this to school?" She pulled her hand away from her mouth. A red welt was blooming in the center of her palm.

"You see what's gone and happened? Now, what if that had been your sister? I'm afraid I'll have to take this." She tucked the handle of the mirror into her waistband, careful to avoid the crack and the raggedy edges of glass, then scowled like a displeased empress. "Now, run along outside."

I ducked my head. Arguing with Miss Sparrow was always a losing gamble. "Yes, ma'am." I hesitated, the tip of my tongue protruding between the buttresses of my lips, then hung my head and shambled out to the schoolyard. Miss Sparrow watched me go, her own lips pinched shut like an old lady's purse. She waited until I was all the way out the door before she pulled out the mirror and held it in front of her, twisting the glass this way and that in order to catch all the angles of herself.

"Mirror, mirror," she whispered, her eyes briefly spreading wide as a girl's. She caught a flash of Serena Jane's flaxen hair framed in the window, then sniffed and tossed the mirror headfirst into the trash. Outside, I heard the thump of the mirror hitting the metal trash can. Morosely, I reached into my pocket, withdrew the deck of cards August had given me, and began to thumb through them. I turned over the six of spades, the three of diamonds, and then the unlovely queen of clubs, her face bloated with a surplus of smug regality. In a round of poker, I knew, that card could be worth gold. It could win you the game, if everything else in your hand cooperated. But in a game of twenty-one, the queen could send you bust with a flick of the wrist as fast as she could win it for you. That was the thing about playing games of chance, I was learning—even when you were losing everything, there was always another suit to turn over, always another facet of the die, where things could add up. It was simple. August had told me so. You just avoided clubs, fished for diamonds, and when in doubt you always, always played the joker.

Outside, Amelia and Marcus were waiting for me on the turtle-shaped rock. "Did you put it on her desk?" they asked, then shut up as they looked more closely at my face.

I shook my head. "Miss Sparrow took it away."

Amelia frowned and stamped at the dirt in frustration. It was Marcus who said the right thing. "Don't worry, Truly," he soothed, "mirrors are just a device for throwing light back at you, and light is just thousands of photons—little bitty particles. Miss Sparrow didn't really take anything from you. Whatever you ever saw in that mirror left it long ago and became a part of you. No one can steal that."

He held out his hand, and I accepted it, choosing—for that moment, at least—to believe him.

Chapter Eight

One of the things you learn growing up in a small town where everyone knows everyone else's business is that desire is communal. And for as long as I could remember, Bob Bob Morgan had only ever wanted two things out of life: to be a doctor and to possess my sister.

Becoming a doctor was no problem at all. History was on his side. Every male in his family from his great-great-grandfather on down had been a doctor. He would be one, too—all of us knew it. It was practically predestined. He could flunk his medical boards, and the school in Buffalo would still have to take him. He could faint every time he saw blood and still get a degree with honors. Serena Jane wasn't so easy to come by, however. Everything about her—from her Kewpie lips to her black-fringed eyes and flossy yellow hair—was like some fancy pony on show parade. No matter how much Bob Bob oohed and aahed, she never spared a glance in his direction.

Not that Bob Bob didn't give it his best shot and amuse the rest of us trying. In the third grade, he climbed the drainpipe up the side of the school building and dangled from it by one arm until he fell and broke his wrist. Serena Jane merely yawned and started picking at the scab on her knee, but I have to say, I was mesmerized by the way the bone protruded sideways out of his arm and his face turned the color of old washing water. When he was ten, he rode his bicycle around and around the school during a violent thunderstorm, risking electrocution, until Miss Sparrow came with a ragged, flapping umbrella and made him go inside. He ate worms for Serena Jane's benefit and tangled with a stray swarm of bees that left his face as juicy and plump as a plum. I enjoyed that week. For once, I could say with confidence that I wasn't the ugliest one in the class.

When Bob Bob wasn't showing off for Serena Jane's benefit, he was thinking up novel ways to torture me. He put thumbtacks in my chair to see if I would feel them when I sat down, then looked blankly amazed when I did. He filled my galoshes with snow, stole my lunches, and routinely peppered my hair with tiny spit wads. The only thing I was glad about was that he left Amelia alone—maybe because she was so quiet—and Marcus, too, because he did Bob Bob's homework for him.

"We could say something to Miss Sparrow," Amelia insisted wanly, brushing flecks of spittle-soaked paper off my collar after class one day, but she knew as well as I did that such a suggestion was fatally flawed. Miss Sparrow loved Bob Bob almost as much as she hated us.

"We could concoct some kind of revenge," Marcus chimed in, rubbing his hands together, his brain already humming with the elaborate machinery of retribution.

"No," I almost shouted, startling the three of us. "That would just make it worse. Don't you think?"

"I guess." Marcus stared down at his hands, depressed by possessing the lore of a thousand comic books and being unable to act on any of it.

"Let's just let time take care of it."

"That could take forever," Marcus almost wailed.

I shrugged. "I can wait."

In the sixth grade, as his hormones kicked in, Bob Bob upped the ante in trying to impress my sister. He stole the pipe from his father's study and learned to blow smoke rings, but Serena Jane just snorted and turned up her nose. By his senior year, Bob Bob must have been getting a little desperate because he kicked up his courting a notch. For three months, he sulked and moped, begging his parents to buy him a convertible, until he hit on an ingenious strategy his father couldn't refuse. One evening at dinner, Bob Bob fanned his fork and knife across his plate like a winning hand of poker, kicked himself back on two legs of his chair, and rubbed his pointy chin with one hand.

"Don't do that with your chair," his mother said without looking up.

Dr. Morgan just glowered at his son. "You heard your mother."

Bob Bob didn't move. "You might want to hear me out." He drew the words from his mouth like a rope of taffy. "I've been doing some thinking."

His father let out a hiss of air and laid his own knife and fork across his plate. "This better not be about the damn car. We're done discussing it."

Bob Bob let his chair fall back to the floor with a thud. "That's too bad. I guess I won't go to medical college, then."

"What the hell are you talking about?" Dr. Morgan's cheeks turned puce.

"Think about it. Without a car, I won't be able to come home very easily, will I? And I know that would break Mom's heart." Maureen fluttered her hands and turned her eyes toward her husband.

A vein in Dr. Morgan's temple began to throb. He pounded a fist on the table. "All right. We'll buy you a damn car. But it won't be new, understand?"

Bob Bob didn't care. He drove it up to the front of school the morning after he got it, one arm hanging out of the side, and immediately attracted a flock of gaggling girls, their knees rubbing together under their skirts, their eyelids fluttering like the tender throats of songbirds. Next to me, I heard Amelia suck a clean whistle of air through the gap in her front teeth, and I knew exactly what she was thinking. At the Dyersons', the criterion for transportation was a little different. We didn't care about spit polish and chrome. If it had wheels and you could push it, we took it.

"It's a ponycar," Marcus breathed on the other side of me, reminding me that he was still a boy and prone to falling under the spell of automobiles, even if they were owned by Bob Bob.

I wrinkled my nose. "A what?"

"A 1967 Mustang. That's a 390-cubic--inch V-8 there under the hood. Mustang won the Trans-Am cup last year with this baby."

I rolled my eyes. Marcus hadn't gotten any better as he'd gotten older. I'd just gotten used to him. There was a rustling among the girls, and then Serena Jane sashayed up to the car. I held my breath, wondering if this was it, if this was the day that she would surrender and swoon into Bob Bob's arms the way we all wanted. But what do you think she did? Nothing, that's what—or not exactly nothing. It was a little worse than that. First she cocked her head like a chicken puzzled by its own egg. Then she swayed up close—so close that Bob Bob could have just grabbed her if he wanted—and reached deep into her pocket and took out a lipstick. She bent over to the little rearview mirror, puckered her mouth like a sour old blackberry, and just barely touched the makeup to her lips.

Just from the angle of Bob Bob's jaw, you could tell he wanted to kill her, and at that moment, I think about half the girls would have jumped in to help him. The thing about Serena Jane was that she was never very good at following other people's rules—especially not the rules of a small town, which said that the prettiest girl must belong to the luckiest boy. No matter how she felt about it, Serena Jane was supposed to be Bob Bob's, pure and simple. It was as bald a fact as her beauty, August Dyerson's bad luck, Marcus's brains, or my enormity.

I was born knowing the rules, which was

why I could see what was going to happen to Serena Jane coming like a freight train on fire. My whole life, people could never understand how someone like Serena Jane had ended up with someone like me for a sister, but the answer was easy, if you thought about it. The reason the two of us were as opposite as sewage and spring water, I thought, was that pretty can't exist without ugly. Even without looking at my puddle-brown eyes first, everyone still would have noticed that Serena Jane's eyes were the promising blue of the Atlantic in July, but I made it a sure bet. I made my sister beautiful without her even trying.

People in Aberdeen may have thought that I was better left a sight unseen, but of course they looked at me all the same. They had to. Even in my flat-soled men's shoes, I was as tall as any of the boys. Had the football team allowed me to, I could have blocked three of the players on the field without a second thought. My hands could have spanned the oblong pigskin with the easy grace of Vince Lombardi. Running could have been a problem, though, for in spite of my robust exterior, my innards were plagued with mysterious aches and pains. Some mornings I woke up with a neck so stiff, turning my head was like pushing a rusty locomotive a mile down a track, and other mornings it was my heart again, skipping beats and flip-flopping in my chest as though it couldn't decide on a music station. But no matter how bad it got, even on the days when my head thumped and the corners of my vision crimped down tight, I didn't say a word, for it always seemed to me that the Dyersons had it worse with their falling-down luck.

Sometimes I thought about going back into Dr. Morgan's office, remembering how kind his eyes were over the tops of his glasses, but the thought of what he might say always stopped me short. That, and the prospect of running into Bob Bob. When you were a girl like me, you stayed away from boys like him at all costs. When I looked at Bob Bob, I saw a dangerous boy with eyes too calculating for his childish nickname. He winced when the soda jerk at Hinkleman's called out his order, scowled when Miss Sparrow replaced "Robert" with "Bob Bob" on the autumn roster, and glowered when his own mother addressed him. In fact, the only people in life he ever forgave the use of his name were his father and my sister—his father because Bob Bob knew he wouldn't think twice about skinning him alive and Serena Jane because she was so beautiful.

And, later, me, but that was different. I didn't really count. I guess I was so unsightly that when I said his name, it was almost as if I hadn't uttered it at all.

Contrary to popular belief, Serena Jane was not a natural blonde. Over time, her hair faded from flaxen to a brackish brown, so that by the time Serena was fifteen, she was expert at dyeing it. No one in Aberdeen knew this about her except me—not Amanda Pickerton, who would have felt betrayed by this visible chink in my sister's beauty; not Miss Sparrow, who would have felt vindicated by it; and certainly none of the other girls, who would have spent the rest of the year huddled in malicious knots, whispering evil little rumors about her. As it was, they sighed when Serena Jane drifted by, her hips lilting, her dimpled chin tilted, and the boys went glassy-eyed, but they never imagined Serena Jane at home in jeans, her regal head bowed over the sink while she combed globs of beer and mayonnaise through her hair. They never in a thousand years would have guessed that the incandescence of her curls came from a simple mixture of chamomile, lemon, and hydrogen peroxide that she put on when Amanda Pickerton was busy attending her committee meetings and Reverend Pickerton was in his parish office and the housekeeper was waxing the floors upstairs.

The only person who might have suspected would have been our father, who gave the recipe to Serena Jane in the first place, never predicting that his ten-year-old daughter would have the wits to gather together the ingredients and then never noticing when she did. Actually, I was the one who gathered the supplies the first time, stuttering that I wanted to disinfect a cut when my father asked why I needed hydrogen peroxide, but Serena Jane was the beneficiary. Her hair came out so shiny and smooth, it was like river water. Dad looked at her a little funny that night, but after his third beer, he didn't see anything different from usual, and that was another reason I supposed Serena Jane was glad our father was dead. Now, no one would ever blurt out her secret. No one would ruin her plans for the future, and she had them all right. Plenty of them.

"I'm going to be an actress," she breathed to me in Amanda's kitchen in early March of her senior year, lighting one of the cigarettes she'd purloined from Reverend Pickerton's pockets. "And not just any old actress, either, but a star. A Marilyn. An Ava. A Rita." I believed her. She had posters of the three of them pinned up on her bedroom wall. One goddess for each color of the hair rainbow.

"Except I'll be blonde, of course," Serena Jane continued, blowing out a lazy stream of smoke. "Brunettes probably have more longevity, but there's just no denying a blonde. You're simply compelled to look at them." I knew what she meant. People were always staring at Serena Jane in long, greedy gulps.

Lately, her friends had taken to drinking beer on Saturday nights, swigging right out of the bottles like the boys. On Mondays, whispers about who had Frenched whom, who had gotten to third base or gone all the way, circled and swirled like witches in flight. But not for my sister and never for me. I didn't have any choice. I spent my weekends cocooned in the Dyerson barn, a deck of cards slipping through my fingers, the warm breath of horses steaming in the air, but Serena Jane was just too good for everybody. Dressed in sleek trousers when the other girls wore jeans, her hair slippery but still neatly arranged, she was as composed and removed as the Buddha. "Let the rest of the girls waste themselves on small-town boys," she said. "Let them sprout little roots in the ground here. I'm getting out."

I handed her a towel and watched her wind it up around her skull. "You look Egyptian," I said.

Serena Jane cocked her neck. "I do, don't I? Liz Taylor wears turbans, and men fall at her feet. Not that she cares, of course. She really only loves Richard Burton." Serena Jane sighed, and I could tell that she wished there were someone like that in Aberdeen—someone heroic and immensely broad-chested. Someone who could light her cigarette with one hand and keep the other one cupped delicately on her elbow. She patted her towel. "All I get is Bob Bob, who has acne on his chin, still drinks milk at dinner, and who's trying to grow a beard and can't."

"Why bother with him?" It was my job to ask the uncomfortable questions between us. Serena Jane merely shrugged and averted her eyes. It was her job to keep her mouth shut, but this time, she didn't. Instead, she guided me over to Amanda's kitchen table and told me a story.

Two weeks ago, she said, she'd finally gone on a date with Bob Bob. She'd wanted to see Zeffirelli's *Romeo and Juliet*, but Bob Bob took her to a party in Hansen instead, where drunken boys lurched up and down the porch steps and tried to grab her hips. Bob Bob punched one of them in the ribs, making the boy go purple in the face, so they'd had to leave, scampering down the sidewalk to his car like rats on the run.

He drove my sister to a diner, where he insisted she order a vanilla milkshake and watched while she drank it—slowly, because she hated vanilla, although only I knew that. When she finished, he wiped her upper lip with the corner of his napkin, as if she were a messy child, then folded her hand inside his long fingers. In the diner's lurid light, I could imagine that his eyes were shining yellow and that his teeth and chin looked particularly pointy, giving him the semblance of a hairless wolf. If it had been me, I would have pulled my hand away, but Serena Jane didn't get that chance because Bob Bob locked his fingers around her wrist, resting his thumb just over her pulse so their blood swam together. Bob Bob didn't know it, but under her blouse, Serena Jane's heart was flapping like a panicked bird. Bob Bob pressed the pad of his thumb deeper into the lattice of veins on Serena Jane's wrist.

He leaned forward. "If my number came up, and I ran across the border, would you come with me?" All over America, young men were on the move—some of them in corroded vans heading north, some of them corralled in the steel bellies of military planes, white-faced and waiting to be dropped into the swampy mire of war. And right there was an opening Serena Jane could have taken but didn't. I would have snapped something along the lines of preferring gunfire in the jungle to a wolf in the forest, but I suppose it's not fair to impose those standards on Serena Jane. She never had to learn to say anything ugly.

Serena Jane snatched her wrist back, tucking it close to her body as if she had been scalded. She pushed the dregs of the milkshake away from her. "I thought you had a deferment. I thought you were safe because you were going to go to medical school."

Bob Bob studied his glass. "I am, but still, you never know. Johnny's going. And so is Marcus."

Serena Jane lifted her watery eyes. "Really? Marcus?" *Poor Marcus*, she thought, which weren't exactly the same words I'd used when I'd found out that he'd enlisted.

"You idiot!" I'd shrieked when he told me. "What the hell were you thinking? Do you know how dangerous it is over there? You'll last about a week."

In the past ten years, Marcus had come along in terms of his appearance. His blue eyes and hair had morphed into handsome features—but he was still by far the tiniest student in the class. For a joke, every Valentine's Day, Bob Bob always cornered me outside the school and wouldn't let me go until I agreed to kiss Marcus. Until just last year, he'd still had to step on the rock in the yard to reach my lips, but recently he'd had a late growth spurt, inspiring his mother to buy him all new trousers, even though she still had to hem them. Marcus was terribly proud of them.

"I'm sorry," I always whispered right before his mouth met mine, and he always muttered, "I'm not," before I closed my eyes and tasted the surprising salt of him. He was good-natured almost to a fault, decent, and you could always count on him to volunteer to do the right thing, which was exactly the reason he'd offered himself up to the military.

The afternoon he told me about his enlistment, we were on the road out to the Dyerson farm. He stepped closer to me and took my hand. Ever since our last Valentine kiss, I'd been letting him walk me home, his fingers entwined with mine. Amelia somehow always managed to go on ahead of us. That afternoon, the air had a bitter bite to it that would haunt me in years to come. "Come on, Truly. Don't be like this. I'm strong enough. You watched me bench-press my own body weight. I've been practicing in the garage, using Dukey's old weights." Dukey, his elder brother by ten years, had missed the draft and was celebrating by living at home, losing one job after another, and drinking his own body weight. "Besides, it's for our country."

"Actually, it's *their* country," I snapped, but I didn't pull my hand out of his. "And anyway, what about me?"

Marcus blinked and took a step closer, his boots squeaking in the last of the season's snow. "You're the thing I'm fighting for," he whispered. Then he squeezed my hand and headed back toward town before I could tell him that I was a battle he'd already won. I watched him go, marveling that while he was so hog confident of victory, all I could feel, pressed into my chest like a heavy, treaded boot, was crushing worry.

"Poor Marcus," Serena Jane said out loud now, interrupting her story, her voice a bell of woe in Amanda's kitchen. "He'll get killed before the plane's even landed."

I clenched my teeth and willed myself not to think about it. "So what did Bob Bob have to say about that piece of news?"

Serena Jane sighed. "He said he wouldn't go."

"But what about his family?" You couldn't grow up in Aberdeen and not know about the Morgan men and war. They excelled at it. Among the four Dr. Morgans, they had enough medals and uniforms to outfit their own private army.

Serena Jane shrugged. "Bob Bob said that his great-great-grandfather was a Civil War deserter. That's how he got here. He walked up from the South. I guess he didn't think war was so great."

"But he served. He went."

"Only to walk away from it and find this place. Where the hell would Bob Bob go in Vietnam?"

I said nothing. I was picturing Bob Bob hacking his way through a South Asian jungle, his skin tinged green, mud flecking his hair. Lush vines twined around his arms and neck, coiling tight as exotic snakes and squeezing until he turned blue, then purple, then a sooty black. Until he knew how it felt to be teased all the time.

What can I say about the events that followed that evening between Bob Bob and my sister? Only that Serena Jane always did want a starring role in something, and she finally got it. Bob Bob drove her home slowly, his arm crouching on the seat behind her neck, his fingers outstretched like spiders. Thinking about all of this—even now—is like watching a movie for me. There's that urge to scream at the person on the screen, to warn them, but, of course, doing so only results in a sore throat and nasty looks from everyone else around you.

She expected him to drive her to the Pickertons', where Reverend Pickerton would be waiting for her, the living room light pooling over his newspaper, but Bob Bob pulled his car up in front of Aberdeen's ragged cemetery gate instead. Serena Jane crossed her arms in front of her chest, making a mummy of herself. "What are we doing here? This is creepy." She reached for the door handle.

"Wait." Bob Bob snatched at the hem of her dress. "You could say thank you for the nice evening. Most girls would." In the dark, I knew, my sister's hair glowed like a mermaid's. When we were very young, I used to use it as a kind of night-light, turning my head toward her to see the reflection of the moon and streetlamps spread out across her pillow. With hair like that, it was impossible not to want to own it somehow, and that's just what Bob Bob longed for—to bury his nose in it and inhale the salt of Serena Jane, making his tongue into a fish that could swim through the mysterious hollows of her flesh.

Serena Jane tried to say no, but the sickly taste of vanilla coated her throat. She clawed at the door but managed only to brush the window crank with her fingers before Bob Bob was on her, his knee wedged between her thighs, his impatient hands plucking at the ribbons on her blouse. His breath rasped out of him in ragged intervals, squeezing between the gaps of his clenched teeth. Under him, Serena Jane twisted and bucked, but he held on, his skinny fingers pinching her narrow shoulders and neck like a savage lobster until he felt the sinews of her relax, until her tendons went slack, and her eyes closed, and she tilted her head back languorously, offering herself up to him just as he'd always dreamed, as he'd always craved. Afterward, he gave her his T-shirt to wipe herself up, ignoring the streak of blood she left on it.

"Forget it," he growled when she offered

it back to him. He was feeling expansive—generous, even. Outside the car windows, the night had stretched itself out like a bride. A gust of wind combed through the trees above the car, dropping pellets of snow on the roof. Bob Bob grinned. This was his night. *The* night.

Serena Jane let him drive her home—a sensible choice because it was better than walking through the muddy slush and gravestones, and besides, by that point it was too late to do much else. She kept her face pointed to the passenger window and tried as hard as she could to ignore the ghostly twin of herself floating morosely in the glass, and in that one gesture, the moment I'd longed for my whole life came true. Serena Jane finally felt what it was like to be me. As she got out of the car, without her underwear or a single word to Bob Bob, she felt as if she had somehow switched places with her reflection and become that other version of herself—translucent, wavering, forever trapped in a small square of black.

As I watched her finish binding her hair up in its towel over the Pickertons' sink now, I could tell she still hadn't forgotten.

She leaned forward toward the window above the sink and blew a foggy circle onto one of its panes, evidence that she was still there, filled with blood, and air, and not about to dissolve. That was one thing I always knew Serena Jane envied about me. She thought I never had to worry that there wasn't enough of me to go around, but she finally found out she'd been completely wrong.

Chapter Nine

After his encounter with Serena Jane, Bob Bob found himself dreaming more and more often of my sister. This wasn't unusual—she'd populated his dreams for years—but the intensity of the dreams had changed. This new, nocturnal Serena Jane was no longer a dimpled teen queen, but a banshee with glowing eyes. It was a facet of Serena Jane that only I knew existed—wild, primal, utterly unforgiving—and he was shocked to make its acquaintance.

Bob Bob always woke from these dreams violently, the tube of his throat tensed, but with the sound still stuck inside of it. Sometimes the moon would be pouring its gauzy light into his window, and he would rub his eye sockets with the heels of his hands and blink up at the ceiling, wondering what his nightmares meant. The stuff in the jungle was easy, he figured. Every day, more and more boys were coming home zipped into the never-ending darkness of body bags. The TV and newspapers, magazines—even comic books—were crawling with the lush horror of Vietnam. When it came to the war, Bob Bob wasn't the only one with night sweats.

But the other dreams, the ones where he was just going about his business only to be blindsided by a snarling and unfamiliar Serena Jane, well, those visitations had him stumped. At school, I watched him watch her, but to him, she didn't appear any different. Her nose still tilted with the charm of Tinker Bell's. Her chin still had a dimple right in its center. And every day, she looked right through him, just as she always had, just as people looked through me.

Then one night, Serena Jane came to him as a crow with a stuttering beak. She perched on his shoulder, gripping his flesh with scaly talons, and clacked her bill in his ear, tweaking the lobe when she was finished as if to admonish him. He twisted toward her in indignation and saw that the crow was holding a small looking glass, the oval of it swaying and glittering like a jewel. He peered into its frame and was surprised to see the wan face of an infant peering back at him, its sloe eyes wet, its tiny fists pummeling the air, as if fighting for breath.

Bob Bob woke from the dream sweating. His room was cold, but his mother had snuck in and covered him with the family quilt that normally hung on the parlor wall downstairs, scalloping him in folds of heat until he almost couldn't breathe. He hated the thing. It was enormous—embroidered in a riot of flowers and vines by Tabitha Morgan, his great-great-grandmother, who everyone said was a witch. Waking up under Tabitha's quilt, Bob Bob could understand why. His skin felt as if it were crawling with sets of bony fingers.

It was the beginning of April, but he could see out his window that a freak snowstorm had blanketed the world, cosseting all its hard edges into sterile white mounds. In the upper corner of his window, the moon was full, reflecting itself ghoulishly against all the white.

It was the same light he'd found in the little county morgue that he'd visited a week ago with his father in preparation for medical college, the kind that left little room for nuance or shadow. The kind of light that belonged to the dead. His father was verifying some last minute work on the autopsy of one of his patients—an old woman from town Bob Bob hardly knew. On the slab in the morgue, her cronelike body was covered with a dingy sheet, but her feet were sticking out, scaly and gnarled as a chicken's. Probably they had looked much the same in life, as had her few pieces of hair and the gummy line of her mouth. If there's one thing I've learned about death, it's that it merely enhances what was already there before it.

"Come here," Bob Bob's father instructed him, putting his hands on his son's shoulders. "Don't be afraid. I want you to see."

Bob Bob shrugged him off. He wasn't afraid—he wasn't even impressed. As far as he was concerned, the old woman was like the dried-up beetle shells that appeared on the garage floor at the end of every summer, their withered legs tucked up into their bellies, their wings desiccated and blown to dust. If he ground his sneaker over the top of her, he bet, she would crunch and crumble, and that would be the end of it. Bob Bob remained as still as he could, counting the woman's waxen wrinkles, until his father deemed he'd seen enough and pulled the sheet back up over the woman's face. He turned toward Bob Bob. "Well?" The question was a fishhook hanging in the air.

Bob Bob shrugged. "It's not that bad." Overhead, one of the room's pallid bulbs flickered, irritating his eyes. He blinked, hating this one weakness.

Dr. Morgan squeezed his son's shoulder. "It gets easier," he reassured him. "Why, after you go through anatomy, death will be like second nature."

Bob Bob didn't say anything, but he thought he might already be way ahead of his father. For the most part, he liked the morgue. It was pleasantly temperate, no one would spend hours yakking your ear off about some stupid problem, and everything was in its place. As far as he could figure, death was no big deal. After all, you had it coming to you whether you liked it or not, and the sooner you got comfortable with that, the better. Really, he thought, it was nothing to worry about.

He followed his father outside again to the car, blinking in the brilliant spring sunlight, brushing a few seasonal midges away from the vicinity of his nose, scowling at a pair of wilted daffodil heads leaning on their spent stalks. Surreptitiously, he flattened them under his sneaker when his father wasn't looking. Death wasn't that bad, but the process of dying was tedious—a feeling I happen to share. He felt the flower bulbs crunch and climbed in the car beside his father, relieved when they pulled away. Bob Bob closed his eyes and decided that it was best to deal with either the living *or* the dead. Ushering people from one state to the other held very little interest for him.

When he was alone in his room, however, freshly woken from his crow dream of Serena Jane, the hard skin of Bob Bob's carefully cultivated emotional detachment began to crack. Confronted with the unreliable moonlight flooding his walls, he suddenly found himself infused with an unfamiliar melancholic longing—as if homesick for a distant shore or the long-absent arms of a lover. He shook his head and turned away from the window, settling the bulk of the quilt over him. It was the unseasonable snow making him turn foolish, he decided, or the drop in barometric pressure. There were no such things as half-truths, or bird-women, or spells. And love was the most ridiculous trick of all. My sister had taught him that. In the end, underneath all the layers of hair and clothes, she had been just like any other girl—an arrangement of skin, and bones, tongue, and teeth. A warm sack of flesh. Nothing more than a little voice he was trying to ignore in the dark.

In contrast, Marcus never got the chance to see that Aberdeen spring. In March he had left for Vietnam with underwhelming fanfare, except for a special trip out to the Dyerson farm to see me. We stood miserably together under the half-rotten windmill, which spun only under the duress of a hard winter wind.

"Why are you doing this?" I demanded again. "You don't have to do this. Just go across the border. Lots of boys are doing it. Or go to college. Maybe the army will give you a cushy job. Like behind a desk or something."

Marcus tucked his chin down against his neck. "Nope. I don't want to do things that way."

"No offense or anything, but how are you going to manage? I mean, how come the army even took you in the first place?"

Marcus scuffed his toe in the dirt and snorted. "C'mon, Truly. I'm small, but I'm not deformed or anything."

I took a wounded step back from him. "You mean like me."

"No, no, I didn't meant it like that." He rubbed one of his hands through his thick black hair. "What I mean is, the army's taking everybody these days. Big, little, they don't really care, just as long as you can shoot straight."

"And what makes you think you can?"

Marcus took another step toward me.

"Don't be like this now." But I knew how enraptured Marcus was by the conflict overseas. His childhood obsessions with Russian space animals and the intricate anatomy of insects had been replaced by a hunger to know all the obscure details of modern weaponry.

"The newest grenade is the M61," he told me, pointing out a mention of it in the newspaper while we shared a float at Hinkleman's. He dug a pen and pencil out of his backpack and drew an oblong shape. "See how it's shaped like a lemon?" He added a squiggle inside. "And this thing here is a notched steel coil. When you pull the pin, the coil explodes into high-velocity fragments. It's lethal."

"I guess that's the point," I mumbled, hogging the last of the ice cream in the glass. But Marcus wasn't finished yet. His hand kept moving, sketching out a rough version of a helicopter with two blades.

"This baby here is the HueyCobra. That's short for AH-1 Cobra. It can go two hundred nineteen miles per hour, which is pretty good considering it's almost seven thousand pounds, empty. It goes up to eleven thousand four hundred feet at a rate of one thousand two hundred thirty feet a minute." He flipped the newspaper page. "Oh, look, here's another story about Khe Sanh." My mind struggled with the unfamiliar sounds of another language, while Marcus ripped out the article and stuffed it in his pocket. In an empty cigar box under his bed, I knew, he was hoarding clippings about battles and attacks. He'd flattened and folded the pages of a *Life* magazine with a photo essay on the soldiers. The black-and-white helicopter blades and rifles sang out to him, and the soldiers sweated and grinned, and every time Marcus looked at them, I just knew that his heart was hammering blood through his body like the blasts of a machine gun. *War, war, war,* the beat pounded, a staccato heartsong as ancient as it was young. A song just for Marcus. His chance finally to do something heroic and big.

So far, Ebert Vickers's son had been killed by mortar, his body shipped home in pieces like a puzzle. His friend Henry's older brother, Frederick, was garroted by a Vietcong spy outside a village and found a few hours later by a local woman, the wound on his neck picked clean by ravenous sparrows. In Vietnam, it seemed that even the birds were starving. Mandy James sent weekly letters describing her life as a nurse. Whenever her mother received another letter, her nose and eyes swelled and reddened like the poisonous berries on a holly bush, and the whole town knew then that things were not going well for our troops. I looked into Marcus's round, expectant eyes, the empty lane leading down the Dyerson farm stretched out like a ribbon behind him.

"Aren't you afraid? You watch the news." I looked for a flicker of fear or uncertainty, but all I saw were my own bulbous features reflected back at me.

"I have to do this, Truly. I'm sorry. I'll write, I promise." He tipped his chin up, and I knew that he wanted me to kiss him, but I was too mad. I turned my back on him and started walking to the farmhouse, so furious that I didn't turn around and didn't even say good-bye.

At first, his letters were full of bravado. *Dear Truly,* he wrote, *lots of fellows have been homesick, but I haven't. I can do fifty pushups now. I know how to clean and oil a gun. Charlie won't get this American!* During basic training, I learned, he figured out how to shoot craps for cigarettes, whistle a hornpipe, and spit polish his boots. Once overseas, he was assigned to drive ambulances. He didn't know how to drive a stick, he said, but he figured he'd tackle that problem when he got to it.

Soon, however, his letters grew shorter. *Dear Truly, I'm alive. I'm still here.* Time had become a game of do or dare to him, I could tell. Even his handwriting started to look tired and pissed. One day, I received a letter with a story in it that finally made me write him back.

In the central highlands, Marcus wrote, the only thing marking the remains of former villages were the skeletons of rice silos. Sometimes ten feet or more of them were still standing, or sometimes the whole structure would be toppled, the rice long since devoured. Huddled in an emergency first-aid post that used to be a barn, Marcus clapped his hands over his ears and bowed his head as yet another shell screamed to an explosion on the horizon.

Marcus looked outside at the smoking sky and then down at the cracked wristwatch banding his arm. Two more hours until nightfall, when he could load whoever was left onto the ambulance and get the hell out. He sank into a pile of straw, settling himself against his pack, and drew his knees up to his chest. It was late spring, but the weather in Vietnam was that of the underworld—pregnant with a heat so wet and heavy, Marcus said some men just gave up and died in it.

"Thompson! Time to load up! The mule train is good to go." Connelly, his section leader, shook his shoulder. Night had arrived, and with it all the paraphernalia of the maimed and wounded. Canvas stretchers. Syringes filled with morphine. Yards of sheer white gauze that could transform a solider into a drugged mummy.

"You've got three down-boys tonight," Connelly barked. The ambulance could accommodate three gravely wounded on stretchers or six sitting soldiers. Connelly grappled with the handles of a stretcher, upon which a human form writhed. "Lie still!" he brayed at it. The soldier paid him no mind and continued twisting on the canvas, as if being manipulated by an invisible puppeteer.

"Goddamn bleeders," Connelly wheezed as he started toward the cluster of cars, crouching as a shell exploded nearby. "They leak all over the damn place. I prefer the corpses. They're less work." Corpses were what they called the almost dead. The ones with open throats, with half their skulls crushed in, with no feet.

Marcus put the car into gear and started down the heavily camouflaged road. The full moon glared at him through ragged clouds, orbital and bright as a fish eye. On either side of him, tall fences of brushes and weeds rustled messages and threats. He patted the tool kit on the seat next to him, making sure it was still there alongside his gas mask, and then foraged in his coat pocket for his flask.

Abruptly, he pulled the car to a halt, idling the rattletrap engine while he assessed the tree branch lying in the middle of the road. Behind him, Connelly braked, followed by Swanson and Smith, their little convoy rounding up like wagons at a hostile pass. "What, ho?" Connelly called through the darkness.

"Tree branch in the road, sir," called Marcus. "I'll remove it."

"Mind yourself, Thompson," Connelly ordered. "Could be a booby trap."

"Yes, sir," Marcus said. As if the thought hadn't already occurred to him. He jumped out of his car, then inched his way forward through the darkness, wishing he could turn on his headlights. At least the moon left enough light to see by. He leaned over the gnarled branch, running his eyes all around it, then took a deep breath and kicked it out of the way. Nothing. Little bullets of sweat clustered on his forehead, slicking him with relief.

Marcus stood up on the road and opened his mouth, but the most enormous percussion suddenly erupted in the air, filling his open throat with a poisonous roiling that stung his lips and eyes before snaking into his lungs, making it impossible to breathe.

"Mortar!" Marcus heard Connelly scream, and he fumbled back to the cab of his ambulance, groping for the salvation of his gun, his tongue blistering, his eyes two bilious swamps. He pulled his shirt over his mouth. He felt his stomach heave, then vomit filled his shirt. Leaning against his ambulance, he let the sick pool up around his chin, breathing through it as best he could. The shell had struck about a hundred yards ahead of them, a little ways off into the woods.

An ambush. It was the worst eventuality, the thing that made even the atheists into believers, the thing that stole life like a quiet thief and replaced it with a death scented with the lingering tropical odors of tamarind and coconut.

The air in front of Marcus began to clear slightly, the haze subsiding enough for him to find his torch and switch it on. Worrying about the light now was pointless with the woods in flames feet away from him. He swung his light in panicked arcs around him, flashing on grisly tableaux with each movement of his arm. There was a pile of soldiers convulsing by the side of the road. Marcus stumbled over a pair of boots and found Swanson facedown in the mud, the back half of his skull smashed open like a candy Easter egg.

Marcus was startled to see that he was still breathing. Swanson's hand dropped the gun and clawed at Marcus's wrist. Marcus peered into the lolling bed of the ambulance to assess the damage. Those men were certainly dead. Swanson's fingers dug into Marcus's arm, as if taking his pulse. He squeezed. He fluttered his eyes—the semaphore of the dying. Marcus squeezed back. He understood.

As fast as he could, before Connelly saw him, he rummaged in his pocket for his handkerchief. He hesitated a moment, then he pressed Swanson's nose, pinching the nostrils closed, and laid his other hand flat over Swanson's mutilated mouth. Swanson gasped and squeezed his arm, but Marcus stayed still. *Maybe*, he wrote, *I could have saved him. Maybe I could have got him out. Maybe I shouldn't have done it.*

In the distance, Connelly was yapping his name. "Thompson . . . Thompson! Why have you left your wounded? Forget Swanson. Get back to your car."

Marcus left his friend and stumbled back to his car. He didn't bother to check whether or not the soldiers he was carrying were alive. He would find out when he got to the field hospital and handed them over to the nurses, beautiful and calm as milkmaids. I pictured Marcus putting his foot down on the accelerator and roaring off through the mist, crunching over sticks and stones, leaving the irritated screaming of Connelly behind him like the crows back in August's fields, and for the first time since he left, I let myself really think about him, and I realized how much I missed him. I was sixteen and just waking up to the peculiar rules of love—how what's left unsaid between two people can be a far more complicated language than what's written on the page.

I tucked his letter in the rough flannel pocket of my shirt and waited for Amelia to go down to feed the chickens so I could compose something back to him. I gazed out over the broken stony fields and wondered what I had that I could tell him about. A line of weak corn that I'd planted? The crows that fed off of it? Maybe something as simple as the earth itself. *When you get back,* I finally wrote, *let's lay ourselves down in the fields outside, and sleep there for the night, whatever the weather. We'll let the crows roost on our shoulders and skulls, let them nudge our necks with their wings, and pick at our earlobes, nibbling all the rotten bits out of us until we're nothing more than sinew, bone, and teeth. Until we're so pure, you can see right through us down to the roots and dirt. Until even our memories are eaten alive.*

I licked the envelope and sent it, but maybe I said too much, for I never got a reply, and the next thing I knew, I heard that Marcus was in a hospital in Maryland, recuperating. I heard his leg got blown apart, and one of his hands, too, changing the whole shape of him, making it difficult for him to walk and even more difficult to write. Or maybe he just had nothing left to confess. Maybe the shell had taken care of that.

Chapter Ten

The morning of Aberdeen's one hundred fortieth official May Day celebration, my sister woke up early, hobbled over to the flowered porcelain basin in her room, and threw up. Then she rinsed her mouth with Listerine, tiptoed down the hall to the bathroom, and quietly emptied the basin's contents into the toilet. She gathered her flaxen hair into a bunch at the base of her neck and peered into the medicine cabinet mirror.

In the dingy square of glass, her eyes looked puffy and bloodshot. Her cheeks were pale, and her lips had a new fullness to them that had absolutely nothing to do with the beeswax lip salve she used at night. Her hands traveled over her clavicles and down to cup her aching breasts. You only had to glance at her to know how plump and round they'd gotten or to verify that her hips were spreading out on either side of her like a pair of misplaced wings. She sighed, pinched some color into her cheeks, and set her mind to the problem of how she was going to squeeze herself into her May Queen gown.

It had been ten weeks since her last period—long enough for her to know that it wasn't likely to arrive anytime soon and long enough to know why. It wasn't long enough, however, to have figured out what to do about it. I was the only one who knew, and every hour of every day, I could feel her problem whorled inside my own abdomen like a question mark. A baby was not what my sister wanted, I was aware. I pointed this out to her as soon as she told me, a week before the festival.

"Truly, I think I'm pregnant," she said, her pretty hands twisting in her lap like a pair of kite strings. We were in Amanda Pickerton's kitchen, which she had just repainted an avocado green. The color ricocheted off my sister's cheeks and turned her hair into fairy moss.

"Are you sure?" *Maybe she's just being dramatic*, I thought, but Serena Jane bowed her head and started crying. A baby, I knew, wasn't going to get her a screen test in Hollywood or her face on the covers of magazines. A baby meant soiled diapers, and drool, and sour milk. It was the most unappreciative audience in the entire world. Of course, it was easy enough for me to think all of that. What did I know about the contorted physics of sex and love? Only that I was too big to enter into them. Every month my period came and went with the blank regularity of the moon, and if the dull cramps in my belly and back ever made me long for the body of a boy, all I had to do was look in the mirror to know that I stood about as much chance in that department as one of August's racehorses winning the Kentucky Derby.

Serena Jane sniffled. "What am I supposed to do? Sal Dunfry had this problem last year, and a doctor in Manhattan took care of it, but I don't have that kind of money.

Besides, I would never get the chance. Amanda would have me crucified first."

I hunkered in my chair and tucked my fist under my chin. "Is it Bob Bob's?"

Serena Jane bit her lip and nodded. She placed the flat of one hand against her belly and pressed inward toward her spine. "He doesn't know yet." She sucked her belly in some more, as if trying to will herself back into her old shape, but it was no use. The evidence was there, as plain as day. Anyone with two eyes and a brain could look at her and know what was happening, and soon everybody would. Everyone except Bob Bob, that was. He didn't have a clue. Every day at school, my sister stared daggers at him, but he never so much as turned in her direction. I imagined that after all this time it must be strange for Serena Jane to have Bob Bob ignoring her—a feeling like cutting off her hair or shedding the heavy weight of a winter coat.

"Why don't you write him a letter?" I suggested, but as soon as Serena Jane seized the pen, the muscles in her palm cramped up. She took to tracking Bob Bob with the zeal of a bloodhound, pacing the edge of the baseball field during practice, and shadowing him on his route home from school. If August didn't need me in the barn, I went with her.

We trailed him like listless ghosts, until Bob Bob startled both of us one day, turning on us with the savagery of a kennel dog. We were on the sidewalk outside of his house. I noticed that the picket fence needed painting but couldn't imagine Bob Bob engaged in such a menial chore. Probably the Morgans hired people to do things like that, I thought.

Serena Jane opened her mouth to tell him about the baby, to let the whole dilemma come pouring out of her like a stream of water, but when she tried to speak, her voice crackled and died. She just stood there, croaking like the enchanted Princess Bugaboo, until Bob Bob snorted in disgust and walked up the path to his house, leaving us on the pavement with the haunting aroma of vanilla seeping down the backs of our tongues. Serena Jane waited till he slammed his door, then leaned over the hedges and vomited while I held her hair.

Inside the Morgan house, the pale moon

of Maureen Morgan's face appeared at the parlor window, her mouth pursed into an O, her breath leaving a vapor trail on the glass. She frowned. Girls that age didn't throw up out of love alone. In her experience, unrequited love never made anyone very sick, but requited love, well, that had its own, corporeal consequences, and it was pretty clear which type she was looking at now. Bob Bob's fascination with my sister over the years had been no secret—his family teased him about it nightly at the dinner table—but the thing that surprised Maureen was that Serena Jane had finally given in, and Bob Bob had said nothing about it. That didn't seem right. Maureen narrowed her eyes and let the swag of heavy curtain fall back into place. From behind folds of velvet, she watched me help my sister wipe her lips with the back of one hand. Maureen turned away. She'd seen what she needed to. She knew what had to be done.

No one in Aberdeen had been surprised when Serena Jane won a unanimous vote for the title of May Day Queen. After all, the crown had practically been hers since the day she was born. By age six, she'd even had the float ride down cold, a spatula cradled in the crook of one arm for a scepter, a tinfoil crown on her head, her right arm waving like a mannequin come to life. Now that the actual moment had arrived, however, I could tell that Serena Jane was finding it difficult to execute the maneuver. For one thing, the bodice of her gown was so stretched, the seams were beginning to pucker. And for another, fumes were frothing out of Dick Crane's car with such vigor that even I felt sick. When my sister wasn't looking, I saw Dick surreptitiously tilt the rearview mirror to get a good view of her magnificent calves. A girl like that was bound to go far, he was clearly thinking, his eyes raking the mirror. My sister probably hadn't been born that blond for nothing. Women never were. He smacked his lips, peeling his eyes away from Serena Jane, anticipating barbecue.

Aberdeen's May Day celebration was the oldest continuous festival in the state of New York, a fact that Dick loved to advertise. Each spring, he had another commemorative object manufactured to mark the occasion—a proud tradition that had led to decorative mayhem in Estelle Crane's parlor. The official May Day platter of 1962 hung on one of her walls, the daffodils on it smeared owing to an uneven kiln temperature (the potter had been a friend of Dick's over in Hansen). And there, plopped on the rocking chair, was the May Day needlepoint pillow of 1965, its bulk covered with butterflies so small and pale, they resembled moths.

The 1959 May Day teacup held pride of place on Estelle's credenza, with the corresponding 1960 tea tray propped just behind it. There was an unfortunate gap between 1965 and 1967, but this year, 1969, was *almost* the start of a new decade. In spite of his wife's protestations, Dick had had a phalanx of T-shirts printed up with beribboned maypoles emblazoned on the front, and on the back, in rows of big blue letters: *May Day Festival! The Oldest Party in New York! Still Going Strong!* Against better judgment, Estelle wore one of the shirts to the postparade picnic on the town green, but besides Priscilla Sparrow (who we all knew harbored an abiding affection for Dick that defied age, position, and common sense), she was the only one. Estelle squinted her eyes in Prissy's direction and sniffed.

"Forget about her," advised Cally Hind from the potato salad station. "Everyone knows she's nuts." She flicked her eyes over to where Serena Jane was seated majestically on her May throne, Dick hovering over her with a platter of spareribs. "I'd worry more about *her*."

"Don't be ridiculous," snorted Estelle. "For one thing, she'd have to wrestle that plate of ribs away from Dick first, and for another, that girl has plans. If she's going to give herself to anyone, it's certainly never going to be to anyone from around here."

Cally plopped a ball of potato salad onto Estelle's plate and leaned forward for a quick heart-to-heart. "That's not what I heard. Unless those plans include Bob Bob Morgan, an aisle, and a big white gown, that girl's not headed anywhere anytime soon. The ring's as good as locked on her finger. All she has to do is finish high school."

Estelle crinkled her brow and watched with relief as Dick returned to the grill for refills, leaving my sister propped alone in her enormous decorated chair, placid as a doll someone had tucked back up on a high shelf for safekeeping. Estelle's face went soft. Maybe she was thinking of the early years of her own marriage, how bewildering it had been to be suddenly left alone in a strange house for the entire day, with nothing on her hands but a pile of laundry and a ticking clock. "That's a shame," she murmured. "After all, she's still just a girl."

"She probably found old Tabitha Morgan's shadow book and put it to her own use," sniffed Madge Harkins, observing the sheen of sun falling on Serena Jane's hair.

Cally Hind shook her head. "Not hardly. From what I hear, she could benefit from a little witchcraft, if you know what I mean. She's in a bit of a situation." Cally rolled the words off her tongue like gumdrops. Estelle and Madge turned their heads toward my sister, resplendent in her satin and taffeta, and sure enough, there in the tight seams of her dress, in the heavy droop of her bosom and the fatigue pooled in her eyes, was all the proof they needed. They remembered what babies did to you right from the start and how it was downhill from there on out.

Madge clapped a hand over her mouth. "The poor thing. What on earth was she thinking? Of all the kids in this town, I'd have thought for sure she'd be one to get out. She just had that look about her."

Estelle jabbed her fork into her potato salad. "Does Amanda know?"

"Lord, no," Cally snorted. "What do you think? Her husband's the vicar, and besides, as far as she's concerned, that girl's a real-life princess."

Madge's eyes went dreamy. "She'll make a beautiful bride."

"Assuming he'll marry her."

"Oh, he will. His folks will see to that. After all, the town doctor can't very well have his own son paddling girls up a creek and stranding them there, can he?"

"Not unless he wants to be the one to take care of the situation."

"Oh, Bob Morgan would never do that, would he?" Madge's eyes widened.

Cally sighed. "No, but I wouldn't put that kind of thing past his son. It's a good thing *he* doesn't have his medical license yet. God help us when he does."

Estelle nodded. "Yes, there's something I've never liked about that boy. Once, he rode his bike right over the petunia beds in my garden when I was standing next to them, and he didn't so much as bat an eye."

Madge flapped a hand at her. "Oh, Estelle, that was ages ago. I'm sure he's grown up ever so much since then." Her gaze shifted and caught the enormous shadow of me hovering on the edge of the food stations. "Now *there's* a hopeless case," she said, rolling her eyes toward me. "Not even witchcraft would do the trick with her. She's a definite candidate for modern medicine."

Cally pulled her eyes off of my sister and turned them in my direction. "It's almost hard to believe they're related."

"Living out at the Dyerson place hasn't helped matters much," Estelle added. "The poor thing. Earl wouldn't take her to the doctor, and the Dyersons can't. They barely have enough to eat on."

I shifted my weight from hip to hip and practiced blending in with the trees behind me, like a boulder in the shade. I stood so still, I could have planted myself in the middle of the town green, along with the statue of Aberdeen's founder, or in the graveyard with all the other frozen souls, inviting open opinion without getting a single feeling hurt.

"She looks like she eats plenty to me," Cally gibed, but Estelle quieted her with a frown.

"It's not her fault she's built like a Sherman tank. Besides, maybe in her situation it's better. Look at Serena Jane. Beauty only landed her in a rat's nest of trouble."

The three women fell silent then, staring into their empty plates and ruminating on the paradoxical connection between opportunity and loveliness that Serena Jane and I presented. Without beauty, I knew, life's possibilities might pass me up, but too much loveliness was clearly a liability. It was like a train wreck, pulling in trouble. So in the end, maybe it really was me who was better off, I thought. I was ugly—no one was going to dispute that—but I was also so big that nothing in life was going to slide past me. And if it did, then maybe I was smart enough to let it keep going.

As Mayor Dick Crane officially announced the 1969 May Queen with salivary glee, I sweltered politely along with the town, applauding when appropriate, the backs of my thighs stuck to a wooden folding chair. I was alone in the very last row of seats set up on the grass and could see the back of Bob Bob's head three rows up. He was perspiring for different reasons. I watched him watch my sister assume her throne on the little dais with her usual grace and a greenish tinge around her lips, and then I saw him reach into his pocket and finger the emerald-cut diamond ring his mother had given him that morning.

Technically, it was his and always had been—his grandmother had willed it to his future wife—but I bet he never expected that he would really have any use for such an object. His mother, however, had had other ideas. She'd barged into his room just as he was waking up, handed him the little green velvet box, and said, "You take this ring, and you make everything right." Bob Bob had looked at the emphatic line of her lips—a line no one ever dared to cross—and hadn't said a word. He'd merely stretched out his arm and accepted the box.

After she'd left, he'd opened the lid and peered at the luminescent gem. It reminded him of the glass pebbles his mother used in her flower vases, and his heart had suddenly contracted in panic as he'd realized that Serena Jane would most likely insist on similar niceties. Linen napkins for eight, crystal vials of perfume, beveled picture frames filled with flaxen-haired children, not to mention that damn quilt his parents had—Serena Jane would no doubt demand her fair share of household loot.

Or would she? The thing was, in spite of his years of scrutiny of my sister, Bob Bob actually knew little to nothing about her. He had no idea that her favorite flowers were pansies, no clue that she snored like a truck driver, that she ate popcorn and not candy at the movies, and that her favorite chocolates were filled with lavender cream. As far as Bob Bob was concerned, girls shouldn't eat, smoke, sweat, swear, or shit. And if they did, he didn't want to know about it. Of course, that was about to change. As soon as he put his grandmother's ring on Serena Jane's finger, I knew, she'd begin her offensive. She would nag him to change his socks. She would throw away his favorite baseball cap. She would insist he wear proper shoes instead of sneakers, drink beer from a glass, and mow the lawn on Saturday. Bob Bob may have thought he was the one holding the prize as he dangled that ring between his forefinger and thumb inside his pocket, but soon enough, Serena Jane was going to be the one pulling the strings.

I thought Bob Bob might have had more finesse in choosing his moment, but he caught my sister just as she was descending the dais steps, her arms full of thorny, uncomfortable roses, her kitten heels skittering on the plywood. He didn't bother to kneel. "Here," he said, thrusting the ring out at her.

My sister blinked at the diamond blazing in front of her like an accusing eye. She reached out a languid, bare arm and plucked the jewel from Robert Morgan's fingers. "What's this?"

The ill will of the moment flushed Bob Bob's cheeks a mild crimson. "It was my grandmother's. My mother thinks you should have it."

Serena Jane exhaled, her breath tinted with the cloves she was chewing to keep nausea at bay. "Oh," she whispered. She wondered who had told Mrs. Morgan or if she'd just figured it out on her own. Bob Bob's mother was spooky that way. She always could tell which kids had been out drinking over the weekend and who had taken up smoking, even if it was only one or two a day, and everyone knew it wasn't Bob Bob who was telling her. He barely even spoke to his parents. She watched him prop an elbow on the dais's banister.

"So, is it true?" he demanded.

Serena Jane nodded, unaware that her yellow hair, capped with its faux tiara, cast off little sparks of its own in the afternoon sun. "Yes."

Bob Bob clamped his jaw tight. *One time*, you could tell he was thinking. *It was only one time.* For a physician's son, I thought he might have been a little better at grasping the basics of human biology. He pulled in his stomach. "I guess my mother's right, then." My sister didn't answer him, so Bob Bob thrust his chin toward her. "Go ahead. Put it on." He watched as Serena Jane slid the narrow platinum band over her fourth knuckle. The ring was a little big on her hand. It teetered on her finger. Bob Bob sighed. "So." The word reverberated between the two of them like a note strummed on a warped guitar.

The wooden seats emptied. On the green, people started packing up their picnics and children, wrapping dog leashes around their wrists, and bidding farewell to their friends. The afternoon was coming to a close, and the party was over for another year. Estelle Crane was tugging Dick away from the vicinity of Priscilla Sparrow. Cally Hind was badgering her son about the amount of beer he'd consumed, and Amanda Pickerton was methodically sealing her leftovers in appropriately sized Tupperware containers. One by one, blankets were folded and wicker hampers closed. Soon, I was the only one left slumped behind a dogwood tree on the edge of the lawn. Through its budding leaves, I watched Bob Bob block my sister on the steps. I watched Serena Jane hold up her hand and tilt it, then bury her face in her two palms as if telling herself a secret.

I waited until they left, walking side by side, but without touching, and crept over to the dais. On the bottom step, I found Serena Jane's May Queen sash, wilted and speckled with spatters of seasonal mud. Every year that happened to the girls. They romped over the lawn, and climbed in and out of boys' convertibles, and then realized too late that they were freckled with Aberdeen's dark soil. It was stupid. I could have told them what would happen, but they never thought to ask.

I glanced around, but no one was paying any attention, so I reached down and picked up the sash, draping it over my neck and one shoulder. I didn't care if the sash was muddy—in my eyes, it was still a prize, something you might hang on a Christmas tree or tie around a present. I thought to run after my sister with it, but Serena Jane was already gone, shuffled off by Bob Bob into her new life. It was a lonely feeling, watching her hobble off with him, like watching a movie that ends badly. *Oh well,* I thought. At least she'd get to be a bride. She'd like that.

I lingered at the little dais for a moment more, one foot poised on the bottom step, contemplating climbing the stage and assuming my sister's throne. But I could imagine the jeers and taunts that would receive. I pulled my foot down and removed the sash—a cheap piece of ribbon that crumpled in my square hands. All along its edges, I saw that little pieces of thread were fraying and that its ends were simply glued together. Just like anything else in life.

I jammed the sash in the pocket of my blue jeans and went on my way, amazed at the elegance of the early evening sky opening up above me. One by one, tiny stars appeared and then the slimmest arc of the moon, transforming Aberdeen from a weedy, upstate town to a twilit garden. I reminded myself that things were not always what they seemed, large or small, beautiful or rough. I resolved to pay more careful attention to the things around me. No matter how they appeared, I reasoned, things could always change, sometimes maybe even for the better.

Chapter Eleven

Serena Jane managed to last eight years with Bob Bob, which, if you think about it, is a long time to do penance for anything, never mind for an evening that wasn't your fault. In all of that time, I saw her only twice. The first time was right after her wedding in mid-June. I wasn't invited—no one was. It was just Bob Bob, and Serena Jane, and his parents, all of them grim-jawed and quaking in Judge Warson's office. Serena Jane wore an aquamarine dress the same color as her eyes, and even from my vantage point in August's truck across the street, the effect was unsettling, making her milk white skin jump out like a ghost's. She carried a half-wilted nosegay of roses and had tied her hair in a severe knot at the back of her neck.

"I'm sorry, Truly, but I don't want anyone there," she insisted when I offered to be her maid of honor. "It's just going to be a quick ceremony, and then we're moving to Buffalo while Bob Bob's in medical school."

"Where are you having the baby?"

Serena Jane drummed lightly on her belly with her fingers. "Why, Buffalo, of course. That's where everything will happen from now on, I guess."

I tried to imagine my sister alone in a strange city with no one for company but Bob Bob. Then I tried to imagine myself without Serena Jane in Aberdeen. Maybe we weren't sisters like those girls in *Little Women* or any of the other books I'd read, but she was all I had of kin. Of the two of us, I figured, she probably had it worse, and I have to admit, a little part of me was glad. *That's what she gets*, I thought, *for going off and leaving me again.* I turned my eyes to her, hoping she couldn't see the tears swimming in them. "When will I see you next?"

"I don't know, Truly." Serena Jane blew a wisp of hair off her face. "Christmas, maybe? I imagine we'll be back for the holidays, after the baby's born."

But they weren't, not for Thanksgiving and not for Christmas, either. The Thanksgiving break was going to be too short, Serena Jane explained in a quick note she sent me in early November, Bob Bob had exams, and the baby was due any minute. They would be home in December, though, for certain.

"What's the matter?" Amelia asked as she watched me fold the letter up and slide it back in its envelope. She had grown tall and thin over the past few years, but her skin was still as pale as ever, and even though her speech had improved to the point where she would sometimes talk to people outside her family, I could always still hear the trouble her tongue had with certain letters. "Bad news?" Her voice, when it arrived, still had the stubborn and rough quality of a tree stump planted in the ground. People were often surprised that her voice was deeper than mine.

We were sitting on the beds in our shared room. I turned to her. When had Amelia's face become more recognizable to me than my own sister's? I wondered. I took in her wet brown eyes and half-bow mouth. If I'd closed my own eyes and grabbed a pencil, I probably could have sketched Amelia to the perfect likeness. Was familiarity as good as blood? I wondered. I laid the letter on my bed, missing my sister, my heart confused.

The baby was a boy named Robert, of course. "Look," I breathed, showing off the three-by-three black-and-white photo to Amelia. He looked like a tiny warrior, with his fists bundled tightly underneath his chin and his eyes alert. "He was born at four-fifteen a.m.," I read, "and weighed seven pounds three ounces. They're calling him Bobbie."

Amelia examined the photograph. "He looks like Serena Jane," she said, "but with Robert Morgan's mouth. That'll be trouble later."

But I thought Bobbie looked perfect—so perfect, I wished he were mine. I wondered what motherhood was like, if having a tiny sack of skin and air to hold every minute was a blessing or a burden. There were different kinds of mothers in this world, I knew. I'd watched the cats in the barn. Some of them lavished maternal pride over their offspring, ostentatiously purring and running their sandpaper tongues over the litter. And other mother cats just did the bare minimum, birthing their kittens, then turning tail and lighting out for the fields. I didn't know what made a cat stay with her brood, nor could I identify what it was in the world that lured the bad ones back to the wild so soon or so hard, but I hoped my sister was more like the former.

I placed the photograph of Bobbie in the shoebox I kept hidden under my bed at the Dyersons', which, in addition to my father's old winnings from August's horses and some more recent ones of my own, contained the single wedding photograph of my parents and a newspaper clipping of Serena Jane as May Queen. It was the closest thing to a family album that I possessed. I was about to place the lid on the box when I was seized by a terrible thought. What if Bobbie turned out to be like me? What if he grew fat and heavy as a melon? What would Bob Bob do with a baby like that? Would he turn all his medical charms on his son, trying to fix a soul that wasn't broken? Or would he just ignore him, like a piece of dough left to rise too long?

I thought about all the comments I'd had to endure over the years: *Hey, Truly, you get any bigger, we're going to cast you in bronze and stick you on the town green! Hey, Truly, my truck needs a push—to Mississippi!* After a while, it seemed as though I had those voices ringing inside me all the time, restless as church bells. It wasn't a music I would wish on anyone, much less a brand-new infant. But you can't worry about what life's going to spit in your direction. Babies would grow up to be what they were, and the world would find a place for them. Spending time with August's cockeyed horses had taught me that. Even the most hopelessly swaybacked among them could throw a race and pull in some cash. I put the lid back on the box and slid it under the worn springs of the bed.

Two years later, I received my diploma, and I even had a little crowd come watch me. Amelia sat in the very back of the audience with Brenda and August, who was smacking his lips, anticipating the special roast beef supper waiting at home. Amanda Pickerton sat front and center, her lips pinched, a gift-wrapped dictionary in her lap. But it was Marcus I missed most of all. Everything felt wrong without him. He would have clapped the loudest, I knew, and whistled when Miss Sparrow handed me the scrolled diploma, her lips stretched tight across her gums. To this day, she is still the only woman I ever knew who could take the act of smiling and make it painful.

"Two points lower, and you wouldn't be receiving this," she stated primly, referring to my final exams. I couldn't tell if she was pleased about the outcome or not.

"Thank you," I whispered, and Priscilla Sparrow surprised me by grabbing my wrist with the sudden fury of a bird of prey.

"Speak up for yourself," she said, her little eyes glittering in the afternoon sun. "Always speak up for yourself, girl. Lord knows no one else is ever going to."

"Yes, ma'am," I whispered, somewhat louder, then snatched the rolled-up piece of paper and fled.

Dear Serena Jane, I wrote later that evening, *here is the diploma I got today. I wish you'd have been here to see me get it, but I know you're real busy now with Bobbie. But Brenda and August were there, and Amelia, too. Mrs. Pickerton gave me a dictionary. When are you coming home? I want to see Bobbie. Can you send more pictures?*

Every week, I checked the mail religiously, waiting for some response, but there never was any. Who knows how long I would have kept running out to the rusty mailbox and peering into its empty mouth, convinced that it was my lucky day, if August hadn't won the unluckiest horse of his life and taught me all over again that the world had different rules for the likes of us?

At first, it didn't look like an unlucky horse. It looked like a winner. It was a Thoroughbred, high-blooded and taut through its withers and neck. August led it into the barn on a worn lead and shut it into one of the stalls. "Name's Lightning," he drawled, pleased with the stunned expression on our faces. "I won him in a poker round."

Amelia's eyes opened wider, and I knew what she was thinking. I said it for her. "You actually won?"

August's grin was as sleek as a fox's tail. "This one's going to change my luck for sure," he said, patting Lightning's flank, then snatching his hand back as Lightning whipped his head around and tried to bite him. Brenda snorted and headed back to the kitchen.

For a few weeks, Lightning was the most honored, if also incredibly bad-tempered, creature in August's stable. He got first dibs on the oats, the sweetest and longest carrots, and extra brush strokes. "As soon as he gets a little more comfortable, we'll race him," August promised, "and then we'll see who's laughing all the way to the bank."

I brushed down the more homely horses and said nothing. Just that morning, I'd risked amputation trying to get a bit into Lightning's gob, and it seemed to me that his contrariness wasn't necessarily going to translate into winning speed. And it turned out I was right, for not three days after that, August went out early in the morning to tend to the horses and made the fatal mistake of getting on the wrong side of Lightning.

Startled out of sleep by the sharp smack

of the barn door opening and a hubbub of horse hooves, I ran outside to find August slumped in a pile of straw, blue in the face, his chest kicked in. Brenda came running when she heard my cries, and between the two of us, we managed to get August into the house, where he fell back on the ragged blankets covering the sofa and struggled for breath.

"Get in the truck and go for Dr. Morgan," Brenda barked, but she knew as well as I did that it would be no use. Even as she spoke, August's breathing was becoming slower and more labored, and the blue around his lips was darkening.

"Daddy?" Amelia squeaked, and then fell quiet, for she had spotted before any of us that August's chest had stopped sinking and rising and that he was peaceful at last.

Brenda sank back on her heels and covered her face with her hands. "God damn it," she said, and then again, slower, as if she wanted to make sure the Lord heard every syllable loud and clear. "God. Damn. It."

I didn't say anything. I had experienced the aftermath of death plenty but had never stared it in the face before, and I was struck dumb by the simple mystery of the process. One minute, life had been coursing through August's body, and the next, he was as still and somber as snow. I stared at his open mouth and his familiar, rotten stumps of teeth, and I found it hard to believe that he wouldn't rise up in a minute or two, brush off his trousers, and wink at us all.

"What should we do?" I finally asked, my eyes wet, and Brenda took her hands away from her face. Her eyes were dry and hard.

"Well, for starters, we can shoot that foul horse," she said, and went to fetch August's rifle herself.

I thought my father's death had been a bare-bones affair, but at the Dyersons' I learned just how elemental death could be. There was no funeral, no burial in the cemetery, just a deep hole in the far field and the three of us shivering together in the wind. Brenda refused to say anything, and Amelia, traumatized by grief, couldn't, so I whispered the Lord's Prayer, and Brenda nailed together a simple cross, which we stuck on the mound of earth before turning our backs on it and giving the place up to the crows. For the rest of the season, we ate horsemeat, our heads bowed in silence over our plates, the stubborn gristle clumped in between our teeth.

After that, I took over many of August's old jobs—hoeing Brenda's vegetable garden into submission, the backbreaking repetition of splitting logs, and, of course, feeding and cleaning the horses. Neither Amelia nor Brenda wanted anything to do with them, but that job was by far my favorite. With horses, I found, there were never any judgments, no sly remarks about my size or appearance. In fact, with horses, my heft was an advantage. A horse could lean its entire weight against my flank and know I would hold.

I sent a short message to my sister explaining that August had died and that I was working on the farm, that I sometimes missed town and school, but that I had the horses to look to now. *Love, Truly,* I penned in the handwriting I'd learned from Miss Sparrow and which couldn't begin to express how big and empty the sky looked to me every night or how, when the wind rattled over the shingles of the farmhouse,

I sometimes wished I could blow away with it to Buffalo, where Serena Jane and Bobbie were swaddled together in a cozy embrace.

"Why don't you go see her?" Amelia whispered one night in the dark before sleep. It was shortly after August's death, and her voice was returning in shaky fits and starts. Sometimes she spoke; sometimes she didn't. Neither Brenda nor I ever pushed her. And even though Amelia and I were both officially women, we still shared a room like the girls we'd once been. I didn't reply. Amelia didn't know it, but I'd tried to go see my sister once. I'd peeled the appropriate layers of bills off the money roll from under my bed and walked all the way to the depot, where I'd stepped up and bought myself a ticket. But when the time came to board the bus, I saw how the other passengers were gaping at me and how the ladies nudged their handbags into the empty seats, hoping I wouldn't come and collapse next to them.

"On or off?" the driver asked, irritated.

The bus wheezed. I stepped down. "Off."

The driver put the engine into gear. "Suit yourself."

"If I was Serena Jane, I bet I'd be real lonely," Amelia said in the dark. "I don't know why she doesn't at least write."

But I knew why. It was because I was an object stuck in Serena Jane's past, marooned down a dusty lane, on a rack-and-ruin farm, and Serena Jane was a person who had no use whatsoever for the past. No bus ride was going to fix that.

"Go to sleep," I told Amelia, and then quickly followed my own advice, my brain muddled with tinfoil tiaras, a cracked looking glass, and the dusty row of my mother's dresses—all punctuated by the faint lost ring of that silver charm bracelet that used to hang from my sister's wrist.

Of course, time has a way of biting people in the ankle when they least expect it, and that's exactly what happened to me when Serena Jane and Marcus came home.

It took eight years, about four years longer than I thought. Bob Bob graduated college, and we all expected he'd return home for the summer before he started his medical training, but he and Serena Jane and Bobbie stayed in Buffalo, and before I knew it, another four years had passed. The war in Asia ended, and boys began making their way home in disappointed trickles, the beards on their chins scruffy, the set of their lips twisting their faces into unrecognizable masks. Marcus was never among them. "Do you think he's okay?" I whispered to Amelia in our beds at night. "Do you think he remembers us?" But the only answer she ever gave me was a squeeze of the hand.

And then one day, he simply came back. I was up on the Dyerson windmill, normally a superior place to see things coming. Perched halfway up its tower, I could easily take in the messy sprawl of the farm—the well, the crazy patching of scrap material I'd put on the roof last winter, and the sagging withers of the barn. I could also see buttercups colonizing the side of the garden fence—a pleasant yellow smear in the afternoon. The household laundry was bright in spite of itself, fluttering on the washing line, and, up high above everything, like a beneficial angel, the pristine trail of a jet feathered. But I didn't see Marcus. He just appeared underneath me, squinting up as if no time had passed.

I dug the hobnails of my boots harder

onto the latticing of the windmill, unsure whether to climb down and embrace him or to stay aloft. It was an unfamiliar dilemma. In spite of my size, I wasn't used to having people at my feet. That was definitely a side effect of living with the Dyersons. The world had gone on growing without us, while we'd gotten smaller and smaller, taking up less of people's imaginations until we were like the litter that blew all over the green after the May Day celebration—a part of things, but not the part that anyone wanted to look at. Marcus placed a hand on the windmill.

"Hello, Truly," he called, but it was a stranger's voice—deeper, huskier, with little currents running through it that weren't there before. When he moved, I could see him limping. His hair had grown longer, and his eyes were deeper set than before. As I climbed down the windmill, I could see how the shadow of a beard was starting to creep around the corners of his mouth, mapping new terrain. I put one boot down in the dust, then the other, smacking the dirt off my hands. Marcus twitched, as if he were about to embrace me, then restrained the impulse. He kept the hand that had been injured shoved in his pocket.

"When did you get home?" I asked.

"Last night." There was an awkward beat of silence, and then he elaborated a bit more. "I've just been wandering since I got out of the hospital. Places you've never even dreamed. Did you know that the catacombs in Paris hold the bones of five million people? And a hundred and eighty-six miles of tunnels, lined with eighteenth-century graffiti. Some of them are flooded, though."

"Oh." On the one hand, I was reassured to find that Marcus's old compulsion for facts had survived his injuries intact, while on the other, I was wondering what he was doing roaming around musty old tombs full of bones. I decided to take a tack toward the future, hoping the outlook would be better. "What are you planning on now?" My vowels twanged in my mouth, and I smoothed a lock of my thick hair behind my ear. Now that I was a little older, my hair was possibly my one nice feature, but it always smelled like hay and the dust from the horses, so I wasn't vain about it.

"I'm going to stay out at the cemetery," Marcus answered. "You know that run-down cottage?" I did. No one had lived in it for two generations. "Dick Crane said I can live there for free if I fix it up and do some work around the place."

"You mean tend the graves?" I wondered if his interest in crypts and bones was perhaps something more problematic.

Marcus shrugged. "Guess so."

"You don't want to stay at your mother's house?"

Marcus stared off into the middle distance. "I think I've been gone a little too long to go back into my mama's house. Besides, she's leaving town soon. Moving with my brother, Dukey, out to Texas."

"Oh." I vaguely recalled hearing something to that effect, although I didn't know that Dukey would have any better luck holding a job in the wide-open state of Texas than he did in tiny Aberdeen. Probably, I thought, he would discover honky-tonk music, Lone Star whiskey, and big-haired women (in that order), and that would be that. A lot of people were jumping town, it seemed, either retiring to warmer climates or relocating for better jobs. Aberdeen was like a party that had gone on a little too long. The people who were left were bleary and half-asleep on their feet. I suppose that included me. I took a deep breath. "Did you—did you ever get that letter I sent you?" My voice wavered, high and unsure, as jittery as the windmill behind me.

I don't know what kind of answer I was expecting, but it certainly wasn't the one Marcus gave me. He merely smiled and said, "Sure, Truly. I read all your letters. Thanks."

But there was just the one, I wanted to say. I remembered my promise to him that we would spend a night in the fields together and blushed, feeling foolish. Marcus surprised me, though. "Your words were beautiful," he whispered, his voice hoarse, his eyes pointed down at his boots. I wanted to answer back, but my breath snared in my chest.

Marcus cleared his throat. "Well, I've got to be going. I want to get back to the cottage and get some work done before it gets dark. I just wanted you to know I'm in town again."

I didn't dare look up as he sauntered off, whistling a tune I half remembered, his bad leg leaving a funny mark in the dirt. Behind me, the windmill thwacked out the rest of his melody. I closed my eyes and listened to it. If I pretended hard enough, I thought, it could almost have been a love song.

People were washing in and out of Aberdeen all right, and after Marcus it was Bob's Bob's turn to make a grand entrance. After a lifetime of tending to the folks in town, Robert Morgan IV was finally retiring, and Bob Bob was all set to take over. He'd passed his medical exams, received whatever qualifications he needed, and was evidently looking forward to becoming Aberdeen's newest Dr. Morgan. In town, it was all anyone talked about.

"I wonder if he's still got that ornery streak," Amanda Pickerton said to Cally Hind while lunching at the counter in Hinkleman's.

"Oh, I reckon not," answered Cally. "He's all grown now. A father and everything. I'm sure he's a fine young man."

"Serena Jane says Bobbie is smart as a whip. He's seven now. I can't wait to see him. Apparently, he looks just like her."

I finished gathering my purchases and took them to the cash register. It bruised me some that Amanda Pickerton knew more about my nephew than I did. She spun around on her stool. “Oh, hello, Truly.” I could hear how hard she was trying to inject a note of surprise in her voice, though I was hard to miss.

“Hello,” I replied.

“So your sister is finally coming home after all these years. You must be thrilled.”

It occurred to me that Serena Jane had left home long before she ever left Aberdeen, but I made myself smile and nod. “Sure,” I said.

“I mean, eight years is an awfully long time, isn’t it?” Amanda continued. “Why, you two won’t hardly even know each other, will you?” Her upper lip sneered a little, and I noticed a smudge of lipstick on one of her teeth. I didn’t bother to point it out.

“I guess we’ll have to see.”

“Well, I imagine so. I mean, Serena Jane is a mother now, and a doctor’s wife, and you’re”—here she paused, as if for effect—“well, you’re still out there with the Dyersons, aren’t you?” She sniffed a tiny bit and glanced me up and down, taking in my mud-spattered overalls, flannel shirt, and boots.

"Yes, ma'am."

"Indeed."

We appeared to have reached an impasse in conversation, and I realized that no matter how big I ever got, Amanda Pickerton would always see me as the awkward, pigtailed child who'd stared her in the eye and defied her judgment about what was good for me. We said our goodbyes politely, baring teeth and squeezing hands, and even though I hated to admit it, I couldn't shake what she'd said about Serena Jane and me becoming strangers to each other. It was the truth, I knew, but it was like a flea bite—itchy, annoying, so tiny that I would have liked to ignore it but couldn't. That night, I tossed and thrashed the thought around my mind until it was as addled and whipped up as a batch of butter.

"What's the matter with you?" Amelia asked when we were feeding the hens the next morning. She scattered a wide handful of grain like snow.

"It's Serena Jane coming home. I don't

know how I'm supposed to act with her anymore. I've missed her, but I feel like the sister I had is gone, and I don't know who all's coming home in her place."

Amelia threw down her last handful of feed. "In that case, why don't you leave all the introductions up to her?" She put down her bucket and smacked her hands together. It was simple and sound advice, I thought, typical for Amelia. A life spent dodging the bullets of creditors had taught her how to get straight to the root of a problem and solve it quick. So I kept my distance, letting my sister sweep back into town with all the glory of a somewhat faded matinee idol. "She'll come out here, don't you wonder," Amelia reassured me. "She won't be able to resist." And after a week, that's exactly what happened.

When she did, it was just me feeding the chickens, tossing out handfuls of corn without even really looking where they were falling, the noon sun bludgeoning my vision so that I didn't see her walk up and then couldn't see her clearly when she did. I stepped into a patch of shade and blinked. "Hello, sister mine," she said, her words crisper than they used to be so that

I wasn't sure if she was being mocking or not. Her hair had grown darker. It was the color of honey now and cut a little shorter so that it no longer flowed over her shoulders like a mermaid's. In fact, from what I could see, nothing much fluid was left of my sister anymore. She was buckled and belted, her slim legs safely encased in nylon, her hem dropped neatly to her knees. There were still some hippies rattling around the state in their death-trap vans, but fashions were starting to change. Serena Jane appeared to have weathered the era with the tired resignation of an old woman.

"Well," she said. Her eyes roved across the sky and caught on the outline of the rusted windmill. "Bob Bob and I are back in town now. We just got in last week."

"Oh." I tried to picture my sister as the wife of the town doctor, essentially taking up where Maureen Morgan had left off. I tried to see her wrapped up in one of Maureen's aprons or bent over Maureen's flower beds, tending the roses, but I couldn't do it. "It seems kind of strange that Dr. Morgan is moving away," I finally said. "None of the other Dr. Morgans ever did that."

Serena Jane nodded. "They're going down to Florida."

I scuffed my boot in the dirt, shooing a chicken. "That's nice."

Serena Jane shrugged, as if after eight years in Buffalo, time and space had ceased to matter much. "I got your letter about August. I'm really sorry." But she didn't sound sorry. She sounded bored.

"Thank you," I mumbled.

Serena Jane sniffed slightly, her nostrils flaring at the chicken stench like flower petals. "Not that much has changed around here. I suppose you know that Sal Dunfry and her husband are living in Papa's old house now. They painted it yellow."

"I know. They planted daffodils out in the front yard. It looks real nice."

Serena Jane sniffed again. "I detest gardening. Do you remember Marcus Thompson? I've hired him to come and do the flowers." I could feel my face grow hot down to the roots of my hair. "He's wonderful with the garden," Serena Jane said.

"Is he?" I tried to keep my voice disinterested.

Serena Jane snickered. "Anyone would

think you're still sweet on his little bones, Truly."

I scowled. "It's not like that. He's just my friend."

"Whatever." She swatted at a fly.

"How's Bobbie? When can I meet him?" I pictured the puckered, newborn face in the one photograph I possessed of him. "Why have you never sent any photographs? Why haven't you ever brought him home?"

Serena Jane stared down at the dirt under her open-toed shoes. "It's complicated," she whispered, "but he's fine, really. He's good. Growing." Motherhood had evidently become routine to her. Perhaps the idea that Bobbie would one day detach himself from her seemed like an unbelievable premise.

I wondered if Maureen Morgan had felt that way when Bob Bob got married and moved off to Buffalo—as though a heavy weight had been cut from her body, freeing it from years of inadvertent torture. Probably she didn't. Maureen was fundamentally opposite from Serena Jane in most things, curved and doughy while

Serena Jane was angular and flat, sentimental while Serena Jane was practical, mousy and faded while Serena Jane was blonder than the sun. Or used to be, at any rate. I wondered if, after a life passed in Maureen's house, sleeping in the same bed, eating from the same plates, Serena Jane would also start to develop plump calves and a small wattle under her chin. If she would list slightly from side to side when she walked, like a ship plowing a gentle and familiar sea. No, I decided. Those qualities—rotundity, a staid calmness in the face of advancing age—came only to contented people, and you just had to look at Serena Jane to tell she was about as far from that as Aberdeen was from the moon.

Serena Jane brushed a strand of hair away from her cheek. "You're staring at me." She scowled and put one hand up to block the sunlight.

I blushed. "You look different."

"So do you."

I had still been half-girl when she got married, but I knew there was no trace left of that person now. Instead, everything on me was square and solid—my cheeks, my eye sockets, even the suggestion of my breasts underneath my baggy man's shirt. I was taller than most of the men in town, but there was no telling if I'd topped out, and anyway, it wasn't so much my height that startled folks. It was more my solidity, the way my larger joints bulged like boulders. Serena Jane must have forgotten all that about me.

She made an O with her mouth—a pretty round shape full of promise, full of all the things she could think to say but didn't—then she choked out an apology and turned and stumbled back to the dirt road where she had left her car. All the other routes in Aberdeen had gradually been sealed up and paved, but not this stretch. After all, it didn't lead anywhere. Serena Jane slammed the door of Bob Bob's new Buick and turned the engine over, her delicate ankle working the gas pedal with an energetic fury. In the rearview mirror, she could see that I'd followed her and was standing next to the farm's single rusted mailbox, my jaw as slack as the hinges. I waved to her, flapping my beefy hands, but Serena Jane ignored me and shifted the car into drive. She put her foot down harder on the accelerator, relishing the hazy dust the car kicked up.

Serena Jane narrowed her eyes, wheels spinning over the road and wheels spinning in her head. Maybe it was no accident that she'd ended up stuck back in Aberdeen, it occurred to me, but maybe she wasn't meant to stay, either. If she'd made a quick check of the mirror, she would have seen my outline wavering in the dust, still there, always there. The bulk of me would follow her wherever she went. But she didn't look. She drove faster, leaving me alone, but not for too much longer. Serena Jane was spinning a plan that would change all that.

Part Two

Chapter Twelve

The morning my sister left him, Bob Bob woke up and knew it without opening his eyes. It was the absence of the usual odors in the house—the cottony scent of her breath captured in hollow of the pillow next to him, the slightly acrid aroma of coffee wafting up the stairs, followed by the grease of bacon frying. He lay perfectly still in the bed, his nose twitching, but there was nothing.

His first thoughts should have perhaps been for seven-year-old Bobbie sleeping two rooms down, or even for himself, but they weren't. Instead, he immediately pictured the expectant plains of Maureen's face crumpling in disbelief, then the stern angles of his father's mouth. His parents were all the way down in Florida, but when you were a Morgan man in Aberdeen, you never fully escaped the tidal pull of familial influence. No one in his lineage had ever died in a war, been anything other than a physician, or gotten divorced. Marriage was a lifelong glue.

Bitch, he thought, even as he stretched his legs wider underneath the covers, savoring the extra space in the rumpled bed. He opened his eyes and scanned the room. Evidently, she hadn't taken much. Her pale silk dressing gown still hung over the latticing of the chair in the corner, its edges pooled on the floor. The random collection of vials and little pots of face cream on the vanity appeared to be untouched, and even her customary shoes—a pair of low-heeled black pumps—were right where she'd left them. Bob Bob hitched himself onto his elbows. The blankets fell around his midsection. He snorted and threw the fabric off his legs, sliding his feet over the edge of the bed, searching for his slippers.

Then he waited.

The house seemed very dull to him, like pond water congealed on a sluggish summer day. He couldn't imagine living with that sensation for long, and it occurred to him that maybe he would miss Serena Jane after all. Perhaps he'd been wrong, he thought. Maybe Serena Jane was simply in the garden with an early cup of tea. Perhaps she'd gone to see one of her old school friends. Perhaps she was downstairs, balancing her checkbook before she started breakfast, or hunched over the sink, working a stain out of one of Bobbie's shirts. Then he spied the envelope.

She'd left it where she was sure he would find it—right on top of his medical bag, which he always stood at the foot of the bed. He tore open the envelope and slid out a sheet of unlined paper. In the middle, scrawled in shaky letters made either in haste or from nerves, were two simple sentences: *Don't come look for me. Just find Truly.* That was it. Nothing about Bobbie. No explanations or reasons. Not even a signature.

Bob Bob crumpled his fist with the note in it, then threw the wad of paper in the bedside wastebasket. *So she's gone,* he thought. *Good for her.* Good for him, even. They'd never really been suited, he thought. First, Serena Jane had been a mystery—luminous and aloof—then an obsession, and, more and more lately, she was just a lump of flesh he'd had to coexist with. Every night, they'd brushed their teeth in tandem, taking turns spitting into the enamel sink, then crawled under the rough cotton sheets together, smacking their respective pillows into submission, before turning their backs on each other. He couldn't remember the last time they'd made love, if he was going to call it that. Ever since the first time, she'd always been a cold fish, nothing like the glamorous, hot-blooded mermaid he'd always expected. In fact, that was the whole problem. Serena Jane had always been a goddamn ice princess.

Don't come look for me, her note said. Maybe he wouldn't, but he wasn't going to sit back and do nothing, either, and that's where Serena Jane had made her biggest mistake. If she thought he was going to let her go like rainwater down a drain, she had another think coming. No one walked out on Robert Morgan. At least, no one ever had so far.

Find Truly. As loath as he was to admit it, Bob Bob finally conceded that this was a fine idea. It was even better than fine. The oxen sister with no future to speak of. The lost cause. Why, Bob Bob bet, I would be more than happy to step into my pretty sister's shoes. He figured I'd be thrilled.

And best of all, he reasoned, I was so big, there was absolutely no danger I'd take flight.

If I was surprised to look through the barn door and spy Robert Morgan (since becoming the town doctor, he'd forbidden anyone from calling him Bob Bob) dragging through Dyerson mud in my direction the morning after my sister left, I'm proud to say that my face didn't show it. The farm had been getting a lot of visitors lately—most of them men of a certain age who found themselves captivated by the sparkling eyes of the widowed Brenda and were more than happy to prove their gallantry by doing a few chores around the place.

It had been years since August's death,

and the farm still had a claptrap air hanging over it, but there were cautious signs of optimism in the fresh curtains Brenda had hung in the kitchen windows and in the recently patched steps. The weeds around the porch had been hacked into submission, and someone had taken it upon himself to remove any intact engine parts from the back of the house. Even the marigolds at the end of the tomato bed seemed to stand straighter.

I was in Hitching Post's stall, brushing his mangy coat, when the thin outline of Robert Morgan appeared in the door. Hitching Post—the last of the losing racehorses—gave a defeated sigh and shifted his weight.

"Hush," I whispered in his ear. In spite of all his physiological flaws, Hitching Post was an excellent judge of character. With unerring instinct, he could ferret out the vainest jockeys on the track and run them into the fence. He always stamped on the crooked veterinarian's instep, and he absolutely disallowed any of Brenda's new suitors near him, sensing, perhaps, the dollar signs they had tattooed on their hearts. Now, he flared his nostrils in Robert Morgan's direction and pulled his ears close to his head. In the dry air of the barn, his breath scuttled like an unsettled breeze.

"Whoa," I whispered again in his ear, and Hitching Post relaxed, leaning his weight against me. I tipped my own head down to him, glad to have the horse's flank between me and Robert Morgan.

"Hello." Under the half-rotten rafters of the barn, Robert Morgan's voice was like a blast of winter. It ate down into my bones and made my breath catch. I peered over Hitching Post's neck and took a good look at my sister's husband. He'd grown a little heavier in the torso and legs, and his hair was cut shorter, but his face still had the same angles. I wouldn't have been surprised to learn that he howled at every full moon.

"Hello," I croaked back, but it came out as a question. When we were growing up, I realized, the only times Robert Morgan had ever spoken to me were when he was trying to get with my sister or when he was teasing me. I didn't see why anything should be different now.

Robert Morgan stepped directly in front

of me and rubbed his palms together. It was the month of August, and even though it was still early, the day was getting hot. Robert Morgan cleared his throat as if he were nervous, but I knew better than that. Reptiles didn't feel fear.

"Well," he began, his voice surprisingly conciliatory, "I guess it's been some years." I said nothing. It was a statement I couldn't argue with, so Robert Morgan continued, folding his lean fingers together into a little temple. "I guess I should just cut to the chase," he said.

Indeed, I thought. The chase was something I knew he relished. It was how he'd caught Serena Jane, after all, stealing her away for eight years and bringing her back all wrong.

"Shoot," I mumbled. It was what August always used to say when his creditors came calling. *Go ahead and shoot*.

Robert Morgan stared down at his impeccable shoes, then took a deep breath. "Your sister is gone. I don't know where. She left a note suggesting I come find you." He glanced up from underneath his eyebrows—a gesture that would have been coquettish on anyone else but appeared calculating on him. He reached into his pocket and pulled out the note, rescued from the waste bin. "See," he said.

It's not going to work, I told myself. It wasn't my problem that Serena Jane had taken off. Then I remembered Bobbie. I reached out and took the note.

Robert scuffled one shoe back and forth over a warped board, waiting while I read the brief words. After so many years, it was a shock to see how like my own handwriting Serena Jane's penmanship was, how she flared out the bottom of her *f*'s and looped the *y* back in on itself, just the way Miss Sparrow had taught us. I wondered if Miss Sparrow had planned this unintended legacy all along—an entire generation of children who formed their letters like hers. I carefully folded my sister's note back up, following the creases, and handed it to Robert Morgan.

"I see," I said. Robert Morgan pinched the bridge of his nose with his fingers. He closed his eyes and sighed. In his stall, Hitching Post responded in kind.

"I don't know what to do," Robert Morgan confessed. "I've got the clinic to run, and Bobbie—he's only seven. A boy that age needs his mother. What do I know about taking care of a house and child?"

About as much as me, I thought. And not everyone was lucky enough to have a mother. I hadn't been. But I remained silent. "No." I shook my head and turned back to Hitching Post. Robert Morgan narrowed his eyes. He cast his gaze up and down the splintering rafters, considering.

"I suppose this place is really like home to you." He turned his neck to take in the sorry picture of the farmhouse framed in the barn's open doors. "It's been with the Dyersons for, what, close to two hundred years?"

I shrugged. Robert Morgan continued, persistent as a wasp. "And yet, it doesn't look like you all are doing too well out here. I guess it's been a little rough since August died. You know . . ." He paused, forming the temple with his fingers again, a smile lurking at the corners of his mouth. "It would be a real shame if all the credit was called in at once, now, wouldn't it? Why, you all might lose everything."

The muscles in my back stiffened. "What do you mean?"

"I'm the town doctor, Truly. I know almost everyone, and they'll listen to me, whether it's advice regarding an ear infection or, say, something more esoteric, like recouping one's debts in a timely fashion. You know, as a matter of policy, I never extend credit to my patients. Everyone pays up front, or they don't get care."

That figures, I thought. "What do you want me to do?"

Robert Morgan's lips curled, as satisfied as two snakes in the sun. He took Serena Jane's note out of his pocket again and dangled it in front of me. "It's not what *I* want. It's what your sister wanted. Surely you wouldn't refuse a request from your own family?"

You're not family, I thought, then I remembered Bobbie again. I put my hands on Hitching Post's back, the uneven bones of him a tonic under my fingers. I worked my tongue around my mouth, careful before I answered. "It won't be before Tuesday."

Robert Morgan nodded. "That's fine. We can make do until then."

"And I want a television in my room."

Robert Morgan's eyes flickered, but he nodded again. "I'll see what I can do."

"A color one. Not too little."

He was edging back toward the door now. Along his hairline, tiny beads of sweat blossomed. "Yes, yes. A color TV."

"Not too small." I turned my back on him first. I didn't think it was an unreasonable request—a television. If I was going to shut myself up in that man's house like a battery hen, I figured, then the least I could ask for was a little window on the world.

"You'll need it," Amelia predicted when I told her I was moving into the doctor's house to take care of Bobbie. We were gathering eggs from the hens.

"Will you and your mother be okay out here, all by yourselves?" I palmed one of the eggs, letting its faint warmth seep into my hand, and wished I could take it with me when I left.

"We'll be fine," Amelia said matter-of-factly, and then shut her mouth to any other conversation.

I looked at her face, hoping I would see a sign of sadness, but I knew I would not. She was too schooled in sorrow to let it show and too familiar with hard times to let them get her down. For once, though, I wished that her exterior were a little softer, a little doughier, like mine. I put the egg in my basket and pictured her alone out here with the creaking windmill and the squabbling hens. "I'll miss you something awful," I said. "You've been like a sister to me."

Amelia didn't crack. She handed me another egg, but I could see the beginning of a tear swelling in her eye. "Better than a sister," I insisted. "Serena Jane only put up with me because we were born in the same house." I looped the basket over my other arm. "What's been your excuse?"

Amelia looked at me, and this time she didn't even try to hide the grief in her face. I put down the basket and hugged her tight, bundling her in my arms as if she were a rare bird. "Don't worry," I reassured her. "My heart will always be here."

Her voice, when she finally spoke, was muffled and confused, as it had been in childhood. "Make sure you don't lose your heart living with Robert Morgan. Make sure he doesn't use up all the very best parts of you."

Like he did with Serena Jane, I knew she meant. But then I thought about

Bobbie and how sad and confused he would be, missing his mother, and I knew I had to go. "I won't," I promised. "You know me best, Amelia. You'll keep me all in a piece." She nodded and put her hand on her chest, as if to pledge fidelity.

It was one Dyerson debt, I thought, that would absolutely get paid in full.

Four days later, Robert Morgan watched as I climbed the front porch steps of my new home. I was remembering how once, in boyhood, his parents had taken him on an automobile trip to see the president's heads carved into Mount Rushmore. From a distance, he'd told everyone at school, they were immense, but he didn't know how huge until he got up close and nothing about them made sense anymore. I figured I was probably exactly like that. Up close to me, Robert Morgan no doubt found it hard to fathom why God made a woman so ugly. My globular nose clashed with my doughy cheeks, which fought a little battle with my inner-tube lips, and so on. I wasn't fat, but I was so solid, I resembled a tree. Feeling my hips shift from side to side as I hauled a cardboard suitcase up the four steps, I found myself wondering how much I weighed. Scales weren't something the Dyersons worried about. In fact, thin was everything that was wrong with the Dyersons: thin clothes, thin meals, thin luck. As for height, I had no accurate idea about that, either. I had a good two inches on Robert Morgan—that much was clear. If it weren't for the way I blinked at everything, or my habit of working my lips before I spoke, I thought that he might even have been slightly afraid of me.

We passed through the front door and into the entry hall of the house, where there was nothing to greet a visitor except a round, empty table with a water stain in the middle of it, a staircase wriggling its way up to a second story, and four closed doors. Robert Morgan dropped my suitcase in the middle of the floor and opened one of the doors. "Kitchen's this way," he said, jutting his chin. "We eat in there. Dining room's in here, this is the den, and this"—he crossed the hall and opened the last door—"is the parlor. No one ever uses it, but if you're so inclined, you're welcome to sit a spell come an evening."

I wedged myself through the door of the

little room, blinking in the shuttered gloom. A threadbare sofa was pushed up against one wall, facing a fireplace, and a pair of tattered chairs occupied the corners. Dust balls hunkered on the floorboards, and the hooked rug was moth-eaten. The only object of any beauty in the room was the floral quilt hung on the wall above the sofa. I walked closer to it, amazed at all the tiny stitches holding the whole thing together. The pattern was one I'd never seen before. The center looked reasonable enough—flowers and leaves in neat rows up and down—but outside the black diamond border, it looked as though the quilt maker had just given up and started sewing vines and plants willy-nilly until she plain ran out of thread. I was so absorbed in my inspection of the quilt that I'd almost forgotten Robert Morgan was standing right behind me.

"It was my great-great-grandmother's," he said. "You know the stories about her. Tabitha Morgan. She made it."

"The whole thing?" I breathed. It seemed impossible to me that one woman's fingers could loop and stitch with such abundance. How many years had it taken her? I wondered. And what kind of fury had she harbored inside of her to make a kaleidoscope like this? In the parlor's gloom, the colors seemed to vibrate, inviting conspiracies and legends. Everyone in town knew about Tabitha Morgan, of course. An old maid at the tender age of twenty-six, she was Aberdeen's primary healer until the first Dr. Morgan loped into town and married her. It was an unhappy union, though, and Tabitha died young—some said by her own hand, and others said by her husband's. And no one had ever found her shadow book.

"Do you think her spell book really exists?" I asked the doctor now, stretching out a finger to tap the old fabric.

Robert Morgan snorted like one of August's horses and bared his long teeth. "That's just a heap of women's gossip—a sin I hope you don't indulge. If you're going to get along in this house, Truly, you will keep what you see to yourself. My patients expect it."

"Of course," I stammered.

He spun on his heel. "You can go on

upstairs, then. Your room is the third door on the left. I'll leave you to manage. It doesn't look like you brought much. Oh, and if you want to"—he glanced over his shoulder at the quilt—"you can take that old thing up with you. I have no use for it." He paused. "We generally like to eat around six. Bobbie's around here somewhere. I imagine he'll be along to say hello. He'll tell you what he likes for supper." And before I could say anything else, he backed out of the room and squeezed the door firmly shut behind him, leaving me alone with the puzzling quilt, whistling as he walked away, as pleased with himself as if he had just sealed a genie into a bottle.

He'd given me the guest room, with its windows overlooking the back garden and fields and a four-poster bed I wasn't sure would hold me. I spread the quilt over it, pleased with the cheer it injected into the room. Come winter, I thought, when Aberdeen's colors ran together into muck, I'd be glad of the embroidered red-and blue-tipped blooms and faded green stems. They would be a reminder that the world outside wasn't gone, just sleeping.

I trudged over to the window and pulled the curtains back a little. The glass in the window was old and streaked, but I still had a pleasant view out over the flower beds Maureen had planted aeons ago. Kneeling in them, his head bowed as if he were praying, I saw Marcus, his hands sunk amid the stalks. Aware that someone was looking at him, he glanced up to the window, his almond eyes startled wide. I half raised a hand to wave at him, and he lifted his chin up at me and squinted. It wasn't exactly a hero's welcome, but it was nice to see at least one familiar face. Just then, I heard a scuttling outside the door. Curious, I walked across the room and cracked the door, only to have it strike against something soft and yielding.

"Ow!" a child's voice cried, and my nephew, Bobbie Morgan, popped his blond head into the room. I caught my breath and took a step back. It was as if Serena Jane had been shrunk into a child again—but a boy this time, with elfin ears and a gravity about him that must have come from the Morgan side of the family.

"Oh," I stammered, "I didn't know anyone was there."

The rest of Bobbie appeared in the doorway—a lanky body clothed in a faded T-shirt, no shoes, and, tipped back in his arms, a vase overloaded with flowers. "Marcus let me pick them for your room," he said shyly, casting his eyes down to the petals. "I thought you might like yellow and blue."

I reached down and took the vase. "They're real pretty. Thank you." I set the vase on one of the night tables.

Liberated from the flowers, Bobbie looked even skinnier, the bones in his arms as brittle as two kindling sticks. He scowled. "What's that doing in here? That goes in the parlor." He jerked his chin toward the bed and Tabitha's quilt.

I turned back to Bobbie. "I'm sorry. Would you like to have it in your room instead?"

Bobbie considered, his eyebrows slanted fiercely in toward each other. "No. My father wouldn't like it." Underneath the hem of his shorts, his knees stuck out like overturned bowls. They glowed as white as spilled sugar. I didn't have any experience with children, but I knew plenty about not having a mother. I remembered all the afternoons I'd spent in my mother's closet, inhaling the diminishing scent off of her coats, her shoes—an odor unlike anything I'd ever known. I patted the quilt.

"Well, why don't we say this? Anytime you want to, you can come in here and lie down on this bed. And we won't tell your father. It will just be our little secret."

I watched as Bobbie weighed the consequences of this one small disobedience. "Okay," he finally agreed, his voice cracking. He tilted his head the same way Serena Jane used to when she examined herself in the mirror. *It's too bad he's a boy,* I found myself thinking. *He's such a beautiful child*. Which was, I would soon come to learn, what scared Robert Morgan the most. Boys weren't meant to be pretty. They were meant to be sturdy, and rough, and rugged as mountains. *Why,* I thought with a tiny smile, *they were meant to be just like me.*

As soon as he got me settled in, Robert Morgan stalked over to his office, double-checked that the handle was locked, then resumed his pacing. On his desk, he had flattened my sister's note, smoothing out the creases, tracing the smudged letters over and over with his skinny index finger. *Don't come look for me*. Like he would ever bother, Robert Morgan thought. Like he wanted her back. Still, my sister's disappearance was a problem. It didn't look good to have your wife making tracks. It suggested certain inadequacies in the marriage that he didn't feel like justifying. He narrowed his eyes. It was time to call in a favor.

One of the distinct advantages to being a doctor's son was that Robert Morgan had all his father's colleagues at his fingertips, including Bernie Briggs, the county coroner. It took a minute to get Bernie on the phone, but soon his bristly voice filled the receiver. A few more minutes was all it took, and Robert Morgan had him eating out of the palm of his hand.

"Of course I'll call you first if something comes in," Bernie promised. "Just as sure as sure can be."

"Thank you," the doctor murmured, making sure to keep his voice dipped low. "It's been a real trial." That taken care of, he hung up the phone and leaned back in his chair, his arms folded behind his head. If he'd had a cigar, I'm sure he would have held it clamped right between his front teeth at that moment. But it wasn't time to rest on his laurels yet. He still had some calls to make.

Putting his feet back down on the ground, he picked up the phone and dialed the police in Hansen—the closest law enforcement to Aberdeen. Once, during the forties, the county had considered putting a police force in Aberdeen, but, as the police commissioner had said, you don't go pouring water over a fire that's not lit. As he dialed the station, Robert Morgan considered this oversight to be a huge advantage. On the other end of the line, a chirpy receptionist answered. Slowly and carefully, Robert Morgan gave his name and address. He spoke distinctly, making sure the girl had all the time in the world to write down the story of his missing wife.

As for the last number he phoned, well, I could have recited it even if I'd forgotten my own name. The line jangled and echoed in the doctor's ear, and then a voice breathed a small greeting into the other end. "Amelia," said Robert Morgan, "how lucky you're home. And always so quiet. I'm counting on that. I need a little favor."

Amelia had reverted to silence on the other end of the line, so the doctor continued. "I'm only asking you because I'm trying to protect Truly. What with her sister disappearing and her recent move from the farm, I'm afraid she might be too emotionally fragile. But you, well, you're tougher than you look."

"Get to the point." When forced to, Amelia would use words sparingly with people outside her family. She had her father's same low tolerance for preambles and prologues. She knew the heart of a deal came when the card was turned and not a moment sooner.

"I might need you to come with me to make an identification. You know, in the worst-case scenario."

"Humpf." Even without words, Amelia could always get a point across.

"What are you implying?" Robert Morgan's voice slid like silk through the phone.

Amelia was silent, so Robert Morgan answered the question for her. "I suppose you're wondering why I'm bothering to look for my wife when she ran away?"

Amelia breathed into the phone. It was, in fact, what she had been thinking. Logistics had never been a problem for her. Robert Morgan clenched his teeth and continued his one-sided conversation. "That's what you're going to help me put to rest. Wait for me to call you. And remember, don't breathe a word."

Amelia sighed. The doctor's voice came out as rough as a lick of sandpaper. "If you help me with this one thing, Amelia, I will make it worth your while, I promise. But if you don't—" He didn't finish his sentence, but he didn't need to. If he wanted to, Amelia knew, Robert Morgan could get his friends at the bank to call in almost every debt owed on the farm for the past fifty years, sending her and her mother out the back door with what little they owned in a wheelbarrow.

She hung up the phone, her heart racing. She didn't have a choice in this matter, she knew, but maybe she could up the stakes a little. Maybe she could wrangle some sort of permanent work out of the doctor. Maybe she could settle her remaining debts once and for all. In situations like these, Amelia had learned, where the deck was stacked against you, the best thing you could do was to take the next card, play your hand anyway, and keep your friends close and your enemies even closer.

Alone in my room the first night, I ignored the television set propped on a chair in the corner and slid my few pairs of dungarees and shirts into a drawer in the dresser. I put my toothbrush and a tube of toothpaste on one night table and then fussed with Bobbie's flowers on the other. Finally, I reached into the bottom of my battered suitcase and withdrew my familiar cardboard box. After settling myself on the creaky mattress, I opened the worn flaps and rummaged inside for the wad of bills that I'd rolled into a tight tube. Over the past few years, as all of August's horses had either died or been taken away, I'd added less and less to the bundle, but there was still a sizable amount of money in my hand. I'd never counted, but it was enough to strain the rubber band, enough to make a gambler's heart beat fast. What would I do with it, though? Especially now that I was bound to the doctor and Bobbie, with his strange stare and skinny arms, missing his mother?

I replaced the money and fished around again for my old deck of cards, soft at the edges and quiet in my fingers. I hadn't had them out of the box since August's death, but here, in this new setting, they seemed tatty and lifeless, so I put them back. Only my old familiar photographs of my parents and Serena Jane were left. There were no photographs of me in the box and none of the Dyersons. There had never been any occasion for any to be taken. People like us didn't make history, even among ourselves.

But maybe that can change, I thought, nestling under Tabitha Morgan's handiwork in the dark. I felt the quilt's cotton batting settle around my bulk and imagined myself covered with the botanical network. Everyone on earth left something behind, I reasoned, even if it was just bone dust. August had left his bow-backed horses, Tabitha her sewing. Serena Jane had left me her son, even if she was just gone from Aberdeen, and my mother had left me. What would my legacy be?

I tried to think further, but a breeze outside set the leaves to rustling, a sound that reminded me of the Dyersons and their farm, and before I knew it, I was pulled away from thought and down into a deep and dreamless sleep like thread passing through a needle.

Chapter Thirteen

After just two weeks, it was as if I'd been bustling around Robert Morgan's house for the better portion of my life. It was astonishing to me, really, that a man I barely knew could so quickly become a source of routine for me, but that was Robert Morgan for you.

Everything in the house was just the way he liked it. Order was the most important thing for him, and along those lines, the doctor had instituted a panoply of domestic rules that could make your head wobble. We ate sweet butter, not salted, drank skim milk, not whole, bought our bread intact and sliced it ourselves, and strained the pulp from our orange juice with a miniature strainer. Bacon was supposed to be served crispy but not burned, the newspaper was supposed to be folded back up into thirds and left on the corner of the kitchen table, and if I got the yolk too hard in his egg in the morning, he'd chuck the whole mess in the trash and refuse to eat again until lunch.

As for the doctor's wardrobe, most of his shirts were solid colored, although he had some checkered ones for the weekend, and he wanted all of them pressed with starch. He liked his socks sorted in his drawer according to color, and every Friday he left his shoes in the hall for me to polish. *It's a wonder all Serena Jane did was run off,* I thought as I ran the iron around yet another pointed shirt collar. *I'm surprised she didn't commit murder first*.

"Truly," Robert Morgan's voice rumbled through the open back porch door and into the kitchen. It was my second Saturday with the doctor, which meant him catching up on paperwork in his office and me ironing and tending to a slow-roasted dinner none of us would really want to eat. "Can you come on out here for a minute?"

I blew a strand of hair off my forehead and set the iron upright. "I'll be just a minute, Robert Morgan," I called. I looked at the clock. Two. Bobbie had gone to visit a nursery with Marcus. They wouldn't be back for another hour. Time in the house without Bobbie was heavier, it seemed. The clock trudged instead of ticked, as if its hands were as big and heavy as mine.

I couldn't get over how like Serena Jane Bobbie was. Too like, actually, for I was beginning to notice some peculiar aspects about him. For one thing, he seemed to be having problems fitting in with Aberdeen's other boys. I was hoping it was just because he was new to Aberdeen. He'd just started school, and it was clear that he wasn't used to the mores and means of a small town.

"Where's the rest of it?" he asked, wrinkling his forehead in confusion, when I walked him up to the schoolhouse. Miss Sparrow stood on the front steps with her hands folded. Her hair looked whiter than I remembered, and upon closer inspection, the knuckles of her hands were as gnarled as old fruit branches, but she still had the same ramrod posture, the same iron set to her neck.

"This is all of it," I answered. "This is the whole school. There aren't that many children in Aberdeen, so you all attend class together. Later, when you're a little older, you'll get bussed over to Hansen, but when I was little, we went here all the way through high school—your mother, and Marcus, and Amelia, and me, and your father, too."

Bobbie's eyes brightened. "Really? That lady was my mother's teacher? Do you think she remembers her?"

I grimaced but tried to make it look like a smile. "Oh, I'm sure Miss Sparrow remembers all of her students, but maybe"—I peeked over to confirm Priscilla Sparrow scowling heavily in my direction—"it's better not to bring up the past. Why not just go in there and let her love you for you?"

Bobbie threw his arms around my knees. "Thanks, Aunt Truly! I'll see you back home at three, okay?"

I watched Miss Sparrow's eyes narrow as Bobbie approached, then her mouth split in half like an overripe melon, and I realized she was smiling. "Why, if it isn't little Bobbie Morgan," she simpered, sizing him up. "Back fresh from Buffalo. My, my, how time flies. Just yesterday, it seems, I was teaching your father geography. Why don't you come inside?" She held the door open wide, and then, because it was still so hot, she lingered a moment, relishing a last blast of air. "Where do you want to sit?" she asked, sweeping her arm to the rows of desks, and Bobbie hesitated before sliding over to the girls' side of the room and plopping himself down next to a very small child with beribboned pigtails. Inwardly, I sighed. *Please,* I thought, *let him get up and go to the other side of the room*. Miss Sparrow's eyes flickered for a moment, but she took her hand off the door before I could see anything else, letting it slam shut.

Bobbie stayed in the seat he'd chosen, and he didn't prove popular with the other boys because of it. He was a will-o'-the-wisp to their thunderclouds, a dented tin soldier to their cavalry. He couldn't kick or throw a ball quite like the other boys, couldn't run as fast as them, and didn't find the same thrill in hanging out of trees.

After school, he walked home alone, relieved to get back to the safety of the kitchen, and if it had been a particularly bad day, I always knew because he went straight up to his room without eating the snack I fixed. I figured he must be missing his mother, but I had no idea how to bring her up, so we just let the memory of Serena Jane hang between us, as thick and tantalizing as the ghostly scent of night jasmine.

"Truly!" Robert Morgan's voice crackled through the kitchen again, a little crosser than before. "I'm out here waiting on you ten minutes already! Did you forget?"

"Coming, Robert Morgan." I hung up the shirt I was working on and switched off the iron, then smoothed my dungarees over my hips and started across the porch, wondering if I should bring up Bobbie's school life with the doctor. Probably not, I decided. From what I had seen, Robert Morgan was mostly a Ten Commandments kind of father. He laid down the letter and line of the law and didn't seem too interested in any problems you had following it.

"What do you need?" I poked my head around his office door. Out here, things were even more severe than in the house. I vaguely remembered the office and examining room from my visit as a child, but Robert Morgan had put some new equipment in and updated the lighting with fluorescent bulbs, with the result that even the healthy patients looked half-dead against the white walls.

Robert Morgan sat behind his desk, his back perfectly straight in his big old chair, so that walking up to him felt like approaching a pharaoh. All he needed was the headdress and a little goatee, I thought, but he settled for spectacles. He peered over them as if he were surprised to find me there in front of him, when wasn't he the one who'd been hollering the walls down for the past ten minutes, telling me to get my butt across the porch? I folded my arms across my chest, glad for once that I was big and that he had to crick his neck to talk to me. He swept an arm out in front of him. "Please, sit."

All I wanted was to get back to my ironing, but I crunched my bones down into one of the little chairs in front of his desk and folded my hands up on my stuck-together knees the way Miss Sparrow had taught us in deportment lessons, most of which I never thought I'd need, but some of which I could see might come in handy now. Suddenly, Robert Morgan wrenched off his bifocals with a savage yank. This close, it left his face too naked, as if I'd just caught him stepping out of the shower. I looked back down at my callused hands. Ugly as they were, anything was preferable to the doctor's come-to-Jesus stare.

He cleared his throat. "I have had an unpleasant phone call from the county morgue. I need you to listen well to what I'm about to say, and to prepare yourself."

My heart did a barrel roll in my chest. I swallowed hard. Of course, I already knew what the doctor was going to tell me. He was going to give me some grievous news about my sister. I'd been hoping for some kind of information about her, and now I realized with a rush that it wasn't going to be good. Robert Morgan put his glasses back on, as if he not only wanted to deliver the message, but also see its impact.

"A woman fitting your sister's description has been found floating in a pond outside of Albany. She was naked, so there's no identifying clothing or jewelry. She'll require a positive ID from someone who knows her. From two people, in fact, but don't worry"—he stuck a hand across the desk, as if to steady me—"I've asked Amelia to come with me. She knew Serena Jane well enough to recognize her. You can stay here with Bobbie. You shouldn't have to do this."

I shifted my hips a little in the uncomfortable chair and didn't say anything. On the one hand, I was grateful for Robert Morgan's sudden and uncharacteristic concern about my emotional well-being. As sure as there were fleas on dogs, I would have crumpled if I'd had to see my beautiful sister's hair streaming across the steel table of a morgue. It just irritated me that Robert Morgan knew me well enough to guess it.

There was a light tap on the office door, and Amelia's head appeared through the crack, her dark eyes calm. She tiptoed over to my chair and squeezed one of my shoulders. It was the first time I'd seen her since the move, and she looked even slimmer to me than usual, her black hair knotted neatly behind her neck. I remembered all the times in childhood she'd called for me to come and kill off a spider in our bedroom, hiding her face behind her long tapered fingers, and it made it hard for me to imagine her at the doctor's side in a chilly, tiled room, watching as Bernie Briggs, the coroner, unzipped a rubber bag. Before I could change my mind, I sat up and spoke.

"Amelia, this shouldn't be your business. I'll go with Robert Morgan. Lord knows I'm big and bad enough."

Amelia threw a panicked glance at the doctor and squeezed my shoulder again. The doctor nodded, and she reassured me in a wavering falsetto, which was what her voice always did when she was nervous beyond belief. "Let me do this for you, Truly."

I should have known better. I was heads bigger than Amelia and about three times as wide around. Without exception, I was always the one who lifted the shovel in the garden, manhandled the meanest horse, picked up the sofa so she could sweep under it, and stacked the bales of hay. But weakness has an insidious side no matter how big you are. It will creep and slide, wrapping around your ankle like a snake until it's up around your throat, squeezing hard, turning you blue in the face. I slumped in my chair, picturing Serena Jane bloated and tinged green, and understood again that if I had to see that image for real, it would undo me.

"Okay," I whispered. "Go." I felt an immediate wave of relief and, after it, the sinking feeling that I was letting the snake get too good a choke hold on my bones and that in the end, like all snakes, it would always be there, waiting to bite me in the behind.

"You're making a wise choice," the doctor said as I stood up to return to the kitchen. "This is how families operate, Truly. We lift each other up when the road gets rough."

If that's true, I wanted to answer, *I'd be in heaven right now. My road has been that bumpy*. But I didn't say that. I didn't say anything at all. The snake had my tongue.

When Robert Morgan came home that evening, it was with the prowling step of a cat guarding a kill. Amelia crept close on his heels, her lips pinched shut, as if what she'd seen that afternoon had left flecks of something malodorous dusted on her soul. I was sitting in the parlor with Tabitha's quilt over my knees. The dishes were done. Bobbie was fed and upstairs, and the house had settled into a twilight stupor, dragging me along with it. First I heard the front door open, and then I listened with astonishment to what sounded like Amelia and Robert Morgan whispering angrily. *What could they ever have to discuss?* I wondered. It was out of character for Amelia to speak to anyone but those closest to her.

"If I'd known, I never would have agreed," Amelia hissed, and the doctor gave it right back to her.

"One person dies, another lives, Amelia. That's the way of the world."

"But this—"

The doctor cut her off. "This is what we agreed. Now you keep your end of the bargain."

"Hey . . ." I came shuffling into the hall, my heart hammering out its usual crazy rhythm, my joints aching the way they always did whenever I sat still for too long. "Well?"

Robert Morgan shrugged off his coat and slammed his keys down on the little round table, where they splayed like a pile of bones. He didn't even look at me. "It's what we expected. Funeral's tomorrow."

I expected Amelia to come over to me, but she didn't. She stayed put in the far corner of the foyer by the front door, gnawing viciously on her thumbnail. I sank down on the stairs, numb to my toes, feeling as if the last living part of me had just been amputated. We'd been separated since childhood, my sister and I, but always, in the back of my mind, I'd told myself that I wasn't alone. Now it really was just me left to walk the earth. And Amelia. I looked over at her, and her eyes flickered uneasily to the doctor.

"Talk about it later," Robert Morgan growled. "Right now, go and get Bobbie. We have to tell him." But I couldn't move. "Get up," Robert Morgan said. "You can fall apart later. Right now I need help telling Bobbie."

I stayed where I was, though, elbows planted on knees. For some reason, all I could think about were the vinyl suitcases Amanda Pickerton had given my sister and me after our father died. Mine had gotten lost in the detritus of the Dyerson farm shortly after I'd moved, but I'd never minded. Serena Jane, however, had always kept hers at the back of her closet, ready for Hollywood. Robert Morgan didn't know it, but on my first morning in the Morgan house, after I'd fried bacon for Robert Morgan and Bobbie, after I'd dried the pans, and made the beds, and swiped a rag around the toilet seats, I went through my sister's things. Most of them I didn't recognize. A pair of midheeled shoes in sensible tan. A silk dressing gown hung over a chair. A string of pearls with a broken gold clasp. In the closet, her clothes were still arranged like soldiers for a battle. She still read movie magazines.

And then I saw her old suitcase sticking out from under the bed, its lid left open like a mouth grappling with an afterthought. Inside, there was a gaudy magazine picture of some Pacific idyll—palm trees, and lots of sand, and, most of all, an ocean as blue as my sister's eyes. Along the horizon, getting as far away as it possibly could, a tiny ship sailed.

I heard footsteps now and sat up straighter on the stairs, opening my eyes.

Robert Morgan was shuffling back into the hall, marching Bobbie in front of him by the shoulders. "Son," he said, remaining behind him, "your aunt wants to tell you some news."

I opened my mouth to protest, but nothing came out. Bobbie tipped his elfin face up to me expectantly, all the sadness of missing his mother pinched up around his eyes, which were blue, just like Serena Jane's. *He knows,* I realized. *He already knows.* Suddenly, I knew what to do. I stood up and stuck out my hand.

"Come with me," I said. "I've got something to show you." Robert Morgan shot daggers at me, and Amelia was shaking her head, but I didn't care. I was damned if I was going to let Serena Jane's memory sink in a swamp of pond water. The world was bigger than that, I decided. It still had me in it, after all. And it had Bobbie, too.

"Follow me," I ordered, marching back upstairs with Bobbie at my heels. I burst into Robert Morgan's room and opened the closet. "Your mother is gone from this world," I said. "I'm so sorry I have to be the one to tell you that. She was my sister, and

I loved her, and the Lord knows I will miss her, too. Here"—I swept my arm toward the closet—"take anything you want."

I watched as he delicately touched the hem of a brown skirt, then the sleeve of a blouse. He ran his fingers across the clothes and back again, then buried his nose in an armful of dresses. "This one," he finally said, pinching the faded aquamarine fabric of a dress. It was Serena Jane's wedding dress.

"That one? Oh, honey, are you sure?"

Bobbie nodded fiercely.

"Okay." I lifted the hanger. "Anything else?"

Bobbie shook his head.

"Okay. We'll put this in your closet in your room, and any time you miss your mom, you can look at this and remember her, all right?"

Bobbie didn't say anything, just clutched the dress to his chest and pressed the satin to his nose—the only embrace he had left with his mother. I longed to go to him and put my own arms around him, but this was clearly a private moment, and he was still getting used to me. I was afraid he would just shrug me off, angered by how little I resembled Serena Jane.

I did what I could. I stood in the same room with him, breathing the same stale air in and out, listening to the trees toss their branches like horse heads in the wind. *Shh, shh, shhh,* they whispered, doing all the soothing for me, making promises I wasn't sure I could keep. That everything would be fine. That I would be able to fill the hollow blue void my sister had left. That in growing up, the gap-toothed, wide-eyed boy I saw standing in front of me wouldn't choke and fade but, rather, root and spread with the savage, persistent glory of a weed.

Chapter Fourteen

At night, its blunt corners dulled by moonlight and shadows, the Morgan house let its ghosts out to roam. In the summer, racked by heat and insects, the interior walls of the house groaned like old dogs left to lie in the sun. And in winter, the radiators howled and clanged with the pent-up fury of banshees. It was during the winter, particularly, that I most felt the presence of the Morgan line. I would draw the curtains of my room tight against the cold and then lie tucked up in bed under the flowery quilt, watching the latest of late night TV and trying to ignore the sensation that the walls were watching me. The door to my room tapped gently against the threshold, pulled to and fro by licks of frigid air racing through the house, making a kind of mournful music.

There was little evidence of me in my room. My toothbrush, hairbrush, and a tube of lip balm sat on top of one bedside table, and a six-month-old *People* magazine was overturned on the other, its pages crinkled and turning to yellow. I took the magazines from Robert Morgan's waiting room before he threw them out, digesting the outdated love affairs of movie stars and the antics of rock singers with sanguinity. I'd never flown on an airplane, never tasted champagne, and never even bothered to open a bank account. What little money I needed was provided in the household account, leaving me to keep my own savings in the box underneath my bed. Occasionally, I added a twenty-dollar bill here or a ten-dollar bill there, until the wad of cash was as thick as my wrist. If I were to unfurl it, I imagined, it would swell and expand like a sail filling with wind, ready to take me and maybe Bobbie across the sea.

I came to understand that life at Robert Morgan's had its inside and its outside components. Inside, there was television, food, and the scraping tick of the grandfather clock, and outside, there was the world of other people. Whereas my size had been a useful benefit at the farm (and sometimes even unnoticeable among the horses), it suddenly made me all thumbs in the china doll setting of the Morgan residence. During my first year there, I think I broke half of Maureen's old dishes, along with two of the spindly parlor chairs, an heirloom teapot, and an entire army's worth of vacuum cleaner parts. Eventually, I just resorted to doing things the way we'd done them at the farm, by the most elemental means possible. A broom replaced the vacuum, and on sunny days I hung the rugs out to beat. I cooked exclusively with the cast-iron pots. Even so, my body still missed its old regimen of physical labor. Trapped indoors all day, I began to feel pangs and pains that I'd never noticed before. In colder weather, the ends of my fingers and the soles of my feet would go stinging numb, as though bees had been feeding on them. Sometimes spots danced in front of my eyes like polka dots on parade, and, of course, there was my stuttering heart. When I bent over and stood up quickly, or when I heaved myself upright in the morning, it contracted and fluttered, sending unfathomable messages down my veins.

And there were other changes, too. My jaw was growing squarer, it seemed, and my brow wider. But the worst was the weight I started to put on. Maybe it was because I wasn't doing farmwork anymore, or maybe it was the extra bites of food I snuck throughout the day, but as soon as I moved under the doctor's roof, I started gaining weight and couldn't stop. In August, I was wearing my usual overalls and rough men's shirts, but by October, springy new flesh cocooned my belly and thighs, wrapped around my shoulders, and began padding out my thighs. My shirts grew too tight, then my dungarees, until finally I had to haul Serena Jane's old Singer out of the closet and run up some loose dresses for myself. Amelia brought me the fabric—the plainest, darkest, sturdiest she could find, the kind she would have chosen for herself to make her even more invisible. It didn't work that well for me, though. The first morning I came down for breakfast in one of my new creations, both Robert Morgan and Bobbie stared at me, slack-jawed.

"Why are you wearing a nightgown? And why is it so dark?" Bobbie asked, his mouth half-full of cereal. Bobbie loved color, much to Robert Morgan's dismay. He thought that boys should pass their lives attired in the sensible, manly hues of khaki, gray flannel, navy blue, and polished leather.

"It's a dress," I stammered.

"What happened to your other clothes?"

I blushed the hard, deep color of a plum. "They're getting too small. I guess I must be getting bigger."

"Cool!" Bobbie shouted, his mouth half-full of toast. "When I grow up, can I be as big as you, Aunt Truly?"

Robert Morgan scowled and put down his newspaper. "You wouldn't want that, son. You have a hard enough time as it is."

It was true. Bobbie was still having problems fitting in with Aberdeen's other boys. During recess, he hung out with the girls his age near the swing or just moped around the schoolyard by himself. He never had any friends over. So I could understand why a boy like Bobbie would want to be as big as me. I could understand it very well. I leaned over his chair. "Maybe one day," I whispered in his ear, and saw his face light up.

"Don't put ideas in his head," Robert Morgan barked, and laid his coffee spoon on his saucer. I glowered at him and swept the dishes into the sink, aware of the doctor's stare on me. I turned around. "You are putting on too much weight, though," he said. "You should let me examine you." His eyes narrowed, as if he were already dreaming of some fancy medical report he could publish to wild acclaim. *The Habits of an American Giantess,* perhaps, with hand-inked illustrations, charts, graphs, and all manner of pictorial data. No wonder my father had chosen whiskey for his cure-all, I thought.

"I feel fine, really." The last thing I needed was the doctor's bony fingers prodding me like a Thanksgiving turkey. But it was too late. I could tell the idea was pinging around in Robert Morgan's head, and once he dreamed up a plan, you had about as much chance of getting him to give it up as you would growing wings out of your back and flying to the moon.

"It's irresponsible not to take care of your health. How much do you weigh now? Do you even know?"

I did not. It was probably a lot—I'd grant Robert Morgan that—but as far as I was concerned, that was my business. Except for my single visit to Robert Morgan's father, no one had ever measured me or weighed me, and I liked this freedom. It allowed me to think of my size with some relativity. With August's horses, for instance, I had been an equal; with Amelia, I was simply solid; and with Bobbie, I knew, I was larger than life.

The doctor's voice broke into my daydream. "One of us is going to lose this argument, Truly, and it's not going to be me. When you come to your senses, I'll be in my office. We can begin an exam whenever you're ready."

I snorted. "The day I walk myself out there will be the day hell has a rainbow hanging over it."

I looked out the window and was reassured to spy Marcus bent into the far hedges, his clippers scattering leaves and twigs. I wasn't sure what I was to him anymore, but I still liked having him near me. Every other day, rain or shine, he showed up to garden, but we interacted little. He was much more heavily muscled now—taut in the cheeks and broad across his shoulders, possessing the body of a man, not a boy. In spite of myself, I remembered all his letters and then thought back to all the kisses I'd had to give him over the years on Valentine's Day, and I wondered if he remembered them, too. I half wanted him to and half didn't, and that indecision made me shy.

I knew that Marcus and I were something deeper and more primal than friends, but we spoke so rarely, we could have been mere recent acquaintances. As a result, I think we were reduced back down to our physical peculiarities. The way I saw it, he'd become a little man whose life had never gotten off the ground, who preferred plants to people, who fussed over his roses as if they were babies. And if I'm being honest, then I have to say that I probably didn't look like a prize myself. I was someone who towered over others but had forgotten about life's smaller blessings. Two or three times during the September hot spell, I'd gone out and offered Marcus lemonade, but it didn't lead to any conversation. None at all. He'd just taken the glass and gulped the liquid fast, and I'd stood there dumb, my cheeks redder than a rooster's comb.

Well, shoot, I thought now, wiping my hands on the dishrag and turning around to check that the doctor really had skulked away. He tended to do that—disappear as soon as my back was turned—and it kind of gave me the creeps. On the other hand, it also left me plenty of time to attend to my own thoughts, and right now I thought that I could use the company of a trusted friend. Before I could think twice about it, I grabbed an old scarf off the coat pegs by the kitchen door, wrapped my throat warm, and trudged outside.

The leaves were half changed, and as a result the air looked dappled. I breathed in, appreciating the chilly edge on the breeze. I'd been living with the doctor only some two months, but in that time my lungs seemed to have forgotten the pleasure of raw air. I scuffed my boots in the grass, crunching a few leaves, relishing the sound. As I neared the back hedge, Marcus heard me swishing through the long grass and straightened up, wiping a streak of sweat off his brow with his bad hand. Today, his gloves were off, and I clearly could see the damage that had been done. He was missing his third finger, and his thumb was fibrous and woody, like a stump of gingerroot. The skin puckered and pulled. It looked painful, but I suppose it wasn't too bad if Marcus was able to work the clippers.

He saw me staring, cleared his throat, and shoved his hands in his pockets. "Hello. This is a surprise."

I hugged my arms around myself, still unsettled by how much weight I'd recently gained. "I'm just taking some air. It's supposed to rain a little later." I coughed a little. "I guess when the weather changes, we won't be seeing you so much."

A tiny smile twitched around Marcus's lips. "I don't know about that. I prefer the sun, sure, but I'm happy to carry on in the rain, too. Water's useful in its own way."

I ran my hand along the neat border of the hedge and tried to keep my voice casual. "Brings out the worms, right? And the spiderwebs?" I blushed, remembering how he had schooled me so long ago in the science of Spider-Man's amazing abilities.

Marcus fingered a leaf. "Yes, but don't say it like they're so unsavory. Most folks tend to overlook the dark, stinking parts of gardening, but that's where they go wrong. People think of gardening as a pastime, a hobby, but it's really more than that." He buttoned up his jacket and glanced at the sky. "A garden is where you can find the whole spectrum of life, birth, and death. It's where poisons meet nectars, where sustenance challenges rot. A garden, in short, is a theater for war." At the word *war,* he stopped short and bent over to pick up the clippers again.

I pinched a pair of the hedge leaves together for courage and kept my voice low and smooth, like a mellow river rock. "Marcus," I urged, "I know we haven't talked in a long time, but I need to know what happened to you overseas. What happened to us?" I suppose the doctor's needling me about my weight over breakfast had made me brave. It just seemed to be the morning for uncomfortable topics. I didn't really expect an answer, and in any case, I wasn't sure I was ready to hear one, but Marcus hefted the clippers from hand to hand and surprised me.

"Close your eyes," he said, and after a beat of silence, I did. When he started speaking again, his voice had a sour tinge in it that unsettled my stomach. He sounded almost like a stranger, and I found myself wondering if his letters (had he bothered to send them) would have been this bitter. "Now, picture a palm-frond village—the prettiest place you ever did see. Bananas hanging in bunches and rice paddies all around. Friendly people decked in the most beautiful colors of cloth you could ever imagine. Chickens everywhere. Can you see it?"

I nodded, and Marcus continued, his voice a little softer. "Good. Now picture it all going up in flames. The rice paddies swimming with napalm, and a ten-year-old boy whose legs are in ribbons because of a grenade you threw." I heard the blade of the clippers snap, and I opened my eyes. Marcus was chopping at the hedge again, savagely this time, and not looking at me.

"I'm sorry," I whispered.

Marcus shrugged. "You and the rest of America. But, you know, when I got hit in my own leg, I was pretty relieved. Not because I got sent home, but because of that kid. I figured we were even."

I plucked a stray leaf off my shapeless homemade dress. Nothing in the world, it seemed, was where it was supposed to be. My sister was cold in the ground. I was living with her husband in his house, and Marcus was still trapped in a fiery hell in Asia. "I didn't think it would turn out like this," I murmured, choking back tears. "For one thing, I think I'm about two times bigger than when you left. I don't know what's wrong with me."

Marcus stopped clipping for a minute. "You look fine to me. In fact, better than fine. Sometimes there's nothing wrong with being big. That's one thing you find out when you're small."

My breath swelled in my throat. "Thanks," I stammered, and turned bright red. I wanted to hug Marcus, but he looked just as embarrassed as I was, so I readjusted my scarf instead and started to inch back toward the house. "Maybe I'll come visit you next time you're here. I'll bring pie."

Marcus straightened up and smiled a little. "I'd like that. Oh, mind the asters," he called as I bumped into a riot of flowers intersecting the hedge bottom. "They're only in bloom another week or so. Here—" He reached over, plucked several of the purple stars, and handed them to me. "Take them inside. They'll cheer the place up, and they're going to die anyway."

I hesitated. What he was offering wasn't a return to what we'd had, I knew, or even picking up where we'd left off. It was more like the line of the thin white scar curling over his blistered thumb—something new laid over something old. I reached out to accept the flowers.

"Thanks." I tucked them safely inside my fist and sniffed their grassy odor on the way back to the house. Once inside, their purple would wither and leach, I knew, but out here, for the time being, it glowed as bright as the bluebells stitched on Tabitha Morgan's quilt. Maybe moments like these were like the threads running over those scraps of cotton, I thought, turning the ordinary fabric of life into something wholly unexpected. And maybe if I wasn't finding new material at hand, it was because I wasn't supposed to. Maybe I was supposed to sow from the seed that was already under my fingertips.

Chapter Fifteen

Who knows how long the doctor and I would have played cat and mouse, but early that December, I opened my eyes to a pain so fierce marauding across the top of my skull that I knew immediately I needed more than the aspirin I usually swallowed. When I sat up in bed, my vision blurred and twisted like the picture on a failing television, making me squint. I realized I was staring at the cloth buds on Tabitha's quilt. They seemed to vibrate and whisper. I cocked my head, trying to catch their song, but a wave of nausea crashed over me, and I let myself flop back down on the mattress, grateful to close my eyes again. A few moments later, I opened them again to find Bobbie's face hovering anxiously over mine.

"Aunt Truly?" His voice seemed to be coming from someplace far away. He shook my shoulder. "Are you okay? What's wrong? Dad sent me in here to see what was taking you so long."

I fumbled for the alarm clock on my bedside table. "What time is it?" My words came out woody and dry.

"Seven-thirty. School starts in half an hour. And Dad wants his breakfast."

At the mention of food, my stomach roiled and lurched. I let out a burp and hauled myself upright again. I waited, but I felt a little better this time. Well enough, maybe, to fry up an egg or two and pour some coffee. I looked again at Bobbie, whose outline was still imprecise and fuzzy. Two weeks ago, I'd walked with him to lay some flowers on Serena Jane's grave, and he had bowed his head in a similar solemn pose, like a leaf curling into itself for the winter. I'd had the urge to wrap him tight in the wing of my coat and kiss him warm, but instinct told me he would only pull away if I tried. He was accustomed to me, but not yet attached. He let me read him stories and peck him good night on the cheek, but he still stiffened when I went to embrace him, and when he left for school, he only waved briefly through the rectangle of the kitchen door before turning around and plodding glumly down the street.

But maybe he was fonder of me than I realized. I recognized an expression of concern colonizing his face now, as if he were contemplating the idea of all the adults in his life shriveling up and blowing away like corn husks. He'd just turned eight, but he was already hovering on the dark threshold of adult cynicism, I saw. One more push from the world, I suspected, and he'd shoot all the way through to the other side of mean, just like his father. Unless I could figure out a way to keep that from happening. I swung my feet onto the floor.

"I'm a bit lopsided this morning," I reassured him while the room righted itself and lurched again, "but I bet your daddy is a genius when it comes to healing. I bet he can make anyone better, even me."

Bobbie frowned and sat next to me on the bed. "I thought you said you'd be hell-bent before you let Dad lay a hand on you."

I scowled. That was true. Over the past month, all through the lead-up to Thanksgiving, Robert Morgan had kept up his pressure to examine me, and so far I'd resisted him step for step, a fact that left him practically frothing at the mouth. He'd wheedled, and reasoned, and finally resorted to out-and-out insults. "You're as pigheaded and mean-minded as your father was, Truly," he pronounced at the table one awful night. "You should be grateful you're living with a person of science and reason, and not still stuck on that mudflat the Dyersons call a farm."

"I liked it there," I replied calmly. "They were good to me."

"If they were so good to you, then why did they let you grow into a behemoth? Why didn't they ever bring you in to see my father when something could have been done?"

I put down my fork. "And pay with what? A good tip at the track? Besides, when I was out there, I wasn't this heavy. It's only since I've moved in with you that I've gained all this weight."

That shut the doctor up for a minute, but it still didn't dissuade him from trying to guess how much I'd put on. He eyeballed me. "I'd say it's thirty, maybe forty pounds. In just a few months. Do you pay attention to how much you're eating?"

I looked down at my plate. The remains of half the roast chicken were piled in a little pyramid, next to a muddy puddle of gravy and a smear of mashed potato. I'd had thirds, but I couldn't help it. As soon as the food melted off my tongue, my stomach screamed for more.

The doctor sat back in his chair and wrinkled up his napkin, confident he'd won his point. "One visit to my office, and I'm telling you we could figure out what to do about your appetite. Besides, you'd be doing me a favor. I've got a bet going with John Hinkleman that you weigh over four hundred." He snickered. "All you have to do is step on the scale and the money's mine."

I threw my own napkin on the table and stood up, my cheeks blazing. "I'll be a baboon's butt before I give you that satisfaction." Bobbie put his hands over his mouth and giggled. I looked at him and winked. "With cherries and whipped cream." Then I'd stomped off to my room and left the dishes to rot, not caring if we got bugs and not caring if the doctor shouted at me all night long.

Bobbie wasn't laughing as he sat next to me on the bed now, though. He looked worried, his narrow face even more pinched than usual. Another jolt of pain arrived, and I clenched my teeth, made weak by pain. "All right," I whispered. "You can run out and tell your father he won this round. Today is his lucky day. I'll be down to his office directly."

"I'll tell him," Bobbie cried, rushing into the hallway. "I'll tell him to get his medicines ready."

"Make it double dose," I murmured to myself, squeezing my temples. "I'm going to need the extra to drown my pride."

To his credit, the doctor didn't outright throw his hands in the air and stomp out a victory dance when I knocked on his door, but it wasn't far off. He certainly didn't waste any time on niceties, just handed me a starched sheet, directed me behind a screen, and told me to strip and then wrap up. "I apologize for the sheet," he said as I emerged. "I just didn't think my regular gowns were up to the task." He rubbed his hands together, not even trying to hide his triumphant grin as he ushered me over to the scale. "At last! Are you ready to see if my bet with John Hinkleman is good?"

I scowled and folded my arms. "On one condition."

The doctor's smile faded. "What?"

"I don't want to know what the scale says."

"What do you mean?" The doctor's face fell, and just then I thought he looked a little like a boy who'd had his football taken away.

"Don't tell me. I don't want to know. And I don't want to know how tall I am, either, or what my blood type is, or how big around my hips are. You can keep all that to yourself. I'm just here because my head is about to blow a gasket."

Robert Morgan fiddled with his clipboard. "It's just a migraine," he sniffed. "We'll get to that in a minute. But how can I treat you if you won't let me give you any information?"

I set my jaw. "That's the deal. Take it or leave it."

The doctor debated with himself for a moment, then threw up his hands in defeat. "Okay, fine, I won't tell you anything. You're as stubborn and stupid as the rest of those Dyersons, but I guess we just are what we are. Now, will you step on the damn scale?"

I hesitated, wondering if he would keep his word, but then I climbed onto the little platform and let the doctor slide the weights all the way to the right. He let out a long, slow whistle. "Wow. That's even more than I expected. You must be carrying a ton of hidden weight to come out that high." I shot him a warning look, and he shut up and scribbled on his clipboard. "Have a seat." He gestured to his examining table, and I sat on it reluctantly, hoping it would hold me while Robert Morgan rapped my knees with a rubber tomahawk, stuck a wooden stick down my gob, lit up my ears, eyes, nose, and throat like the Empire

State Building, and shimmied the cold disk of a stethoscope all around my chest.

"What does it sound like?" I asked. My heart was the one organ I did have some curiosity about, wondering if it was like everyone else's on the inside, but the doctor just held a rigid finger straight up in the air as if he were testing the wind, and I knew that I'd broken some sort of medical commandment. He pulled the round circle of metal off my chest and slinked his fingers up and down my windpipe. "Swallow," he ordered, before pulling a tape measure out of his pocket and winding it around my breasts, hips, and upper arms.

"I've always been big. You know that." I blushed, watching as he jotted down numbers on his chart. "Your father said it was something inside my brain. A little clock." I remembered the way his father's fingers had pressed into the base of my skull so gently, telling me about the mechanism inside of me that was ticking too fast, and I wondered if that's what Robert Morgan heard when he slid that stethoscope against my skin. Or was it just the slow sludge of my blood, confirming everything he thought he already knew about me? "Maybe that's why I have this headache."

Robert Morgan's eyes swam into focus, as if he were reeling his thoughts up out of a very deep, very cold lake. "For now, just take some aspirin. You'll get over it. Migraines happen to women sometimes. But in your case, I think it could be linked to something else." He frowned.

"What is this exam for," I stuttered, "if you're not going to help my headache?" Outside, I noticed, the day was growing darker, the trees shedding leaves and dead twigs, slimming down for snow and ice.

Robert Morgan blinked and slid a needle into my arm for a blood sample. The pinch was sharp and familiar, just like all his thumbtacks I'd sat on years ago. I wondered if he was enjoying sticking me with a needle as much as he'd enjoyed tormenting me in the schoolroom. The little gleam in his eye told me yes, but it also spoke of a bigger, more adult anticipation.

Suddenly, all the breath in my body seemed to stop. It was a spooky sensation, like God putting down His fury for five minutes in the middle of a storm to think up something even worse. "This isn't about my headache," I said. Maybe if I'd been better practiced in the art of anger, I would have recognized the symptoms of rage and would have released some right then on the doctor's head, like hail dumping on a tin roof. But when you're raised by Dyersons, you learn not to do that lest the whole damn house falls in and crushes you. I uncurled my palm and watched the test tube fill with blood.

Robert Morgan slid the needle out of my vein and stuck a cotton ball in its spot. He pressed down, harder than he really needed to, I thought. "Did you really think I'd keep you in my house and not take the opportunity to examine you? You're about as normal as a dog with two tails, Truly. To be honest, I don't even know if I can cure whatever's wrong with you." He let my arm go.

"Well," I said, my cheeks burning, "you said it yourself. We are what we are in this world." I dipped my chin and thought about my sister, who had been born beautiful, and then Amelia, predisposed to silence. I was strong and square, I knew, born to brush the horses down in the barn. But I *liked* August's horses. I missed the comforting smells of their hay and dung. Even just the memory of the barn's dusty air could make my breathing slow and all the muscles in my back relax. I looked back up at the doctor. "Anyway, what makes you think I want to be cured?"

"I'm sorry?" Robert Morgan seemed distracted, probably by all the collaborations with big-city doctors he was no doubt imagining. A case like mine, I realized, would do wonders to help broadcast his name in the world beyond Aberdeen—a world he probably missed, a world my sister and Bobbie had yanked him out of before he'd gotten to taste of it.

I crossed my arms. "What makes you think I have any intention of letting you try to fix me?" It seemed ridiculous to be locking horns with the doctor when one of us was all but naked, but if there was anything I'd learned so far in life, it was that you didn't get to pick your moments.

Robert Morgan stared at me as if I had just grown an extra toe in the middle of my forehead. "Of course you're going to try to let me fix you." He leaned down close, his voice a snake hiss slithering into the tight chambers of my heart. "Admit it. You want it as much as I do. You'd let me turn you inside out and back again if you thought I could make you as pretty—or even as small—as your sister."

I didn't bother to respond, just left his office with hunger pains erupting in my belly with the ferocity of fireworks, my headache all but vanquished. I scuttled from his clinic door to the kitchen as quickly as I could, and flung open the icebox, soothed by its electric hum and the blast of cold air. Hot dog relish, leftover chicken, parsley leaves—I tamped my mouth as full as a cannon. It didn't matter with what as long as my gullet got filled. I suppose I might have appeared greedy, but my gorging offered no relief, no reprieve. I spread my hands wide on the table's yellow oilcloth and swallowed with difficulty, tears budding in my eyes, and then, because there was nothing else left to eat in the immediate vicinity, I swallowed those down, too.

One day, I vowed, Robert Morgan would know what it felt like to be pricked, and prodded, squeezed, and studied. He would know what it felt like to be one of his own experiments. Of course, the difference between the doctor and me was that Robert Morgan would always be divining for some cure, whereas I knew better. And so there you have it. Long before I ever did it, I'll admit that I thought about killing Robert Morgan. Right then and there I promised myself that if I ever found the occasion, I'd give him such a good dose of his own medicine, he'd never have the backbone to survive it.

Chapter Sixteen

That February, the line of hedges around the doctor's fields transformed into huddled heaps of snow, and the blue air was so frosty, the jays were preening ice out of their wings. Even the feral cats gave up and took shelter in the nooks and crannies of people's woodpiles, and still, Bobbie hadn't made any friends. After school, I watched the town children knot together and run shrieking to one another's houses, but Bobbie always trudged home alone, his chin resolute in spite of himself. I'd fix him cocoa, and he'd head up to my room, where he'd climb under the quilt on my bed and snuggle back against my pillows. "Tell me a story," he'd demand. "Tell me something I don't know."

"Do you want to hear more about Princess Bugaboo?" I stuck my coffee cup under my nose, comforted by its steam. It had been Amelia's suggestion to tell the stories to Bobbie, and he seemed to like them, but I wondered if he was perhaps getting too old for Princess Bugaboo. Recently, I'd stumbled on to him washing in the bath. The door had been half-cracked, and over and over again, he'd stubbornly pushed the single finger of flesh between his thighs down into the water. No matter what he did, however, out it popped, bobbing like a marine specimen—a puzzling cadence that both was and was not part of him.

I'd darted down the hallway before he could spot me, then immediately regretted my cowardice. I thought about sneaking back, knocking, even, and having a sit-down talk with him, but life doesn't give us the option to remake our decisions, only the power to reconceive them. I knew that better than anyone. All I had to do was look down at the blubbery columns of my thighs and the wilderness of my abdomen, or think about Marcus's scarred hand and limp, and I was reminded of how his body wouldn't let him forget what it used to be or the things it had done, and how my body wouldn't let me forget what it was always going to be. And now, it seemed, Bobbie's bones were beginning to write a complicated story of their own.

"No Bugaboo," Bobbie said. "Tell me something else today."

I smoothed the quilt over our bodies and pulled Bobbie closer. "Make sure you're warm enough." I reached behind me and rearranged the pillows, and after a moment, Bobbie let himself sag against them. His child's weight barely registered on the mattress, and as he nestled against the bulk of me, I could feel the sinews of his body held taut. It was like sheltering a spooked horse, and I thought back to all the days I'd spent combing down August's nervous animals. The trick had been to move slow and speak easy, avoiding the quick spike of a hoof or the sudden pinch of teeth. You had to maneuver as if you were carrying a secret you were just about ready to let spill.

"You know," I began, smoothing my hand along the jagged inner border of Tabitha's quilt, "time was when the only doctor fifty miles around was your great-great-great-grandmama Tabitha."

Bobbie didn't move a muscle, but his breathing lightened, as if he were waiting for me to continue. *Probably,* I thought, *he's never even heard these stories*. Robert Morgan certainly wouldn't have told them, and Serena Jane never had any interest in anything as plain sewn as Aberdeen's folklore. I hitched my elbow up a little so Bobbie could rest even closer.

"Time was when the people of this town found their health in spells and in the jars of Tabby's balms. That all changed, though, with your great-great-great-granddaddy. He was this town's first real medical man.

"Some folks said he was a blessing with his black bag of instruments and powders, but others insisted they were better off with Tabby's elemental cures. They'd worked for decades. Why stop now? But stop she did. No one knows why. And when she died, still so young and pretty that bees made honey on her grave, everything she knew died with her. No one's ever found that spell book of hers, and the good Lord knows more than one Morgan man's spun this house into a heap looking for it."

Bobbie's eyes widened. "Do you think it's really still here, Aunt Truly, do you? Maybe up in the attic? There's tons of stuff up there."

I shook my head. Half of what I'd just said was nonsense, but it sounded so good, even I half believed it. "Maybe, but I don't think so. I think old Tabby was smarter than that."

Bobbie nodded, emphatic. "You're probably right. She probably put it somewhere no one would ever think to look."

Just then, a slash of winter sun shot through the windows in my room, unexpected in its harsh brilliance, a needle of light pricking the triangular edges of the quilt's inner border. Inside of it, appliquéd cloth leaves and flowers were lined up in assiduous rows, pieces of flora embroidered on a series of stitched white squares. Outside of the border, however, the blooms ran rampant in no sequence whatsoever, as if they were born wild right onto the cotton backing. How many hours had it taken one small woman to sew such a quantity?

I wondered. I pictured a smooth-haired wife bent over her own lap, frowning as she threaded yet another needle in snowy gloom, the evening's late fire dying, her fingertips raw from the cold but determined to set out in pictures what she couldn't in words. I gasped and sat up, splashing a drop of coffee onto my sheet hem.

"Aunt Truly? Are you okay? Are you getting another migraine?"

How had I not seen it before? Here I had been sleeping under that damn quilt for coming up on six months, yet I never once thought of it as anything more than an extra layer of warmth. Of course, I had been attracted to its lively design, but only as a bright spot in an otherwise colorless room. It was more than that, though, I saw now. Much more. I ran my hand over the weft of the fabric, marveling at how clever Tabitha had been and how stupid the generations following her were. I glanced down at Bobbie.

"Think about it," I muttered, my thumb lingering over a threaded stalk of what looked like a mint plant. "If you wanted to hide something very precious to you, where would you stick it? Some dark place where maybe it would get found and maybe it wouldn't, or would you do something even trickier? Like put it right out under everyone's noses in such an ordinary way that no one would even bother to look at it twice?"

Bobbie wrinkled his forehead. "What do you mean?"

Downstairs, the kitchen door scraped open and banged shut, forced by the wind. Bobbie and I fell silent as Robert Morgan's stern footsteps rapped over the floorboards into the foyer. It had grown late, I suddenly realized. I kissed the top of Bobbie's head. "Never mind. I'm just talking a foolish woman's nonsense. We best get downstairs and get some supper on the stove."

Bobbie reluctantly peeled back his nest of covers and withdrew his legs from the warm cocoon of the sheets. He paused for a moment, studying the quilt. "Why are the flowers so crazy on the edges and so straight in the middle? It's almost like old Tabby couldn't make up her mind."

I cupped the warm dome of his head, smoothing his hair, reluctant to let him go for the evening. "Maybe. That's a possibility.

Or maybe she was saying there are two sides to every story. I guess it just depends on which way you look at it."

That night after the dishes were wiped dry as whistles, and two loads of washing were sorted and folded, and the kitchen floor was swabbed with two parts water and one part vinegar, and after Bobbie had done his homework and washed behind his ears, I closed my door and spread the quilt out on the floor in the middle of my room. Bobbie had been right, I thought. The quilt did look like the work of the left hand and the work of the right attached together by the black inner border. I squinted. It reminded me of something—a place. Someplace where the chaos of life met stillness and order, a place I was all too familiar with. I sucked in my breath. Of course. The graveyard, with its spiky iron fence punctuated with weeds. And inside, squares of immortal stones set neat with flowers. My heart hammered. The quilt wasn't just a piece of handiwork. It was a kind of map. But for what?

Breathing shallowly, I tipped the shade of my bedside light so it could better illuminate the fine web of needlework quilted across the expanse of the fabric. And there, so faint you'd never see them if you didn't know to look, specific forms began to swim their way out of the play of light and shadow, slowly at first and then with more and more clarity. A bone. A flame. An eye. A heart. A set of lips. A single hand. And all along the wild edge of the border, repeated over and over again, what looked like the feathered spread of wings.

I exhaled and sat back on my heels. My hips ached from squatting, and my eyeballs felt used up, but my pulse was racing with the exhilaration of a horse in high gallop. Had Maureen, Robert Morgan's mother, ever noticed this? I wondered. Or any of the other Morgan wives? Tabitha Morgan hadn't had any daughters, I remembered. Only sons. And those sons had had only sons. But those boys had married, and each one of them had lived in this house with the quilt on the wall. Hadn't any of them seen the designs?

Of course, in the end, it really wouldn't have mattered. Tabby was dust in the ground, and her shadow book was a silly legend. No one would have believed it. The legend had to have come from somewhere, however, and, looking at Tabitha's quilt, I thought I knew where. It sprang from a secret squeezed inside a rib cage for too many centuries, like a long, deep breath. And the thing about secrets is that they multiply. Once you have one tucked under your belt, it's easy to add a couple more. I found that out, too. In fact, I only ran into trouble when I forgot that everyone around me might have been doing exactly the same thing.

Chapter Seventeen

It took me until the tail end of spring to figure out the quilt. At night, my bedside lamp tilted at an angle, I studied the ghostly outlines stitched across the floral surface, wondering what they could mean. Bones, and lips, and hearts, disembodied and floating. They, too, must be a kind of map, I finally decided, a topography of the body overlaid on top of specific leaves and blossoms, indicating a relationship. Viewed like that, the quilt began to make perfect sense. Tabitha was showing what herbs worked on what parts of the body, and the jagged border, which so recalled the cemetery's iron fence, said where to go to get the ingredients for her cures.

Next, I had the guesswork of identifying all the plants. For two weeks, I copied stems and flowers into a notebook in the evenings, making sure I'd drawn all the lines right, double-checking the proportions. With the darkness sucking up against my windows and the sound of late ice melting off the eaves in the roof, I thought I could taste a little of the awful loneliness that Tabitha must have felt as she sat sewing with the moon eyeing her up like a big bald baby. During the day, I put Marcus to work, pestering him in the garden with my pictures and questions, but, truth be told, I think he enjoyed the distraction. It gave him a chance to return to his former role as a know-it-all.

"How about this one?" I demanded on a particularly balmy spring afternoon. "What do you call this flower?"

Marcus squinted at the sprig of blue blooms I'd scribbled on my notebook page and bent over closer to me. "Foxglove. *Digitalis*. It's Latin for 'fingerlike,' because you can slip a blossom on the end of your finger so easily." Then he frowned. "But it's not much more than a weed, and you don't want to mess with it, anyway. It's toxic. I don't plant it in the flower beds. What are you asking me all this stuff for, anyway?"

My own heart lurched at being so near to Marcus. Up close, his skin smelled both familiar and exotic, like the stand of woods behind the Dyerson farm. I slammed my notebook shut and stepped away from him, surreptitiously wiping my sweaty palms on the rough wool of my dress. "Never you mind."

Marcus grinned and switched the spade in his hand for a pair of clippers off his tool belt. "Are you sure you're not gunning for my job?"

I blushed. In the time since he'd been home, Marcus had become a horticultural celebrity. Good on his word, he lived at the cemetery in the caretaker's cottage that had been abandoned for the past forty years. At first, keeping up the cemetery was nothing more than a chore, but soon he found pleasure in the labor.

Sal Dunfry found pleasure in it, too, as she watched him chopping weeds along the cemetery fence line one hot afternoon. "What do I do about my hydrangeas?" she asked him while laying flowers on her mother's grave. "They used to be purple. Now they're faded and dull."

"Coffee grounds," Marcus told her. "Just around the stems."

Sal batted her eyelashes. "Maybe you'd better come take a look. I've got trouble with my tulips, too."

Is there anything more irresistible to a woman than a man who can get things to grow? From her kitchen window, Sal observed Marcus coaxing tomatoes, then chrysanthemums from the ground. She remembered that he'd once been the smartest boy in town, then she wondered if his current occupation was a sign of intelligence or stupidity, before concluding that she didn't care. She watched him peel off his shirt to let the sun speckle his back and brown it and decided he was perfectly formed, even if he was tiny and lame in one leg.

"Do you think it's scarred?" Vi Vickers whispered to Sal as they spied on Marcus outside of Sal's window the next week. "Do you think he's lost sensation in it?"

"Would it matter?"

Sal giggled. "You wouldn't think a man so small would be so strong."

Vi sighed. "Look at his hands. Look at the scars over his thumb."

"I don't get it," Sal sniffed. "Why is he always hanging around Truly at Dr. Morgan's house? I see them sitting on the porch together like mismatched lovebirds. She's always asking him about plants."

"They were always friends. Don't you remember? We all used to tease him, and her, too. But he's definitely changed, and Truly, well . . ." Val's voice trailed off.

Sal finished the thought for her. "She'll never change. It's the law of inertia. You just can't alter something that big."

Vi giggled. "You mean someone."

Sal just shrugged, as if to say what's the difference, and I guess she had a point, but she was wrong about the law of inertia. You can throw something huge off course, and it doesn't always take something—or someone—big to do it. Interesting results can be achieved with very little effort. Sometimes, all it takes is the smallest push from a pair of damaged hands to make even the driest bulb burst.

And Sal was wrong about me. I was changing in ways I didn't recognize. My weight was continuing to climb, no matter how little I ate. After the incident with the migraine, I'd finally succumbed to Robert Morgan's weekly examinations—not because I believed they would do any good, but because in the end, curiosity got me just as the doctor said it would. What if one day Robert Morgan *did* find a way to minimize me? I wondered. Wouldn't I take him up on his offer? I thought of Marcus, and my pulse quickened. If I could make it so that he could reach out and not up for my hand, wouldn't I do it? Of course I would.

These days, all I had to do was step on the scale, and both lead weights toppled all the way to the right. Robert Morgan scribbled the numbers in a folder, still abiding by his agreement to keep the numbers to himself, and nodded. If I gained a pound or two, he would chuckle a little and write a line to himself, as if finally confirming some long-held suspicion. Then he always told me that stupid story about the hippo.

He kept an eye on every inch of me, illuminated every pore with his flashlight, stroking it up and down my skin like a lighthouse beam seeking out shipwrecks. "But, my God, you're ugly," he once stated, clicking off the penlight and squeezing the glands in my neck. "And that's a professional opinion. In fact, you're so goddamn off the charts that I had to order this." He produced a cardboard box and pulled a blood pressure cuff out of it. "It's a leg cuff," he explained, "but we're going to just wrap it around here." He fastened the material around my biceps, inflated the cuff, and noted down what the little dial said. Then he got out his needle, tied rubber tubing where the blood pressure cuff had been, and proceeded to jab at my veins.

"What do you do with all of it, anyway?" I asked when he was done. He had six vials lined up in front of him. I daubed my forearm with cotton.

Robert Morgan capped the last tube. "Not that you need to know, but it goes to a university lab. I'm starting to see some interesting results." I was tempted to ask what they were but didn't bother, for we had our agreement, and anyway, Robert Morgan was about as forthcoming with information as August had been when you asked him for the location of his favorite fishing hole.

"You'd tell me if I was dying, right?" I joked, turning my back and starting to gather my shapeless clothes. I stepped behind the three-part screen in the corner and threw my dress over my head, waiting for his reply.

When he finally answered, it was with all the humor of a corpse. "Why would I end a study just as it was getting good?"

My mouth fell open, and I stepped back around the screen. "Out of concern for the subject?" I suggested, my cheeks flaming with anger. "Because it would be the right thing to do? Because you're dealing with people, not rocks?"

Robert Morgan shook his head and stuck his pen in his breast pocket. "Don't worry, Truly—yet." He leaned forward, mouth agape in a jack-o'-lantern grin, and patted my arm before retreating to the safe harbor of his desk, leaving me sputtering mad.

"Damn doctors," I murmured, and stomped across the porch to the kitchen to char his Wednesday roast until it became one with the pan. Hacking apart tomatoes for a sauce, I blinked back tears. It was hard to hurt me. Robert Morgan's needles didn't do it, and neither did the hot iron I'd singed my forearm along last week. Once, in August's barn, Hitching Post had reared up and landed square on my forefoot, but all I'd ended up with was a pretty, purple bruise and a broken toenail. I was even getting used to my migraines. My body, it seemed, sponged up the world's pain like bread in the bottom of a gravy tray.

But I was unfamiliar with the kind of ache I was feeling now. It seemed to start in the center of me and steam outward until even the ends of my fingers tingled. I looked down and saw that I'd sliced my finger. A line of blood spurted out and mingled with the tomato pulp on the board. That explained the stinging. I glanced through the window and thought about going out to the doctor, but the thought of his fingers crawling on my flesh again gave me chills. Besides, I had a very different kind of remedy waiting for me in my own room, I realized. Without thinking twice, I swept the tomatoes—blood and all—in a pan and set them on the stove to stew. Then I threw down my knife and stomped upstairs to read Tabitha's quilt.

I had a choice, it seemed. The hand or the heart. The hand suggested touch, and therefore skin, to me, but the heart had to represent blood. I scowled, then decided to combine the two. But how? I wondered. In a tea? A pulp? Was I just meant to eat the leaves raw and whole? Tabby's embroidery didn't recommend a delivery system—just the raw ingredients. I studied the plants on the quilt some more. I didn't know all of them yet but could pick out comfrey, chickweed, and prickly ash underneath the heart and hand. Well, that would have to do, I thought. And even better, I could find them anywhere. I wouldn't have to go out to the cemetery. In fact, that was one of the remaining mysteries of the quilt for me. Why had Tabitha included the jagged fence of Aberdeen's cemetery? Half the plants she'd sewn grew willy-nilly anywhere you could spit in Aberdeen. There was no need to trek all the way to the town graves. I tilted my head and stared at the quilt from a different angle. *Maybe*, I reasoned, *the graveyard is simply the one place where all the plants grow*. It was the answer I came back to again and again.

My eyes lingered on the tiny set of lips puckered over sprigs of peppermint and chamomile. *The mouth,* I thought. Gateway to the stomach. Peppermint was good for digestion. Almost everyone knew that. Then my heart leapt a little in my chest. What if Tabitha had known something more? I wondered. What if she could take away the appetite as well as cure it? I thought back to my humiliating examination with Robert Morgan. What if I could beat him at his own game? What would I need? Peppermint, the quilt suggested, and chamomile. Rosehips and dandelion greens. But would these make me hungrier? I had no idea. There was only one way to find out.

A pulp, I finally decided, would be the easiest thing to make for both my problems: the cut on my hand and the hunger rumbling in my stomach. I could mash up the respective stems and leaves, smearing one paste on my wound and infusing the other mixture into a sort of tea.

I waited until the household was asleep,

then snuck into the garden by the light of the moon. I hadn't been outside at night in longer than I could remember, and the wet air was a welcome shock along the walls of my throat. I inhaled in big, greedy gulps, my ears keening to the rollicking of crickets, letting my eyes get used to the dark. Up in the house, the doctor's window was still illuminated, the curtains squeezed tight, so that the glass glowed in a muffled way. I moved quickly, hoping he would attribute all the noise I was making to the restless shenanigans of a skunk or opossum.

Back in the kitchen, I found the mortar and pestle and mashed up handfuls of twigs and leaves into a slick green mess. "Truly?" The doctor's wooden voice floated down the stairs. "Is that you making all that ruckus?"

"Yes, Robert Morgan," I called back, scooping the paste into a bowl. "I'm just fixing a little snack."

I thought I heard him snigger, then the house fell silent again. The cut on my finger throbbed and oozed under its bandage, as if it were literally crying out for a poultice. I ripped off the bandage and applied a generous blob, wincing against the heat that started to build up. I smeared more on and then more again and even daubed the burn on my forearm, then wrapped my hand in a clean dish towel, setting the empty bowl in the sink for the morning.

I poured boiling water over the second mixture and watched it cloud. A pleasant steam rose up from the rim of the cup, redolent with mint. I inhaled the vapor and took a cautious sip, expecting to taste bitterness, but not so much of it. I pulled a face and tried another slurp, then poured the rest down my open throat.

That night I dreamed about my sister, but in my imagination she was all mixed up with Tabitha Morgan, her long hair tucked under a silk bonnet, her hips swathed in pleats of calico. She was laughing and spinning, and when I tried to reach out and touch her, she danced away from my grasp. "Wait," I called, but she just spun faster and faster until the sprigs on her skirts turned into huge cabbage roses, and I woke to the cloying scent of their oils seeping under the crack in my window.

It was quite late. The sun was already up over the lilacs and headed toward the clouds. I sat up and unwound the dish towel from my hand. The green paste had hardened to a kind of glue, but when I rinsed it off in the bathroom sink, I found that the skin around my wound was puckered up as tight as a pair of lips for a kiss, and the place where the burn mark had been was pink and smooth once again. I flexed my hand and noted that the pain was gone as well. The cut would almost certainly leave a scar, but that didn't bother me in the least. I could just add it to the list of all my body's other indignities.

I walked into the kitchen, whistling. The doctor was already at the table, legs crossed, sipping a glass of orange juice and perusing the morning paper. "What's that in the sink?" he asked. He was either sneering or reacting to the lemon juice I'd mixed in with the orange juice—I couldn't tell which.

I hustled over to the sink and quickly swabbed the remaining paste out of the bowl. "Nothing. Just my snack from last night. Remember?"

Robert Morgan snorted. He was definitely sneering, I decided. "What in heaven's acres was it? Looks like something you would have fed August's beat-up horses. Don't tell me you're on some kind of crazy diet. Because I doubt that much you do in that department will ever help."

Anger crackled in my nostrils and ears like static. Inside my boots, I curled my toes, then did the same with my tongue. I would have liked nothing better than to tip the jug of juice over the doctor's head and watch it ooze down his collar, but with a man like Robert Morgan, you were better off keeping your elbows close to your sides, your head down, and your feelings to yourself.

"A diet?" I echoed. "No, no. Nothing like that. Of course you're right, Robert Morgan. I was just trying a recipe that didn't work out, that's all."

But he was uninterested in my explanation. Already, he was folding the paper back into thirds and shrugging on his coat, his mind racing ahead of him to the appointment book on his desk.

"It's going to be a hot one today, Truly," he crowed as he opened the back door. "Make sure you open all the windows."

I reached for the eggs. "Wait, don't you want your breakfast?"

"You have it. I'm not hungry." He swept across the porch, and I was alone once again save for the empty bowl in the sink and the odor of roses lingering like a sweet dare.

Chapter Eighteen

I consider myself guilty of plenty of things, but probably not the crimes you'd assume. I don't regret sending Robert Morgan to meet the Maker, for instance. I don't regret it a bit. After all, it was his original idea. As for the other two souls I've doctored, well, each case came with its own dark face for me to stare down.

Is what I've done right? Maybe. Some people in Aberdeen call it a mercy. Some mutter that it's the doing of witches and devils—the work of Tabitha Morgan and her infernal quilt all over again. And in a sense, they're correct. It is, after all, her recipes that I use, both for giving comfort and for darker purposes. But here's something I've never done—I've never made a decision for anyone one way or another. People come to me first and foremost, sometimes for healing, sometimes for more, but they are the ones who do the asking. Why don't I refuse? you might wonder. Why don't I just say, "No, I won't, end of story"?

Believe me, I think about it sometimes, but there is this to consider: There is the unrivaled power of death to even out the past. In particular, my past. I used to think I couldn't change my history, that the things that happened to me were as good as grooved in my bones, but each time I take a life, I find otherwise. I uncover another long-lost layer of my past, another strip of my soul.

Usually, it's no mystery why someone wants life to end. Sickness, for the most part. Sometimes debt, although I won't take those cases. It's not my business to judge, only to determine. But I can't discount the weight of the past on the present moment—it's nothing I can see, but always there all the same, like an invisible stone sinking a ship. And it's never the people I suspect of meddling with the past who are guilty of it, either. Friend or foe, anyone is capable of scuttling a few innocent details, omitting one or two facts, and changing a life forever. It's another thing entirely whether they choose to admit it.

Before I moved in with the doctor, I wouldn't have called myself vengeful, but the longer I was under his roof, the more I began to feel spite tugging on my sleeve like a fitful child. Mostly it was because of the absence of my sister, which lingered in the house like a rank odor we all tried to ignore. The doctor accomplished this by alternating vast periods of silence with harangues about my weight, my looks, my cooking, and my general existence.

"A big bird for a big woman," he snickered when I brought out the turkey I'd roasted for Thanksgiving. "Your sister always made Cornish hens, but I guess that would be nothing more than a light snack for the likes of you, Truly. Son"—he lifted up a piece of breast meat and turned to Bobbie—"pass your plate and prepare to be stuffed!" He chuckled a little at his seasonal joke, disregarding the tears hanging in the corners of Bobbie's eyes and completely overlooking the fact that Bobbie was still getting over the loss of his mother.

"Thanks," Bobbie mumbled, his voice as dry as the meat on his plate, and then proceeded to eat nothing, not even the pumpkin pie or the fudge I'd made special for the day.

After every maddening meal, after every one of the doctor's humiliating medical exams, I took the opportunity to retreat to the warmth of my bedroom and Tabitha's quilt, studying its strange botanical whorls and lines while I tried to pound the malice inside me back down to a manageable ball.

Thanks to Marcus, I had become familiar with the names of the herbs, but the overall design of the thing still puzzled me. The plants in the middle of the quilt were easy. Everything I expected to be there pretty much was. There was peppermint, and comfrey, sage, and lavender, borage, chamomile, and rosemary. Lined up in neat little rows, sewn demurely on neat white squares, they suggested a host of remedies. With Marcus's help, I had dried a measure of herbs in individual jars and stored them in the pantry next to the spices. During my quiet evenings, I went over the lists of plants and body parts I had made, trying to decode the quilt.

The stitched eye stood for vision, I figured, so the herbs underneath it must have been good for sight. I wrote down bilberries, chrysanthemum, honeysuckle, and horsetail. And sure enough, when I developed a sty on my left eyelid, a poultice of these plants soon took down the swelling. Encouraged by my success, I used the mixture I'd made for the cut on my own finger to soothe Bobbie's scraped knees, warning him not to tell his father. I hadn't yet gotten a chance to try any of the remedies underneath the quilt's bone, but I figured Tabitha had meant those plants to be used for fractures and breaks. Likewise, I was guessing that the heart stood for circulation and blood. The hand denoted skin to me, and the lips suggested eating and therefore the stomach. Every night before I went to sleep, I drank a cup of peppermint-chamomile tea, as the quilt suggested, and while my digestion was always just fine, I was sorry to find that the size of my appetite remained the same.

The only motif I couldn't figure out were the wings that fluttered along the edges of the quilt. Maybe they were just a decoration, I reasoned. Or maybe they meant nothing at all. The plants on the outskirts of the quilt certainly weren't as well behaved as the ones in the middle. Actually, they were more like weeds. They twisted and seethed, tangled their roots, seeds, and bulbs, and spread themselves into a snarl. Furthermore, not one of them could boast of anything but a bad reputation—like devil's trumpet, a white scoop of flower whose seeds could pickle a hippo. And there were hemlock leaves, and belladonna, the oblong shapes of oleander leaves, and raggedy nightshade. Marcus had refused to dry any of these plants for me.

"I don't know what you're doing with all this stuff," he said, dumping a long fistful of rosemary on the kitchen counter, "but there's no way I'm bringing you a heap of hemlock leaves. Between you and the doctor, I don't know, one of you just might take it in mind to kill the other one. That's how Socrates committed suicide, you know, after the Athenians put him on trial."

A fluttering started up at the base of my skull right then, and for a moment I thought I might be coming down with one of my migraines, but an image of the quilt's unkempt border swam into my mind's eye, along with the pale host of wings, and with it came a clarity of understanding so sharp, it was almost eye-splitting. I knew that hemlock was fatal from reading one of the herbal guides Marcus had brought me from the library, but it was also sometimes used as a sedative. And belladonna and digitalis, just as deadly as hemlock, were also sometimes used for medicine. The art, of course, lay in getting the dose right. Or maybe not.

"Oh," I breathed, and reached out for the edge of the counter. "Oh, my goodness."

Marcus was immediately by my side, tender concern unfurling across his face. "What is it?" he asked, and lightly put one of his hands on the small of my back.

I straightened up, surprised by how simultaneously familiar and strange his touch was. Part of me wanted him to put his hand on my back again, but another piece of me was scared I would bust. I smoothed my apron over my hips. “Nothing. Sorry. I’m fine. I just remembered something, that’s all.”

Marcus looked at me quizzically but then shoved his hat back on his head. He hesitated as if he wanted to say something more, but the moment passed, and he flung the door open to the wind and the garden. A faint, moldy smell of compost trickled under my nose. It was the same smell I always caught out at the graveyard—an odor of burial and decay, but also of rejuvenation and life. A subject Tabitha Morgan had apparently known plenty about and which I was determined to learn.

We in Aberdeen are pure creatures of habit. Saturdays, for instance, are for gardening committee meetings and library outings. Fridays are street-sweeping days. Wednesday is garbage collection, and on Sunday mornings, while the rest of Aberdeen was praying, or sleeping, or loading leather bags of golf clubs into the trunks of their cars, I got a chance to reunite with Amelia. Sunday mornings were her hours to clean Robert Morgan’s clinic, but we always took the opportunity to flap our gums a little afterward and catch up.

She brought her own equipment from the farm—buckets, mops, and dusters and bleach, vinegar, and baking soda. Amelia held no faith in modern concoctions for the household. She simply cleaned the way her mother had—with lemon oil, and salt, and old-fashioned elbow grease. Still, as a concession to the doctor's medical ways, she consented to swabbing the floors and surfaces of the examining room with the pine-scented disinfectant he ordered from one of his catalogs, her face screwed up in protest the whole time and both windows thrown open.

After work, she always sat in the kitchen with me to drink a cup of bitter coffee, the steam rolling over the rims of the mugs and misting up our eyes until everything looked better. It was a trick we'd learned at the farm—an optical illusion of necessity that was still serving us well. Amelia would give me the news, and the worst news of all came on the day she told me that she'd had Hitching Post put down.

I sloshed coffee on the table. I'd been living at the doctor's house for four years by then, and of course some things around town had changed, but not as much as you might imagine. The firehouse bells still clogged up in the summer. The newspaper still had the same masthead, and even the neighborhood dogs and cats rarely ventured away from their haunts. An image of Hitching Post's crooked forelegs and swayback rose up so powerfully in my mind that I could almost believe he was standing before me, runny nostrils and all. I had almost come to think of him as an extension of the barn, I realized. I took a slurp of coffee. "What was wrong with him?"

Amelia sighed. "He was starting to go lame, and we just couldn't take it anymore. Besides, hay isn't so cheap. And Ma's getting older, and I don't like the horses. Never have."

I bit my lip. "Still."

"It was quick, though. One bullet. And then we buried him."

I frowned. "Where?"

"Right next to Dad."

At that, my lips twitched. I pictured August in the underworld, frantically juggling chits and bets, inviting all comers. “He would have liked that.”

Amelia smiled, too. “I know.” She lapsed into silence, then swilled the rest of her coffee and slid her red bandanna off her hair. The doctor made her wear it. He was particular and didn’t like her to drop any hairs in his clinic. Sunday was Amelia’s longest day, but she got paid by the hour, so the additional labor meant extra cash. More than that, she enjoyed the extended period of quiet it granted her.

In spite of Miss Sparrow’s years of torturous dictations and elocution lessons, Amelia never did become a chatterbox. Far from it. In fact, as if to spite Miss Sparrow and prove herself the victor, Amelia generally spoke only under duress—sometimes even with me. That’s why cleaning suited her so well, for it allowed her the time and space to pay attention to life’s tiniest details, leaving nothing undusted, nothing unscrubbed. The thing about cleaning for Amelia was that it was a delicate business. People wanted their spaces made fresh and new, but they also didn't want anyone snooping around in their personal dirt, and that was the true genius of Amelia. She could give the illusion that absolutely nothing had been touched, nothing moved—that the sparkling light fixtures and gleaming tabletops simply happened by magical accident—even while she turned entire rooms upside down.

Precision was particularly important for the doctor. Once, Amelia moved a canister of cotton balls from the left to the right side of the counter in his examining room, and Robert Morgan met her at the clinic door the next Sunday, his jaw locked up tighter than Fort Knox. "Do you see the order in which these are arranged?" he asked, pointing to the glass containers of cotton balls, cotton swabs, tongue depressors, and individually packaged alcohol swabs. He spoke slowly and loudly, as if Amelia were stupid or from a foreign country, but she was used to that. It was the way most people spoke to her.

Amelia nodded and gave Robert Morgan the thumbs-up sign. "No problem," she croaked. "It won't happen again."

Her chapped voice surprised Robert

Morgan, but I knew her better than he did. For Amelia, words were something to use sparingly. They were like vinegar or bleach. A tiny amount could clean up almost anything, but dump out more than that, and you could have one ungodly mess on your hands.

After that incident, Amelia was more careful to measure the distance of the canisters from the counter's edge, to put the doctor's chair back in exactly the same spot, and to memorize the order of the books on the shelves before she restacked them. Amelia loved books, and other people's books offered a world of information above and beyond what was printed on their pages. I never would have guessed, for instance, that the ancient Reverend Pickerton and his wife were hiding a copy of the *Kama Sutra* under their bed or that the twin-setted Vi Vickers checked trashy science fiction novels out of the library. "They're for my son," she said, blushing, when Amelia ran her duster over the stack of them. "He just keeps them on my desk." But Amelia said nothing. What was it to her if Vi Vickers wanted to lose herself in Amazon space warriors?

Robert Morgan's shelves, however, harbored no such indiscretions. With the doctor, what you saw was what you got, and after Amelia perused the books once, she quickly grew tired of looking at cross-sectioned illustrations of internal organs. I've often thought that people would be better off if they left nature well alone, but I guess it's a matter of personal preference. Amelia, for example, used no cosmetics, dressed in a black skirt and white top every day, and hadn't even trimmed her hair in six years. Nevertheless, the skin on her cheeks was as taut and shiny as an apple, and her eyes were as clear as well water.

"What's your secret?" Vi always begged her, but Amelia just smiled and pressed her lips together. Vi wouldn't have liked the answer anyway, which was hard work and harder living. That and a general avoidance of mirrors.

The day she told me about Hitching Post, however, Amelia was rushing through her work. As she reached for the last book on the doctor's shelf, she leaned so far over the top of the stepladder that she fell off balance and dropped it. She watched it thud to the floor, facedown, and then saw a bundle of envelopes slide from its pages. She climbed down and retrieved them, turning them over one by one, an expression of alarm and surprise scribbled on her face. Suddenly, without any warning, the doctor's black shoes appeared in her peripheral vision.

"I don't pay you to snoop."

Amelia's cheeks burned. She tried to hide the wad of papers in her fist, then gave up and simply stood shaking. The doctor's nostrils flared—always a bad sign. "Now that I think about it, however, I'm really quite happy you found them. It's serendipitous, really. Because now you can get rid of them for me."

Amelia blanched. "Sir?"

"Isn't that what I pay you to do? Clear out my trash?"

Amelia bowed her head. She worked her mouth, forming words with difficulty. "But these—"

The air exploded as the doctor flung a crystal ashtray—a wedding gift—across the room. It didn't shatter, however. Merely cracked with an ugly fracture running down its underside like a scar. Without taking her eyes off the doctor, Amelia picked it up and replaced it on the desk. She was August's daughter. She didn't scare easily. She worked her gums for a minute, wetting her tongue, and then her voice rose up thick and determined, like a cloud of mosquitoes. "I want what you promised me. I've been waiting for four years, and now I want the papers to the farm. I know you have them in your desk. I seen them there."

The doctor waited a moment before responding, as if he were trying to decide between a display of righteous fury or icy disdain. In the end, he surprised Amelia. He smiled, flashing those long teeth of his like a bear that's set on winning you over before it digs into your hide. "Well, well, well," he droned, the tight set of his eyes a dead contrast to the honeyed lilt coming out of him. "I must say, this is a real surprise. I seem to have finally found myself a worthy adversary here in Aberdeen. And in quiet little Amelia Dyerson to boot. Maybe you have more of your father's genes in you than I previously thought."

At the mention of her father's name, Amelia cocked her chin and pointed it straight at the doctor, like a gun. Robert Morgan rubbed the back of his neck. "Fine.

You've got yourself a deal. But on one condition. I want you to burn those papers. While I watch. Only then will I sign the deed over to you."

At that moment, the buttery scent of apple pie wafted through the clinic's open window. Startled, Amelia looked through it to see me waving at her from the kitchen, a hot pie balanced on the sill. I remember I swept an arm through the air to tell her to hurry, to come on over. Amelia crooked a finger in the air back at me and, without my noticing, dropped the bundle of yellow paper at her feet, sweeping it together like yesterday's ghosts.

I've often considered what would have happened if Amelia had made a different decision that afternoon, but it's easy to solve the past in the present, and when you do, you sometimes forget to leave room for forgiveness. What kind of a mess would she have made if she had brought that bundle of paper inside and shared it over a piece of pie, I wonder, and what price would she have had to pay for it?

Glancing through the kitchen window, I didn't notice anything out of the ordinary. All I saw was Amelia cleaning up the way she always did—straightening out the books and streaking beeswax on the shelves while the doctor watched, his usual sour expression pickling his features. I watched her line the books back up in order, their spines all level, the tops of them brushed free of cobwebs, taking special care with the last book. She stepped off her ladder and surveyed her work, then swept a pile of rubbish into a brown grocery sack. The doctor followed her into the house, leaving the room empty, and soon I heard them conversing in the parlor and smelled the rich smoke of a fire being started.

"What are you doing in here?" I poked my head through the door. "Why are you making a fire so early? I've got pie."

Robert Morgan hastily threw a log onto the crackling pile of kindling, sending blue smoke curling up the chimney. When he turned to me, it was with the snarling, open-toothed determination of a hyena. "Did I ask for you?"

I took a small step back. "No, but—"

"Then leave before I make you."

I wrinkled my brow. Something was definitely wrong, but I couldn't put my finger on what. In the far corner of the room, Amelia was crouched at the doctor's feet like a much-maligned serf, silent as ever, watching the growing flames lick and swallow the log with a curious expression of grief washed over her face.

The doctor paced across the room and put his hand on the door. "Amelia will be out shortly. Right now she's busy tidying up a few of the household's loose ends. After all, isn't that what I pay her for? A clean slate." And with that, he slammed the door, leaving me alone with the nostalgic, hopeful scent of pie filling up the air around me.

Across town, Priscilla Sparrow was beginning to have trouble squeezing her foot into its spectator pump. Every morning she twisted and wriggled it, but to no avail. The shoe refused to accommodate the bunion on her left metatarsal, and she was given no choice but to don the pair of wide-toed black oxfords she'd purchased two days before the start of Aberdeen's new school year—her twenty-third in the classroom, but her first in ugly shoes. Her feet weren't the only things slipping. Some mornings she had trouble twirling the wiry shock of gray hairs into a respectable chignon. Some mornings the Satin Primrose lipstick looked a little garish on the thin set of her mouth; and some days she even needed to band a girdle around her little paunch of belly. Already, she'd twice replaced the tweed skirts in her closet with one size larger, but every year her body betrayed her and spread another inch. This month, she was following the cabbage diet, and in the depth of her bowels, she could feel a rebellion brewing. She belched discreetly, then blushed, even though she was alone.

Just as I was learning the ropes of loneliness, so was Priscilla Sparrow. At one time, in the early sixties, the little schoolhouse at the edge of town had boasted a full range of pupils, but these days the town offered only ten children to instruct. Now, after the third grade, the pupils were bussed to the middle school in Hansen, where they were able to socialize with children their own ages and take advantage of art classes and a physical education program. If Priscilla Sparrow was going to be honest with herself, she'd have to admit that her current students would also probably be in Hansen if it weren't for the intervention of the late great Dick Crane, who'd played poker with the superintendent of education. To thank Dick, Prissy had knitted him a particularly fine Shetland wool cardigan, but when she'd gone to drop it off at his house, Estelle, his wife, had answered the door with a sour look and raised eyebrows, and Priscilla never saw the sweater again.

She sighed and gave up her struggle with the spectator pump, kicking it under the bed and reaching for the hated black oxfords. She smoothed her hair along her temples and hooked her pearl earrings through her lobes. She'd bought them for herself as a present to mark her five-year teaching anniversary. She'd spied them in the window of the jewelry store in Hansen and had known immediately that they were just the kind of thing Dick would have picked out, had he been at liberty to do so. But, of course, he wasn't. Despite her best efforts, he'd gone home every evening to silver-framed wedding photographs, afghans draped over easy chairs, and a martini mixed by Estelle exactly the way he liked it.

In her darker moments, it pained Prissy

to have to admit that she had no idea how to blend a martini or any other cocktail, for that matter. She stuck mainly to sherry and a glass of port at Christmas. She cleared her throat and reached for the heavy telephone on her vanity, finally resigned to calling Dr. Morgan and doing something about her darned foot. Really, she thought, she ought to get one of those lighter touch-tone phones, but one hated to waste, and this phone still worked fine. Everyone has one lie they tell themselves, and that was Prissy's—that everything still worked fine, just fine. As fine as fine could be. Still, a visit to the young Dr. Morgan couldn't hurt, she reasoned. What could he possibly tell her that she didn't already know?

When Robert Morgan's patients came to the house, sometimes they'd step onto the porch if I was sitting out there and make a little conversation. Priscilla Sparrow, however, wasn't one of those people. The day of her appointment, I watched her mince up to the clinic door without even saying hello, her eyes as pinched as ever at their corners, and I immediately knew in my heart—time was not on her side.

Inside the office, she changed into the paper gown provided for her, remembering when Robert Morgan had been a chattering boy with gangly elbows. It must have been strange for her to see him attired like his father and running a medical office, but with the same chin and eyes he'd had as a child. There was a tentative knock on the door, and then Robert Morgan's gravelly voice asked if she was decent. Priscilla cleared her throat and twittered, "Yes. Of course. Yes."

She tugged the gown a little tighter around the back of her, feeling even more naked than she would have without it—a feeling I knew well. All around Prissy's shoulders, the stiff edges of the garment stuck out like wings, and whenever she moved, she crackled. She looked around the room, uneasy with the hard edges and metal. She was used to the knotty wood of the schoolroom and its heady smell of chalk dust, pencil grindings, and bananas. On the table, Priscilla slumped a little as Robert Morgan prepared a dizzying array of instruments with which to check her, none of which looked at all familiar. She felt her head swim and put a hand down to steady herself, and I recognized that feeling, too—when you realize that the future has gone on and happened without you.

Robert Morgan thumped her clavicle with his knuckles. "How long has it been since your last medical exam, Miss Sparrow?"

The inside of her chest rang and reverberated like a hollow urn. "Years."

"I couldn't find your records in our files." Robert Morgan put his stethoscope in his ears and averted his eyes while he slipped the disk between her wrinkled breasts.

"Oh, I used to go to a doctor in Albany, but it's so far. I thought I'd just come here. I'm only having a little bunion trouble, you know. I have to wear those ugly shoes." She tilted her chin toward the hated black oxfords squatting in the corner.

Robert Morgan turned his head and removed the stethoscope. "They don't look so bad."

"Oh, but they are. They really are." How could Prissy explain that the awful black shoes were insinuating themselves into her life with the brassy arrogance of crows? She opened her mouth to elucidate but saw him frowning while he ran his fingers over her spine, the oxfords already forgotten as he concentrated on something in her back.

"Does this hurt?" He pressed on one of her vertebrae, eliciting a small universe of pain.

"Oh!" A ball of fire rumbled down the tracks of her central nervous system. It was the same sensation she'd been having in her foot, only from the top down, as if by switching direction, the pain were trying to cheat her—and Priscilla Sparrow hated cheaters.

"Sorry." Robert Morgan pulled his fingers away and closed the edges of her gown back together again. He frowned some more while he made notes. "Do you ever have dizzy spells, or breathlessness?"

Well, come to think of it, lately she had. "I've been on a diet," she explained. "Cabbage."

Robert Morgan stared down the length of his nose at her. "That's not healthy."

"Neither is being fat, young man." Her

voice smacked like a ruler. By now, the unyielding corset of a schoolteacher's voice was easy enough for Prissy to slip into.

"I think you need to see a specialist."

"What? Why?"

"An oncologist. I can give you some names, but you'll have to travel. There isn't even one in Hansen."

Priscilla scowled. "An oncologist? But that's for cancer. I just have a little problem with my foot."

Robert Morgan shook his head. "I don't think so." He paused, giving the news time to sink in, then flipped open his prescription pad and wrote down a name and phone number. "I'd call this guy first. He's the best, and if you tell him you're a patient of mine, he'll fit you in right away." He tried to hand the paper to Prissy, but her fingers were stiff, and she dropped it. Undeterred, Robert Morgan bent over and retrieved it, making sure she held on to it this time. Every time he broke bad news to a patient, it was the same thing. They dropped the name of the referral or they lost it. Quite often, he had me call the person to make sure he or she followed up. Robert Morgan wouldn't have that problem with Priscilla Sparrow, though. She was a rule follower through and through, right down to her cancerous bones. Just the kind of patient he liked.

"If he absolutely can't fit you in, call me, and I'll give you the name of someone else," Robert Morgan said, and swept out of the room.

I watched Priscilla Sparrow emerge into the afternoon stunned, her face crumpled at its edges like a wad of wrapping paper waiting to be burned, and although it seemed impossible that the two of us would ever share anything in common, I somehow knew just how she felt.

Chapter Nineteen

Death is a kind of quilt in itself. We're all alive in this world together, and we're also all mortal, but when one person pulls his thread through to the other side, it can start a chain reaction you never in your wildest dreams saw coming. Maybe you'll be left with nothing more than an unholy knot to unpick. Maybe a new design. Sometimes a whole new perspective on yourself.

Marcus's refusal to bring me any of the herbs from the wild border of Tabitha's quilt began to sting in my craw. "Doesn't he trust me?" I fumed to myself as I sorted laundry or mixed a pot of mashed potatoes on the stove. "What does he think I'm going to do? Slip them in the doctor's dinner?" Although to be honest, the thought had occurred to me when I was watching my murder mystery shows on my little TV late at night, the rooms of the house an open conspiracy around me. At that time of night, plans just seem to get darker and rougher around their edges.

The puzzle of the deadly knots of plants on the quilt began to bother me more and more. I tossed and turned under them when I slept, and during the day, I had a hard time keeping my hands from going round and round in circles over their stems and leaves. It occurred to me that Marcus could probably take one look at the thing and figure it all out, but it seemed wrong somehow to share Tabitha's secrets with anyone else. All that winter, I fretted and schemed, and when spring burst, my curiosity was so great, it was all I could do to wait for Tabby's nasty weeds to hurry up and bloom so I could see if my suspicions were right.

I took a few samples of everything I found on the quilt: hemlock and oleander leaves, nightshade, daffodil bulbs, and foxglove. A little devil's trumpet and a single castor bean seed. Thorn apple. Once again, I waited for the household to sleep, and then I crept downstairs. The mixture, as I mashed it with a mortar and pestle, turned from a mossy green pulp to an almost black paste. I held up the bowl and took a cautious sniff, expecting foulness, but was pleasantly surprised by how sweet it smelled. So sweet, I thought, it might just do the trick.

All through the winter, I had pondered how to test Tabitha's quilt. All joking aside, I knew I couldn't disguise a mixture of fatal plants in the doctor's food because I wasn't sure what such a combination would do: sicken or kill. I thought about setting some out for birds or rabbits, but they would be hard to observe and follow, and we didn't have any pets. I thought about giving up on the idea, but the maze of vegetation on the quilt maddened me more and more, and then, after one particularly miserable night's sleep, I came up with a solution.

I slipped out the kitchen door now, a pair of rubber boots on my feet, the black coat I'd found in the doctor's attic thrown over my nightgown. There was a half-moon up and a few moth-eaten stars hanging in the sky, as if Aberdeen had gotten the left-overs from a long-dead vaudeville show, but they were enough for me to navigate by, and for that I was glad.

It took about five minutes for me to walk to Amanda Pickerton's house, and when I arrived, it took another moment for me to catch my breath outside her gate. All the Pickertons' lights were turned off, even the porch light, and I pictured Amanda and the reverend tucked upstairs in their antique bed, their pillows angled in the same direction, their blankets pulled up high over their bony hips. I wondered if Serena Jane's room was still covered in primroses, the vanity ruffled within an inch of its life, or if Amanda had converted it into a sewing room or an upstairs den, and how she could bear to go in it if she had.

The gate barely squeaked when I pushed it open, but the noise was enough to rouse the ancient Sentinel from his perch on the porch. If any creature had the secret of life, it was surely Sentinel, for he was nearly as old as I was. In the darkness, his eyes glittered like a younger cat's, and his outline was once again sleek and dangerous. In the daylight, he had a gray muzzle and bald patches on his rear, but his temperament was ever the same, even if his claws and vision were no longer as sharp. Moving slowly so as not to spook him, I edged closer to the Pickertons' front steps, pulling the jar of Tabby's mixture out of my coat pocket as I did so and unscrewing it stealthily.

To make the concoction more palatable, I'd added some leftover tuna and raw egg. Sentinel's whiskers twitched, and he let out a hoarse meow. "Good kitty," I whispered, trying to copy Amanda's singsong rhythm, and set the jar on the top step.

Sentinel paused, as if considering whether to attack my ankles or accept the offering, but finally chose the latter. He finished the pulp off in three bites but took an extra moment to lick the inside of the jar clean, his back arched with pleasure. He walked a tight circle around the jar, tail upright, as if it were a kill he'd made all on his own and dragged home. One circle, then two, and then, on the third circuit, he faltered, listing dramatically to the left, a look of cross bewilderment passing over his face. His legs buckled under him, and he meowed once—a punitive, accusing sound—before collapsing, paws twitching.

Watching him writhe on the porch was both worse and better than I had imagined it would be. It was horrifying, of course, to see his furry stomach lurching and heaving and his chin tucked into his chest, but after it was over, he was beautiful in the silvery light—an object of perfect stillness. I reached over him and plucked the jar back up, putting the cap back on, and tucked it in my pocket again. Then I glanced over my shoulder once or twice. I felt as if I ought to say a little prayer or something, but my mind was empty, and my feet were growing numb from squatting. I heaved myself back up to standing and rearranged my coat around me again, being careful not to touch Sentinel. I made sure to latch the gate and began to walk back to the doctor's house, keeping in the shadows as best I could, my head ducked low.

I felt little satisfaction as I skulked home in puddles of darkness. My suspicions about Tabitha's quilt had been correct, but now I wasn't sure what to do with that knowledge. I cupped my hand around the empty jar in my pocket and tried not to think about the foam that had collected around Sentinel's mouth.

From now on, I imagined, a part of me would always be keeping in the shadows.

Having been told she was going to die, Priscilla Sparrow wanted nothing more than to get it over with as soon as possible. In her opinion, her entire existence had been narrowed down to the fine art of waiting, and she was frankly a little tired of it. In her teaching career, she had waited for children to return from recess, then she had waited for retirement, and in love she had waited for Dick Crane to leave his wife and claim her, and now she was just waiting for an ending.

Except that it never arrived. Dr. Morgan's diagnosis of bone cancer didn't finish her off, and neither did anyone else's. For months she woke up skinnier, more wrinkled, pale around the chops, and mad as hell at the world. She visited a series of doctors. The last doctor she'd seen had actually shown up on her doorstep. He was young—barely out of medical school—and he'd sat in her little front room, a cup of tea trembling on his knee, shaking his head over and over again. "Are you sure the diagnosis was correct?" His voice rustled like a reed.

Priscilla shrugged. "Three different doctors said it was."

She knew how the young man felt, for at first she, too, had been dismayed and amazed by Robert Morgan's news. She had come home and peered at her face in the mirror, running her polished fingertips over and over the plain bones of her cheeks and nose. When she came back to the house to visit Robert Morgan, he scowled at her lab results again and thumped and massaged her, hitting all the sore spots. In the end, he was unable to give her any answers. She certainly wasn't in remission, but neither was the disease progressing, he said. It was merely idling in her body.

Prissy sat on the edge of the examining table, her bare feet dangling like a child's. "So what you're saying is that this could go on indefinitely?"

Robert Morgan peered over the tops of his bifocals at her. He had a nasty cold, and he curled his hand into a fist and coughed. For the first time, he felt like one of his own patients. His head ached, and his bones ached, and he just wanted to go lie down. "We're in uncharted waters here, but yes. It's highly unusual, however."

Prissy shifted her weight. Her sinuses throbbed. Her mouth was always dry. She'd entirely forgone makeup, spectator pumps, and her narrow tweed skirt. She looked Robert Morgan in the eye. "Can things change?"

He frowned. "What do you mean?"

"You're a doctor. You must know how to hurry things along."

Robert Morgan turned down the corners of his mouth. He thought about the mouth-watering temptation of holding the power of life in the pocket of his hand, but, in the end, rules were always rules for the doctor. The body had its own laws, and he was bound to follow them. He sighed. "I'm afraid I can't do that. It's totally against medical ethics. I could lose my license."

"I see." Priscilla hung her head.

"You shouldn't be thinking in those terms, anyway." Robert Morgan pulled his glasses off his nose. "You should be staying positive. Try some gentle exercise—swimming, or gardening. Get together with a reading group. Enjoy this time you've been given. Also, I can give you the number for hospice."

Priscilla blinked at him. The nearest swimming pool was ten miles away, and she didn't have a car. Her cottage had a garden the size of a postage stamp, and the only people she knew who would be interested in a reading group were the remaining friends of Estelle Crane. For the first time in her life, Prissy could see her days floating in front of her as empty and useless as children's party balloons. She didn't know whether to pop them or just let them rise and disappear.

Priscilla sucked in her gut. "Yes," she said. "You're absolutely right. Of course." She climbed off the table, got dressed, and went home, where she made herself a cup of tea, retrieved a forgotten deck of cards, and dealt herself a winning hand of solitaire. She reached for a tattered notepad and scratched another tick on it, adding the forbearance of sorrow to the paltry list of her life's accomplishments.

Everyone has a personal breaking point, and the day Priscilla Sparrow woke up to find her hair falling out in clumps was the day she decided she was fed up. Clusters of hair fanned over her pillow when she lifted up her head, and most of the rest of it came out in the shower, sliding off her scalp like rain off a roof before clogging up the drain.

Alarmed, Prissy turned off the water and stepped onto the bath mat, bald and wet. When she finally got up the courage to peek in the mirror, she was shocked. Without hair, she finally saw what all of us had been looking at for years and years. Her brows were spindly and uneven. Her mouth was a ragged gash. And her nose—her nose was a pointy beak. Had she always looked like this, Prissy wondered, or was it simply age playing a trick, enchanting her mirror to reflect all her fears and miseries?

She reached for a tube of lipstick, drew on a smile, then put her hands over her face and wept. Her bones throbbed. The corners of her eyes always felt as if they were filled with sand, and her heart buzzed and banged in her chest like a furious bee. *It's just a matter of time,* the doctors all said. *Time will take its toll.* It was their answer for everything, but they knew about as much as a barrel of chimpanzees. For Prissy, time and pain ruled like two competing queens, the map of her body rolled out between their feet.

She wound a chiffon scarf around her head, then removed it and tried her winter hat, but it was too warm for a felt cloche. She knotted on the scarf again and added a brooch—something Dick had given her. A mermaid in gold and pearls with two emerald eyes. She'd pinned it to her lapel the afternoon he'd presented it to her but then had taken it off almost immediately and never worn it again. It was too girlish, she told herself. And secretly, she was afraid Estelle had one exactly the same. It would have been like Dick to buy them identical baubles, then turn hangdog when he got found out. *Shoot,* he would have said, grinning. *It was too pretty to buy just one.*

Forgetting to lock her door, she rounded the corner, relieved to see the doctor's house looming at the far end of the street. She put her head down and made for it. Come hell or high water, she vowed, this time she wouldn't be leaving empty-handed.

When I answered the doctor's door, I could tell right away that Priscilla Sparrow barely recognized me. I was about three sizes bigger than I'd been on Bobbie's first day of school, for one thing, and no longer wearing men's clothes. My hair was bundled up in a bandanna, my feet were bare, and in my eyes there were pinpricks that Prissy had never noticed before. She put a self-conscious hand up to her turban and adjusted the mermaid pin. "Hello, dear," she said.

To be fair, I almost didn't recognize Priscilla Sparrow. Her voice was the only unadulterated thing about her. High and clear, it still rang with authority. She fixed me with her cloudy stare. "May I come in for a moment? I have something to discuss with you."

In the front parlor, Priscilla Sparrow perched on the spindled edge of the Victorian sofa and glanced around the room. Almost no one ever came into the main house, and I could tell Prissy was surprised by the austerity of it. Plain wooden planks shone under her feet. The duck-egg walls glowed, and bare windows let in the sunlight.

Prissy closed her eyes and took a deep breath. If she had been by herself, I thought, she might have been tempted to slip off her orthopedic shoes, stretch her legs on the sofa, and take a nap. Instead, she interlaced her knobby fingers, making a temple out of her hands for luck, knelt as best she could on the waxy floor, and started begging woman to woman.

It's strange to see what time does to your adversaries. Here I had the indomitable Miss Sparrow kneeling in front of me, but with a couple of teeth missing, yellow eyeballs, and a head as bald as a plucked goose. As she spoke, I remembered the day she'd confiscated my mother's cracked mirror and the sound it made hitting the metal trash can, the tinkling of the glass splintering. Even now, that was still the noise I imagined a heart made when it gave up on life. For a moment, I wished I had that mirror back so I could hold it up to Priscilla Sparrow's face and invite her to take a good long look. *See,* I would have said, *ugly fits into anybody's skin. Size doesn't have a damn thing to do with it.*

The truth of it is, though, size has plenty to do with forgiveness. Staring down at the measly-boned Priscilla Sparrow, I realized for the first time that maybe my enormity was an unintended gift. All that fat and muscle hanging off my frame—the very same flesh that Robert Morgan seemed so determined to chip and whittle away at—was like a suit of armor laid overtop my spirit. And so far, I'd taken all the misery thrown at me and absorbed it like salt sucking up water.

Without taking my eyes off Prissy, I leaned close to her. Gently, as if persuading a mean dog into a better temper, I took her clawed hands into my own. "I'll take care of it," I whispered, my voice as supple as the surface of Tabitha's quilt. "I promise. One way or another, I'll take care of it."

The doctor was not exactly congenial to seeing things in my fashion. I'd decided to try him first. "Absolutely not," he sputtered when I informed him about Priscilla Sparrow's visit. "I've told her I won't. It's completely unethical." He worked a bit of ham gristle out from between his teeth. It was after dinner. Bobbie was upstairs doing homework. For supper I'd made all the doctor's favorites—cola-glazed ham, two-fried potato hash, and sour patch tomato salad—but it wasn't helping. He was crabby, and dangerous, and not inclined to agree with me about anything, especially when it involved his work.

"But maybe it's more unethical to prolong her life." I slid a cup of overly bitter coffee across the table, trying to ignore the image of Sentinel's pinched gray muzzle going slack in the moonlight.

"It's murder."

"It's still an option."

"Which is murder."

"Or peace." I eyed the doctor. After putting up with his pronouncements and orders, it felt like liberation to voice an opinion of my own, even if he was shooting it down. I put my hands on my hips. "Listen, you may know a lot about how the human body hangs together, but you don't know doggone about the soul. People get tuckered out. They get tired of hanging around waiting when the finish line's in plain sight. You ought to know that better than anyone."

The doctor shut up and slurped at his coffee. His hair was beginning to thin out, and what was left of it stuck up in tufts off his head. For a moment, he looked just like

Bobbie. "It's illegal," he snapped, accusatory and mean, just like his old self. *But maybe he can't help it,* I thought. Maybe his cells were just programmed that way.

"Well now, that all depends."

"On what?" Robert Morgan was not a man who appreciated the easy morals of August Dyerson, but I was pleased to note that they were still alive and kicking in me—just like one of his hobbled old racehorses.

I raised my eyebrows. "On not getting caught."

I was preparing to make my grand exit, sweeping out of that kitchen with all the dignity of the Queen of Sheba, but the doctor was a man who'd never lost out on the last word, and he wasn't about to start now, even if it came at the cost of tarnishing his honor.

"Not so fast. Sit," he ordered. He kicked a chair out for me, then licked his lips and spoke with the sweet slowness of a man who had all the time in the world. "I didn't want to have to do this now," he said, running his hands through his hair, "but you're leaving me no choice." He looked back over at me. "Tell me, Truly, if it was you sitting on the other side of the fence, do you think you'd be making the same argument? Because what I'm about to say to you may change your mind." I hesitated, a bad feeling rising in my chest. "Now, do you have any idea of the name of what afflicts you?"

I refused the seat. When I'd decided to go to bat for Priscilla Sparrow, I hadn't counted on nitpicking my dimensions, but if the doctor wanted to go that route, I figured, it was one I could follow. "Well, I'm guessing the word *giant* is in the title somewhere," I said, "and if it isn't, I'm sure you'll petition to put it there."

Robert Morgan drummed his fingers on the tabletop, unperturbed. He appeared to debate something inside himself for a moment, then he nodded, satisfied, and continued speaking. "The precise term is *acromegaly*. You're a kind of giant, Truly. Do you know what that means?"

I sighed. How many times in my life, I wondered, was I going to have to have this conversation? I thought back all those years to my first day of school and Miss Sparrow's incredulous assessment of me. It made me feel as dull and heavy inside as a rusty old barrel. Maybe I would take that chair, after all. I sank into it before answering, "It means I'm bigger than average, Robert Morgan."

He shook his head. "No, it's more than that. How did my father explain it to you when you were a child? A little clock?"

"Yes. A clock."

"Well, that's not technically accurate. It's more like a stopwatch, or a kitchen timer. Most people's pituitary quits sending out hormone after puberty, but yours never has, probably due to some kind of tumor. Your timer is infinite. In other words, you've never stopped growing, and you probably never will."

I sat back in the chair, absorbing this new information, wishing I had some more coffee to go with it.

"There's more," the doctor continued. "I never told you before, but given our topic of conversation tonight, I believe now is the time. You need to know that there's a high probability that this condition will be terminal for you, Truly."

"What?" The word *terminal* flapped in my throat like a duck trapped in lake ice. I tried to take a breath and found I couldn't.

The doctor lowered his gaze, slipping into professional mode. “Your heart won’t be able to keep up with your growth. Your organs will become enlarged and stressed. Inevitably, your vital systems will start to fail.”

I shifted on my chair, aware for the first time of precisely how much the wood was bending and bowing under me. More than last week? I wondered. Much more than a month ago? I put a hand on my chest. “Oh. Oh my.”

Robert Morgan folded his hands. “I realize this must be a shock.”

He had no idea. My mind swirled with questions. How big would I get? How long would it take? How would I know if my organs were failing? But there were a few questions that were larger than any of the others and one in particular that couldn’t be ignored. “How could you keep this a secret all these years?” I finally blurted.

Robert Morgan sipped his muddy coffee and considered. “I was always going to tell you. You have a right to know, of course.” He hesitated a moment, then cleared his throat roughly. “I was waiting for the right time. A better time.”

I slammed my hands on the table. "Better than what?"

To give him credit, the doctor didn't even flinch. "Better than now," he replied, calm as cabbage. He ran his fingers through his hair and elaborated. "Look, Truly, it's always tricky giving someone bad news, and it's even more so when that person is a member of your household. I suppose I didn't like the idea of rocking our little boat. Not while you were still healthy, and not after everything Serena Jane put us through."

"But what if something had happened to me in the meantime? What if, what if—" *What if I died?* I couldn't say it.

Robert Morgan held up his empty palms as if he were offering all the blame back up to the universe. "Then it wouldn't matter that I'd never told you, would it?" That sounded about right, I thought. Plus, it gave him a few hidden benefits. If I didn't know about my condition, Robert Morgan would be able to watch me like a lion getting ready for a kill, tail twitching, eyes all narrow and tight. He would be able to keep measuring every inch of me right up until the end, notating all the changes, and when

I was gone he would be able to write all those numbers up in a nice, fat medical article with his name signed in red.

"What about treatment?" I finally asked. "Can't you do anything?"

The doctor shook his head slowly, almost a little sadly, it seemed. "Under ordinary circumstances, yes, but in your case, our options are limited. Surgery, I am almost certain, would be futile and far too dangerous. Radiation has its own drawbacks, which leaves only medication. I'd like to start you on a series of pills and injections right away."

"And what if I say no?"

The doctor shrugged. "Then you'll die sooner rather than later."

I pushed my chair back from the table, my stomach queasy. Was that a symptom? I wondered. The beginning of the end? And what about all my headaches? But when it came down to it, none of it mattered, I decided. All I wanted was to get away from the doctor's house. I longed to go back to the farm and lie in my old room, the itchy weft of a horse blanket scratching my hips and knees. I wanted never to see the doctor again.

Just then, Bobbie came stumbling into the kitchen, skinny arms pocked with insect bites, his tongue poking in between his teeth. He had just crossed the brink between boyhood and adolescence but hadn't entirely left youth behind. "Aunt Truly?" He blinked, confused to see that the dishes hadn't even been cleared yet. "I have a question about my history homework."

My head snapped to attention. *Bobbie*. Towheaded, berry-lipped, prettier than any of Aberdeen's girls. But lonely and still carrying puddles of sadness in the depths of his eyes. A boy so different from his father, he might very well have been a gift from the angels. If for some reason I weren't here, what would happen to him? Who would he talk to when he came dragging his heels home from school, his lip bust open again by the bullies at school? Who would fix him dinner, and fold his socks, and make sure he brushed his teeth?

"Aunt *Truly*," Bobbie whined, "are you listening?"

I put my hand on my heart. In spite of what the doctor had just told me, it was throbbing just like always, regular and true under my breastbone. Maybe it was large, I thought—bigger than average—but that just meant it matched the rest of me. It was as tough and stringy as that twice-boiled ham hock still lying on the bottom of the pot on the stove. I reached up to my face and felt a streak of salty tear. *Turns out there's some grit in me yet,* I thought, then I looked across the table at Robert Morgan. Evening had fully fallen, and shadows were descending on us like cobwebs. If we didn't move soon, they'd eat us alive, and one thing I knew for sure was that I wasn't going to let it happen to me. I stood up. For that night, at least, I wasn't going anywhere.

"Of course I'm listening," I said, beginning to collect the dishes. "I'll be with you in a single minute. Your father and I were just talking, but we're finished now. In fact, I just realized that we never even got around to dessert. Who wants peach cobbler?"

Bobbie smacked his lips, and the doctor looked up and blinked, mild and surprised as a child. "Why, thank you. That would be kind."

I snorted. "That's not kindness talking,

mister. Just hunger." I turned my back on him and flipped on the light. *Facts are facts,* I thought. None of us were built to last, but that didn't mean we could ignore the here and now. After all, I had a stomach, and it had a mind of its own, and right then it was telling me to get up, stop feeling sorry for myself, and get to the work the good Lord had given me.

Chapter Twenty

Sometimes I think we'd all be better off if we took a cue from horses and treated our fellow humans accordingly. When a horse goes and breaks its neck, you don't sit around debating the merits of keeping it alive. You go and get your shotgun, and you shoot it right between the eyes, hard. Anything else would be cruel. But when a man teeters on the brink, folks are apt to start philosophizing. They start asking questions that don't have any answers, like What's a life for? And what comes afterward? And how many of our actions are we supposed to answer for, anyway? Horses don't have to live up to any of this, and if you ask me, they're the luckier for it—free in their hearts and pure in the moment. Even August's worst horse, the cockeyed Hitching Post, had a touch of the noble in his crooked old bones.

In the end, though, a man is different from a horse. You can't get around it. For one thing, men talk back at you. They blather a lifetime of opinions. And they're fickle, for another, always changing their mouths to change their minds. You can pretty much always guess what a horse is going to do, but don't ever gamble on a man. There's just no telling. August found that out the hard way during his life over and over again, and I found it out, too, when I decided to help Priscilla Sparrow die. I had watched Sentinel. I thought I understood what would come to pass, but the universe always holds a few tricks up its sleeve, even for a veteran card turner like me who's used to getting the cruddy hand. I guess it's the world's way of making sure we never get so comfortable in our skins that we quit asking ourselves the hard questions. At least that's how I explain things to myself.

When someone gives you bad news about the future, you basically have two choices in the matter. The first is to stew yourself a big pot of worry and despair, and the second is denial. In my experience, the first option just leads to bellyache. So, in order to take my own mind off my personal demise, I started focusing on Prissy's instead.

After giving me the bad news, the doctor immediately started me on a new medical regimen, which involved swallowing fistfuls of pills and being stuck like a pincushion, as well as the taking of even more vials of blood and endless examinations. By the third week, I was starting to feel a little like a laying hen getting groomed for a new henhouse, but whenever I started to think that way, I just pictured Bobbie's wan face moping over my grave, and remembered Priscilla's situation, and it made it easy to choke down the next handful of bitter capsules.

Much as I hated my latest routine, even

I couldn't deny how much my body had changed in recent months. My words were coming slower and slower now, as if my tongue were growing—which, the doctor assured me, it was—and the gaps between my teeth had never been larger. Also, I sweated all the time, even if it was chilly, and my skin always had a fine sheen of oil slicking it.

"Now that we have a better idea what we're dealing with, the medication will start to ease those symptoms," the doctor claimed, but he wasn't the one enduring them. At night, when Bobbie and Robert Morgan were sleeping, I tiptoed down to the kitchen and cooked up a few of Tabby's remedies. For the nausea the pills brought on, I boiled more peppermint and chamomile tea. For the eczema that broke out on the tops of my feet, I made a paste of calendula and elderberries and mixed it with soft beeswax; and for my headaches, I tried dried feverfew. After only a few days of my home remedies, the doctor squinted at the clean skin on my bare toes and beamed.

"I see the eczema is clearing up. Soon you'll start to see results in other areas as well."

I examined my feet, certain that it was Tabitha's beeswax balm that was making them better. "I wonder what your great-great-grandmother would have prescribed?" I asked, flexing my arches.

The doctor snorted and clicked on a pen flashlight. "Eye of newt, probably. With a side of spiders. But I guess we'll never know now that all her so-called spells have been lost. Turn your head this way." He pointed the beam of light into my eye.

I blinked, then forced myself to keep my eyelid open. "Didn't she come from a whole line of witches?"

The doctor moved the light into my other eye, then clicked the button again, satisfied. Spots swam before my eyes. "That's what they say. Apparently one of her ancestors was burned at the stake in Massachusetts. But it's all hogwash."

"What, the burning?"

Robert Morgan frowned. "No, that probably really happened. But the rest of it is nonsense. For all we know, she could have just been making moonshine with her brother until my great-great-grandfather made her stop."

"Hmm." I crossed my ankles.

"You sound skeptical. Don't tell me you believe in the poppycock of an old woman. Trust me, Truly. There is no shadow book, and I should know." A blush swept across his face, and he scribbled something very fast on his clipboard. "Okay, okay," he said, scowling, when he saw that I was still staring at him. "I might have searched for it once or twice when I was young. Purely out of scientific curiosity."

I tried to keep a straight face. "Of course." I was remembering a time shortly after my arrival, when I'd found him searching through the drawers of the little chest in the parlor and feeling the tiles around the fireplace. "Nothing," he'd snapped when I'd asked him what he was doing. "Just checking the mortar, which is a job I should leave up to you, really."

He ripped yet another prescription off his pad for me now. "This should help with your arthritis. You mentioned that the joints of your fingers are growing stiffer. I'll fill it, and get it to you by the end of the week."

Already, my mind was whirling through the lexicon of Tabby's quilt. What cures were embroidered under the stitched bone? I tried to think. Horsetail, I thought I remembered. And arnica. I waited while the doctor stepped out of the room so I could retreat behind the screen in the corner and change into my baggy dress.

"What's for dinner?" the doctor called through the doorway of his office just as I was about to leave. For such a thin man, he had an unaccountable appetite. Not that it couldn't maybe be dampened down a notch with some of the herbs from Tabitha's quilt, I suddenly thought—herbs that could bring either suffering or salvation or maybe just common misery.

"Eye of newt," I called back, "with a side of spiders." And I bustled off to see about ruining his supper, not to mention his stomach, with some lily-of-the-valley leaves.

Here's what I know about small towns: People in them are either all-forgiving or intolerant as mules, and the way they choose very often comes down to the issue of what you're willing to sacrifice. I think Tabitha Morgan understood this, and I think that's why she married the first Robert Morgan and sewed her secrets into a quilt. After all, you don't carry a burned ancestor around in your lineage without a certain amount of anxiety about future recurrences. No matter how friendly the people of Aberdeen were to her, no matter how grateful for healing their sick children, she still must have sensed an undercurrent of danger best remedied by the twin conventions of marriage and motherhood. After all, spinsters have always been a social problem all up and down history, and spinsters with spells are even more unappealing.

I have it easy in some ways. No one's ever really expected much of anything out of me—certainly not snagging a husband or children of my own. My size makes me speak slowly and move slowly, and it's also paradoxically enabled me to slip through cracks no one in Aberdeen would ever think possible. Like testing out Tabitha's mixtures. Or killing off Prissy Sparrow right under Robert Morgan's pointy nose.

Based on what the doctor had told me about my own condition, I thought the chances were pretty good that I might one day require the same grace I was about to extend to Prissy. It gave me comfort to know that if Robert Morgan's medicines didn't work, and if I couldn't find cures in the quilt, I still would have a more comfortable option than the smoking end of a pistol or the long drop of the train trestle outside of town. But the real reason I took so much time poring over the scattered wings and vines of the quilt almost pains me to admit now. Much as I would like to think so, my intentions weren't totally altruistic. In fact, they were the absolute opposite. They arose from pure, unadulterated revenge.

I knew Priscilla Sparrow was sick and aging, and I knew she'd gotten down on her knees in front of me to beg, but I can't lie. There was a tiny part of me that thrilled to see those things. It was as if the child inside of me were standing with arms akimbo, bottom lip stuck out, sulking. I was glad that the woman who'd first labeled me a giant, and had stolen the one thing left belonging to my mother, and had never given me a drop of praise, was ill. I was happy to watch her die heartbroken and in solitude. In fact, I was happy to see that even dying wasn't working out for Miss Sparrow. *Finally,* I thought, *she's getting a taste of what it's like to have your body betray you.*

Well, that lasted all of about a week. The problem was that I couldn't reconcile the ferocious Miss Sparrow of the past with the turbaned lady propped on her bony knees in front of me. If I were better at holding on to a grudge, I'm sure I could have managed to pin down her ghost, but, as it tends to do, the present won out, and I let my school memories dissolve like tarnish in a vinegar bath. *Release,* the wings on the quilt seemed to urge, the edges of them so faint that they shifted when I tried to trace them. *Release*. And so, on a Saturday in early summer, I found myself scouring roadsides, empty fields, fence lines, and even the weedy thickets of the town green. Any neglected spot where deadly plants might happen to grow, all the way out to the fence of the cemetery.

It was the kind of day that asked you to take off your shoes and go creek walking or wriggle your toes in the grass, not a day for collecting the ingredients like these. I had made a list. Oleander and nightshade. Foxglove, and thorn apple, and devil's trumpet. Nettles for sting and bite. All the herbs that Marcus had warned me against. All the ones I'd used on Sentinel—and more. That night, it took me four hours to cook them into a kind of sludge. I made some of my own improvements, adding peppermint to ease the bitterness, and chamomile to make the drink gentle, and then some sugar to make what I was about to do go down a little sweeter. I let the mixture cool and then strained the liquid into three small jars, capping them tight and setting them on the table. How much would it take to do Prissy in? I wondered. A spoonful? An entire cup? The whole jar? When it came to questions of dosage, I was beginning to realize, Tabitha's quilt was more a blueprint than a handbook. It didn't have all the answers.

In the morning, I woke early and made sure Bobbie and the doctor were still sleeping before I stole back down to the kitchen and fetched a basket from the pantry. I wrapped one of the jars in a clean tea towel and laid it inside the basket, then I sat down and wrote a quick note. *This is what you've been waiting for,* I wrote. *Drink it all at once. Don't hesitate. God bless.* I shoved the note into an envelope and tied it to the basket handle with red ribbon. There were two jars left. I put them in the pantry, where the liquid shimmered and glowed with an unsettling light. Two jars left for me just in case the doctor's worst-case scenario came true. Or maybe not just in case. Maybe for when it did.

Priscilla's newspaper—folded into thirds like the doctor's—was sitting on her stoop when I arrived, along with a bottle of milk. I glanced up and down the sidewalk, but all I could see were ticking sprinklers, her neighbor's newspaper stuck in his hedge, and a calico cat. I nudged the basket up against her door, then turned and walked away.

On the way back to the doctor's, I imagined Prissy tearing open the envelope, reading my note, and then tossing it away. Then I pictured her uncapping the jar and inhaling the grassy concoction before leaning her head back and pouring it straight down her gullet. Summer would fizz along the back of her tongue, I hoped—fresh hay, and the nip of lemonade, and the smoky blare of fireworks. A time when everything in the world was youthful and plump and full of lazy grace. Maybe the faces of her students—every one of them, right from the beginning—would swirl before her eyes, rising up to meet her. I like to think so. I like to think I was even marching at the front of them, leading the show, my stocky legs scissoring, my hair flying, my hands clapping out the joyous overdue music of the seraphs.

Chapter Twenty-one

After Prissy's death, I fell into a kind of limbo where it seemed time went on without me, like a river bending its way around a mountain. For one thing, I stopped growing. I don't know if it was the doctor's pills or maybe the cures from the quilt, but something halted my increases so that for the first time in my existence, I knew the suffocating equilibrium of absolute stillness. A series of winters came and went in Aberdeen, snows piling deep and then melting away again, the lilac hedges on the side of the house creeping higher and higher until Marcus arrived to hack them back, but through it all, I was just a bored observer, my viewpoint perfectly fixed, the world around me so distant and small, I felt as if I were looking through the wrong end of a telescope all the time.

"What's the matter with you?" Marcus asked as I was hanging out the washing one afternoon. We had all the modern conveniences, but I loved the way the sunshine made the sheets smell, so I used the chance of good weather to air the household linens. I couldn't remember the last time I'd done it.

"What do you mean?" I mumbled, my mouth full of pegs.

Marcus reached up gently and removed them, then held his hand open so I could pluck them from his palm, one by one. "This is the first time I've seen you outside in weeks this year. You mope around the kitchen all day, but you barely cook anything anymore. You've gotten pasty as a ghost. You're avoiding Amelia's and my company, and Bobbie says you can go whole days without even speaking. I think he misses you."

I missed him, too. A full-blown adolescent now, he was like a leaky bucket getting emptier by the day, the soul dribbling out of him in a steady stream. Over the past few years, his voice had cracked and deepened, and he had sprouted wisps of hair under his arms and in his groin, but I was pretty sure the normal path of his development had ended there.

The truth was, Bobbie was more like a teenage girl than a teenage boy, and I wasn't sure what to do about it. He spent hours in the bathroom tweezing and grooming, relishing the sting of each and every pluck, and I knew he kept a stash of stolen makeup hidden under a loose floorboard in his room. On rainy afternoons, when his father had appointments in the clinic, Bobbie would sweep an arc of Tangerine Dream over his bottom lip before anointing his eyelids with the glittery mystery of Midnight Blue. Holding a mirror so close to his face that his breath fogged the glass, he would watch as his real self emerged—the willowy one with sooty eyelashes. The one whose hips swung like a delicate bell. The one he kept trapped in a fairy-tale tower, awaiting a handsome prince.

"Am I as glamorous as Princess Bugaboo?" he'd ask, peeking his head around my door and fluttering his eyelashes with the efficiency of a harem vixen. The first time I caught him painted up, I have to confess, I was just the tiniest bit revolted. Not shocked. Not outraged or even embarrassed, just a little repulsed—the way I would have been if I'd come across weevils frolicking in the flour bin.

"What have you got on your gob?" I cried, my reflection rearing up behind his in the bathroom mirror like a mountain hogging the sky. My own hair was threaded with gray, I saw, and there was no definition left in my face anymore. My cheeks melted into my neck, which rolled and spilled onto the butts of my shoulders, which rounded into my arms and wrists. My breath scuttled around inside me like a ragged animal trapped in a cage.

Bobbie cringed. "Don't be mad, Aunt Truly. Please. I think I'm *supposed* to look like this."

I was about to make him wash it off, but I looked again and saw that he was right. He did look better—more alive. I reached out and cupped his chin. "It's okay," I said, gazing into his adorned eyes. "Let's just keep this quiet, though. I don't think your dad needs to know. It'll be our little secret."

And it was, until Robert Morgan came stomping in from work early one afternoon and ruined everything. Panicked, Bobbie tried to smudge the blush off his cheeks, but when he descended the front steps, he saw his father gaping at him.

"What the hell is on your face?" Robert Morgan demanded, and Bobbie, with a quick wit I didn't know he possessed, told him it was pink highlighter.

"I fell asleep on my books and smeared ink on my face," he said, which made no sense but seemed to satisfy his father.

"Go and wash it off," Robert Morgan ordered, and then added, "And why don't you use blue ink, like a normal boy?"

"Hinkleman's was out of blue," Bobbie mumbled, slinking back upstairs, sweat slicking him like spring rain. He stepped into the bathroom and washed his face, then picked up one of the rough towels, rubbing his eyelids and lips raw, rubbing that side of him out of existence.

I know how that feels, I wanted to tell him, but lately if I tried to talk to him, tapping on his door gently or luring him into the kitchen with cookies, he always rebuffed me, saying he had too much homework or that he just wasn't in the mood.

"It's not like you're my *mom*," he sneered once, grabbing a fistful of the fudge I'd set out on the kitchen table. I sucked in my breath as if I'd been slapped.

"I'm the closest thing you've got left," I snapped, and then it was Bobbie's turn to look stunned. "Wait, I'm sorry," I called after him as he stormed out of the room. I'd never before spoken harshly to him, but it was too late. The damage was done. After that, he grew even more distant and sulky, avoiding eye contact with me at dinner, giving one-word answers to his father's questions about his day.

"What's going on with him?" Robert Morgan wanted to know. "Does he talk to you? Is he on drugs?" His face clouded.

I looked up, startled. Was Bobbie? I didn't think so—at least not on a regular basis. But what could I tell Robert Morgan about Bobbie's particular brand of heartache? That his son was more comfortable in lipstick than jeans? That he wasn't growing out of his pretty stage? And why should I have to say anything at all, I wondered, when the truth was right in front of all our eyes?

Marcus saw it, as he saw all facts. "The boy's just different," he said, shrugging, when I tracked him down by the lilacs to ask him his opinion. "It's hard in a town like this, the size of a cricket wing. Anything the least bit out of the ordinary seems about five times worse than it really is."

Amen to that, I thought.

He squinted. "You know, in Vietnam, they had these bars in the cities, where the boys dressed up like girls and danced and sang and everything." I tried to picture Marcus in a place like that, his fist unscarred and curled around a dirty bottle of whiskey, but I couldn't. His eyes were too peaceful these days, and the strongest thing he ever touched was hot tea. He shrugged. "After a while, the fellas kind of forgot who was who and just enjoyed the show."

I twirled a leaf. "So what are you suggesting?"

Marcus smiled. "Enjoy the show, Truly. Don't try to direct it." His hand brushed mine, and I blushed and jerked backward a few inches. He ignored my reaction, his gaze focused on the middle distance. "Say, what would you think about putting in a proper garden out here? I've been studying some old designs from the nineteenth century that would really complement the house. You and the doctor could have your own vegetables."

I looked around at the stretch of lawn, hedges, and the borders of perennials. As long as I could remember, these things had always been the same. Every spring, daffodils and irises shot up in alternating bands, and every summer, primroses lazed along the back fence.

"I don't know," I said. "The doctor won't even let me change my brand of shoe polish. And these were all his mother's plants."

Marcus's face darkened. "I suppose you're right. It's just that, well, damn it, I really want to do a little something more than clip other people's boxwoods."

Suddenly, I could see how important building a garden was to him, how maybe he actually wanted to put down some roots rather than just dig at them. I wondered if he ever got frustrated knowing all the fancy Latin names for the bushes around him, not to mention the complicated biology of photosynthesis, but in the end being just a kind of janitor for other people's yards. "Why don't you plant yourself a garden at the cemetery?" I suggested. "There's acres of space out that way."

Marcus shook his head. "Municipal land. It's not allowed. Besides"—he cast an eye across the grass, avoiding my gaze—"I also sort of wanted to do it for you."

I looked down at my hands—swollen, mottled, the fingers clumped like sausages. Hands no man in his right mind, even Marcus, could ever love. "Thanks," I choked, "but you're probably better off trying someone else's yard." I sidled another few inches away. It was almost noon. Time to see the doctor for another injection. Two sets of pills and one needle a day were apparently all that was keeping me from floating away like a hot-air balloon. "I have to get back inside now. The doctor needs to see me for something."

Marcus looked as though he wanted to say something else, to add a thought, but I didn't give him the chance. Frankly, I didn't want to hear it. At that precise moment, I didn't think I had any more room inside me for the weight of anyone else's secrets.

❧

During Bobbie's last year of high school, he finally made a friend. Salvatore was a year or two older than Bobbie but was struggling to graduate. He lived in Hansen but started coming home with Bobbie in the afternoons, and where Bobbie was fair and flighty, Salvatore was all lean muscle and bulk, sleek as a bull and about as proud. Right away, I didn't like him.

"He refused to shake hands when he met me. He doesn't eat any of the food I fix for you boys, and his eyes are shifty," I complained to Bobbie. "He looks nervous all the time, like he's just stolen something, or he's thinking about it."

Bobbie sneered. "Salvatore's never stolen anything in his life. You just don't like him because you know how much *I* like him."

I wanted to argue with Bobbie, but he had a point. You couldn't watch them together and not see it. When they sat at the table, their feet always got to touching underneath it, and when Salvatore walked through the back door to go home, it was with Bobbie's hand nestled in the small of his back.

"What are you going to do if your father sees?" I asked Bobbie, and he frowned.

"He won't."

"But what if he does?"

The attic fixed all that. During a freak autumn hailstorm, Bobbie and Salvatore went looking for a place to smoke a joint. Bobbie's room was out. I was barricaded in my room down the hall, watching TV, and he didn't want to risk it. The rest of the house was out for obvious reasons, and Bobbie was just about to suggest they give it up when Salvatore asked, "Don't you, like, have an attic in this place, man?"

When he and Bobbie emerged into the peaked room, he lit the joint, sucked in a plume of sweet smoke, and surveyed the jumble of wooden steamer trunks, pyramids of boxes, garbage sacks, and a pile of what looked to be gardening implements. "Very cool," he declared. "I bet some of this shit is valuable, man. You should try to sell it."

But Bobbie had no interest in making a profit. Instead, he was concentrating on the lace edge of a parasol peeking from underneath a roll of carpet. He took the joint from his friend's hands and lifted it to his lips, inhaling with a glee that far exceeded the thrill of pot. He picked up the parasol and spun it over his head.

"Beautiful," Salvatore said grinning. Then he leaned forward and kissed Bobbie. Shocked, Bobbie dropped the parasol, then quickly leaned in for another kiss, his mouth broken open like an egg, everything inside him oozing out. Next to him, the smoke rose and broke apart, turning to wisps that were fragile as cobwebs.

After that, every afternoon I heard Bobbie and Salvatore sneaking up to the attic, where they would lose themselves in a world of chiffon and satin, velvet, and fur. Tucked away in trunk after trunk, folded into frail squares of tissue paper, and buried under camphor were flounced petticoats and plunging tea gowns, plumed satin hats, and corsets with ribbons so slippery, they kissed Bobbie's skin like a mermaid's scales.

Occasionally, Bobbie unfolded a soldier's greatcoat, triumphant with military braid, or one of his great-grandfather's shooting jackets, but these he merely set aside, dropping them as if they were yesterday's newspapers. Bustles and ruffles were what he was after. Slips and stockings. Garments that flirted and flipped when he moved. Clothes that unmade the man.

By the time winter came, his fingers had become adept at handling the tiny eyelet hooks of petticoats, the minuscule buttons of tea gloves, and he knew the difference between organza and tulle, sateen and watered silk. He learned how to sit wearing a bustle, how to bend over and tip a silver teapot while encased in whalebone. He learned that women's clothes, far from being frivolous confections for the male eye, were actually work to wear.

It wasn't hard to see. The evidence was written all over him. I watched as he began moving in a new way, conscious of his hips and the backs of his knees as he poured himself coffee in the morning, so careful of his shoulders as he carried the cup across the room. Something in the way he tilted his chin before drinking reminded me of Serena Jane, and I wondered if things would have been different if Bobbie really had been born a girl. Maybe Robert

Morgan would have been nicer to him. Maybe his standards would have been lower for a female child. But things were what they were. Any way I looked at it, there was no getting around the problem of the annoying truth Bobbie carried between his thighs—the ugly, unwanted root that kept him planted in Aberdeen and which I knew would only reseed and replicate if he didn't do something about it.

Chapter Twenty-two

Winter in Aberdeen is a terrible season. Stinging. Biting. So cold, it stuns the truth right out of people's veins. The winter Bobbie finally left his father's house was worse than most. The ground was frosted up so hard, it rang like stone, and everybody in Aberdeen pulled in deep and close. No one went out, and if they did, no one spoke in passing. No one lingered over the counter in Hinkleman's—no one even waved across the street from the safety of windows. Up and down Conifer Street, all you could see were drawn sets of drapes and chimneys puffing like steam engines.

In the very worst of the cold, Marcus chose to argue his case with Robert Morgan about planting his vegetable garden in the spring. Robert Morgan received him, as always, in the kitchen, while I brewed up coffee and tried to hide how pleased I was by Marcus's visit. It had been a long few months, and even Amelia hadn't made it out from the farm for weeks. Anyone's company was welcome. I peered over Marcus's shoulder as he unrolled the set of plans he'd drawn. "Nothing too delicate, like lettuce, and nothing too exotic, either," he was saying. "But some strawberries might be a nice touch. Or how about some Japanese cucumbers?"

Robert Morgan accepted the cup of coffee I handed him and shook his head. "Vegetables attract pests. They're unsightly. And anyway, the last thing Truly needs is any more food around her. She's already plump as a watermelon. Right?" He winked at Marcus, and I blushed. Marcus looked away, embarrassed, but the doctor continued, oblivious, then asked the same question I had. "If you want to grow a garden, why don't you just do it out at the cemetery?"

Marcus frowned. "Municipal land. It's not allowed."

Robert Morgan rubbed his spindly hands together. "Well, Marcus, I don't know what to tell you. I'm happy with the work you do on the flower beds, but I'm not ready for any changes at the present moment. Maybe one day you'll find a little plot of your own, but until then"—he clapped Marcus on the back—"I guess you're just stuck doing my bidding." He stretched his lips back over his teeth, his version of smiling.

Marcus was quiet as a church mouse. If you didn't know him well, you might think the insult had gone over his head, but I could see from the way he twisted his scroll of plans back up that he was angry. I opened my mouth to try to defend him, but Marcus shot me a warning glance and shook his head just the smallest bit, so I just sloshed more coffee in my cup. Maybe if Robert Morgan had shut up then and there, too, things would have been fine, but deep inside, Robert Morgan was still the boy who would poke a sleeping dog with a stick, still the boy who would throw stones at a bee's nest just to see them swarm. He leaned all the way in to Marcus and spoke so softly that if I hadn't been standing right there at the stove, I never would have believed it.

"Who's the smart one now?" he whispered, then patted Marcus on the shoulder as if he were a child, rolled up his newspaper, and shuffled out to his office.

I turned the burner off under the pot of water I was boiling and turned around. My first impulse was to follow the doctor out and pound him, but then I saw Marcus's flushed face, and I wanted to stroke it instead. "Don't let him start on you," I said. "You know he's always been mean as a snake."

Marcus shook his head. "Why do you put up with him, Truly? How do you stand it?"

I wiped my hands on the dishcloth. Marcus knew nothing about my medical condition, and neither did Amelia. I had made a point of keeping that news to myself, along with everything I'd learned about Tabitha's quilt. I looked at Marcus now and was tempted to tell him everything, but I knew he'd be horrified if I confessed what I'd done for Priscilla, and I didn't think I could live with his condemnation. Instead, I fibbed a little.

"Easy," I said. "For Bobbie. Can you imagine what would happen to him if I weren't here?"

Marcus shook his head again. "A boy like that, with a father like Robert Morgan. I guess the only thing those two have in common is their blood type."

"No, not even that. Bobbie is O positive, like me and his mother. I know that because I personally held him down for stitches and a blood test when he sliced his arm open that time he was fixing the fence in the garden with you."

Marcus nodded. "I remember. Bobbie was the only person Robert Morgan wasn't able to treat." He hesitated a moment and then went ahead and asked what he really wanted to. "But what about you? Is he still sticking you full of needles, Truly? Is he writing up files on you? I know how much you hate that."

I didn't say anything.

"Why did you let him start?" Marcus said. "Why don't you just tell him no?"

Because if I did, I might die, I wanted to say, *and I'm not ready to go yet*. I waved a hand. "It doesn't matter. It gives the old coot something to do. Besides, it's never good to cross him." I didn't know how to explain Robert Morgan's temper to Marcus. It wasn't the blustery, volatile kind that blew itself up like a thunderstorm, but more sinister and steady, the north wind trailing its ribbons of frost and ice. Once provoked, his rage might linger for days, chilling everything around him, dropping temperatures until it hurt to breathe. I'd seen him go after the patients who were late with payments, and he wasn't kidding. The north wind always meant business.

Just then, I noticed that Marcus, who was so small that he never had to look anyone in the eye if he didn't want to, was staring at me as if I were the sun come out after the Ice Age. Flustered, I smoothed a strand of hair behind one of my ears. Marcus reached up to my cheek and cupped it with his bad hand. I was surprised that I couldn't feel his scars. His breath lingered between us. "What if it was just us here?" he asked, his voice low. "What would you do then?"

I shook my head.

"Come on, Truly, haven't you ever wondered what it would be like?"

My skin was on fire. I cleared my throat.

"That's ridiculous. We're polar opposites, for one thing. Salt and pepper. Water and dirt."

Marcus sighed and took his fingers away from my cheek. Immediately, I missed them. "So? Who says all the lines of love are supposed to match up?" I'd never thought about it that way before—that maybe your perfect other wasn't everything you already were, but everything you were never going to be. Marcus scuffed his boot on the floor. "You're not ready to hear this."

"No."

He pulled his hat back on his head, then his gloves, hand by hand, not looking at me. "I'll go, then. You know where I'll be." He opened the door, letting in flurries of snow.

After he left, I saw that he had left his plans on the table, so I unrolled them, carefully, tenderly, and stared at the penciled whorls and arcs. As far as I could tell, he wanted to plant vegetables in the beds by the back fence in an oddly beautiful, spiral pattern. He wanted to dig up a line of hedges and put in maize. He wanted to try cultivating a pear tree. I closed my eyes and tried to imagine the papery sound of corn leaves rustling messages in the dark. I pictured Marcus's strong bare back bending over a bed of raw earth, and then I envisioned globes of fruit hanging on a branch at dusk, pale as moonstones, heavy as babies waiting to be born.

"What are you looking at?" Bobbie had come in the kitchen without me hearing him.

"Nothing." I quickly rolled the plans back up. "Just something from Marcus."

"Let me see."

"No." I pulled the plans closer to my chest. "They're nothing. Just some ideas he had for the garden." Marcus's words were still shimmering in my head, however, like tentative bubbles.

"Come on, what's the big deal?" Bobbie stuck out his arm. It was as stark as a pylon, with milky skin. Each month, it seemed, Bobbie was getting thinner and paler. For the life of me, I couldn't figure out why Robert Morgan hadn't hauled him into his office for a battery of tests and shots the way he did me, but for some reason, things were different with his own flesh and blood. Marcus was right. Robert Morgan never had been able to treat Bobbie. They went to see a doctor in Hansen instead.

I looked up and saw that Bobbie's eyebrows had turned into two angry slants, just like his father's, and for the first time, I was a little afraid of him. Maybe I'd made a mistake, I thought, never telling him no, always giving him what he wanted all these years, keeping the secret of what was going on in the attic for him.

His lips stretched over his teeth in perfect imitation of his father, and suddenly I realized where I'd gone wrong with him. It was something I should have known better, me of all people, something I didn't see until right that moment, but it was plain as day: Bobbie was like a lopsided equation. The inside of him didn't match the outside of him. He had Serena Jane's nose, Serena Jane's blue eyes, her lips, and her cheeks, but somehow, when you added all the features together, you still ended up with one more Robert Morgan. It was amazing, I thought. Maybe biology really was destiny.

I took a step back, still clutching the plans. "They're really not very interesting.

Why don't you sit down, and I'll make you some eggs?"

He snatched the scroll away from me before I had time to object and opened it. He blinked down at the plans, disappointed. "Oh, you're right. They are boring. Everything's boring." He tossed the plans aside and slumped into a chair while I went to the stove and started his breakfast.

"Well, I expect all that will change next year when you're studying medicine at Buffalo, like your father did. You'll be too busy to be bored."

Bobbie snorted. "Yeah, right, like they'll accept me with my grades."

"They'll take you. They have to take you. Four generations of your family have gone there. Every Robert Morgan in this family has graduated a doctor, and you will, too." In the pan, the eggs shimmered like giant knowing eyes. I broke the yolks and turned down the heat. "After all, your father won't be around forever. He'll need you to take his place one day."

Bobbie shook his head. "That's never going to happen."

I considered Bobbie's shadow-ringed

eyes, his willowy neck and wrists, the bony shoulders hunched under his T-shirt. He looked as if he were half skeleton, like a specimen to be studied. I couldn't imagine him sequestered in a morgue, puzzling over the contents of the human body, but I supposed he would do it. All the Morgan men did.

"Don't be silly." I poured out two glasses of orange juice. "Here, a toast to the bright path of the future Dr. Morgan." Bobbie sullenly clinked glasses with me and sulked, not looking at all certain that such a road led anywhere he was willing to follow.

That night, Bobbie woke with an erection so powerful, it was almost painful. He hobbled out of bed, grasping at himself, but his penis refused to deflate. He released it, and it sprang upright again, defying him. He removed his boxer shorts and stared at himself in his dresser mirror. Everything else on him—his hips, his long slender thighs, the dips and hollows in his chest—was supple and smooth, until he got to the nest of hair between his legs and the cylinder of flesh throbbing out of it. It wasn't that he was particularly well endowed (at least, he didn't think he was); it was merely the fact that the thing existed at all.

He ran his hands through his hair and sighed. In the spring, he would be required to walk down aisles of folding chairs with a silly cap on his head and collect a rolled-up diploma—an event for which he was none too eager. Robert Morgan and I would arrive late, he knew, and shove into the back of the auditorium, where his father would glower at Bobbie, pissed that he hadn't even come close to being valedictorian, and I would heave myself to half standing, waving. We would take posed photographs and mill around, and then we would all come back to the house and eat platters of food that had gone half-cold. Without warning, as quickly as it arrived, his erection disappeared, and Bobbie sighed with relief.

Still naked, he ruffled his hair. Over the past few weeks, to his father's intense annoyance, he'd been growing it. Little tendrils were starting to sprout down over his ears, fluffing around his jaw, softening it. It looked almost gamine. But not over the stern lapels of a blue blazer. Not over the regulated stripes of the necktie he would be required to wear at fraternity mixers in college.

He pulled his boxers back on, then a T-shirt, and opened his closet. There, nestled in the very back against his winter coat, was his mother's blue dress. He pushed the other clothing aside and stroked the silky fabric of the skirt, ran a thumb along the sweetheart neckline. If he put his nose to the material and breathed deeply enough, he knew, he would still find a musty scent buried in the threads. He slipped the dress off its hanger and slid it on over his head, savoring the cool lick of the garment against his bare skin. He turned back to the mirror, and his cheeks flushed with pleasure. If only he could prolong this moment, Bobbie thought, stretching the secret hours of night out long and thin enough that a few tendrils might remain with him in the day. So often, we believe we are alone in the privacy of our fantasies, but that is a delusion as well—and perhaps the most dangerous kind. For in letting ourselves forget about the common threads of our innermost wishes, we erode our foundations and lose the keystone of our souls.

Bobbie remembered only fragments of his mother. Her dusky hair tickling his cheek. The press of her lips against his neck when she tucked him into bed. The musical clicking that the heels of her shoes made on the parquet floors, a sound he could never reproduce no matter how hard he tried. At the edge of the cemetery, in a little clearing by the west fence, her square granite headstone squatted—a deliberately ugly memorial chosen by Robert Morgan, carved with the bluntest letters possible, plain in the extreme. On the afternoon of Serena Jane's burial, the sun was high and bright, Bobbie remembered, but the wind was already filled with a bitterness so mean, it dried his tears before they formed.

"May she rest in peace," the Reverend Pickerton had whispered, ashen around the lips.

"Amen," Robert Morgan had spat through gritted teeth.

After that afternoon, we rarely visited, but I can only give you the reason for my own absence. Even when we were supposedly laying my sister in the ground, her grave seemed anonymous to me—a rectangular hollow that would still be empty after it was filled. Once a year, I went to lay flowers on my mother's and father's graves, but I avoided Serena Jane's altogether. I simply missed her too much. Marcus told me he weeded around the stone regularly and that noisy crows liked to perch on the top of it. "I don't know why," he reported, "but they always go for that one spot. You don't normally see them do that."

Maybe it was the image of his mother's dress clinging around his shoulders, or maybe it was the culmination of years of missing his mother, but at that moment, Bobbie suddenly determined that Serena Jane's grave was the one and only spot in the world he wanted to be. He slipped out of the house without anyone hearing him—his overcoat bundled over his mother's dress, boots still unlaced. The frosty air stung his bare calves and thighs, but he didn't notice. The anemic moon illuminated his trail of footsteps, lonely little cavities chipped in the snow, close together at first and then strung out farther and farther apart until they lost their form completely. In the tottering house on Conifer Street—

the house of his father and all the Dr. Morgans before him—Robert Morgan and I slept, gnashing our teeth, unaware that the chain of history had just been broken and a new thread of events, one we couldn't control, had begun.

Part Three

Chapter Twenty-three

Sometimes I think I collect souls to make up for the ones I've lost over the course of my life—the string of disappearances that started with my mother and spread outward like a raven's wing, darkening everything beneath it. Sometimes it's possible to see misfortune coming and prepare for it, I guess, but most of the time, when a person disappears, it's as unexpected and shocking as hail in the middle of June.

Bobbie never came back from the cemetery to his father's house. Instead, Marcus rang the front doorbell the next morning and kept his eyes lowered when I answered the door, twirling his hat in his hands. "Why, Marcus," I exclaimed, throwing open the screen, "come on in. Are you here to argue your garden some more?" I was surprised to see him at the front door. Normally he just came to the kitchen.

Marcus wouldn't look at me. *He's mad*, I thought, *because he tried to say he loved me and I couldn't say it back yet.* But I was working on it. I thought I might be able to say it one day. Maybe even sooner rather than later.

"I need to speak to Robert Morgan."

I shut the door. "I'll go get him. But, Marcus . . ." Now I was the one who couldn't look up. "About the things you said to me last—"

Marcus waved a hand. "They'll wait. Just go get Robert Morgan. Please. It's important."

"What's the matter? Is everything okay?"

Marcus rubbed the bridge of his nose. "It's about Bobbie. I found him out in the graveyard this morning, sitting on Serena Jane's grave. What's going on with him?"

I put a hand to my heart, remembering how I'd needled him about his educational plans. In some ways, I thought, he really was still a boy. Even though his future was bearing down on him, he still had both feet in the past. Suddenly I felt guilty. I looked at Marcus's patient but questioning eyes and found I couldn't hold his gaze. "I'll fetch the doctor. You wait in the kitchen," I said, and bustled off to find Robert Morgan in his office.

"What's the problem?" Robert Morgan coolly examined me over the tops of his bifocals. They were new and made him look even more medicinal, I thought.

"Something about Bobbie. Marcus is in the kitchen. He'll explain."

Robert Morgan scowled, but he put down his pen, grabbed his doctor's kit, and followed me across to where Marcus was waiting, tapping his good foot.

"Don't worry. He's at my place. He's fine," Marcus began, "but I thought you should know, I found him sitting on his mother's grave. He'd been out there all night."

The doctor cut right to the point. "Was he drunk?"

"No. Not that I know of. In fact, I think he was clear as a bell."

"Well, thank goodness for that. Although, between you and me, it wouldn't be the first time a Morgan man tied one on." I could hear the wink and nudge in the doctor's voice, but Marcus ignored it.

"Listen, I don't know how to tell you this, exactly, but Bobbie wasn't—*isn't*—himself."

All the humor left Robert Morgan. "What do you mean?"

"Well, for one thing, when I found him, he was wearing a dress."

There was woolly silence for a moment, and when Robert Morgan finally spoke again, it was in such a low voice, I had trouble hearing him. "Did anyone else see him?"

"No, it was too early. Just barely dawn."

"And where is he now?"

"In my cottage. Sleeping."

Another pause, then, "Good, that's good. I'll give you some clothes to take back to him. And here . . ." Robert Morgan fumbled in his doctor's bag and shook a series of pills out of a plastic bottle. "When he wakes up, give him two of these. Give him the pills first, then the clothes. Wait about twenty minutes in between."

There was a stretch of silence. My heart hammered in my chest as I wondered what Marcus would say. Would he stash the pills in his jacket pocket, no questions asked, or hesitate, his palm half-uncurled? I guessed right. Marcus shook his head firmly, his eyes cast down to his boots, but resolute. “No sir,” he said. “I don’t think that’s the right answer.”

Robert Morgan glowered and closed his fingers tighter around the pills. “With all due respect, he’s my son. I get to call the shots here.”

But Marcus wouldn’t be moved. “I guess we’ll just have to agree to disagree, then. I’m not giving him those pills.”

The doctor sputtered, “You can’t just let Bobbie stay with you. I’ll call the police.”

Marcus folded his arms across his chest. “Didn’t Bobbie turn eighteen two months ago?”

Robert Morgan sputtered again, and Marcus put his hat on his head. “Like I said, I guess we’ll just have to agree to disagree.”

Before he could open the door, however, Robert Morgan slammed his hand against it. “Know this. When you walk out that door, you are finished in this house. If you ever set foot on my property again, I'll have you arrested."

Marcus shrugged. The doctor's face turned a dangerous puce. "You were a little shit growing up, Thompson, and you're still a little shit now. No war wound is going to change that."

I sucked in my breath. It was the worst, meanest thing Robert Morgan could possibly say. A gust of wind kicked up outside, rattling dead tree twigs, and it was a final sound, empty and dull. To his credit, Marcus kept his cool. "You can insult me all you want, Bob Bob, but it isn't going to change the finer points of your son. I guess I'll see myself out the front." Marcus twirled his hat once more, glanced at me for a moment, and shook his head. It was enough for me to understand that he was saying good-bye.

"Wait!" I followed him into the foyer, the floorboards bowing under my feet. "Marcus! Don't go. Not like this. What about Bobbie?"

Marcus looked up at me. His eyes were wet at the corners. "He's just across town, Truly. We both are."

"You know it's not as simple as that." My voice came out rough and bumpy.

Marcus reached up and cupped one of my cheeks the way he had before, and it felt like the sun kissing my skin. "I'll take good care of him, I promise."

I was trying hard not to cry. "I know. And maybe in a little while, Robert Morgan will come around."

"I don't think that's too likely."

"No. I don't guess it is."

The thing about leavetakings, I've come to learn, is that they're harder to deal with when they're finished. It was only after Marcus closed the front door gently behind him that it occurred to me that my chances of telling him I loved him back were about as big as a flea and shrinking. For the first time since I'd arrived, I let myself dream about what it would be like to leave the doctor's house and not even take a suitcase or an extra pair of shoes, but simply to slam the door behind me with a good, hard shake and point my hips out of town and back toward the Dyerson farm. Or maybe toward the cemetery and Marcus.

Behind me, the dark shadow of Robert Morgan was a smudge across the wall, interrupting my thoughts. I sighed. It was useless to dream. No matter how far I went, I would never be free of Robert Morgan's bad temper, and I would never, ever outrun my own problems.

The doctor's voice swept across the room like an arm drawing a curtain. "I want you to clean out Bobbie's room by tonight. Then close the door and leave it that way."

I turned around. "He's still a boy, you know. He's confused."

Robert Morgan held up the flat of one hand. "By tonight."

"What do you want me to do with his things?"

"Give them away or throw them away. I don't care."

The doctor could scatter Bobbie's possessions to the four winds as if they were bones, I thought, but the ghost of him would still always be under his skin. I tried to put my thoughts in terms the doctor would understand. "He's still your son," I said, "no matter what. Your flesh and blood. You can't change the fact of blood."

Robert Morgan blinked, and for the first time, I saw that his eyes reflected light the same way as Bobbie's. *Maybe*, I thought, *there's some common thread still strung between them.*

But I was wrong. When Robert Morgan opened his mouth to speak, his lips were set as solid as a gravestone, and I knew that the thread had snapped. "You're quite right," he said. "I can't change biology, but I can change history." He held out his hand as if to introduce himself. "Pleased to meet you," he said. "I'm the first Robert Morgan in five generations without a son."

As the weather began to change from hard snow and ice to the halfhearted slush of spring, I started to wonder if the past and the future were hinged together like a hip socket, one grinding up against the other until something wore out. I had tried so hard not to hate Robert Morgan. For most of my life I'd tried, and now that I saw that Bobbie had hated him, too, I regretted so much ill will. Or maybe not regretted. Regret might have been too strong a word. Repented was a better choice. It implied that while I was willing to atone for certain things, I might not be all that sorry about them.

I still wasn't sorry for what I'd done for

Prissy, for starters. The doctor had been livid when he'd found out Prissy had taken her own life, but he'd had no idea it was me who'd helped her do it. Prissy had been careful with the evidence. Now, he started bringing it up again more and more frequently, however, maybe because after my sister and Bobbie, it was one more thing that had gotten away from him or maybe because it was easier for him to focus on an event that didn't matter as much to him. "I think someone in this town was working against me," he seethed. "Someone must have helped her die. She could have kept fighting. Old women don't just drop dead on their kitchen floor with their lips stained, even if they are sicker than a fish on land."

I shrugged, glad that the quilt was safe up in my room, away from the doctor's diagnostic eyes. "I guess. At least she found peace."

But the doctor continued to worry and fret over the problem until the topic was as frayed and full of holes as one of August's horse blankets. Every night at supper, Robert Morgan hunched over his plate and ruminated, while I tried to stay as quiet as possible. Without Bobbie in the house, conversation had quickly been reduced to a running monologue on the doctor's part.

"It couldn't have been Reverend Pickerton. He's a godly man," Robert Morgan surmised, tapping his fork on his plate of roast beef. "And it wasn't Sal Dunfry. She's so dumb, I doubt she could even mix her own piss in water. Amelia's a possibility—she has all those cleaning solutions—but, no, she's too timid. My money's on that little shit gardener. He still thinks he's so smart, even though I'm the one around here with the medical degree."

At the mention of Marcus, I sat up a little straighter. "That's ridiculous," I interrupted, daubing a smear of pan drippings from my lips. "Marcus was in a war. The last thing he'd want to do is take someone's life. Besides, he's a gardener. He makes things live." But wasn't it also true that gardeners were always wrestling with death, whether in the form of drought, or blight, or hungry insects? In a garden, Marcus always said, death was the first, last, and only fact of life.

The doctor peered at me. "Look at you, all riled up. Don't tell me you're still stuck on that little creep. Explain to me, exactly, how you think that would ever work out?"

I hung my head. "No, it wouldn't. Besides, it's nothing like that." But I couldn't help remembering the warm sensation of Marcus's hand cupping my cheek and the happy glow of his eyes when they met mine. *What do you know about love,* I wanted to ask the doctor, *when everyone you've ever loved has left you?* I laid my knife and fork side by side on my empty plate.

The next night, just to make the doctor shut up, I packed his meat loaf so full of hot peppers, he couldn't get two words out before his eyes widened and his brow broke out in a sweat. "Sweet mother of the saints," he choked. "What the hell did you put in here?"

I blinked at him mildly. "Oh, is it too hot for you? It just has a little cayenne." Also some dried and powdered hyacinth bulb, but he'd find out about that later in the evening when his stomach started cramping.

The doctor gripped his fork tighter and clenched his teeth. "If you dished it out, I can surely eat it." And he did. Silently. Every last bite.

On his birthday, I laced his turkey roulade with cascara, causing him to spend another evening sequestered in his bathroom, and three weeks later, feverfew leaves (so helpful for my headaches) made his tongue swell when he ate them raw in salad. I distilled borage oil into his coffee and watched his eyes turn a sickly yellow in two flat weeks and then witnessed sores erupt on his lips after he spooned down a pudding rife with jack-in-the-pulpit.

He started eyeing my meals with some suspicion, sniffing at them the way a dog noses a handout. "What in tarnation has been wrong with your cooking lately, Truly?" he demanded. "Nothing you're putting on the table is agreeing with me."

I fluttered my hands in the air. "Oh, I'm sorry, Robert Morgan. Without Bobbie around, I've been so distracted lately. I guess I'm not good for anything."

The doctor snorted. "What else is new?" But at the mention of Bobbie's name, his eyes narrowed. "You haven't been sneaking out to see him, have you?"

He popped another bite of meat in his mouth and chewed ponderously. Tonight, it was just plain meat. It occurred to me, however, that I still had two jars of the deadly mixture left in the pantry. If I wanted to, I could just brew it into the doctor's coffee and end this charade at once. I could set Bobbie and myself free. I blinked, snapping myself out of my thoughts, hoping none of them showed on my face. "No, of course not."

The doctor set his jaw. "Good. If he wants to be out there on his own, let him. But don't you give him any help from us. If I find you've gone out there"—he fixed his glassy eyes on me—"so help me God, Truly, you won't even be able to whisper your apologies. Understood?"

I pushed my chair away from the table. "Understood." I thought about all the things I knew about Bobbie that Robert Morgan didn't, not to mention all the secrets I'd discovered about Tabitha Morgan, and then I decided that when everything was said and done, I wasn't sorry about keeping any of that information to myself. In fact, if Tabitha Morgan had provided a recipe for blissful ignorance, you couldn't have paid me to take it just then. I wasn't anywhere near through with the doctor yet. It was time to up the ante.

What started off as occasional experiments with Tabby's remedies on Robert Morgan turned into a regular onslaught. Soon I was trying out a new element on the doctor almost every day, incorporating Tabby's dangerous herbs into the doctor's meals the way you disguise medicine in horse feed. I gave him minuscule but repeated doses of oleander, nightshade, and even a little hemlock. At first, nothing seemed to happen. He slurped down his herb soups and scooped his berry pie with relish and then left the table whistling. One morning, though, about a month after I began fooling with his food in earnest, he appeared in the kitchen looking drawn and exhausted, the skin around his eyes pulled into shadow, his neck a wrinkled sack of tired blood.

"I think I'm going to take the day off today, Truly," he rasped, wrapping his dressing gown tighter. "Cancel my appointments, if you please, and could you bring me up some tea?"

"What's the matter, Robert Morgan?" I asked, trying to hide my smirk behind an expression of concern. "Feeling under the weather?" I knew I was. Maybe it was all the pills the doctor had me swallowing, but my stomach always felt sour these days. I tried brewing some of Tabitha's teas off the quilt, but even they were no help. My joints ached in spite of the arnica I took, and my eczema just persisted under the cream I'd made up for it. It was as if the more I used the quilt's ingredients for malice, the less they worked for the good.

He coughed into his fist. "Must have caught some sort of bug. Say"—he frowned—"does this porridge taste funny to you?" Moments before his appearance in the kitchen, I had personally pounded a clutch of wormwood leaves—so renowned for their hallucinogenic properties—into a pulp and scraped their juices into the cereal.

"No," I said around my teeth as I made a show of swallowing one tiny bite. "Tastes regular to me."

"My tongue's been feeling funny lately." The doctor scowled. "Like it's swollen or something. Maybe it's just this infection."

"Maybe," I agreed, "but you never know, do you? Maybe it's witchcraft." I winked.

Robert Morgan appeared stupefied for a moment, then he snickered. "And maybe fairies frolic on the lawn at night. Still . . ." His smile faded. "A checkup wouldn't hurt. I have a colleague over in Hansen. Maybe I'll give him a call. I haven't been feeling myself lately."

I smiled, the picture of ignorance. "Sure, Robert Morgan. Sounds like a good idea. You medical men should stick together."

He gave me an odd look, but then another coughing spasm rattled his bones. He'd lost so much weight over the past three weeks that even his bedroom slippers looked too big. If I wanted to, now would be the time to finish him off, I thought. Half a jar of Tabby's potion would probably do it.

But what would happen to me if I did that? For one thing, whether I liked it or not, he was the only one who knew what was wrong with my body, the only one with half a chance of curing me, and I wanted to get better, I decided. Marcus had given me a reason to hope. And there was always Bobbie.

I rinsed the pulped wormwood leaves out of their bowl and then emptied the doctor's half-eaten cereal into the sink. Maybe I would ease up on using Tabitha's cures, I mused. It was true that I still had a kettle of resentment against the doctor set on hard boil in my heart, but fanning the flames of it hadn't really made me feel any better. It hadn't changed anything at all, in fact. I was still stuck in Robert Morgan's house, still big as a barn, and for all they were worth, Tabby's herbs were lately proving about as useful to me as a dram of water pulled up from a tainted well. Maybe it was time to come clean again.

Chapter Twenty-four

When it was clear that Bobbie really wasn't coming home, I knew it was time to do what Robert Morgan was urging and pack up his belongings as neatly as I could in cardboard boxes. Amelia came over to help me take them to the farm for safe-keeping. I promised myself that one day Bobbie would get them back, but as we bumped along the road to the open fields and weather-eaten barn, I temporarily forgot all about Bobbie and stared around me in amazement.

This was the first time I'd been back since I'd left. Two years before, Brenda had married one of her creditors and moved to Saratoga Springs, where she drove a Cadillac, learned to drink wine, and routinely tried to convince Amelia to sell off the farm. Amelia wasn't likely to, though, not while August's bones were still sunk in the fallow fields. There are some things in life too painful to let go of, much as we want to. Instead, Amelia had somehow found the means to mend the fences, patch the chicken coop, repair the windmill, and rewire, repaint, and refurbish the house. The only thing that looked remotely similar was the old barn. In August's time, it had already been an open proposition for owls and mice, but now I found the sight of its rotten beams and exhausted roof too melancholy to bear.

"How much longer do you think before it tumbles back to the ground?" I asked, unloading one of Bobbie's boxes from the truck bed.

Amelia glanced over her shoulder and shrugged. Out here, away from the scrutiny of town, her lungs filled easily with air, and her voice rang true. "It's leaning all right, but it won't fall. Daddy's ghost is still in there some."

I saw what she meant. Just like August, the barn wasn't quite ready to throw in its hand, even when all the odds looked to be bad. I set Bobbie's box on the front porch. "Well, the place looks great. You must have worked so hard."

Amelia blushed. "I didn't do it all on my own. I had some help."

"What do you mean?" Besides me, I couldn't think of any of Amelia's friends. There were her clients, of course—most of them people, like Vi Vickers, that we'd both known forever—but I don't think any of them thought of Amelia as anything more than someone who scoured their homes and then slipped away for another week.

"Come on, I'll show you."

She took my hand and led me around the back of the house. As we rounded the corner, I sucked in my breath. Gone were the rusted auto parts that no longer fit any specific machinery. Likewise the rotten picket fence, the hillocks of weeds, and the bald patches of scratched-up dirt. Instead, a garden was just beginning to poke through the early spring ground—planted in a round, gentle spiral. I instantly recognized the design.

"It's Marcus's garden," I breathed, and Amelia blushed again.

"He's only been working on it a few weeks, but he's sure got a lot done. He said he's been scratching around for a place to plant, so I told him I had more than enough room. Look . . ." She walked in between a narrow row of sprouts. "We're going to have peppers, and beans, and eggplant, I think." In spite of the chilly air, her cheeks were a vivid pink, and her eyes were aglow. I thought I could suddenly see what had attracted Marcus to gardening out here besides a free plot of land.

Seething with jealousy, I turned my back on the plants. "Can we put these boxes inside now? I'm freezing." It was a lie—nothing made me cold—but I didn't want Amelia to see the envious set of my mouth.

She looked confused, then hurt. "Okay."

What I really wanted to do was linger in the tidy lines that Marcus had scored into the earth. I wanted to sit in the exact center of the spiral and wait for the plants to unfurl themselves. I wanted them to climb and rove over my limbs until I burst into bloom with them. But it was Amelia who was going to get to harvest the thick-skinned peppers and gather up baskets of waxy beans. It was Amelia who would be waving to Marcus through the kitchen window, inviting him in for a plate of her fresh-cooked succotash and smoked ham. A column of bile rose in my throat.

"Truly, what's the matter?" Amelia put a hand on my forearm, but I shook it off.

"I have to get back soon. I've got the doctor's dinner to fix."

Amelia looked as though she wanted to say something, but a lifetime of swallowing words is a hard sea to swim against. I wonder now if she recognized jealousy in my glare or if she chalked my mean mood up to some flaw in herself; but knowing Amelia, I figured it was the latter. She may have had a whole lovely garden spread out at her feet, but in her heart, she still thought of herself as a weed—unlovely, uncultivated, unwelcome even in her own backyard. Everything in the world has its two faces, however. Weeds sometimes blossom into artful flowers. Beauty walks hand in hand with ugliness, sickness with health, and life tiptoes around in the horned shadow of death. The trick is to recognize which is which and to recognize what you're dealing with at the time. At any given moment, you can tip the balance just a little, one way or the other, if you're paying attention, but that afternoon I wasn't. I was too preoccupied with the hard stones rolling around inside my own heart.

"Come on," I sighed. "Let's go inside."

After ten years away, the brass handle of the Dyersons' back door still felt familiar in my palm. I wondered if the house still smelled like beeswax and vanilla, and the icebox still made a whining noise like a mosquito. I so badly wanted to take in one more gulp of Marcus's garden before I entered, but I didn't want to give Amelia the satisfaction, and truth be told, I didn't want to give it to myself, either. For years I'd been caught up in my memory of the place, and now here it was in front of me, real, and I wasn't sure what to think.

Amelia deserved an explanation for my mood, I knew, so I screwed up my courage and attempted to provide her with one. "It's the garden," I choked. "It's the same one Marcus wanted to plant at the doctor's. I thought—it's just that . . . well, I thought it was supposed to be special."

Amelia's eyes filled with comprehension. "Special for you, you mean."

I ducked my head. "Something like that."

She smiled. "But it *is* special. Don't you see that? Just because it's planted here doesn't make it any different. He still planted it. He still brought it into being."

I raised up my head, still slightly dizzy with the swirling design of Marcus's garden. "Oh," I breathed. A tiny pulse of hope began to throb in my chest.

Amelia stepped closer across the porch to me. "Truly, he cares for you. It's obvious. He always has. Why don't you do something about it? Bobbie's gone now. He's not coming back—you know he's not. What do you have left to stay at the doctor's for? Why don't you move back out here with me? It'll be like the old days. Come home."

Home. The word reverberated down my bones. Most people had one definite place they called home, but for me, it was different. Did I choose the doctor's house, where Bobbie used to be and where I'd lived so long? Or the Dyerson farm, where August's bones lay and where there was enough space to make me feel small; or was it the cramped wooden house of my childhood, where my mother and father had both died? I reached again for the brass doorknob, anticipating the familiar wave of aromas that would envelop me when I opened the door. I thought one last time of Marcus's garden, sorry to leave it behind me.

The only thing holding me at the doctor's house now was the addictive bite of revenge, but its teeth were long and hooked, and I wasn't at all sure anymore how to extricate myself from them. I was dependent on the doctor for the medicine he gave me, but I was also finding that I had sprouted unexpected roots under his roof, and the thought of tearing them up to move—even somewhere as familiar as the farm—gave me pause. I guess I was like a creeper strangling a tree with slow determination. Now that I had reached the very top branch, I saw, there was nowhere left to go but back the way I'd come.

When I arrived back at the doctor's, Robert Morgan was sitting in the kitchen—unusual enough for him, but doubly so because all the lights were turned off. He was sitting so still, I almost didn't see him.

He waited until I had my coat off, and then his voice scraped the air with the precision of a razor. "You've been out a long time."

I shook my black coat off my shoulders and laid it over the back of a chair before sitting down. Predictably, the wood groaned beneath me. I wanted to shout, to spit sparks and brimstone, but I was so tired, I managed only gruff irritation. "I took Bobbie's stuff away."

Robert Morgan didn't reply, and I shifted my weight to my other hip. I still wasn't used to the house in its new incarnation. Without Bobbie, the rooms felt positively funereal. I yearned to flip on some lights and start cooking, filling the kitchen with good smells and the happy sound of pots bubbling, but there was no need. The doctor had helped himself to a plate of cold beef, crackers, cheese, and celery.

I stared at the desiccated stalks on the doctor's plate and thought again of the garden Marcus had planted, imagining how lush it would look when it was ripe and how good the tomatoes and peppers would taste straight off the vines. I imagined him feeding me sweet peas, pulled from their shells one by one. I thought about the rest of the farm, too—how there weren't any horses left now, but maybe come spring I could raise a graceful foal I would train to gentleness. Nothing like the buckle-kneed animals I used to care for, though. I wanted a little elegance for a change. I flattened my hands on the table and looked the doctor in the eyes. Amelia was dead right, I decided. Perhaps it really was time for me to open the door to my own future. There was nothing keeping me here anymore but the ugly lure of comeuppance. It was time to leave. But informing the doctor was a different matter.

I thought about it and decided it was best to do it sideways. Butting your brains up against the doctor's iron will was never a good idea. Better first to parrot what he wanted to hear. I took a breath and repeated, "Well, I did it. I took Bobbie's things away like you wanted." I didn't mention what I'd done with them, and Robert Morgan didn't ask, so I continued, throwing out more and more words as if I were filling up a pot for stew. "They're gone now all right. His room's empty. But, you know, he's still right here in town."

Robert Morgan scowled, and I backed

off, guessing he wasn't ready to entertain the possibility of reconciling yet. Time to get on with my own concerns, then. "Speaking of moving on, I've been thinking. You won't really be needing me anymore, and this afternoon, Amelia offered to take me back at the farm. Not"—I raised a finger—"that I couldn't still come in once a week or so to cook up some dinners for you, or tidy up. That kind of thing. And, of course, I'll need to come back for my medicine." I folded my finger back into my hand, wishing I could just make a clean break and leave the way Bobbie had but knowing that was impossible. I sat back and waited for the storm I was sure was coming, but it never arrived.

Resigned silence widened around us in arcs like pond ripples. Through the gloom, I noticed that the dark smears under the doctor's eyes had grown more purple, the cracks in his lips deeper. He appeared as worn out as an old front porch, and this suddenly alarmed me. Maybe using Tabby's recipes on him hadn't been a good idea, I reflected. It hadn't made me feel any better. It was a good thing I'd stopped. I leaned forward and put out a conciliatory hand across the table. "I'm sorry," I said. "Please try to understand."

"I always thought you'd go before me," he whispered.

I squinted at him. "I know. It's time for me to leave."

"No, that's not what I meant." He shook his head.

"What are you talking about?" I pulled my hand back.

He closed his eyes. "I finally got around to seeing the doctor, and he finally got his tests back. I have acute myeloid leukemia."

There was a beat of silence. Even I could tell that sounded bad, but I asked the obvious question anyway. "What is that?"

"A type of cancer. My white blood cells are multiplying too quickly. They're choking out the red ones." I hadn't realized you could divide blood into opposing colors, but I supposed if anyone could turn something as elemental as his own blood into something that seethed and fought, it would be Robert Morgan. It seemed that after all these years, he was finally finding out what the rest of the human race already knew—

that he was a man at serious odds with himself.

I let out my breath in a long, slow stream. "How long have you got?"

"Weeks. Maybe months. It's highly individual." He avoided my gaze. "There's really nothing anyone can do. Nothing I want them to."

I thought about Priscilla Sparrow's last visit and seriously doubted that. When the sick got sick enough, I'd learned, there's nothing they *wouldn't* let you do for them. But the doctor was going to find that out for himself sooner rather than later, it seemed. And when he did, I wanted to be around to witness it. My future would have to wait—again.

Chapter Twenty-five

A body can bear anything for a few months, which is the only explanation I can give for the uneasy and unexpected peace the doctor and I managed to forge in the final weeks of his life. On the surface, it was as if nothing between us had changed. He spent hours in his office, sorting files and cleaning out a years' worth of prescriptions and medicines, and I busied myself in the house. Even without Bobbie, I had plenty to keep me occupied, and though Robert Morgan's natural pace might have been winding down, he seemed determined not to act like it. He still stuck his shoes out in the hallway for a spit polish, and demanded knife-sharp creases ironed into his trousers, and wanted extra starch on all his shirts. He chastised me when the water at the bottom of the flower vase in the foyer got cloudy, reprimanded me for accidentally buying salted butter, and found the new brand of hand soap I'd switched to less than satisfying.

"I just don't like the smell of it," he snapped when I asked him what was wrong with it, and then he watched as I dumped all the new bars in the trash and replaced them with the old cakes.

I suppose that if there was anything different between us during this time, it emanated from me instead of him. I wasn't exactly done hating him, but I couldn't muster up quite the same amount of ire as before. It would have been too much like taking a swing at a scarecrow when what I was really after were the crows.

After he told me about his illness, I'd crept back up to my room, my stomach lurching, where Tabby's quilt draped my bed, the orbs of its blossoms pointing at me like dozens of accusing eyes. *What if I'm the one who caused his illness?* I wondered. Fighting off a wave of nausea, I tugged and pulled at the quilt until I'd made a ball of it, and then I carried it downstairs and restored it to its original place on the wall in the parlor. There would be no more mixtures, I vowed. No more steeping herbs for hours—not even for myself. No more blending foul-smelling pastes. I was done with Tabby's spells. From here on out, all the doctor would be getting out of me was sweet charity.

But no matter how solicitous I was, no matter how many times I refilled his hot-water bottle or changed his sheets, no matter how many times I emptied the basin of vomit next to his bed, the question of Robert Morgan's sickness wouldn't leave my mind. It rubbed and irritated me like a grain of sand stuck in my shoe, until I finally couldn't take it anymore and flat-out asked him.

"Why do you think you got sick?" I put a cup of tea—just a cup of tea, plain and simple—on his bedside table and folded my hands, awaiting an accusation or, at the very least, some kind of suspicion.

But Robert Morgan just blinked, sorrowful as an owl. He had lost more weight than I thought he had on him in the first place, and his cheekbones had gone from stark to skeletal. I turned my eyes away. "I thought I explained it," he answered. "It's a disorder of the white blood cells."

"No. I know that. I mean, why do you think you have it? Did something cause it? Like something you ate, maybe?"

The doctor peered up at me. "Why do you ask?"

"No reason." I shifted.

"No, Truly. It's not because of something I ate. It's not because of Bobbie leaving. It's just because some of the cells in my body have decided to reproduce too quickly. That's it. If I knew more than that, I wouldn't be sitting in this chair right now. I'd be sitting in front of the Nobel Prize committee."

"But, that can't be *it*," I replied. "There has to be more to it than that. There has to be some kind of reason."

The doctor shook his head. "I'm afraid there isn't. The body is just the body. It has its own structure, its own laws. It's a thing unto itself. When it breaks down, that's it."

I breathed out and glanced out the window at the blue, blank sky. "Is that what you think? We simply are the way we are?" I remembered him speaking those words so long ago, the first time he ever examined me. "What about me? Will I ever change?"

He waved his hand vaguely. "You—you're a thing of exception, Truly. I don't know what to tell you." The doctor closed his eyes and took a sip of tea. Outside, wind rustled the leaves. "Sickness doesn't mean anything," he finally said. "It's either something you can fix or it's not. All I've ever tried to do is to give people a way to live with it."

I pictured Marcus's garden, planted in a slow spiral that would leaf and bud into sustenance. "What do you think happens when we die?" I asked. "Do you think we go back to the earth?"

The doctor frowned. "You mean ashes to ashes, dust to dust?"

"I guess."

"Biologically speaking, yes. I'm not sure about anything else."

But I was. All of a sudden, without doubt, I knew that everything and everyone on earth was one and the same. I thought about Priscilla Sparrow, and what I'd done for her, and how one day I might need the same favor myself. And though Robert Morgan and I had radically different casings, we were still stuck together by Bobbie and my sister, and there wasn't a damn thing we could do about it. But still, for all that, we weren't exactly alike, the doctor and I. He was wasting away while I'd gotten a double helping of what the universe was serving, and it hadn't killed me yet.

Instead, it was teaching me to live.

Amelia didn't share my newfound grace. "He's got a house full of medicine, let him dose himself," she said when I told her I wasn't moving to the farm and why. "He's a mean so-and-so, and always has been. Let him get what's coming."

Her venom shocked me. "That's not very Christian," I responded, and Amelia snorted.

"Tell me what the Lord has ever done for us."

I stared at her. She was spring cleaning, and she'd been acting strange all morning, like a snake about to shed its skin. Now that the doctor was confined, and there was no one around to hear her but me, she often hummed while she worked and sometimes even had conversations, like now. Irritated with my lack of an answer, she wiped a layer of dust from one of the kitchen shelves and began swabbing the floor.

"You can't really be suggesting that I leave him here all alone to die? Besides, did it ever occur to you that I might have other reasons for staying?"

Amelia shrugged. "What goes around comes around." She paused in her mopping. "You don't know the half of it with the doctor," she said, "and, trust me, you don't want to, either."

I opened and closed my mouth. "You don't know the half of it, either," I finally said. I still hadn't told her about my condition. She thought all my pills were a vitamin program.

Amelia looked up at me. "What's that supposed to mean?"

"Nothing." I wanted to come right out and tell Amelia about my illness, but something stopped me. *I'll tell her later,* I vowed, *after she's done cleaning*, *when we're hav-*

ing our coffee. Today, I was particularly eager for Amelia to be finished with work so I could ask her for news about Bobbie.

Ten times a day I imagined myself walking across town to the cemetery to visit him, but there was the issue of Marcus. The doctor had made it clear what would happen if I let Marcus back in my life, and I didn't want to make trouble for him. Also, I wasn't sure where we stood with each other. Were we friends? Back to old acquaintances? Or were there still some unopened buds left on our branches? *He'll come to you,* a voice inside my head urged. *Just wait*. I randomly wondered if Tabby had sewn any love charms into the quilt but quickly squashed the idea.

Amelia waited a beat to see if I'd give in and pour out what was sitting heavy on my heart, but I didn't, so she shook herself, offended as a rooster. She wrung out her mop and leaned it in the corner. "That's that," she said. "I'm going out to tackle the office." I watched her march across the porch to the clinic and throw open its windows. All afternoon she scrubbed and polished, but by the end of the day, her breath was coming in shallow scoops and her heart was skipping beats. She finally returned to the kitchen to switch disinfectants.

"What's the matter?" I asked, alarmed at how flushed her cheeks were.

"This stuff's no good," she said, dumping the cleaning fluid and grabbing a jar of vinegar from the pantry. "I think I'm allergic."

Next, she tried tying a bandanna over her nose and mouth, but after only an hour, she tore it off, her heart hammering, frantic as a landed fish. She vacuumed and dusted the blinds, scrubbed at the upholstery in the desk chair, and took apart the light fixtures, but none of that appeared to help. Then she dusted the doctor's books. I peered through the kitchen windows, watching as she stood frozen halfway up the stepladder, her pink feather duster gripped in one hand, a single book clenched in the other. I saw her lips move and her finger trace a line across the cover, then she shook her head, clamped her lips, and stuck the book back on the shelf.

Moving carefully—she'd inherited her father's dodgy back—she pushed all the books back into their original places and maneuvered herself backward off the ladder. She didn't bother to fold up the ladder, however, and she didn't position that last book very well, and I remember thinking that was out of character. The book remained stuck out on the shelf, its spine cracked from rough handling. I considered pointing it out to her, but I was too eager for news about Bobbie, so I let it go.

"Tell me how he is," I urged when we were finally settled in our usual places in the kitchen and I was pouring her out a cup of strong black coffee. "Tell me if he's happy."

Amelia seemed less waspish now that she was finished with her chores, and I was glad. *Maybe it's just the pomp of the doctor's death she's dreading,* I thought. Waiting around for someone to make up his mind and die, I knew, could wear the living out. *Maybe she wishes we could just put him in a hole at the farm like her father.*

Amelia slurped her coffee and gave me the skinny. "His friend Salvatore just got him a job at that men's bar in Hansen. I've read about that place in the paper. The church folks picket out front sometimes, and a couple of times now, the police have been called in for a fight."

I raised my eyebrows. "What does Bobbie do there? He's not of age." I held my breath, hoping it wasn't anything illegal.

"He works in the back, I think. They serve food, I've heard, so he helps out in the kitchen. Turns out he's a prodigal whiz at the stove."

I exhaled. "What's he dressing as these days?" I thought back to my own early childhood of rough-hewn boy's clothes and how I still preferred plain garments to frills or fluff. Did we dress ourselves from the outside in, I wondered, or was it the other way around?

Amelia shrugged. "Boy, mostly, but Marcus says he's not giving up on that blue dress of his mother's."

I nodded. "He must miss Serena Jane fierce. Robert Morgan never let us mourn her right."

Amelia looked uneasy all of a sudden. She shifted in her chair a few inches, opened her mouth as if to say something, then closed it up tight again. At the mere mention of Marcus's name, it was as if vines were choking us both. "And how is Marcus?" I finally asked, my heart squeezing into a familiar fist in my chest. "Garden going good?"

Amelia avoided my gaze. "Real good. We've already got bean vines halfway up the poles. Why don't you come see sometime? He's out there most days of the week. He could tell you more about Bobbie. Besides, I know he misses you." When it came to Marcus, it seemed, Amelia never minded being wordy.

I tilted my chin down toward my chest. "Maybe."

Amelia went funny again, as though she had a pound of lead she wanted to get off her tongue, but she still didn't say anything. We see what we want to see in life, regardless of whether it's really in front of us or not, and what I saw at that moment was how Amelia's braid hung over her shoulder like a bell pull, how her birdlike clavicles rose and fell with each breath she took, how tiny and precise her fingers were. In short, I saw everything I was not, and I was jealous. I looked down at my own rough arms and my thunderous legs, and I wished they were as petite and neat as Amelia's. *Maybe then,* I thought, *Marcus would come to my door and plant a garden, no matter what the doctor says.* Then I thought about what might happen between Marcus and Amelia if I disappeared, and my heart grew even more pinched. I longed to go visit Marcus and see what could be between us, but then I checked myself. I was a ticking time bomb. How could I offer myself to a man who'd already had his fill of death?

Of course, this memory makes me sorrowful now, for if anyone ever knew the shape of me, it was Amelia—and not just the outer lines of me, either, but all my innards as well. She was as necessary as the sun to me. She was the quiet heat that shimmered inside my shadow and made it live, and without her, I am a little darker. Amelia stood up and gathered her bags and buckets. "I have to go," she sniffed. "I need to get back and feed the chickens before dark. At least *they're* some company."

I rose with her. "Okay." I walked her to the door and watched her climb into August's old truck. She started the engine and drove off, pulling all the unspoken tension between us taut, then tauter still, until, like a rubber band stretched too thin, it went flying.

Chapter Twenty-six

The doctor warned me that he would grow sick quickly, but it was still hard to believe when the exact morning arrived that he couldn't get out of bed. It was the middle of May—high spring—and the birds were chirping so loudly that I didn't hear the small pewter bell the doctor was ringing, our prearranged signal for help. Soon, however, the metallic sound became hard to ignore. I followed it down the corridor and found the doctor half-covered and blushing all the way out to his ears.

"Truly, I need help going to the toilet," he said with as much dignity as he could muster, which, given that it was Robert Morgan, was actually quite a lot.

"Why don't you let me fetch Bobbie?" I asked as we shuffled down the hallway. "You must miss him. Wouldn't you rather your own flesh and blood do this?"

Robert Morgan grappled with the bathroom doorknob and looked sour. "He made his choice. He gave up everything this family holds dear, and now he's out of the circle." He turned around. "I can manage from here."

I blushed. "I'll wait outside."

"Thank you."

I was far from ready to let the matter drop, though. As I plumped pillows and rearranged covers, I regaled the doctor with the latest news about Bobbie, straight from Amelia's mouth. "He's in love," I crowed, tucking the doctor's feet up tight in the sheets and figuring that it was best if he heard it from me first. "You'll never guess with who."

"Whom," Robert Morgan corrected, but I ignored him. *He must know,* I told myself. *He must realize about Bobbie by now, even if he doesn't want to admit it.* I took a deep breath and got ready to explain.

"Do you remember his friend Salvatore, who used to come by and spend time with him?"

Robert Morgan turned his face away from me. "No."

"Of course you do. Tall boy with dark hair. A few years older." *Not to mention Bobbie's only friend,* I wanted to add but didn't.

Still, the doctor refused to play along. "No," he repeated.

I waved a hand. "Oh well. It doesn't matter. But that's who it is. That's who Bobbie's with."

The doctor was so quiet, I thought I might have killed him right then and there, but then he spoke, and what he said shocked me all the way out to the hair on my head.

"Is he good to him, this Salvatore?" he asked, still not looking at me.

And then I shocked myself. Without thinking, I took the doctor's hand and squeezed it, as if we were old friends instead of barely tolerable in-laws. "Very good," I whispered, imagining Salvatore's coffee-colored fingers intertwined with Bobbie's white ones. "He's the best."

"Okay, then," Robert Morgan rasped, "I guess I can live with that." And he fell into a deep, rapturous sleep—the first one, I believe, that he had ever earned on his own.

As summer warmed, the doctor grew weaker. "Don't we have more blankets?" he chattered one evening, a plaid wool wrap flung around his bony shoulders. "I'm freezing. I need another cover." His eyes suddenly lit up, and he half sat. "What about the quilt in the parlor downstairs?" he croaked.

My heart flip-flopped as I shook a pair of his pills into the palm of my hand. I snapped the bottle lid back on tight and tried to sound casual. "Oh, you don't want that old thing. It's probably all musty." The last thing I wanted was the doctor cozied up under the very catalog of spells that may have started him on this road in the first place.

But the sick have minds of their own. They want what they want. "I don't care," the doctor insisted. "Go fetch it for me."

I tried again. "Here, take your pills." I'm

ashamed to admit that not all my appetite for vengeance had been quelled by Robert Morgan's actual illness. Temptation sometimes triumphed over my contrition, and I would find myself withholding water from him or giving him only one pill when he could have had two. He was getting so addled, though, that he was starting not to notice. Today, hoping to distract him from the quilt, I gave him both pills, but it didn't work. He swallowed them down, then immediately resumed pestering me.

"Please, Truly, my bones feel like they're going to grow ice. That quilt is just the thing to warm them." I pretended not to hear him, which turned out to be a mistake. Next time I glanced over, the doctor was half out of bed, his stick legs dangling over the edge.

"What are you doing?" I cried. "You'll break your dang hip, and that's the last thing I need."

He shot daggers at me. "If you're not going to do what I want, then I'll do it myself."

He swayed a little, and I propped him up with one arm. "Okay, okay. For the love of the devil, I'll bring you the quilt. Just get back into bed." He allowed me to tuck the covers back over him, a cat-who-ate-the-cream smile tugging at his lips.

When I returned, he was already dozing, his mouth hung open like a puppet's, and I was half in a mind to turn around and take the quilt back downstairs, but I didn't. The doctor was sick all right, but he wasn't putty in my hands. He still had his memory and his eyes intact, and if he woke up without that quilt, I knew, there'd be no end to it. I sighed and tucked the corners of it gently around him, folding it back on itself a little so the designs didn't show quite as much. Robert Morgan snorted and opened one eye. "Thank you," he grumbled, and nodded off again. I watched him sleep for a moment, unaccustomed to the ragged new arrangement of his face. He grimaced and moaned, fretful even in rest, and for a moment, I was tempted to soothe his brow the way I used to with Bobbie.

The doctor was going to get worse than this, I knew. He had warned me. "Toward the very end," he had said, his jaw clenched, "I'm afraid you will have to do all the heavy lifting, and for that I apologize."

"Good thing I have big arms, then," I'd answered, but I was starting to question what I had gotten myself into—nursing a man who had tortured me for years, a man my sister and nephew had hated and from whom they had fled. When the time came, I wondered, shouldn't I maybe just give him Tabby's drink? Wouldn't it be easier? And, if I was being totally honest, wouldn't it also be a little bit gratifying? For once, I would beat the man at his own game. I could give him the cure he hadn't been able to give me.

Stop it, I told myself as I brought Robert Morgan yet another tray of chicken broth in bed. *You said you were done with the quilt. It's just cotton and batting now, and a million little pieces of tangled threads.* Except it wasn't, and I knew it. Tabitha's quilt was more than pieces of fabric sewn together. It was a patchwork of souls. I gasped and almost dropped my soup. The phrase had jumped unbidden into my mind. *A patchwork of souls*. Suddenly I understood the significance of the angel wings. They were more than random symbols—they were markers, as clear as any in the graveyard. Tabitha Morgan had done the same thing I had done for Prissy.

The border had been a record of the deaths.

"What's wrong?" The doctor peered up at me groggily.

"Nothing." I spread a napkin out over the quilt, hoping the doctor would never see what was covering him and make me explain. What would I say? I wondered. What would I do if he asked? I didn't know, but it turns out I didn't have to. The day was soon coming when the doctor would make that decision for me.

⁂

To witness a conversion is not always to recognize it. In Robert Morgan's case, it started with time. More than softening him, more than breaking him, the doctor's leukemia gave him opportunity to pay attention to the seemingly insignificant details of Aberdeen. "I never noticed those yellow roses in the back corner of the garden," he drawled, pumped as full of narcotics as a baby after a feed. "They're just the color of butter. And that tree across the way over there. What kind of tree is that? An elm? Did you ever notice that the jays just love that tree?"

I peeped out the window at a pair of birds perched on the elm's branches. "Why, yes, they surely do, Robert Morgan."

His head lolled on the pillow. "Why did I never notice the jays, Truly? Why did I never walk out and smell those roses against the fence?"

Because you were a tight bastard, I wanted to say but didn't. "Because you had your mind on higher things," I suggested instead.

The doctor nodded, emphatic. "That's right. Higher things. My head was in the clouds. But no more. I'm putting my head down to the dirt now."

"You mean you're burying your head in the sand?" I smiled, but Robert Morgan scowled. It was an appropriate comment, I thought, considering denial was his main method of handling Bobbie.

"Laugh all you want to, woman. I'm serious. The little things—they're all I have left."

"I wouldn't know about those," I sniffed, "what with being a giant and all."

Later, though, when he was sleeping, I went outside and cut some blossoms for him, propping them up in a bowl of water by his bedside so that when he woke he would be able to catch their sweetness. *They're as much for me as they are for him,* I told myself. After all, I was in there about twenty times a day. I thought I deserved a little burst of summer where I could see it.

Men can regress when they're desperately ill, and this certainly happened with the doctor. First he quit moving, then he quit speaking much, and finally, with his mind snipped free like a bone cut from a rigid cast, he slipped back and forth in time, careening from childhood to the present with awful frequency. Sometimes he called me by Serena Jane's name, which always made me laugh to myself, and other times, like the rainy afternoon he grabbed me by the forearm and forced me to sit on the bed beside him, he thought I was his mother. "Please," he begged, tugging on my hand, "stay awhile, Mother."

I tried to free myself from his grip. "I'm not Maureen. I'm Truly, remember?"

Robert Morgan blinked and released my hand, his face turning cross. "Of course you are. Why are you telling me?"

"No reason."

He shifted under the covers. "But while you're here, maybe you could get me a fresh pajama top." I had to strain to hear him. His voice was as hollowed out as a termite tunnel.

"Of course." I reached into the bureau and pulled out a striped pajama set.

"Just the top."

"Right."

"Now look away."

"But don't you want me to help you—"

"Look away!"

"Okay, fine." I turned around and busied myself with the teapot I'd brought up. "But it's not like the view is outstanding, trust me."

I waited a beat for him to shoot a barb back to me, but silence ruled the room. Curious, I turned around, and what I saw froze me to the core. The doctor was inspecting the folds of the quilt, his mouth stretched as flat as a pin, and I knew in an instant that he had discovered its secret. I quickly tried to shake out the quilt, but I was too late. In his eyes, I recognized a gleam of comprehension.

"My God," he wheezed, "it's Tabitha's shadow book! After all these years, I've found it. It's real!" He leaned his head back against his pillows momentarily and closed his eyes, breathing deeply and evenly, the balance of his life's convictions wavering inside of him.

What could I say? I picked up his teacup and added hot water, and as I did, Robert Morgan rasped and pointed. I looked over my shoulder to see what he was indicating, but it was nothing. The air had filled with steam. That was all. I nodded to show that I could see it, too—a weightless alphabet, the language of the soul. Silently, we watched it rise heavenward in loops and curls.

The doctor spent the better part of the next two hours muttering over the quilt, studying each stitched sign and determining its meaning. He lingered on the wings, as puzzled as I'd been by them, but his knowledge of medical botany was better than mine, and he quickly figured out the relationship between the wings and the clutch of deadly herbs that they covered. His eyes narrowed, and he slapped his hand on the mattress. He couldn't shout anymore, but he could still smack up a ruckus, and just now he looked as mean as he used to when he was teasing me in the schoolroom all those years ago.

"Priscilla Sparrow," he spat. "How did you do it?"

Hoping to distract him, I went over the various emblems on the quilt with him: the hand, the bone, the little set of lips. And finally the wings, spread like broken hearts across the tangle of plants on the border. He wasn't dissuaded.

"How?" he insisted, so I gave in and told him about the drink and how I'd walked it over to Prissy's in the cool of the early morning and laid it on her doorstep in a basket as if I were depositing the baby Moses. I didn't say anything about the extra liquid I'd stored in the pantry, though. That was my secret. Nor did I bring up the various concoctions I'd snuck into his food over the past few months. I saw him eyeing me cautiously, however, and I could tell he was calculating up all those odd-tasting meals on his own.

I think I knew at that moment that he was going to ask me to make the drink for him. I could see the idea spinning all crooked in his eyes like the sails going round on the Dyerson windmill. Not sure they wanted to, but doing it anyway. "Truly," he gasped, "promise me you'll listen carefully, and do exactly as I say, no matter what."

I had more than a hundred reasons not to. Prissy had been a sick woman, for starters, to whom no one had paid much attention. The risk of anyone being suspicious of her dying had been slim. Plus, she'd been careful. She'd thrown away the note and then the jar before succumbing. The doctor was a different story, however. He was ill, it was true, but he was also a force to be reckoned with. Anyone who knew him knew how much he was fighting his demise. No one would expect his death to be short and quick.

And why should a man who'd spent his whole life scorning Tabitha's cures reap the benefits of them now? I wondered. He'd chosen to mock and disbelieve her during his life, and it seemed only fitting that he should die with those beliefs intact. "Please," the doctor repeated, folding his hand into mine as if he were conceding a losing set of cards.

I tried to refuse, but my tongue wouldn't

listen. The image of the old blades on the Dyerson windmill kept running through my mind. They kept turning, coming back to the same place they'd started. Not sure they wanted to but doing it anyway. Just like me.

Chapter Twenty-seven

I would make the doctor's drink different from Priscilla's—I knew that right away. It would be harsher. More acidic. I wasn't planning to include even a drop of sweetness. At first, I picked only the plants that were on the border of the quilt. I collected sprigs of nightshade and delicate devil's trumpet. I dug up daffodil bulbs and laid them gently in my basket. Soon, however, my hand started straying, collecting sprigs of rosemary and cellulose strands of chive. Everywhere I reached, it seemed, my hand knew where to pluck bitterness.

I made a circuit of the town green, remembering the year when Serena Jane was May Queen, then I ambled down State Street, until, before I knew it, I found myself at the gate of the cemetery. I hesitated, then passed through the gate and rambled inside. The older tombstones tilted and leaned, but the more recent ones were still resolute in the ground, not ready to give up yet on the world of the living. I knew where to find Serena Jane's grave, but I didn't want to visit it. Instead, I wished to linger in the more distant past, so I wandered among Aberdeen's older stones, idly reading names and noting how few of them had changed in town over the years. And soon, I reflected, Robert Morgan would rest among them.

I was adding more nightshade leaves to my basket when I heard rustling in the long grass behind me and a throat clearing. My heart hammering, I turned around and saw Marcus. I stood up, brushing weeds from my thighs, trying to hide how stiff my joints were from the unaccustomed exercise. "Marcus. Hello."

"Hello back." He tipped his chin down. He was wearing his familiar wide-brimmed hat, and because I was so much taller than him, I had trouble seeing his entire face. I wondered if he knew that. I could feel the blood creeping up my neck.

"It's been a little while," he said.

"Yes." My voice came out squeaking.

"You've been taking care of the doctor."

I shifted the basket onto my other arm and sighed. "It's almost at the end now."

Marcus nodded, then looked up at me. His eyes were nearly the same color as the sky. He glanced at the basket slung over my wrist. "What's all this?"

I stuck my hand into the plants to try to rearrange them and felt the stinging graze of nettles along my thumb. "Nothing. Just collecting some things for Robert Morgan."

Marcus scowled and peered closer at the basket, making a quick inventory of all the plants I had collected. "Nasty bunch of weeds you've got yourself there. Real nasty." His scowl deepened into a frown as he studied the basket further.

I put down the basket and stuck the edge of my thumb in my mouth. Welts from the nettle were beginning to sprout on it like wasp bites. I didn't want Marcus studying the leaves too closely.

His face darkened. "You sure have been a stranger. You haven't even been out here once to check on Bobbie. And Amelia says you hardly even speak to her anymore."

I bit down on my thumb. "Since when are you and Amelia so close?" I thought of Amelia's glossy braid and of how well her petite fingers would fit with Marcus's, and I felt my stomach lurch.

Marcus's cheeks reddened, whether from anger or embarrassment, I couldn't tell. But then he spoke, as if reading my mind. "Oh, Truly, is that what you think? Is that what you really believe? You've known us our whole lives. I thought you knew us better than that. Or at least me."

"I don't know what to think." I closed my eyes. *Let what he's saying be true,* I thought. *Let Marcus really still feel the same*. I opened my eyes. "The past season has been rough. I miss seeing you."

Marcus stepped a little closer. "I miss you, too, Truly."

My heart pounded. Once we had been so close, it seemed, to working everything out, but now it felt as though we were back at square one. Marcus picked up my basket, and I felt a brief pang of guilt, wondering if he had any idea what kinds of plants I was collecting and why. I knew deep in my bones that he wouldn't approve. *It doesn't matter, though,* I told myself. *Soon the doctor will be at peace, and then I'll be free.*

Marcus stepped even closer, until I could see the familiar gold flecks dancing in his eyes. "Truly, bend down a little." He pulled me near to him, and finally kissed me, shocking me with the tart, lemony taste of his tongue. "You don't know how long I've wanted to do that," he said, smiling, and I beamed back.

"Yes, I do." It was ridiculous, I thought. On the face of things, we were hopelessly mismatched, but somehow we fit together perfectly. I inched my leg back. How could it be, I wondered, that I was standing in a cemetery, gathering the means for the doctor's death, but at the same time felt so alive? A fly buzzed close to my ear, pulling me back to reality. I couldn't do this now. No matter how much I wanted to, I couldn't forget about Robert Morgan. After he was gone, Marcus and I would have our chance. I pulled back from Marcus, sobered. "We should wait," I said.

I wanted him to reach for me again and to argue his case, but he didn't, and maybe that was the right thing. After all, I chastised myself, we had lived too long in our small town for any kind of easy romance to bloom. There were so many people between Marcus and me, for starters. The doctor. Amelia. Bobbie. I took another step back and straightened my dress, one of my hands still clasped in Marcus's. "What did you tell Bobbie about his father? How much does he know?"

Marcus scuffed a boot on the ground. "He knows he's dying. He knows it's bad, but he doesn't know how little time he has left." I blushed and cleared my throat uneasily. Marcus peered at me more closely. "Truly, do you know how little time he has?"

I looked away, thinking not of the doctor's remaining days on earth, but of my own. Did I owe it to Marcus to confess my condition? I wondered. After everything he'd seen and been through during the war, would he really want to go through the trauma of illness with me? And what if he found out about what I'd done for Prissy and what I was about to do for the doctor?

Telling him could ruin the one chance I had with Marcus, I knew, but at the same time, I didn't know how I could keep a secret of that magnitude. Marcus's fingers were tempting and warm around mine, however. They promised that they could forgive anything. They almost made me loosen my tongue, but at the last second, fear tied it up again. More than anything, I didn't want him to let go of my hand.

"Of course not," I finally answered. "How would I know a thing like that?"

Marcus seemed easier. "I don't know. It was just a thought. But you should go see Bobbie. He's in the cottage now. He doesn't work until later in the afternoon. I'll just be down that hill, doing some weeding. The door's unlocked." He squeezed my hand and let it drop. We stepped apart, and Marcus handed me my basket. "Watch out for those nettles," he said, running his thumb along the welts on my skin. "They're nasty things, Truly. They'll flay you alive."

My veins crackled with heat. "Thanks," I whispered, drawing back my hand, "I'll try to be careful." I wanted him to kiss me again. I wanted to say that his touch could cure the rash, could cure everything about me, but there was nothing to do now but wait, I knew. I'd been bitten by a witch's mouth, and I was going to have to let nature run its idle course.

A short walk brought me to the cottage, and as Marcus had promised, I found it unlocked. I'd never been inside it before, and I expected it to be spare, but it was surprisingly warm and comfortable. The main room had a small kitchen in the back corner, an oversized sofa, a rocking chair, and a fireplace stocked with well-seasoned wood.

"Hello?" I called, sticking my head in the door.

"Aunt Truly!" Bobbie bounded across the room. "Finally! I've been wondering how long it would take you to come out here. I've missed you so much."

I staggered a little as he threw his arms around me. I couldn't bear to tell him how much I'd missed him, so I patted his shoulders instead. It was amazing what a difference a few short months had made in his appearance. The lanky, sulking Bobbie that I remembered had been replaced by a glowing young man with light in his eyes.

"I wanted to give you time," I lied. "But I've been thinking about you every minute of every day." I didn't want to tell him about his father threatening me or about my troubles with Marcus. In some ways, I still thought of Bobbie as a child. Looking at him now, I wondered if it was time to give that up.

Bobbie sniffled and squeezed me once again. "Come on in." He detached himself and waved a muscled arm, beckoning me forward.

"Okay." I ducked my head going through the door. The ceiling was low, making me feel even bigger and more awkward than I usually did. I moved slowly, worried I would knock over one of Marcus's stacks of gardening catalogs or sideswipe the cracked pitcher stuffed with cattails and reeds.

"Come and sit down," Bobbie insisted, patting the sofa cushions and giving me an opportunity to study him more closely. He looked older, I thought. His hair had grown long enough for him to pull it into a small ponytail, and it gave his face new and interesting angles. I sat down gingerly, waiting to see how much the cushions would sag. Surprisingly, they held me well.

"You look good," I said.

Bobbie blushed. "Thanks. I guess you know I've been working at a bar over in Hansen. Garth's, it's called." He shifted and twiddled his thumbs. There was a beat of silence. "I guess you've also heard what kind of bar it is."

It was my turn to blush. "Bobbie, honey," I said, "it's fine with me. However things are, they're fine."

"I guess you heard about Salvatore, too, then." Bobbie stared down at his hands and blushed.

I didn't know quite what to say. It seemed so strange to be discussing love with a boy who was still eight in my heart. I cleared my throat. "Well, the way I see it, honey, love's love, whatever shape it comes in."

Bobbie half smiled, relieved. "Does Dad know?"

I nodded. "Yes." He sat back against the cushions, solemn. I couldn't tell if the expression on his face was relief or regret. Maybe a little of both, I thought. I cleared my throat. "He surprised me, you know. He was more okay with it than I thought he would be. He wanted to know if Salvatore was good to you."

Amazement swam into Bobbie's eyes. "And what did you tell him?"

"I said he was." I was silent for a moment and then leaned forward, hoping what I'd just told Bobbie would influence him. "Listen, your dad's real sick now. I think you should come by and see him. He's—well, he's not going to be here much longer." I didn't go into how I knew that with such certainty.

Bobbie shook his head. Stubbornness reclaimed his face. "I'm sorry."

"Just come by and hold his hand. You don't have to explain anything to him."

Bobbie pinched the bridge of his nose. "I'm sorry, Aunt Truly. I don't think I could go back. Besides, it's not like he made any effort to come and see me."

"You know what that would take out of him. And lately, he hasn't even been able."

"Still."

I turned so I was facing Bobbie square. I put a hand on his shoulder. "Your father's dying. You understand that, don't you? You won't ever be able to ask him anything or tell him anything after this. Are you sure that's what you want?"

Bobbie's eyes glistened. "Maybe." He

turned his face away from me and mumbled, "I just want it to be over."

"It will be. Soon. But you'll be alone then. Are you ready for that?"

Bobbie put his arms around me again and laid his head on my shoulder. He still smelled the way he had in boyhood, like Ivory soap and grass. "I won't be totally alone. I have Marcus. And Salvatore, and you. I'll always have you, right?"

I smoothed the yellow strands of his hair, so like his mother's. *It's about time*, I thought, *that we start to hold on to one another better in this family*. I was tired of losing people. I squeezed Bobbie back, hard. "Of course. You'll always have me." But that was a lie. In spite of everything the doctor had tried, I was still getting bigger. I wondered which part of me would bust first. My heart, as Robert Morgan had predicted? Or my stomach? Or would everything go together? I pulled back from Bobbie and examined him again, pleased to see that his father's glare was gone from his eyes. In the end, his mother's spirit seemed to be winning.

"Don't worry," I reassured him, patting

his hand. "No matter what happens, I'll always be around you somehow."

I didn't tell Robert Morgan about my visit with Bobbie, but it wasn't out of any sympathy or innate goodness on my part. I just figured there's no point in snapping kindling that's already cut. Over the next few weeks, I made two more trips to get the right amount of herbs. "Start with the nightshade," he said, "then add the foxglove. Did you know it's still used in heart medicine today?"

"So if it doesn't kill you, it will make you stronger?" I said.

He wiped a trail of saliva from his chin. "Maybe."

"I guess we'll see."

He grimaced. "I guess we will."

Robert Morgan didn't go as easily as Priscilla Sparrow. He clearly wanted to stick around and give orders. It was as if after years of bossing and tormenting me, he couldn't just give it up. He lost his voice completely, but he took to constantly ringing the bell I'd left by his bedside. I'd no sooner fetch him a fresh glass of water than he'd want a mint to suck on, and when he had that, he'd want me to give him the newspaper, trying to pretend that the print wasn't swimming and bobbing before his eyes.

"Robert Morgan, you should just rest. Let me handle this," I told him, but he wasn't having any of that. He made me sit on the quilt next to him while he pointed at all the different plants, double-checking what I put in the drink.

Finally, on the last night of July, I helped him to one of the lawn chairs in the garden and covered him with Tabitha's quilt. He'd chosen nighttime, I knew, because he wanted the stars to be the last thing he looked at. "Ready?" I asked. In my hands, the jar of green liquid sloshed and rippled like a dangerous emerald sea. I uncapped it and released the mossy aroma. The doctor was so weak that he could almost not lift his own arms. He merely nodded and gazed at me with sunken eyes. I took one of his stringy hands and wrapped his fingers tight around the jar. "Hold on," I told him. "You don't want to spill any. Here—" I pulled out a napkin. "For under your chin."

It was a perfect twilight—the kind that

tickles you with the promise of autumn lurking right around the corner, when the crickets are alive and yakking and the day's heat lingers in the flowers and trees, scenting the air. It could have been an evening for almost anything—eloping, birthing a child, a simple, good rest—but instead, here I was killing a man, and not just any man, either, but Robert Morgan, who'd housed me for the past ten years, doctored me, riled me, and who, nevertheless, I'd strangely come to love a little bit lately.

I tipped my head back, gazed at the spangled sky, and wondered if people's souls ended up there or stayed sunk down in the earth with their bones. I squinted, and the stars blurred until they looked almost calcified. Maybe the heavens were a kind of celestial grave, I thought, the way the earth is a repository for our flesh, and when we stared at the stars, we were really beholding a million lives twinkling back at us, asking us not to forget. I sat forward and cleared my throat.

"Is there anything you want me to remember, in particular?" I asked. I tried to think about the things I carried around with me from my mother, my father, August, and my sister. My name, I decided. Certainly the genes that made me bigger than everyone else. From August I could say I'd gotten the ability to spot the losing horse at the racetrack and a winning hand of cards, and Serena Jane had entrusted me with Bobbie. I wondered what the doctor's legacy would be, then reflected that maybe he'd already given it to me. He'd told me the truth, after all, about why I was so big and what it meant for my existence, and he'd shared the secret of Tabitha's quilt with me. It sounds funny now, but in a nutshell, I guess you could say he'd granted me the secret of death and, by extension, life.

The half-empty jar in Robert Morgan's hand quivered, and I reached out and steadied it. "Don't worry, I'm right here," I said. There was a weak moon overhead, and it cast enough of a glow that I could just make out Robert Morgan's profile. Even sideways, you could tell how much weight had fallen off him. Now, all the angles and lines of his body were even clearer than before, as if the Maker had wanted to whittle him down to his absolute essence before He let him into the afterlife.

Something strange happened then. At the time, I thought it was just delirium. Men have been known to do all kinds of bizarre things before they pass to the other side, and it's a busy fool who would sit around trying to unknit them. But the doctor wasn't mad, and he wasn't desperate, either. He was confessing.

"California," he wheezed.

I patted his shoulder. "No one's going to California," I assured him. "Everyone's right here where they've always been." *Even Bobbie,* I wanted to add, but I held my tongue. A dying man should be able to spout off whatever nonsense he wants.

"No . . ." He lifted his head off the chair and half rolled toward me. *"California."*

"Hush." I pushed him back down, and with that, he seemed to give up. I can't say exactly how much longer we sat together—half an hour or half the night—but it seemed more like the latter. Every now and then, the doctor's head would loll, and he would murmur a name: my sister's, Bobbie's, once or twice even mine. For my part, I didn't say much. I figured anything I did would come out sounding either petty or dumb. Instead, I just sat there and let the stars do all the talking for me until they, too, started to fade, and the red fingers of dawn started crawling across the sky, and I realized that the night really had gone for good and taken Robert Morgan with it.

Chapter Twenty-eight

Two deaths under similar circumstances, and then two funerals in the same town, and yet Priscilla Sparrow had had exactly zero attendees at hers, while the doctor's was oversubscribed. I can't explain the dearth of mourners at Priscilla Sparrow's grave, only perhaps to suggest that habitual bitterness reaps emptiness in this life. Of course, the doctor had his own emotional issues, but he still had plenty of folks flocking around his grave at the end. Somehow, he managed to have it all the way he wanted, exerting influence from the grave. I guess death changes less about a body than you'd imagine.

One thing it didn't change was Robert Morgan's relationship with Bobbie. The whole time the town was muttering its prayers and dabbing its eyes, I was searching and searching for a sign of Bobbie, but in the end, I had to concede that he wasn't coming.

"He knows Robert Morgan passed away, doesn't he?" I asked Amelia.

She scowled, and I corrected myself. "Of course he knows. Marcus wouldn't keep something like that from him. Besides"—I jutted my chin toward the grave—"I think it's pretty obvious." I fell silent. The air between us had been chilly ever since our falling-out on her last cleaning day, and I shifted, uncomfortable and unsure about how to clear it.

"The doctor said some mighty odd things the night he died," I finally mused, at a loss for what else to talk about.

Next to me, Amelia stiffened and stretched her neck.

"Something about California," I continued. "You think he could know anyone in California?" Amelia looked white. I waited to see if she would answer, but she didn't, so I shook my head. "I didn't think you would. I guess some things about Robert Morgan will always stay a mystery."

I moved up to the gaping hole that contained Robert Morgan, Amelia staying by my side, and we stood silently for a moment, sunk in our own private thoughts. Amelia took a deep breath and almost started to say something, then closed her mouth.

"Were you going to ask if I'm going to the wake?" I filled in for her. It was as though we were back to our early days together, I thought, where I carried all the conversational burden. "Because the answer is no." It was going to be at Sal Dunfry's house—my old childhood home—but the thought of crushing together with the whole town in those familiar rooms was too much. Besides, I had some other, unfinished business to which I wanted to attend. Amelia suddenly grabbed my elbow, however, her words falling out pell-mell, her tongue so thick, I had trouble understanding her.

"Truly, I'm sorry for what I did. I let years go by when I should have said something."

I wrinkled my forehead. "Why, Amelia, whatever are you talking about?"

Amelia was about to continue, but Vi Vickers's loud voice interrupted her. "At least we don't need to worry about her falling in," Vi was snickering to Sal.

Sal giggled and rolled her eyes toward me. "She'd get stuck halfway down."

Amelia sucked in her gut, and for the first time in her life, she looked prepared to make a mess instead of clean one up. "I wouldn't talk like that, Vi," she said loudly and distinctly. "I know some ugly things about you, too."

Vi gasped when she heard Amelia speak and then blushed about a hundred different shades of red, but before I could thank Amelia, she disappeared into the trees. Having her stick up for me like that was so against her nature that it melted something in me. I realized how constant Amelia had been in my life, from the first day she'd snatched the doll leg from me in Brenda's kitchen, to all the times she'd tagged home from school behind Marcus and me, to our coffee-fueled chats in the doctor's kitchen. *I'll catch her later*, I thought. *I'll tell her everything, from what the doctor said would happen to me to what I did for him and Priscilla.* We had a whole summer's worth of talking to do, me and Amelia. First, though, I wanted to pay my respects to Priscilla Sparrow. In the years since her death, I had resisted visiting her grave, figuring what was over was over, but the doctor's dying had brought Prissy back up in my memory again strong, and I knew that it was time to lay her down to rest in my own mind, along with the doctor.

Her grave was on the opposite end of the cemetery from Robert Morgan's, but you had to know where to look. There wasn't even a headstone—just a painted wooden cross—and I wasn't sure if that was because stone had cost too much or because she had no one to do those things for her. I plucked a clutch of Queen Anne's lace—a weedy flower, true, but also prim and mannered as Miss Sparrow had been—and laid it on top of the grass under the cross. I crossed my hands and bowed my head, and then, because I was pretty sure no one else had said it, I started whispering the Lord's Prayer.

"It's a little late for that." Marcus's voice

floated through the air to me. I opened my eyes.

"Marcus. You scared me."

"Seems your natural reaction to me these days." He grinned, but his eyes remained sad.

"That's not true." But even as I spoke, I could feel my heart hammering up a ruckus against my ribs, as if it wanted to be let out into the wide blue world. I put a hand on my chest. "How did Bobbie take the news about his father? I didn't see him today."

"He hasn't said much the last few days. Just goes to work, or out to meet Salvatore. He helped me dig the grave, though, if you can believe that. Just grabbed an extra shovel, put his neck down, and set to work. You never saw anyone dig so hard."

I was silent for a moment, remembering my first weeks in Robert Morgan's house with Bobbie and how fiercely he'd clung to his mother's blue dress. "We were never very good with death," I finally said. "We never talked much about his mother dying. Robert Morgan wouldn't let us dwell on it."

Marcus worked his tongue over his teeth. "Well, now he's got two dead parents locked up in that head of his. One of these days, something's got to give."

I shrugged. "Maybe he'll move back to the house now." My throat tightened with anticipation of how good it would be to have him under the roof again, to hear his footsteps clattering up and down the attic steps.

Marcus shook his head. "No. I already asked him about that. Says he's not ready."

"Oh." I tried to keep the disappointment from coating my voice, but Marcus picked up on it.

"Solitude can be a blessing, Truly. You just haven't tried it. It might do you some good. It did me good after the war, I can tell you. Just me, and a backpack, and the open road."

Not when your body is a ticking time bomb, I thought. *Solitude is not good then.* I bowed my head. "I guess. Seems like I might be a touch lonely, though."

"Well, it's not like the doctor was great company."

"No."

Marcus stared down at the dirt heaped in front of us on top of Priscilla Sparrow's grave. "Now there was a lonely woman. Do you remember how god-awful strict she was back in school?"

I nodded. "But inside, she wasn't as bad as you think. Especially later, when she got so sick. Why, when she came to see me last—" I clapped a hand over my mouth, realizing too late what I had just said.

Marcus narrowed his eyes. "Go on," he said.

"I was just going to say that she was tender inside, that's all," I stammered, but it was too late. The wheels and dials were turning lickety-split in Marcus's head. "Truly, what was in your basket that day you and I met in the cemetery? Tell me you weren't gathering the kinds of plants I think you were."

I opened my mouth, prepared to deny everything, but one look at Marcus and I knew that among all the people on earth, I'd never be able to lie to him. "It wasn't my idea," I croaked, "it was Priscilla Sparrow's. I found Tabitha's shadow book. It turns out it's really an old quilt that's been in the family for years. Maybe you noticed it? The one hung in the parlor with all the plants on it?"

Marcus furrowed his brow. "That thing with all the twisting vines?"

I nodded. "They were sewn there for a reason."

Marcus frowned. "So the legends about Tabby are true, eh?"

"Maybe. Who knows?"

Marcus kept his face pointed to the ground. "You gave the drink to the doctor, too, didn't you?" He squeezed his lips tight.

Miserable, I nodded. Marcus put his hands flat down at his sides, and in that moment I finally saw that he wasn't small so much as compact. Like a coil burrowed into itself. For such a slight man, he suddenly looked surprisingly tall. He glanced up, startling me. "Do you know why I became a gardener?" he asked, white around the lips. "Do you even know why I choose to live out here among all these rotten old tombstones?"

"Well, you get the cottage for free, and—"

Marcus cut me off. "It has nothing to do with money. Nothing at all." He stared over the graves. "I know when I came home you thought I was nuts, going on about the catacombs of Paris and their five million bones, but look at all these rows of people here, tucked up beside each other like they're lying in a giant bed. That's all the earth really is—a final resting place. But it's one we need to tend, because one day we'll be there, too. I learned that all too well in Vietnam. You know, once I had to make the same choice you made for the doctor. I think I did the right thing, but it's something I never want to do again. I can't imagine why you would even do it once."

I set my jaw. "It'll have to be live and let live, I guess."

Marcus screwed up his mouth. "I don't think that's quite the correct terminology for this discussion."

I took a step toward him, unwilling to let the subject turn into a swamp between us. "But it's over now." I remembered the extra jars I'd stored in the pantry for myself—just in case—but figured I didn't need to say anything about them. It wasn't as though I were planning on giving out the potion to anyone besides myself, and it wasn't doing any harm all bottled up, dusty in the dark. "No one knows," I said. "No one will ever know."

Marcus eased away from me. "You don't get it, Truly. *I'll* always know, and you will, too. There will always be ghosts between us. You'll see." *Isn't that part of love,* I wanted to ask, *carrying someone else's ghosts for them?* But before I could, he wheeled around on his good leg and hobbled across the grass, leaving a ragged, vegetative trail I was sorry I could not follow.

Much has been documented about the soul's response to death, but I think the human body's reaction is just as inscrutable. Is it such an outlandish concept, I wonder, to imagine that the body has its own rituals and protocols for loss and that those rites remain mysterious and distant from what goes on in our minds? And maybe it's necessary and proper that they should be so, for without that gap, we would probably never let ourselves be transformed. I know I wouldn't have, but I didn't get to make that choice—or maybe I should say I didn't have to make it. Either way, something began happening to me right after the doctor died.

He'd given me the name of a new doctor in Hansen—a Dr. Redfield. He was a man about the same age as Robert Morgan who'd worked in Albany for years but liked country life better. "I've given him copies of all your records," Robert Morgan assured me a few weeks before he died, "and he knows all about your case. He can provide you with your medication, and oversee your symptoms. He'll even travel out to the house. Just call him."

A few days after the doctor's funeral, I found the number and began to dial. I still had about a week's worth of medicine, but I would need to get more, and sometimes it could take a few days. As I was about to push the last button on the phone, however, I caught a glimpse of myself in the foyer's oval mirror, but where a glimpse was all I could ever catch of myself before, this time I found that the narrow frame was able to hold my entire reflection. I examined the newly bared planes of my cheeks, tilting my face first one way, then the other, then lifting my chin to see how much more neck I had. The fresh summer air licked and tickled my throat, and I shivered. *Is this how it is for everyone,* I wondered, *to be so plain to the world?* I remembered when Marcus had comforted me after Miss Sparrow had taken my mother's mirror. What was it he had said? That reflections were just little particles of light? I liked that idea—that even I consisted of tiny fragments that could be rearranged.

As if in a trance, I slowly lowered the receiver back into its cradle and dropped the paper with Dr. Redfield's number. I turned my face from side to side, but every angle confirmed what I suspected. I had shrunk a little. I couldn't imagine how it was possible, especially since the doctor had told me I would keep increasing in size, but the mirror wasn't lying. Instead of spreading as wide and thick as the chestnut tree outside of the schoolhouse, here I was with the flesh on me limning the general shape of my bones. I rushed upstairs and dug the farm clothes from my youth out of the back of my closet, and for some inscrutable reason, they fit again, the plaid flannel and soft denim nestling against my skin like old, familiar sheets.

To celebrate, I gathered up all the balloonlike rayon dresses I'd worn over the years, balled them together in the downstairs fireplace, and watched them singe and cinder. It was so satisfying watching them burn that before I half knew it, I'd gathered up a whole other load of junk and set fire to it, too. Recipe cards, the yellowed stacks of magazines from my room, the dried flowers off the parlor mantel—all of them went up in smoke. The next morning, I washed the quilt in lavender soap and hung it in the sun to dry, its wet batting pulling the line low. I took down the curtains to wash them, too, but decided the windows looked better without them, so I rolled them into a ball, shoved them in the fireplace, and ignited them. I added the flattened needlepoint pillows off the sofa—grungy from years of dust—and the doilies off the backs of the chairs and then ran for dear life when the room erupted in a choking cloud of noxious smoke. When I finally got up the courage to reenter the parlor, the fire had gentled down to a glowing heap of ash, and the floorboards in front of the hearth were pitted and scarred from live embers.

By week's end, I had burned the oilskin from off the kitchen table, the ancient pack of playing cards August had given me in childhood, and most of the doctor's clothes. My fires grew too noxious and large for the little hearth in the parlor, so I moved my operation outside and set off my blazes in Marcus's flower beds, pleased to see them scorch, too. *Serves him right,* I thought, though for what, I couldn't really say. Every day, I came up with a different reason.

Who knows how much more I would have burned if I hadn't burned myself first? Again, it's the old lesson of bitterness eliciting like. To anyone else, I would have looked like a larger-than-average woman clearing the detritus of decades out of a house no one had much use for anymore, but if you'd come closer, you might have been disturbed by the way the reflected flames danced and leapt in my eyes. You would have noticed me standing smoke side to the fires when I didn't have to, just so I could gulp in one more acrid taste of the past before it floated upward without me. With every crackle and snap of heat, I could feel myself getting tighter and smaller, until I felt so immune to the world's ills that

I grew reckless. I fed the fires higher and higher until one afternoon a rogue ember burned a crescent into my palm.

Hissing with pain, I went to the dispensary, to see if the doctor had any old cream or balm. Away from the fire, my cheeks cooled and tingled, even though the air was moist. The center of my hand throbbed and beat—a rhythm my temples picked up and began to copy. With my good hand, I groped along the top of the doorjamb for the hidden key, then shoved open the screen door and unlocked the doctor's office. It was the one place I had avoided since his death, and even though it had been only about a week, the air inside was as thick and stale as old rubber. I groped my way to the light switch and flicked it on.

I opened the door to the medicine cabinet and found a sample tube of antibiotic cream and a roll of gauze. Winding the white fabric around my hand, I continued to inspect the room. The doctor and Amelia had pretty well cleaned it out at the beginning of his illness. His desk was bare of his usual files and folders, and he'd either destroyed all his old patient records or sent them on to the clinic in Hansen. I idly pulled open one of the metal drawers and was surprised to see a few files remaining. One of them was Priscilla Sparrow's, and one of them was mine.

Mine was so thick that I had trouble holding the whole thing in one hand. I flipped it open and right away saw a decade's worth of blood test results, measurements, and other numbers. I scanned through this information quickly, not daring to let myself put an actual number to my weight and height after all these years. I still didn't want to know. The back of the folder held his notes, and I read these more thoroughly. *Subject recalcitrant,* one sentence read. *Refuses to follow dietary advice.* I turned the page. *Subject's bone structure more in keeping with a male's. Subject shows increased musculature. Subject's heart shows evidence of gross enlargement. Prognosis poor.* I sighed and shoved the papers back into the folder, then set the folder on top of the filing cabinet. The doctor's history of me was like a faulty, oversized shadow. One more thing to be burned.

On the wall above the doctor's desk, his books still held all their old posts on the shelf. Anatomy texts, drug indexes—there were enough words, I thought, to write the human body into existence ten times over, a hundred different ways. I ran my fingers down the spines of the books then back again. Each time, my fingers kept hooking on the last book in the row. It was slightly out of kilter with the other volumes, as if someone had recently taken it off the shelf. I peered at it more closely. Someone *had* taken it down. I scowled. Who could it have been? The doctor? But he hadn't left his bed before his death. Bobbie had keys to the house, but as far as I knew, he hadn't been back. That left only Amelia. But she hadn't been in the doctor's office since he'd died, I didn't think, and it would have been totally unlike her to move only one item in a room and then not clean it up properly.

Curious, I fanned the pages open in my hand. Pen-and-ink drawings—precise and delicate as spiderwebs—wavered, depicting all the mysteries of the body. The beefy heart. Clusters of cauliflower buds on the lungs. Blood vessels that narrowed into fronds of capillaries, looking more like ferns than part of the flesh. But then something stuck in between the pages caught my eye. A small bit of paper—the corner of an envelope. I plucked it out and held it up, and then gasped. It was a return address, and the name I was reading, in very familiar handwriting, was my sister's.

What was a letter from my sister doing in Robert Morgan's bookcase, I wondered, and when would she have had the occasion to send him a letter? As far as I could remember, they'd never been apart after their marriage until she'd left him. I took down the next book and flipped through it, but there was nothing—just pages of ink. I did the same with all the other books, until the desk behind me was full, but there was no other sign of any correspondence from my sister. Bewildered, I stared down at the scrap of paper again and saw what I hadn't before. The envelope had been torn so that half the address was missing, but there was enough left for me to make out some of the words—*11 Palm* something—and the state that the letter had been sent from. *California.*

All the air left my body, and I slumped against the desk. I remembered what the doctor had said the night he died. Had he really been talking about Serena Jane? It didn't make any sense, though. My sister lay in the Aberdeen cemetery, boxed, buried, and weighted down right next to all the other Morgans. I could go there anytime I wanted and touch the heavy block of stone with her name on it. But the grieving mind is an irrational thing. It tricks us, overlooks details, stops paying attention halfway through the story, and thus ignores all other potential endings.

Seized with curiosity, I yanked open the center drawer of the doctor's desk and dug around. Except for a few yellowed receipts, it was empty. Same with all the other drawers, except the last one. There, underneath a copy of his will, which I'd already gone over, was something I never even knew existed—the deed to the Dyerson farm. I pulled it out and examined it. What I was holding was a copy, I surmised, and it had been amended several times. At one point, the doctor had possessed the farm, I saw with surprise, but now, under *Owner,* there was a new name, one I never really expected to see scrawled on a Morgan document. *Amelia Ann Dyerson*.

Like a frame stilled from a moving picture, an image of Amelia frozen halfway up the stepladder in the doctor's office with a bundle of papers in her hand suddenly stuck in the reel of my mind. I remembered all her recent stop-and-start, partial confessions, her paleness when I'd brought up the topic of California at the doctor's graveside, and instead of the anger I expected, I felt the blood run as cool and calculating through my veins as Robert Morgan's had done in his life. Amelia had had something to do with the disappearance of my sister's letters and the secret of her existence—the only thing I didn't know was why, and I wasn't sure I cared to, either. Some betrayals are so huge, nothing can ever whittle them down.

Locking up the doctor's office and sliding the key back into its hiding place, the mysterious scrap of paper tucked safely in my pocket, I began racing through a mental slew of wild possibilities. What if my sister was still alive? What if I could find her again? What if Bobbie could have his mother back? Was there such a thing as redemption?

Outside, evening had begun to come on. The first bats were tickling the pale sky, and the fireflies were getting ready to light themselves up and dance. It was still hot, though. Across the yard, my fire had mellowed but gave out an occasional crackle, like something alive. The burn on my palm throbbed, keeping time with the blood pounding in my temples, my ears, and I knew for certainty that my heart was shrinking and that I would take Amelia down with it.

Chapter Twenty-nine

Some people, when confronted with a mystery, will go forth immediately and scour the earth for answers, overturning furniture, comparing the angles of doors and windows, checking under flower pots, certain they're on the right path. Maybe they're impatient, or maybe they've read too many detective stories. They've gotten so accustomed to getting the solution that they think it's their natural-born right. It never occurs to them there might not be one—not a good one, at least. Not one that makes any sense. Me, I've never been a big reader. I figure that if a secret has an answer, it'll out on its own if it's meant to, and if it doesn't, then maybe providence has a better reason for keeping it hidden than you think. But some mysteries are too big for one person to hold on to for long, and some are too tantalizing to let lie fallow, and those are the worst kind of all, for they end up being the real heartbreakers. They are the ones where once you know the story, you wish you didn't.

I didn't go chasing after the truth right away—it was like the burn on my hand. Too recent, too raw, still oozing and sore. It needed time to set and heal before I went digging in the coals again. I needed to grow a second skin. To compensate, to keep my mind tethered to the present, I continued my efforts of cleaning out the doctor's house. I ventured into the attic and dug through all the boxes and trunks, setting aside any treasures I thought might be valuable. I polished the banister and the mahogany dining table and chairs. I even got out a toolbox and tightened up the washers on all the sinks.

The burned spot on my palm gradually turned into a congealed, red lump of a scar, but it itched like the dickens. Nothing

I put on it—the doctor's cream, petroleum jelly—helped. So one afternoon, I threw whatever calming herbs I could think of—chamomile, mint, comfrey—into a pot and brewed out the oils, catching them with one of the doctor's glass beakers. Then I mixed all of that into some softened beeswax, and spread it on my hand. Immediately, my skin settled down and felt cool and regular, and in a week, the scar was beginning to fade. I'd promised myself that I was done with the quilt, but this wasn't technically going back on my word, I figured. I had made up this mixture on my own. Still, it was close enough to Tabby's cures for me to fold up the quilt and put it away in the back of the linen closet. *You've been enough trouble,* I said to it. *History's done with you now*.

Who knows if I would have left it there, but Vi Vickers dropped by with a case of hives the next day, wanting to see if the doctor had anything left over in his office she could use. "Please," she howled, her eyelids crusted and swollen. "I can't drive all the way out to Hansen like this, and Art's out golfing for the afternoon. Besides, it's Sunday. Everything's closed."

She was right. She did look awful. So what I did next, I did without thinking—grabbed the tin of balm I'd made and held it out like an offering. "Here—" I pried off the lid. "Try this. Maybe it will work." Vi smeared some on her cheeks and tried to give back the container, but I shook my head. "Keep it." I closed the door, smiling, understanding that where I had hidden the quilt didn't really matter because it was already mapped in my mind. It was up to me, I realized, to decide how I would navigate it. History didn't just happen. It was made.

The next day, I decided that if I was finally going to bring everything on the quilt out into the light, I was going to do it whole hog, in front of God, the town, and everyone. I went upstairs to fetch Tabby's handiwork out of the closet. It could use some more sunlight, I decided—an entire day hung on the line. As I stepped out onto the porch, I found a potted geranium propped on the boards with a note attached: *Thanks for the balm, Truly. It also cures circles under the eyes! Love, Vi.* I smiled and nudged the container with my foot, happy to see something growing after all the weeks I'd just spent staring at ash.

Vi must have a big mouth, because word got around, and soon I had people dropping in for all manner of minor aches and pains, asking if I could do something about indigestion or if I knew any way to get rid of three-week cough. "I'm not a doctor," I protested. "I really don't even know the first thing about this stuff."

"I know," Sal insisted, seeking to cure a patch of eczema on the back of her hand, "but you worked wonders on everyone else. Couldn't you just give it a try?"

I studied the quilt and made up another balm—the same as Vi's but with more comfrey—and dropped it off at her house, which was really my old house. "Why don't you come in?" she asked, swinging the front door open wide to reveal glossy floorboards and the rich smell of something with cinnamon in it baking. I peeked around her and saw gingham-checked chairs in the living room and a porcelain umbrella stand next to a chest of drawers. I remembered the dingy wallpaper we'd had when I lived there with my father and the way a week's worth of letters used to cover the floor, and I shook my head. Time had gone by, it was true, just not nearly enough.

“Maybe another day.” I waved. “I have to go.”

“Well, thanks again,” Sal called after me. “And you look good, Truly. Are you losing weight?”

“Nah.” I grinned. “You’re just getting used to me big.”

Sal shrugged and closed her door. But I went home and looked in the mirror again, not daring to believe what I saw. I hadn’t had any medication for days, but I could tell I hadn’t grown. I certainly wasn’t any taller, and my hands hadn’t become the size of baseball mitts. In fact, I was cinching my belt one hole tighter and then one more, and none of my buttons ever busted open anymore.

That was all guesswork, though. To definitively test my mass, I knew there was only one way. I would have to step on the scale in the doctor’s office, and so I did, moving the bar for myself for the first time ever, astonished when the weights didn’t slide all the way to the end. I peeked at the number, then compared it with the ones I remembered from the doctor’s chart and found a small difference. Don’t get me wrong. I was still the same old me, but what the doctor had predicted—my bones getting so big that I'd just sink my way into the earth—not only wasn't happening, it was all going the other way. How would Robert Morgan have explained what was happening to me? I wondered. He no doubt would have had some fancy medical theory for my shrinking, but as far as I was concerned, the lightening of my body came as much from being free of him as anything else. At last, with no one measuring me or sizing me up, I was finally free to be whatever size I wanted.

During this time, I saw Amelia. Of course I did. In a town the size of Aberdeen, people are as like to stick in your craw as not, even when you don't want them there. Even Marcus couldn't keep from running into me from time to time, though when he did he would just tip his hat and move to the other side of the street. I accepted his coolness, understanding the reason for it, but with Amelia I was more calculating, drawing her in closer and closer while I considered how and when I would confront her.

She began visiting me more and more regularly, amused by all the concoctions I was making and impressed by the gifts folks left on the back porch. Baskets of peaches. A loaf of fresh bread. A hand-knit scarf with a note that said it would match my eyes. In the house, jewel-colored bottles of tinctures lined the windowsills, and the air continually smelled like wet grass and peppermint.

She seemed amazed by the quilt. Now that my secret was out, I always had it on display. She paused in her dusting now to regard Tabby's handiwork, draped over the back of a kitchen chair, then she drifted into the pantry and began tipping bottles up to the light. I glanced over to see what she was holding. "That's for headache."

Her fingers roamed to another bottle.

"I'm not sure yet about that tonic. Maybe for sore muscles."

She reached up to the top shelf and hefted one of the emerald jars of Tabby's potion in her hand. The liquid was dusty now, dulled down but no less potent for all that.

"Put that one back," I snapped. "It's for no one." It was like the scrap of letter that I'd put in my bedside drawer upstairs, I thought. It was merely a relic, a fragment of something I didn't want to think about. Amelia looked hurt but set the jar back in its place. *Good,* I thought. *Now we both have our secrets.*

"Did you hear about Bobbie?" I finally asked, keeping my voice matter-of-fact. "He got some write-up in the local paper about his cooking. Apparently, he's got a real gift."

Amelia's eyes swelled with pride, and she nodded.

"I think he's going to be okay," I continued. "Why, I bet Marcus puts on five pounds having Bobbie live with him." At Marcus's name, I frowned and shut up, and Amelia, sensing my ire, closed the door to the pantry and resumed her dusting.

We spent the rest of the afternoon more or less in silence, nursing lemonade on the front porch. I was tempted that afternoon to confront her, to lay the whole puzzling mess of Serena Jane in her lap and see what she had to say for herself, but I wasn't done punishing her yet. The longer I stayed sullen and sulky, the more uncomfortable she grew, and it pleasured me to watch her nervous fingers tug on her braid. I relished the times she knocked and knocked at the front door, then finally slunk away like a banished dog when I refused to answer, or the awkward silences between us whenever she brought up Marcus. *And that's another thing,* I thought, the unfamiliar sensation of rage swilling through me, making me feel all-powerful. *Marcus belongs with me. That garden should have been mine. Even if I'm dead and gone, they shouldn't be together.*

No matter how I imagined it, it peeved me to picture Marcus kneeling in the dirt in back of Amelia's house, just as it galled me to think that somewhere out there, my sister might be trailing her bare feet through the sand and rough water of a California beach, wondering about the cracked sidewalks and crooked fences that she'd left behind in Aberdeen and wondering about Bobbie, too. *What if she hears about the doctor's death?* I wondered. *What if she comes strolling back into town?*

The days of summer continued to heat up, and the scrap of envelope in my drawer curled and dried until I thought it might float away, but it didn't. Instead, the notion of it billowed and swelled like a thunderhead until I finally couldn't take it anymore. If I kept all the questions I had inside of me, I knew, they would multiply and multiply, until I really did come apart at the seams. And I didn't want that. Quite the opposite. No, I decided, the time had come. I needed to let the clouds inside me burst.

At the end of August, on the last real dog day of the year, Amelia came knocking as sure as the sun, two paper sacks full of vegetables clutched in her skinny arms. She had her on usual black-and-white attire, and there were little stray hairs curling at her temples. But whenever I picture Amelia, it is her mouth I always think of—lips as crooked and thin as her father's, but at the same time as resolute and hard as her mother's, for they gave nothing away very easily, especially a confession.

"What's in the sacks?" I asked, unlatching the kitchen screen door for her.

Today, Amelia was effusive. Her words tripped out of her mouth lightly. "Beets. Lettuce. Baby carrots and greens." She put the bags on the counter. The heady smell of fresh dirt swam through the air.

I kicked a chair out from the table, refusing to look at her. “Have some coffee. I’ll put a pot on.”

Amelia blew a wisp of hair off her shiny forehead. “Too hot. Got any iced tea?”

I opened the icebox. “Orange juice or lemonade.”

“Lemonade.” Amelia sank into the chair. She squinted at me. “You look different. And what are you doing at the back of the house? Looks like a war zone.” Now that my hand was better, I’d resumed my burning of decades of the house’s trash, in spite of the heat. Watching the flames dance and spit somehow dampened my sense of rage and made me feel calmer.

I sloshed lemonade into a pair of glasses. “Spring cleaning.”

“It’s almost autumn.”

I shrugged. We sat in silence for a moment, watching our glasses sweat. Finally, I took a deep breath. “You know, there’s still a whole heap of stuff out there in the doctor’s office.”

Amanda stared down at her lemonade. “Autumn’s around the corner. I could get to it then.”

I took a sip from my glass and set it down,

back in the precise spot it had been. It seemed important in that moment not to alter anything more in the world than I had to. “I’ve been out there already, you know. When I burned my hand.” I held up my palm, healed now but for a faint half-moon.

“Oh?” Amelia’s eyes were definitely her father’s, I decided—heavy-lidded, thick-lashed, built for gambling.

“Seems the doctor tidied most things up himself.”

“I’ll scrub the room for you, then.”

I continued on as if I hadn’t heard her. I felt terrible toying with Amelia this way, but at the same time, I couldn’t contain my fury. “I mean, not everything is gone, of course,” I said. “His books are still there. And there was this.” I reached into my pocket and pulled out the scrap of envelope with *11 Palm* and *California* written on it. “Along with this.” I pulled out the copy of the deed to the farm.

It’s an interesting sensation when intense anger is finally realized. It’s as if after watching a top spin for hours, it suddenly stops and falls over. Your eyes keep darting and twitching, not wanting to believe what they see. I waited. There was an uncomfortable wall of silence between us, and then Amelia stretched out a hand and touched the scrap of envelope with the tip of one finger. "Where was it?" she breathed.

"Inside a book. Is this what I think it is?"

Amelia nodded, her eyes still downcast. I leaned back hard against my chair, and it crackled and groaned. "I don't understand. I thought she committed suicide."

"It was someone else." Amelia's voice was a whisper—a mayfly skimming the surface of a pond. "Not Serena Jane."

"But how did Robert Morgan get the body?"

"He said it was her. He made me say it, too. He said if I didn't, he'd take the farm." Amelia cupped her head in her hands, and that action told me enough. It was Robert Morgan, after all. How had anything in this town ever happened but through his lies, intimidation, and tall tales?

I pictured my sister's square, blunt headstone. "So that's not Serena Jane buried in the cemetery." Amelia shook her head again, and her passivity infuriated me.

Amelia sniffed. "He—he said that if you ever knew, *he* would know. He said he'd call in every last creditor in three states. I tried to get him to give the letters to you, or at least to Bobbie, but he said what was done was done, and that should be the end of it."

I sat back again. Her pragmatic answer shocked me. All this time I had assumed she'd kept the location of my sister a secret out of a kind of jealousy, but I had only been flattering myself, I realized. When it came down to it, Amelia was a Dyerson through and through, wheeling and dealing, always dodging the bullet of debt. *She did it to save her own skin,* I thought, *not mine.* I remembered Robert Morgan leveraging the same threat to get me to move in with him and wondered what Amelia would have done in my place. Would she have made the same sacrifice? I suddenly hated the Dyersons and their long-faced hard luck. No wonder they were such sad cases, I thought. They all but opened their arms to the world's abuse. They never even tried to change a thing. I smacked the table. I would never be like that, I knew. I couldn't in the body I'd been given, and this, more than anything, made me realize that whatever Amelia had been to me, it was never a sister. I laid my head down on the table. *So much for trying to keep the universe in place,* I thought.

Of course, what was done was done. Wasn't that what I had been telling myself? Had I been wise to bow to the greater pull of the past, I wondered, letting it suck me into the mystery of the quilt and now of my sister? I didn't have an answer at that moment, but the time had come, I thought, to address the question and begin living in the present. I couldn't stay angry forever, or I'd burn myself up. I knew that. I needed to try to forgive Amelia.

I unfolded my fingers and took a breath. "I'm angry, Amelia. So angry I can almost not see, but too many years have gone by. What I figure we need now is a fresh start. No Robert Morgan. No creditors. Tell me where the letters are, and we'll go from there."

Amelia's mouth froze into the shape of a zero, and I remembered how much trouble she'd had reciting her elocution lessons for Miss Sparrow, how no matter what she did, she could never get any part of the story straight. "Sorry, Truly," she babbled. "So, so sorry." She covered her face with her hands.

My stomach churned with a bad premonition. "Amelia, what have you done?" The past was so tantalizingly close, it seemed, all I wanted to do was reach out and bite it. "Tell me, where are the letters?"

Amelia heaved a huge sigh. "Burned."

"Burned." Neither a question nor a declaration, but an echo, hollow and loose.

Amelia elaborated. "The doctor burned them. I watched. We built a little fire in the parlor, and he threw the envelopes in."

Inside my chest, my heart flapped ragged and sere. "Why would you help him? How could you? And where was I?"

"You came into the parlor, remember, to tell us there was pie? You didn't know what we were doing. Robert Morgan shouted at you, and then you went back to the kitchen." I thought briefly back to that afternoon, when Amelia had been crouched in the corner, ash dusting her hair, and the doctor had snapped at me so suddenly. Amelia took a deep breath and continued her explanation with difficulty. "I was trying to get him to give me back the farm. All I've ever wanted is for you to come back there and live with me like it used to be. . . . Truly, please say something."

I stared at the scar on my hand. All this time I'd been trying to cinder the remnants of the past when the item I most wanted was already up in smoke. I closed my eyes and pictured waves washing sand off a beach. "I will never forgive you for this, Amelia," I finally said, my voice as low and rough as it's ever been.

I heard a sob catch in Amelia's throat. She stretched a thin arm across the table toward me, but I jerked my hands away. "Get out." I turned my head and closed my eyes, wanting her to go more than anything, wishing she would disappear and leave my beautiful blond sister in her place. When I opened my eyes, however, Amelia surprised me. She was standing in front of me with the jar of Tabby's herbs, a calculating glint in her eye. She shook the jar, loosening sediment and small particles, sending them swirling.

"Give me that." I lunged for it.

Amelia widened her eyes. She mimed drinking the concoction, then pointed toward the doctor's office, a question hanging on her lips.

I gasped. "How do you know about that?"

Her voice croaked out rougher than I'd ever known it. "I heard you and Marcus talking about it on the day of the doctor's funeral. You thought I'd gone, but I hadn't. You just didn't see me."

"The doctor asked me to do it," I said coldly. "It was his idea."

Amelia worked her mouth. She was thinking.

"He was sick, and confused," I said. "He was going to die anyway."

Amelia jutted out her chin, defying me to contradict her. She pushed out her words with difficulty. "So tell me, Truly, was it mercy or murder?"

I rounded on Amelia and snatched the jar out of her hands. "Does it matter? He never had a chance anyway. I just hurried nature along. And if it evened up some old scores, so what?"

It was still better than what she had done, I reasoned. I had merely taken life, but she had gone beyond death and erased my sister's existence. Her accusations niggled at me, however, reminding me of the price Marcus predicted I would have to pay for following the doctor's wishes. Mercy, I was discovering, was a heavy blade that could cut both ways. It wasn't always kind. I set the jar on the kitchen table and folded my arms. "We're done. Get out."

Amelia knew all about mercy, though. She'd spent a lifetime courting it. I watched her sink to her knees. When she looked up at me, her eyes were as shiny and black as the graveyard crows. "Please," she whispered, "forgive me. You're all my family. I don't know what I'll do if you don't forgive me."

On a different day, perhaps, when the air wasn't hot as a crucible, when there was a little lick of breeze, I might have relented, but the kitchen was close, and all I could feel was my own sweat, welling up so fast, it threatened to choke me. I was sick of life, sick of the cicadas shrilling all through the night, sick of the twists of vines crawling over all the fences when they would only drop their leaves in a few weeks and die. I closed my eyes. "Go," I seethed, and waited till I heard the back door close as softly as a sigh.

I went through the house, pulling the shades down in all the windows and turning off the lights, so mired in sorrow that I didn't even notice that Amelia had taken the jar of Tabby's herbs with her. It wasn't until the next morning that I learned of their absence, and remembered her anguish, and, with my heart in my mouth, asked myself if I would have gone after her if I'd known, dragging the heavy, burdensome sword of mercy in the dirt behind me.

Chapter Thirty

I wish I could say I was the one who found Amelia, but it was Marcus who discovered her curled like a snail in her vegetable beds when he showed up to weed. Already, the bugs were feasting on her. A conga line of ants was parading in and out of her left ear, and a spider was tentatively exploring the cavities of her nostrils. A trail of green liquid ran down one side of her mouth into the vegetation. Marcus reached down and brushed the insects away from her cheek, then straightened up, parked his hands on his hips, and limped over to his truck.

The sound of frantic knocking woke me, then I heard Marcus's voice calling me, and I rushed downstairs. "What is it?" I asked, my dressing gown half-open over my pajamas. "Has something happened to Bobbie?"

Under the last fingers of dawn, the shadows under Marcus's eyes were deeper and his irises were the color of a pond right before it freezes. He put a fist to his mouth and coughed. "It's Amelia. You need to come with me. Oh, Truly, what have you done?"

We didn't say a word to each other the whole bone-rattling ride out to the farm, but when we arrived, I was surprised that Marcus drove past the house and straight out to the barn. "What are we out here for?" I asked, slamming the truck door, but Marcus still didn't say anything, and when I entered the barn, I saw why.

He had laid out Amelia the old-fashioned way, on a board between two trestles. In spite of the plentiful holes in the roof, the light was still dank and dim, but Marcus lit a kerosene lantern that smoked and sputtered, then set it up high to spread the light. At Amelia's feet, I saw the empty jar.

"Oh, my God." I turned away, but Marcus was behind me, and he forced me to face Amelia.

"I moved her in here. I found this lying next to her." He indicated the empty jar. "How could you do it again, Truly? I thought you were sorry! Why did you give her that stuff?"

A fly buzzed near my ears. The sun was coming up, and the heat would soon begin to bring pests, I knew, as well as a stench. We had to call someone. "I—I didn't give it to her," I whispered. "I swear. She took it."

"Why?" Marcus's voice was a hammer driving a nail.

I bowed my head. "We had words. Well, I did. I didn't give her the chance to have them back."

Marcus walked closer to Amelia. A ray of light was beginning to stroke her hair. "Over what? What could she have possibly done?"

I wrapped my arms around myself. Where did I start? I wondered. With the fact that my sister was really alive? Or that Robert Morgan had buried someone in her name? Or maybe with the welt on my hand and the day I'd found the scrap of a letter? When it came down to it, maybe words were what had fueled this mess. After all, my life under Robert Morgan's roof had started with a note from Serena Jane, just as Amelia's life had ended because of one.

"I guess you could say that our words undid us," I finally muttered.

Marcus cocked his head. "I don't understand."

And so I told him then in the close air of the barn about Robert Morgan whispering, "California," and Amelia helping the doctor burn the letters and how one small fragment had slipped out of the past like an ember shooting up a chimney. And I didn't stop there, either. I told him all about the doctor's diagnosis of me, and how I'd let that secret isolate me from the very ones I loved the most—Amelia and Marcus, but especially Marcus—and how Robert Morgan had been wrong in the end. I explained about the quilt being used for better and for worse, and how, even though I wanted to, I knew I'd never be able to untangle myself from its mess of threads and roots. I told him about how the angel wings that Tabitha had sewn had seemed to become embedded in my own flesh.

When I was finished, tears the size of raindrops were sliding down my cheeks, and my breath was coming in such jerky gasps that I almost didn't even notice Marcus taking me into his arms.

"Hush," he whispered. "It's all right. I'm here." And for the first time since that afternoon in the cemetery, he put his lips to mine.

There are some confessions you must make face-to-face, some truths so painful that you must utter them not eye-to-eye, but directly into the other person's soul. "You were right," I said, my mouth pressed against Marcus's. "I should never have made the drink. This is all on my hands."

Marcus squeezed me. "No. You couldn't have known this would be. You aren't responsible." He backed away from me but kept my hands gripped in his. "Listen, Truly," he began, "about what you did for the doctor and Priscilla Sparrow—"

"I should have listened," I interrupted. "I shouldn't have ever done it."

He stopped me with another kiss. "No.

You did right. I know it better than anyone. I did the same thing, remember?"

I nodded and was silent, remembering his letter and what he did for his wounded friend. "Is it murder or a mercy when one of the needs in life turns out to be death?" I whispered, remembering Amelia's final question, but Marcus didn't have an answer. We just stood together, heads bowed, hands clenched, our hearts pushing blood through our bodies—mine large, his small—in the same languid cadence.

"We need to do something," I finally murmured, turning my head toward Amelia.

"You stay here." Marcus unwound his fingers from mine and headed toward the barn door. "I'll be right back, and then I'll let you handle the details."

He returned with a bucket, and vinegar, and sponges. Powder, and oils, and a sheet. Dried herbs, a coin, and a length of red yarn. Candles to keep the flies at bay. He replenished the kerosene in the lantern, then left me alone. Working in small patches, I first bathed the length of Amelia's arms with vinegar, then slowly moved down her torso to her legs and feet. I oiled her brow with the essence of rose, anointed her cheeks and chin, and fixed a coin under her tongue. I loosed her braid and combed powder through her hair, then bound it again with the red yarn, snipping off a lock for a keepsake. I rubbed beeswax into her fingernails, daubed each palm with ashes I found in the corner, and made sure the hollows in between her toes each held a sprig of dried forget-me-not. When I was finished, I folded her hands on top of her chest and laced the stem of a purple thistle in her fingers for divine protection and luck.

There was peace in washing the dead, I discovered—a preternatural quiet absent from any other activity. As I moved around the examining table, I hummed the half-remembered hymns of childhood, joining phrases and melodies into a ragbag of devotional noise. The only religion the Dyersons had ever followed had been the path of hard luck, and its golden rule was simple. You did what you had to do when it needed to be done. I smoothed the last pieces of Amelia's hair down along her brow and stepped back to review my work. Outside the window, I could see Marcus hacking at a thicket of bushes like a sour angel, already resenting the first licks of autumn. The winters drove him crazy, and it occurred to me that he needed a greenhouse—a condensed universe where the laws of nature were suspended.

Of course, the world doesn't really work that way, but it helps if you imagine that it does. With every breath, there are choices to make—sometimes to take a life and sometimes merely to ease the pain of it—and sometimes those choices have consequences that you never foresaw. Nevertheless, I decided right then that I would keep doing what I could, brewing separate infusions for life and death and putting them up on the shelf until someone asked me to take them down. I leaned down and kissed Amelia. I finished winding a bit of thread around the tip of her index finger, binding it tight so she wouldn't ever forget me, and then I stepped out into the day, making sure to leave the door ajar for the souls among us who wished to enter and for the spirits that had chosen to go.

A young, ponytailed official from the coroner's office came to cart Amelia's body away, shaking his head at the string tied around her finger, the red yarn in her hair, and the thistle wound in between her fingers.

"We haven't seen this shit since the nineteenth century," he said, zipping Amelia into industrial plastic. "We'll let you know when you can come get her," he told me, slamming the van door and gunning the engine. Marcus and I walked out of the barn together and watched the van drive away, and I was glad he was standing behind me, his knees pressed into the backs of mine, keeping me straight and strong.

"We need to tell Bobbie," I murmured. "One of us should. He ought to know about the letters."

"He leaves for work at four," Marcus said. "He's around the cottage until then. I can make myself scarce. Here's my key in case he's not there."

"Thank you." I turned around to face him, shy in front of him. "Marcus . . ." I lowered my eyes. "About earlier in the barn—"

He cut me off. "Let's not worry about what's done anymore. When all this is over, let's make a fresh start, the right way." He slid his wounded hand out for mine, and I accepted it, matching the scar on my palm to the patches and lines on his, wondering what kind of seed we would plant together and how tall we could coax it grow.

Bobbie greeted me with the uncomplicated enthusiasm of a puppy, flinging open the cottage door and clapping his hands. He was wearing shorts and a gauzy linen shirt that showed off the new muscles in his chest. "Aunt Truly! Can you believe how hot it still is? Do you want some water?"

"No." The air in the cottage was thick, and I immediately broke out into a sweat. Amelia's death was still too heavy. I didn't want to be inside, where the walls seemed to press and accuse me. "Let's go for a walk," I suggested. "I need to talk to you about some things."

"Sure. Let me grab a hat." Bobbie plucked a straw boater off the coat tree and swung the door shut behind him, then immediately cringed. "I forgot the keys," he moaned. "Let me just see if I can squeeze through one of these windows."

"No, no." I stopped him. "It's okay. I've got a set."

"Oh." Bobbie wrinkled his forehead. "Um, fine. Why do you have Marcus's keys?"

I blushed, but Bobbie didn't seem to notice. I steered him down a shaded lane and toward the Morgan section of the cemetery. My footsteps fell heavy and leaden, matching my heart. I felt my way slowly forward into conversation. "Bobbie, what do you remember when you think of your mother?"

He stiffened beside me. We rarely ever discussed Serena Jane. Robert Morgan never had, and I'd merely sighed and rolled my lips like the lid of a sardine can whenever Bobbie had asked. Serena Jane's favorite color, her favorite song, her favorite movie—those bits of information were never revealed to Bobbie, I realized. Instead, what was pressed home was the simple moral of her. She was a black sheep too uppity for her own good. A peacock strutting in a henhouse. A swan that had it coming.

"I think of her blue dress, mostly," he said. He bowed his head as he walked. "It's the only thing I have left. I think of the way her hair smelled like talcum powder. I remember her singing to me when I was sick."

My throat tightened. I had never tried to do that, I realized. It had never occurred to me. I remembered my first week in the house and my attempts to feed Bobbie. *Don't you want your eggs?* I would ask every morning, my brow furrowed, and Bobbie would simply shrug. An image came to me of him kneeling in the plants shortly after I arrived, the crouched figure of Marcus at his side like a benevolent gnome. They'd spent hours digging, Bobbie squatting on his heels, striking the tip of a spade in the ground over and over again.

That's good, Marcus used to mutter, stealing a glance from the corners of his eyes. *You're aerating the soil real well.* Bobbie never answered back. He looked as though he didn't care what he was doing as long as it didn't involve his father or my hulking shadow. He didn't know yet if he could love me, only that I was different from his mother in every possible way, huge where Serena Jane had been delicate, rough where she had been as soft as a goose feather. Every day at the breakfast table, he examined the crags and hollows of my face, seeking a family resemblance, and every day he went away hungry. The only one who never asked anything from him, I suddenly realized, not even a single sound, was Marcus. Occasionally, he would put his fist over Bobbie's fingers and show him where to prune back a flower or direct him to burrow in a new patch of ground, but mostly he let him be, watching as Bobbie combed through handful after handful of dirt.

We arrived at the Morgan plots. The earth around Robert Morgan's marker still looked tumbled and raw, as if the doctor were having some trouble settling into the afterlife. Bobbie edged away from me and looked as if he were trying to think of some appropriate eulogy, but the only words that came to his lips were "I'm sorry," whispered as faintly as a moth grazing a pane of glass. It occurred to me as I watched him that he was Aberdeen's last Robert Morgan, and that thought made me shiver a little. Maybe he really wasn't so different from any of the men lying in the ground around him, I thought, but I sort of thrilled to the idea of him being historical. It made me appreciate the gravity of the late summer sun falling across the grass and the first traces of red and gold sneaking into the trees. It made me wish he would stay in Aberdeen forever. It made me wish I had given him life.

"Bobbie . . ." I angled around to Serena Jane's headstone. "Come here a minute. I have some things to tell you, but I don't quite know how." Bobbie stepped carefully across the grass, avoiding the graves. "Well, the first thing is"—I put my hands in my pockets—"I feel I ought to explain something to you about how your father died."

Bobbie was a good listener. He let me tell him about the quilt, and how the mixture was first Priscilla's idea and then his father's, and how I foraged for all the herbs and boiled them myself. "So I guess I'm as guilty as anyone," I explained. "It doesn't matter that the idea wasn't mine if my hands were in the pot, so to speak."

Sensing I had more to tell, Bobbie remained silent, waiting for me to continue. "The thing is," I went on, "that stuff's turned out to be kind of like a genie escaped out of a bottle. It gives people choices they shouldn't always make. For Priscilla and your father, it was the right decision. But for Amelia"—I watched as a shadow of comprehension began to cross Bobbie's face—"it wasn't."

"Amelia's dead?" Bobbie's face was white.

I nodded.

"You mean, she drank the herbs?"

"I'm so sorry." I wasn't sure anymore to whom I was apologizing, and no matter how much I wanted to, I found I couldn't look up. For the first time in my life, I found out what it was like to feel small.

"But, *why*?"

How do you tell a boy who's grown into manhood without his mother that she was really there the whole time? And how do you do it without making him hate the people who kept her from him? Truth, I was discovering, is like a blunted hoe. Inadequate for hard ground.

"Bobbie," I said, "you know what it's like to keep a secret so big that it presses every inch of you until you can't stand it anymore." Bobbie lowered his own head and didn't answer. He knew I was referring to his penchant for makeup and the women's clothes in the attic while he was growing up and to his boyfriend—all of which we thought we'd hidden so well from his father. "Well," I continued, "it turns out Amelia was hiding something from you and me, something *about* you and me. It turns out that your mother isn't buried under that stone after all." Bobbie's head snapped up. "She ran away years ago. I guess for your father, it was just easier to pretend she was dead."

Bobbie's breathing was shallow. "How do you know this?"

"She wrote to us. Years ago. Your father hid the letters in his office, but Amelia knew they were there."

"So why didn't she say something? Why didn't she give them to us?"

I folded my hands. "I think your father would have made things difficult for her if she had. You know the farm was the thing she cared about most in this life."

Bobbie rubbed his palms over his eyes. "I don't believe this."

"I know."

"Is there an address? Does anyone know where she is?"

I shook my head. "Amelia and your father burned the letters."

"Oh."

We were silent then, contemplating the various graves around us. I searched Bobbie's eyes, anxious for his reaction to everything that had come to pass, but there was none. He was simply too stunned to process what he was hearing, but later, when it finally did hit him, I resolved that I would be right by his side, along with Marcus and Salvatore.

"There was this," I finally said, pulling the scrap of envelope out of my pocket and handing it to him. "I found it in the bookshelf. Maybe it's enough to start a search."

Bobbie reached out and plucked the paper from my hand with trembling fingers.

"Eleven Palm," he read. "It's not much to go on."

"It's all we have," I said.

"True." He shoved the paper in his own pocket.

We stood a moment longer, watching the tops of trees toss and crows swoop in and out of them, then Bobbie said he had to get going. "Work," he explained. "And Salvatore."

"How is he?" I vaguely remembered the width of the boy's shoulders, and it pleased me now to imagine how well they would shelter Bobbie.

Bobbie nodded. "Fine. Better than fine." We set off back to the cottage. The light was very strong, and it dazzled us a little. "Do you think it's this bright in California?" Bobbie asked, and I looked up, shading my eyes with one hand.

"I don't know." *My poor sister*, I thought. She never could seem to resist the featherweight lure of glitter and glare. She never understood that love—especially that of a child—was the most necessary weight you can endure in life, even if it hurts, even if it tugs bags under the skin of your eyes. Without it, the soul skitters to edge of the world and teeters there, confused.

"This light's like heaven," Bobbie sighed, and I pondered on that. Maybe heaven really did exist, I thought. Maybe it was just the perfect realization of all one's dreams—an impossible realm of suntans and muscles, where a magic elixir could heal you and make you strong, where men could make roses bloom with the single touch of a thumb, and where the bigger the women were, so much the better.

When we reached the cottage, Marcus

was framed in one of the windows. He was washing dishes—his hands making soapy circles with a sponge, then rinsing everything clean. I watched him fetch plates and lay them on the table with a savage solidity, as if to prove that he wasn't going anywhere. Not today, and not tomorrow, either. The smell of stew drifted out across the grass, and Marcus turned and saw us. I watched him straighten. He appeared to consider and then thought, *What the hell.* He stumped his way to the door, the change in his pocket rattling along with the beats of my heart. My mouth was dry, but I swallowed hard and knocked, knowing he was setting one more place at the table. There was just time for me to breathe one last wish down into the roots and worms under my feet, where it would either flourish and survive, I knew, or sink into the afterlife. But I hoped not. I hoped it would grow. Love always seemed to.

Epilogue

Death almost always rearranges life, sometimes for the worse, many times for the better. A month after Amelia's death, Marcus and I moved into the farmhouse together. No one wanted the place, so after half a lifetime, I finally found a use for all the earnings from August's screwball horses. I got to scrawl my name in the space above *Owner* on the Dyerson deed, Marcus sitting next to me, my pen making the perfect loops and whorls Priscilla Sparrow had taught us so long ago.

On our first drive out to the farm together, Marcus told me he had a surprise waiting.

"Close your eyes," he bossed, and led me across the bumpy ground toward the barn. "Okay, open them," he said, and when I did, I saw a leggy brown colt standing in the newly repaired paddock, its lithe neck bent down to the rich grass. Startled, it reared its head, and I saw the unusual marking spread across its forehead—not a star, exactly, more like a pair of feathered wings. Angel wings.

I put a hand over my mouth and made a small sound. I reached for Marcus's hand to say thank you, but he had dropped to his knees in the dirt in front of me. "Truly," he said, looking up at me with his warm eyes, "we're not exactly a match made in heaven, you and I, but I figure we're good enough for here on earth. Will you have me?" He reached into his pocket and pulled out a rough-hewn gold ring. "I had it made special"—he blushed—"so it would be sure to fit."

"Oh," I breathed, sliding the ring over my knobby knuckle. "Yes. A hundred times, yes. But there's someone I have to ask first."

"What took you so long?" Bobbie grinned

when I told him that evening. "You two should have gotten together years ago."

"But what about you?" I blushed. "Won't you be lonely living here all alone?" After Amelia's death, Bobbie had moved back into his father's house, but it was different with just the two of us—more peaceful, certainly, but a little empty, too.

"Don't worry about me." Bobbie smiled. "I have some plans."

And he did. The first thing he did was move Salvatore in with him, which ruffled more than a few feathers in town, but not as many as when the carpenters descended on the house and began tearing up the clinic in the back. "What in thunder hill is going on behind that tarp," Vi Vickers scowled, trying to peek around the blue sheets of plastic that blocked everyone's view. "You can hear the noise all the way out to Hinkleman's. It's a damn distraction."

"You'll just have to wait," I said, smiling. I knew, but then, the work going on was partly my doing. Bobbie had needed money for his project, and after all these years, I had been more than happy to find a permanent home for the bundle of bills under my bed.

A month later, Vi got her answer. Bobbie had transformed his father's office and clinic into a small restaurant. Bobbie cooked, and Salvatore worked the dining room. The Dispensary, it was called, and soon the boys had critics traveling all the way from Manhattan to swoon over their recipes. *Incandescent*, his food was called, and *a tonic for the soul*. Marcus provided all the fruits and vegetables, and many of Bobbie's dishes included locally foraged herbs. Diners were always charmed to find that the front of the menu was printed to look like an antique quilt.

I took the real thing with me to the farm, intending to hang it as decoration, but I quickly discovered that my days meddling with the quilt were hardly finished. People in Aberdeen were more stubborn than I gave them credit for. I guess they were so used to having a Morgan tend to their aches and pains that they were fully prepared to brave the potholes and dirt road out to the Dyerson farm. Soon I had a regular stream of visitors knocking up a storm on the front door. At first I was a little hesitant about treating them.

"I'm not a doctor," I reminded Sal Dunfry, who'd come out to see if I could do something about the liver spots on her hands. "Not even close."

"I know," Sal answered, plopping herself down in the kitchen and helping herself to the coffeepot, "but whatever you're doing is working, and besides, this isn't brain surgery." And then she made the most sensible suggestion of all. "You lived with Robert Morgan for all those years. You must have picked up a little something from him. Why don't you just find yourself another doctor around here and see if he'll help you?"

So I finally phoned Dr. Redfield, who turned out to be not at all what I was expecting. He was almost as tall as me, for one thing, and had the easy laugh and manners of a harlequin. He was fascinated by the remedies on Tabitha's quilt and agreed to check up on the people I treated, taking the cases I couldn't solve and making sure the ones I did stayed that way. Once again, my pantry began to fill up with infusions for everything from ulcers to general despair, and the pots on the stove were always bubbling. There is one cure I never show anyone, however. The last jar of Tabby's green liquid is stowed in the darkest corner of the root cellar, tucked under a shelf, where the glow of it can't get into anyone's thoughts. I'm not saying I would never do it again, but ending an existence, I know now, isn't like closing the covers of a book. It isn't as simple as folding down the top corner of a page and putting it aside for later.

There are some things in life, however, you can do that with, and the letter I received from Serena Jane was one such item. Bobbie and I hired a private detective to help us find her, and after a few weeks, he hit pay dirt with a working address. "Should we send one letter between us, or separate ones?" Bobbie puzzled, his pulse racing. Salvatore put a calming hand on his shoulder.

I thought about it for a moment. "Separate," I finally said. "But let's put them together in the same package when we mail them. And let me be the one to tell her about your father."

Bobbie wiped a tear from his eye. "Do you think she ever loved him?"

I considered, remembering the circumstances of Serena Jane's single date with Robert Morgan, followed by her somber wedding. I wanted to lie, but Bobbie wasn't a child anymore. He deserved to know the truth. I shook my head. "No, I can't say she did. But I know she loved you."

"How?" Bobbie scowled. "She didn't leave any evidence of it."

I opened my eyes wide and held out my arms. "Why, Bobbie Morgan, of course she did. It's been standing right here in front of you all along." Bobbie looked stumped for a moment, and then he broke out into laughter and threw his arms around me.

When I received word back from Serena Jane, it arrived with a postcard. She sent a picture of a beach with a boat heading out to open water and on the back signed *Love, SJ.* I opened her letter and began to read. She had left because she wanted to get lost for once in her life, she said, so she'd bought a Jeep and set off with no maps. She'd figured she'd recognize the Pacific when she hit it. She was hurt when no one ever replied to her letters, but it was understandable, she thought, when she had been the one to leave. Once or twice she thought about coming back, but then she got a job managing wardrobes for one of the studios and met another man, who sadly ended up leaving her a few years ago. I read each and every one of my sister's words twice—lingering over her descriptions of sand and pelicans, absorbing her continual amazement that in Hollywood, the stars were right there under her feet. Serena Jane's last sentence ended with a plea for Bobbie to forgive her, to remember that she was his mother, in spite of everything, and that she loved him.

"Are you going to see her?" Marcus asked me after I got the letter. It was still early, the winter light of dawn breaking over us like a wave. I blinked, my eyes rimmed as red as roosters. I thought about the false gravestone carved with my sister's name and how its edges had yet to be scoured by centuries of wind and rain, how the letters on it were still as sharp as thorns and as black as spiders. No matter what the season or how many flowers I left at the base of it, the stone had never seemed a final home for Serena Jane. Not a proper one, at least. Robert Morgan's matched it exactly.

"I don't think so. Not yet," I replied, and nestled my head into the crook of Marcus's arm.

"Don't be sad," Marcus whispered, nuzzling my neck. "Not today, of all days." I smiled. It was our wedding day. We were going to be married by a judge in Hansen, and then Bobbie was making us a feast. "Let's start getting ready," Marcus urged. "I want to see you in your dress. I don't care if it's bad luck."

I snorted. "When it comes to bad luck, we've got nothing on this place. It's steeped in it."

"Not anymore it's not." Marcus shook his head, and I realized he was right. We had made changes. For one thing, we'd dragged the furniture into new arrangements to suit us and us alone. There were armchairs in the kitchen now, and we'd relegated an old, nicked table to the front hall—giving us a place to dump mail and park boots and where each of us could leave a note for the other, even if we'd only walked out to the windmill to check on the day's weather. But I rarely do. I don't care if it rains down molten arrows. There are days like today when the snow is heaped in piles, but I don't mind as long as I'm with Marcus. At night, the valleys of my body curve around him, creating a geography I never knew existed before, where size is relative and more is always better, and I can't seem to get enough of it.

I threw back the covers and stalked over to the window, to see three ink-feathered crows perching on the blades of the old windmill, squawking at the sky. I wrapped the blanket closer around my bulk. "Between us, do you think we make enough racket to scare all the crows off this place?" I asked, grinning at Marcus.

He glanced out the window. "No. They were here long before us, and they'll still be here when we're gone. This place really belongs to them."

"I guess you're right. I guess we'll have to learn to share."

Marcus tiptoed up behind me. "Come back to bed for a minute." His hands were warm on my back. With my eyes closed, it was easy to forget about his scars.

I shook him off. "There's something I have to take care of. Something I've been meaning to do for a while." I kissed his damaged thumb. "You go start breakfast. I'll be down in a little while."

While Marcus went downstairs, mumbling the names of some plants to himself in Latin, I gathered up Tabby's quilt from the chair in the corner. Over the past year, its flowers had become increasingly worn and faded, but I was so familiar with the design, I could have reproduced it with my eyes shut. I knew each and every bud, all the leaves, and each pointed tip of the black diamond border.

I pulled aside the curtains even farther and rummaged in a bureau drawer for a needle and thread, snaking a long piece through the tiny hole, and then sat myself down in the rocking chair in the corner. To the untrained eye, Tabitha's quilt appeared to be a full canvas, but I knew better. There were some blank spots yet on it, but not for long. I had already prepared everything, tracing my design with pencil, and now I pulled and tugged the fabric through my hands until I found my drawing. Three interlocking sets of wings spread out along the very edge of the inner border. I took a deep breath, poised the needle, and began sewing.

At first my stitches were uneven and shaky, but soon my hands found the rhythm, and as I pulled the thread back and forth, my mind found quietude. When I was done, I held my work up at arm's length. Even amid the cacophony of the competing flowers, my handiwork still stuck out. Three sets of wings that pulled all the other ones out of relief and into focus. The first set of wings was for Priscilla. I had embroidered them in purple, for dignity. The second set was for the doctor, and I made those plain black, and for the last set—Amelia's—I used the deepest blue I could find. From now on, I vowed, everything added to the quilt would be done in full color. Everything would be brought out to the light.

I stuck the needle back in the pincushion and wound the quilt around my shoulders. Moving slowly so Marcus wouldn't hear me, I made my way downstairs, pulling on my boots in the hall, and wound a scarf around my throat. In my hand, I carried the plain wooden box that contained the ashes of Amelia. For months I had been holding on to them, unable to scatter them, but today was a day for new beginnings. I took a deep breath of the cold air and set out across the fields.

Even though it was the middle of January, the sky overhead was as clear as a June lake. As my boots crunched through the snow, I surveyed the land around me. Across the paddock, the renovations that Marcus was beginning to make on August's old barn were becoming manifest, and even better, beside the barn, a new structure was starting to rise—glass panes instead of walls stuck up to the sky and strong new beams spanned across them for a glass roof. Eventually, Marcus will have an oasis in the middle of winter. We will have sweet peas and lettuce all season. Roses will scale the windows in February, crazy with heat.

Inside the barn, the foal, Seraph, was tucked up snug in his stall, a pile of fresh hay mounded at his feet. He nickered when he saw me and stamped a foot. In time, he will grow, too, but I will never race him. He is purely a creature of pleasure, made to prance and canter through the fields, streaking the world with momentary beauty. I patted his flank and swung his stall door shut again. I still had one last thing to accomplish.

In the snow, it wasn't easy to find August's marker. It had fallen years ago, but after shuffling around, I stumbled on it and cleared it off. Holding my hands steady, I slowly slid open the box lid and reached inside. It was time to lay Amelia to rest—not sunk in the ground and surrounded by Aberdeen's grim-whiskered ancestors, but scattered by the handful, fodder for the ravens and crows, fair game for the north wind. I reached into the box again and again, finally withdrawing the last handful of silt, letting the grain run across my palm and stick in between my fingers. I will have pieces of Amelia clinging to me forever, ground into the smallest spaces of me, I know, but I will also always be able to find her here in the stubbled pastures I've come to love. When dealing with the long lost, I've learned, it's best to let them lie where they will. Some, like Bobbie, find their way home in the nick of time. Some, like Amelia, remain lately departed, and some are so light, so easily replaceable, that their coffins could be holding anyone.

I wrapped the corners of the quilt tight around the ample curves of my arms and smiled. At least I will never have that problem. When the day comes to slide me into the ground, the earth will certainly recognize me. The hole will have to be wide and deep, a veritable canyon, bigger than anyone else's by far. Then, I'll know if we're really joined as one, linked bone to bone like stitches in a quilt. I'll pull the final thread from my soul and see what happens next.

COUNTY LIBRARY
DISCARD
TILLAMOOK, ORE.